Forever Faithful

Years of America's Great Cultural Change

MARILYN L. REICKS

King James Bible Version

Douay Bible Version of the Old Testament

Confraternity Bible Version of the New Testament

WestBow Press books may be ordered through booksellers or by contacting:

WestBow Press
A Division of Thomas Nelson & Zondervan
1663 Liberty Drive
Bloomington, IN 47403
www.westbowpress.com
1 (866) 928-1240

ISBN: 978-1-9736-3828-5 (sc)
ISBN: 978-1-9736-3829-2 (e)

Print information available on the last page.

WestBow Press rev. date: 11/06/2018

World War I and World War II brought changes to the self-sufficiency and independence of farm life. Note the land for: crops, gardens, trees in the fruit orchard and the many farm buildings for milk cows, beef cattle, pigs, chickens, and any other animal the family might raise for food and to sell for income.

How thankful I am that State Aerial Farm Statistics, Inc. has preserved vintage aerial views of numerous farms. Their photo of my childhood home on Old Mill Road in Winneshiek County in Iowa recalls unforgettable memories. This farm became the setting for *Forever Faithful*. In the book, I attempt to show how life in America has changed in so few years from being quite self-sufficient and independent to being more globally interdependent. A farm family used to be able to produce most of their food and were quite self-reliant. They raised many kinds of food and animals. Today farms are focused more on single crops or the raising of a specific animal. By doing so they are no longer able to raise much of their own body needs making them more dependent on others.

I wanted to include this picture to show how many buildings used to be on one family farm. There needed to be many buildings to house the milk cows, beef cattle, horses, hogs, baby pigs, laying hens, baby chicks, sheep, and the watch dog. Some structures were for storing grains such as oats, barley and loose hay. Machine sheds provided shelter for horse drawn farm equipment including a plow, disc, drag, grain drill, corn planter, corn plow, mower, hay rake, hay loader, grain binder, grain box wagons and buggy. At threshing time, a huge threshing machine powered by a large tractor was moved from farm to farm to thresh the grain.

From birth until I married I lived there with my father, mother and two brothers. I am the only one left of my original family. The farm has been in the Stortz family name since 1858. The original log house no longer looks the same as it has been boarded over on the outside and the interior of the house has been sheet rocked and remodeled over the many years of its existence. The house is over one hundred sixty years old and is still lived in.

The log cow barn burned to the ground in 1962 and the large horse barn and tall silo have been torn down. Gone are the following buildings: the granaries, the slotted walled corn cribs, the smoke house for curing ham, bacon and other meats, wood shed to store stacked split wood to burn in the large stoves in the house for heat and for the kitchen range to cook food and heat water in the stove's reservoir from which warm water was used for washing dishes and for washing ourselves. I must not forget the little house outback with its two holes in a seat and supplied with the Sear Roebuck catalog or soft tissues from around individual peaches packed in crates.

This farm inspired me to portray ordinary farm life before and during the WWII years. Hopefully, my readers will visualize and realize how our culture has greatly changed from those turbulent years.

The over a mile-long road to the farm home was named Old Mill Road in memory of the Springwater Mill my grandfather owned and operated on Canoe Creek, another mile down the hill from the house. My grandfather ground grain for humans and animals. Bags of grain marked Springwater Mill were sold to housewives in Decorah.

Grandfather sold the mill in 1912 and purchased wheat land in Eastern Montana. My father told me the old wheat was high in protein and low in starch whereas genetically modified wheat today is high in starch and low in protein. All starches change to sugar in the body and are the suspected cause of many health problems today. Other parts of grain have been altered creating concern about our food supply.

Grandmother wondered how she would feed her family without the grain and the income from the mill. She gave birth to fourteen children, the first-born son died as an infant, a ten-year old girl's health failed, a son gave up his life in the military and eleven sons and daughters lived a full life time. One son, my father was the one who stayed on the farm and farmed it all his life. This is the background for my story to show the huge rapid shift in the way people live.

Even though the story is motivated by my memories of life on a northeast Iowa farm during World War II, it is portrayed through fictitious characters. Unlike me, Julia has two brothers and a boyfriend who serve in WWII.

Springwater Grain Mill 1912 Picture How could life change so much in only a hundred years?

To the memory of my parents, Alfred and Nellie Stortz, whose lives inspired me to write this historical fiction book. My mother's excellent farm financial records from 1924–1946 were used to give authenticity to the historical and fictitious writings of the book.

1936 picture in front of the family home that started as a log house in 1858 and memories of it led to the story for *Forever Faithful.*

Until the 1940s into the 1950s there were one room country schools in many rural areas where children went to school close to their homes. One teacher taught all the subjects to all the grades kindergarten to eighth grade in one room with rows of seats sometimes nailed to the floor. The teacher opened the school each morning, took care of the stove or furnace and she swept the floor at the end of the day.

A large water cooler stood in the entry way with tin cups one for each student on a wall nearby. On the walls were hooks for students to hang coats and a shelf above on which to put their dinner pails, some were Karo syrup gallon tin cans or black metal buckets. The teacher rang a brass metal bell on her desk when it was 9:00 and time to begin classes. At recess time, mid-morning and mid-afternoon, the children might have a snack and play outdoors in nice weather. They played ball or games. There were little houses behind the school, one for the boys and one for the girls as there were no indoor bathrooms.

Introduction

Dear Reader,

Do you wonder how life in the US was affected by WWII? In *Forever Faithful* I take you into the lives of a farm family—their hardships and heartaches suffered during the war. The fictitious characters impart evidence of great cultural change in beliefs and behaviors. American life concerning traditional religion, Constitutional politics, debt finances, health and society drastically changed.

Besides war references, much has been helpful in writing this book including my mother's well-kept home and farm financial records from the Great Depression years to 1946. I became interested in finances of that time because they are so different from what we are familiar with today.

United States ration books with stamps, old sheet music from the 20s, 30s, 40s and 40s movies helped me tell the story. I used articles on history from the *Decorah Journal*, church history from St. Benedict's church and writings in the *Catholic Girl's Guide*, on piety for young women, edited by Rev. Lasance. Julia's teaching was described from the teaching experience of my mother and myself in Canoe #8, a one room country school. Places mentioned in the book and experienced by the author include: canoeing the Upper Iowa River, enjoying the Decorah area parks, the Passion Play (closed 2008), Spearfish, SD; Yellowstone National Park, visits to and brochures from: Wonder Cave (no longer open), the Winneshiek Hotel, Decorah, Iowa; the

Bily Clocks in Spillville, Iowa; Vesterheim, the national Norwegian-American museum and heritage center, Decorah, Iowa.

The past is interesting—and it should be---it is our legacy for life to today and the future.

Acknowledgments

Heartfelt thanks to Gary Reicks, Joyce Reicks, Darel Reicks, and Margie (Reicks) Nienhaus, my children for their encouragement and suggestions.

Special thanks to my husband, David Botterbrodt for his support in the preparation of this book for printing.

A book is the knowledge and work of many people.

I wish to show my appreciation for the remarkable people who have helped me make my book a reality.

Check-in Coordinator Anthony Lim.

Publishing Services Associate Tim Fitch.

Any Westbow Press team member involved in layout, proofing, printing, and marketing of my book.

Most of all I wish to thank my publisher for the publishing of my manuscript and giving me the opportunity to share my memories of yesteryears.

Luke Davis, Main Street Studios, Siloam Springs, AR for personal portrait and permission to use the portrait.

Charlene C. Selbee, Executive Director, Winneshiek County Convention & Visitors Bureau, 507 W. Water St., Decorah, Iowa for history of local parks.

State Aerial Farm Statistics, Inc. for permission to use the vintage photo of the farm that inspired me to write *Forever Faithful*.

Contents

1

The Family

Summer 1940

Dad, looking up from reading the Dubuque *Telegraph Herald*, in a worried tone of voice suddenly announced, "I hope we don't get into another war. Hitler and his Nazi troops already control the European mainland countries west of Russia. Now they are zeroing in on Great Britain with German bombers making aerial raids on England."

Mother looks up from her crocheting a doily, a decorative lacy mat. "God have mercy on the British…their families, industries, and businesses that are being bombed without mercy."

"Lettie, just so we don't get involved in this war like we did in 1917. It would be hard to see our sons have to go to war."

"Sam, I pray that our country does not get into the war. Besides how could they take our sons? We need them to help farm our 280-acre farm."

"Dear, I am sure if the war gets bad enough, we will have a draft, and yes, our sons could get drafted into the war."

Mother laid down her crocheting and looked at Dad. "I would hate to see John or Bobby have to fight in a war. I shudder to think what another war would mean to our country. After the last war, we had so many cultural and moral changes in our country. I hate to think what changes another war would bring."

My mother and father Sturloff continued to talk in hushed words about the war brewing in Europe. I sensed their deep concern about the possibility of the United States being pulled into the war. I know Father does not want to lose the help of his sons on our 280-acre farm, but most of all, I realize, both Mom and Dad do not want to see their beloved sons have to go off to war in another country so far from home with all the dangers that war means to the brave fighting men.

Then I listened to my father telling a story that I did not remember hearing before. "My father was a first-generation German to be born in the United States. While he was doing his banking during the First World War, he said bluntly that we should not be fighting the Germans. I do not like remembering that my father's bold declaration was overheard in the bank by a clothing store owner who reported him. Dad was forced to pay the heavy fine for his remark as the listener called it unpatriotic. Dad was fined five hundred dollars."

My father went on to add, "In my spirit, I feel Dad was right. In the early 1850s, his father, my grandfather and our children's great-grandfather, left southern Germany to immigrate to the United States. To my dad, I am sure it was like we were fighting our own kin…a terrible thing once one thinks about it. Doesn't it seem unthinkable to fight one's own blood relatives?"

Understandably, Mom laid her hand on my dad's arm and inquired, "How did your mother, Maggie, feel about the five- hundred-dollar fine your father had to pay?"

"Sure that cost was a heavy weight to Mother and her twelve children when Dad had to cough up that amount of money."

Dad looked at my brothers, my sister, and me. He explained, "Five hundred dollars was a lot of hard-earned money in those days. My father, your grandfather, had to ship a whole carload of hogs by rail to the stockyards in Chicago to pay his fine."

Then Dad lowered his head and in a barely audible voice told us, "It is sad but true, one of my older brothers, Louie, died that fall in October. He was serving in the US Army near Boulder, Colorado. He was not well but had to go anyway on maneuvers all day long and died in his tent that night of pneumonia.

"In January, my mother, your grandmother, died from the flu that was so bad during the winter of 1918 to 1919. At age forty- five, just two months before her death, she had given birth to your aunt Lillie. Lillie was the only one of her fourteen children to be born in a hospital as there was no hospital before 1918. Because of the flu epidemic, Dad thought she should have the baby in the hospital."

I responded, "Dad, that is so sad that your brother and your mother died so close together. Your mother left so many children, never to see them grow up."

"Yes, those were sad years. After word had come through that Louie died, Mother received a pretty hanky that he had mailed to her. My mother lost her first baby as an infant. Two years after Mother died, my ten-year-old sister Lucy wasted away and died, but the remaining eleven children are still alive and doing well."

Deep inside me, I felt sorrow for my grandparents and yet proud of them. I was happy to be living in their home place.

Over the years, Great-grandpa Sturloff 's original log house had been added on to to make room for my grandfather and grandmother's large family. The 1860 original home hewn log house and the newer additions were both sided alike so now the house looks like any other white frame house.

I continued to listen to my mom and dad talk seriously about the possibility of war. My mother's concerns over the drastic moral and cultural changes after World War I scared me. If my parents saw so many changes after WWI, what would another war do to affect transformations in my life? I don't want to have to deal with radical adjustments. I think about the security of my loving family. I do not want any of them to die. I want this familiarity of life to go on into my future years.

Tonight, my eight-year-old sister, Marian, is snuggled down behind our large round stove in the parlor, soaking in the heat as she reads a small paperback book.

Brother Bobby, a youthful fourteen-year-old, his mouth open and his tongue almost hanging out, is concentrating intently on whittling a whistle from a piece of wood. His jackknife is slicing chips off the willow stick into a pail.

Mother looks up and asks me, "Julia Ann, what are you reading?"

I reply, "I am reading *Song of Years* by Bess Streeter Aldrich."

"Dear, I am happy you enjoy reading. I liked that book very much. Did you know that the lady who wrote it was born in Cedar Falls, graduated from Iowa State Normal School there, and became a teacher? Her story is so true to life."

I replied, "Just like the author of this book, I want to be a schoolteacher. In my senior year of high school, I hope to take normal training and do my practice teaching in a one-room country school so that the next year I can teach school."

"Dear, you would make a good teacher. You love to read, and you are a good student. If you want to be a teacher, I am sure you will become one. Just think in two years, you could be a teacher."

Later in the evening, Bobby is studying the *Sears Roebuck Catalog* intently reading the information about guns. Dad looks over at him and asks, "Son, are you planning to spend your gopher money on a gun?"

Bobby answers shortly, "Yep."

"Well, you are a clever trapper. I have been watching you. You look for fresh dirt mounds that a gopher has made in making an underground dwelling by removing soil, carrying it above ground, and piling it up to make the mound. Every morning all spring, Bobby, you have set traps just below the mound in the hole leading into the gopher's home."

"Yep! Dad, you taught me well how to trap."

Then, I think to appall the rest of us, Bobby went on to say, "If I have a dead gopher in the trap, I cut off the gopher's front feet and put them in an old Calumet baking powder can I got from Mom. Dad, I am glad you showed me how to sprinkle some salt over the raw-looking bony feet to help preserve them and keep them from stinking so much. When I had a good collection of feet, you took me to the courthouse to receive money for each pair of front feet, the ones with the digging claws."

"Bobby, I am thankful that the government is encouraging the trapping of gophers to help conserve the soil and help stop the damages that gophers can do to crops."

Bobby proudly says, "From the money I received from the gopher feet plus wages I will receive for helping the neighbors hay this summer, I believe I soon will have enough to pay for a gun. By fall I will hunt squirrels, raccoons, and rabbits with my own gun."

This spring, my older brother John trapped muskrat and mink on the banks of Uncle Roy's creek. He got up at five o'clock on school days to check his traps before he ate breakfast and went to his high school classes. He brought the trapped animals back to the house and threw them in a shed. After school, he skinned them. He is hoping to buy a car with his earnings from the pelts.

It makes me feel sad. The boys are making money to buy what they want. Can I find some way to make some money this summer? Do I have to wait until I can teach school to make some spending money? Right now, I could use two dollars to buy a new pair of summer white-strap sandals to wear. Oh! Why is money so hard to come by? Wouldn't it be nice if it really did grow on trees?

I turned to face my mom. "If I was one of Aunt Millie's girls, I would be helping some young mother when her baby was due, taking care of the other little children and helping with the housework. Sometimes Aunt Millie's girls work six weeks or more for a woman before and after childbirth. They make some good money helping like that."

"Dear, you know that Aunt Millie has seven girls and three boys, so she can permit some of the girls to help other families in need of extra help in the home." My mother went on to claim, "I need you in the summertime to help in the garden, pick berries, can, and care for the chickens. I cannot spare you to help anyone else. Marian is learning to help, but there is plenty for all of us to do at home."

I went on halfheartedly to explain, "It would be exciting to help when a baby is due. Just last Sunday after mass, cousin Mindy, my age, told me her experience last week while she was working at a farm home near Fort Atkinson. Right after coming out of church, Mindy quickly recounted to me:

"Last week, I worked helping with the wash, getting meals, and taking care of a little girl. In the afternoon of the fourth day, the mother went to rest in her upstairs bedroom. While lying on her bed, the mother went into labor, and I heard her cry out for help. I ran to the machine shed to tell her husband. He ran for his mother who lived in a house nearby.

"It was just minutes after they reached his wife that the baby was born. It was crying. I quickly ran for whatever the lady told me to get. I saw the woman clear the baby's mouth, cut the umbilical cord, wash the new little one, and lay her new grandson on his mother's stomach cuddled in a warm, fuzzy blanket. The excited father rushed to the kitchen, cranked the handle on the large wall oak telephone, and called the doctor's office. When Doc Koontz came, he pronounced everyone in fine shape."

"Mindy, were you scared?"

"Julia, there was no time to be afraid. I did my best to get the husband and the man's mother as quickly as I could. I must run because my dad is taking me back to work again this week for that family. Bye, cousin."

"Julia, I am sure that was an exciting time for Mindy, but nowadays, most women go to the hospital to have their babies. I had all of you kids in the Decorah Hospital, even your sister who was born in 1932 during the Great Depression. As money was scarce, some mothers could not afford going to the hospital. Women who went to the hospital were kept up to ten days to ensure that there was no infection and the mothers, as well as their babies, were in good health before going home."

Mother left the room and soon returned with a large ledger. She opened her 1932 account book. "Julia, look at this."

I saw a receipt for the payment when Marian was born on May 10, 1932. The payment was for ten days in the Decorah, Iowa, Hospital for the delivery room, my mother's room, the nursery, medicines, and dressings, and the total bill was $47.20. It is sad to think that during the Great Depression, some mothers could not afford that much money to deliver their babies in a hospital.

Then I remembered that my grandmother Maggie had the last one of her fourteen babies in that hospital when it was just new in 1918. Before that, all mothers had their babies at home as there was no local hospital. Imagine Grandma Maggie having thirteen babies at home sometimes with just a woman present who helped with home deliveries.

When I thought about it, maybe my present lack of spending money wasn't so bad. There are things that happen in life that are worse than scarcity of money for wants.

Sunday evening, Dad let us know, "All this week, we will be haying. Tomorrow I will be mowing the hay. I hope the barn cats do not go into the clover field looking for mice. I heard of someone mowing and tragically cutting the back legs off a kitty."

"Oh! Isn't that just awful? I don't want my cats losing their legs," I told Dad.

At dinnertime, Dad informed me, "Julia, this year it is your job to drive the horses on the hay rope to pull the hay into the barn. You must be very careful when you turn the horses so that they do not get spooked and start to run. Remember that Bud, a few years ago while rolling on the ground, got caught in barbed wire and injured his legs. Ever since then, he has been very touchy about anything touching his legs."

Dad said to Bobby, "This afternoon, you will hitch the team to the side rake and rake the dry hay in nice long rows across and around the hayfield, ready for the hay to be lifted up onto the hay wagon.

"John, I want you to get the hay wagons ready, check the barn pulleys and hay ropes."

On Monday afternoon, Dad and John lowered the big barn door through which the hay will be lifted by rope up to the pulley where it will then go on a track into the hay mow. A man will release the hay from the hay fork and the hay falls in a heap. Loose hay will pile up as each load is lifted and dropped into place.

That evening, Dad listened to the tall standing wooden radio in the dining room. We have no electricity, so the radio is powered by a large battery. Dad let us know, "We are to have rain in a few days, so we must hurry to try to get our hay in before the showers come. If the cut hay gets wet, it can grow mold, and the barnyard animals will not eat it."

Dad decided to ask Mr. McDonald, our neighbor, if he could come with his son to help us. The McDonalds finished their haying last week.

Another wagon and two extra pair of hands could mean we would finish before the rain on Friday.

I was excited. Mark's father and Mark were coming to help. Since grade school, I had always had a soft warm feeling for Mark. He was tall with dark-brown hair and warm brown eyes. He was in the same grade as John. This fall they will be seniors, and I will be a junior. *Maybe this week, haying will be fun and not so much just work to get a job done.*

It made me feel good to think that I would be driving the team, Bud and Bill, hitched to the doubletree to pull the hay rope and lift the hay into the barn. *Maybe I will get to see Mark often if he brings the hay loads in.*

With two wagons alternating coming in with hay, I was kept busy with the team of horses pulling the hay into the barn. Mark drove one team, bringing in a loaded hay wagon, and John drove the team on the other wagon. I felt a thrill to see Mark as he rode on the top of the hay up to the barn. I watched as he strongly thrust the hay fork into the load of hay. I felt happy to drive the horses away from the barn, lifting the hay up the side of the barn to the top where it would then go on the track into the barn. Dad was in the barn to unhook the hay fork and send it back down for another load to be lifted.

In midafternoon, Mother and Marian brought out lemonade, home-cured ham sandwiches, and oatmeal cookies for us. We all took a much-needed break. With the warm June day, we were very thirsty as well as ready for some nourishment.

The conversation between the men and older boys turned to the war in Europe. Dad asked Mr. McDonald what he thought about the war news.

Mr. McDonald answered, "Sounds like the United States is trying to stay out of the war, but they are sending aid to Britain. How long will Hitler allow the United States to give help to Britain without drawing us into the conflict?"

Dad nodded in agreement. Mother couldn't help but say, "I pray that we do not get into war. Our families have young sons that could be drafted."

Mark gave a quick look my way. He smiled then boldly said, "If our country goes to war, I will enlist. Hitler's Germany must be stopped in their thrust for power over other nations."

From Mark's smile, I felt a warm feeling, which was quickly replaced with a cold chill that swept through me despite the hot weather. Everyone became very quiet. It hit me—war could be felt close to home. I did not want to think about that. I do not want anyone whom I care about to have to face military forces in battle. I do not want anyone to be wounded or worse—be killed.

Oh, how glad I am that I am a girl. Women have traditionally been protected from war. Girls do not go into combat. No, but we can face death sometimes in childbirth. Does that kind of balance things out for the two genders? Each one can have life-threatening forces that can come against them.

After lunch, we went back to work. Bobby and Marian sat on the tall wooden fence by the barnyard gate where I turned the team. Mark was on the loaded hay wagon, thrusting the hayfork into the loose hay. He turned and smiled and with a wave told me to turn the horses and start pulling the hay up into the barn. I started slowly turning the huge workhorses and all the while attempting to keep the doubletree away from their large feet and legs. Just before the horses turned their blinders on their horse collars, one or both caught glimpses of Bobby and Marian wriggling on the fence. Bud jerked, the doubletree hit him on the leg, and he reared with his front feet thrashing the air.

Bud's rearing frightened Bill, and he started forward pulling Bud with him. Both terrified horses took off frantically running.

The sudden jerk threw me to the ground. Dazed, I felt myself being dragged over the hard ground. Mark yelled, "Let go!"

I let go. My right-hand leather glove fell to the ground. Now Bud and Bill were wildly galloping as fast as they could go. The powerful animals reached the end of the rope. For seconds the team seemed stunned at the sudden forced stop. Their forward straining on the rope was futile. Realizing they could not go on, they abruptly turned.

Mark, while hastily getting down off the wagon, screamed, "Julia, run!"

In that instant, I saw Bud and Bill tearing at top speed back toward where I lay on the ground. Immediately I froze with fright. Just as the thundering hooves approached, I scrambled out of their path. Almost to the high wooden fence, the team in unison turned and again ran the length of the rope. This time when they reached the end of the rope, they side-stepped and pulled it around the corner of the granary. They kept pulling and pulling.

The wood on the corner of the granary gnawed the rope into dangling shreds and finally broke.

The startled team, now free of the rope, again roared back to the barn and directly toward the wooden fence where Bobby, Marian, and I clung to the high boards. Within six feet of the wooden fence, the frightened team reared into the air. Stomping the ground, Bud turned, dragging Bill with him. The wide-eyed pair ran downhill and through the open cow yard gate. Dragging the bouncing doubletree behind them, the terrified team raced across the grassless barnyard, broke through the wooden gate to the cow pasture, and ran downhill out of sight.

Dad hurriedly came down the ladder out of the hay mow to see what the commotion was all about. "Julia, I am relieved you were not dragged." Glancing at Bobby and Marian, he added, "It is a miracle not one of you were hurt. Thank God."

In the small woods behind the log cow barn, Dad found Bud and Bill standing under a large walnut tree. They appeared to be as calm as could be just as if nothing had happened. He led the subdued team home.

"We won't be doing any more haying today. When John comes in with his load, I will send him to town for more rope. I will start working on repairing the harnesses for Bud and Bill. Mark, you and your dad might as well go home until we get the repairs made. Hopefully by tomorrow afternoon, we will be ready to hay again."

In the morning, Dad cut more hay. He came in at noon. With a sad look on his face, he approached me. "Julia, I am sorry, but I think Blackie was in the hay field and got caught in the mower. I don't know if your cat is still alive. The first that I knew he was there was when he cried out in pain. I could see the unmowed hay move as he tried to get away from the mower."

"Oh, Dad, no! I hope he is still alive."

"If he is alive, he might have lost one or more of his legs. It could be hard for him to live like that."

With tears in my eyes, I said, "Dad, I hope he is not cut up so badly that he is somewhere dying all by himself." *That's too terrible to think about. I will believe he is still alive somewhere and not too badly hurt.*

"Farm machinery and work can be dangerous. I thank God that yesterday you or no one else was seriously hurt when Bud and Bill ran away on the hay rope. Dear daughter, you are more precious than any cat, but I know that you think a lot of your cat." Late Thursday afternoon, we pulled the last of the loose hay into the hay loft. Mother and Marian had lunch ready for us in the shade of the porch. They served us ham sandwiches, date oatmeal cookies, and lemonade for a lunch. Everyone was in a jovial mood as our task was finished before the rain.

Dad was especially thankful and asked, "How would it be if we have a picnic at the Phelps Park on Saturday to celebrate and have some fun?"

We all were taken by surprise. Mother, Mr. McDonald, Mark and all of us nodded and acknowledged our agreement. So we planned that each family would pack a picnic lunch and meet in the park on Saturday at noon. Dad said he would try to arrive early enough to get one of the shelters.

Oh! I was so excited. This was going to be so much fun. I took my old sandals out to the slanting cellar door where I sat to polish my shoes with white polish so that they would almost look new again. I decided to wear the dress Mother made this spring for me, the blue polka dot with short puffy sleeves and a large sash of blue cotton.

Mother told me, "Julia, wash your hair in the rain water from the rain barrel by the milk house. The barrel caught rain running off the roof of the milk house, so it is soft water. The soft water will leave your hair silky soft. The water pumped by the windmill comes out of the ground and is hard water from seeping through the limestone rocks below and picking up minerals that harden the water. That water would leave your hair a sticky, tangled mess." After drying my hair, I twisted a strand around my right forefinger, held the pin curl down with my left hand; with my right hand, I opened a bobby pin under my left-hand forefinger, and I thrust the open bobby pin under and over the pin curl to hold it in place. I continued that way until all my hair was in pin curls. I wanted my hair to be curly for the picnic.

While I was pinning up my hair, Mother told me, "Julia, pin curls came into popularity when women started bobbing their hair in the

1920s, so the pins used to hold the bobbed hair in place were called bobby pins. Before that, a woman wore her hair long or wound in a bun at the back of her head. The Bible says long hair is a glory to a woman and is a covering for her."

Wondering, I asked, "If God's word teaches long hair is a covering for a woman, why did that change in the twenties?"

"After World War I, traditional life changed to modern ways. Society got swept up in the vogue of the day. A craze for gambling, alcohol drinking, wild dancing, and painted faces under bobbed hairstyles overtook the populace. Women's dresses became shorter with no waistline and wide, straight, flat-looking bodices. I feel women's styles made them look more like men… short hair, flat-chested look, and no defined waistlines. About that time, women started wearing knickers, pants for women, which grew in popularity. As far as modesty, the pants were more decent looking than the high skirts, low necklines, and flaunting looks of the flappers.

"According to the Bible, men are to dress like men and women like women. It seems the twenties led us away from many traditional lifestyles."

I worry sometimes what is ahead of me in life. Mother often mentions that since WWI, there have been many changes against Christian beliefs.

Friday afternoon, Mother whipped and whipped egg whites into a frothy thickness while she slowly added cake flour and sugar. She baked a beautiful angel food cake frosted with boiled egg white frosting. She cooked a picnic ham to slice and made a potato salad with tiny pieces of green pepper and topped with slices of hard-boiled eggs. Over the top of the salad, she sprinkled paprika.

After supper, Mother explained to us, "Phelps Park was built in 1911. It is a beautiful park overlooking the Upper Iowa River." Mom went on to describe where we are going tomorrow. "In the park, there is a trail through the woods and over the hills running parallel to the Upper Iowa River below. There are lookout places where you can gaze over the tree-blanketed hillside to the river below, snaking through the lowland. One can sit on benches and peacefully enjoy the woods, rocks, and the scenic view."

Just before going to bed, I took a bath in the summer kitchen. Mom heated the water in a large copper boiler placed over two of the kerosene stove burners. Mom always says that copper boiler was so worth the $3.39 she paid for it a few years back.

Marian, being the youngest, always gets to be first to bathe, then I can. I love getting down in the metal wash tub at least as much as I can. The water is soothing to just sit there, but I can't stay long as Mom is next. Then Bobby, John, and Dad follow in their turns. More hot water is added as the water cools so the last one still has some warm water.

I laid out my dress, clean underwear, and my socks on the chair by my metal bed already for the fun day at the park. I wondered if I could sleep; I was so excited about tomorrow. Marian and I pulled back the chenille bedspread, then we laid back the gray wool blanket, which was made from wool sheared from Dad's sheep. We would not need its warmth tonight as we probably only needed a sheet over us.

Marian was just as anxious as I was for the next day to come. Mother had told her there were swings, teeter-totters, and a slide in the park. She kept talking to me about sliding on the tall slide at the park and riding the push iron merry-go-round with a wooden floor to stand on. She said she wanted to see the pond with the lily pads on it.

After Marian fell asleep, I was still thinking. My mind couldn't seem to shut down. It just kept wondering on. I thought of the wool blanket on my bed. I remembered going with Dad to take some of his bundles of sheared wool in a small trailer he pulled behind the car to Mabel, Minnesota, to sell. The rest of the wool bundles Dad took to the large brick woolen mill at Decorah where it was made into wool blankets and wool battings for inside of the quilts Mother made.

I think I was trying to avoid what I really wanted to think about. I was afraid to trust that it might happen. *Maybe tomorrow, I will have a chance to hike the trail in Phelps Park with Mark. It would be so much fun to walk and talk with him, just the two of us. Of course, it is likely that John and Mark will rush off without me. Hopefully, we will walk together.*

Dear God, I pray that we do not get into war. How can I imagine what life would be like if Mark and John left for the military? My days would feel so empty. I know that I would feel like a limp Raggedy Ann with holes in my heart. How could I go on living? Losing Blackie was bad enough, I could not possibly think of losing Mark or John.

Finally, my mind stopped turning thoughts over and over, and I slept.

2

The Picnic

The bright sunshine was shining through the thin lace curtains on the window. I stretched, and as soon as I thought this is the picnic day, I quickly got out of bed. Marian stirred. I told her to get up, this is the day we will have fun.

Arriving in the summer kitchen in the milk house, we realized the rest of the family are already at the table. Mother had stacks of fluffy pancakes with fresh strawberries and whipped cream on them. Marian and Mom had picked the berries the day before.

Earlier, Father and John had milked the dairy cows, but they still had to feed the hogs and the chickens. Marian and I cleared the table. Marian put the butter and cream in a tightly lidded metal can in the large tank in the milk house. That is where perishables are kept lowered in the cold water pumped by the tall windmill beside the milk house.

I took two large dishpans from hooks on the wall. One pan was for washing dishes, and the other for draining the dishes. Because of it being summer and not much need for heat except to cook, the kitchen cook stove fueled with wood was not often used. I put a teakettle over one of the three burners on the kerosene stove in the milk house to heat the water. Mom had used the kerosene stove for making the pancakes for us and the coffee for her and Dad.

When the water was hot, I turned the knob on the stove to shut it off. I poured the hot water into the dishpan on the table. Soon I was stacking dishes to drain in the other pan. I like getting my hands in the soapy hot water. It feels so good, but often Mom wants to wash. She says the hot water makes her arthritic hands feel better.

Marian grabbed a white feed sack dish towel to dry the dishes while I washed them. I wrung water out of my dish rag so that I could use it to wipe clean the colorful red, yellow, and green oilcloth on the table.

While Marian and I did the dishes, Mom baked a batch of yeast buns. She had let the dough rise in the cool cellar overnight. I added to our picnic a jar of homemade sweet pickles and tomatoes freshly sliced from our garden.

Mother got the picnic dishes ready to place in our large wicker basket with two wooden handles. She placed some things in a wooden peach crate. Last July from the Buy Rite, we had purchased Arkansas peaches wrapped in soft tissues to keep them from bruising and packed in a wooden box. The wooden box comes in handy for many uses.

I combed out my curls made from the bobby-pinned curls yesterday. I am glad that my clothes are all laid out. I quickly dress. The picnic basket and crate are loaded in the back of the stark black Model A. Bobby and I must sit with our feet across the top of the crate. John holds the picnic basket on his lap. Marian is squeezed in between Mom and Dad.

Joyously Dad toots the horn, and we are off. We live on a dirt road a good mile off the gravel road that leads into Decorah.

We plan to get to the park about 11:00 a.m. On the way, Dad says, "I will buy a dollar's worth of gas, so we have plenty for Sunday so we can go to church. No stores are open on Sunday as it is the Lord's Sabbath."

At the filling station, Dad pulls up to the pump. An attendant comes out. "What will it be today, Mr. Sturloff?"

Dad replies. "Put in a dollar's worth."

The man pumps the gas and then wipes our high straight windshield. "Have a good day, Mr. Sturloff!" he cries as he waves us on.

The car slowly climbs the hill up Broadway and curves toward Phelps Park. My legs are getting kind of sore leaning on the wooden crate, but we are almost there.

Dad spots a shelter house, and we park. Our neighbors have not arrived yet. Mom places two oilcloths on the tables and gets out our dishes and food. Then she starts to tell us more about the park.

"I want you to know the history of this park so that you will enjoy it more," Mother explained.

Mother impressed on us to value this park built by the foresight and hard labor of other people for us to enjoy and treasure. I am glad my mother always stressed to us the importance of appreciating what others did to make our lives happier.

Just then our neighbors' 1932 Plymouth four-door sedan came into view. We waved to them, so they would know where we were. We had put two picnic tables together, so we had plenty of room for all twelve of us. John and Mark sat together across from Mark's sister, Melanie, a year younger than me. I sat next to Melanie with Bobby on my right and Jimmy across from him. Janie and Marian sat with our parents at the first table.

The food was passed. Mrs. McDonald had brought a large platter of deviled eggs sprinkled with red paprika, pickled beets, a lettuce salad, and two apple pies. Her fare, in addition to Mother's dishes, produced so much to delight the eye and fill the empty place inside.

After our apple pie dessert, the two youngest took off for the playground. Mother warned them, "Marian and Janie, be careful on the high slide. Hang on tight to the handrail going up the steps to the top and sit down carefully on the slide so you don't fall off."

Mother and Mrs. McDonald put the food away and cleared the tables. Dad and Mr. McDonald started visiting. They started talking about the improvements in the last few years.

Dad pointed out, "Why, it is already eight years since the paved highway from Decorah to the Twin Cities in Minnesota was finished. The last of the unpaved portion in Minnesota was completed in 1932."

Mother, after listening to the men, commented, "Twenty years ago, my sister put in electricity in her Decorah home. Lydia claimed it only cost thirty-five dollars to wire her whole house. The money paid to have a pull chain fixture in the kitchen, a switch with a fixture in the following areas—the living room, the dining room, the bedroom, and on the porch…all of it…the wiring, fixtures, lamps, and labor—all of it cost thirty-five dollars. Isn't it too bad we cannot have such modern conveniences in the country?"

I know my dad feels bad for Mom and deeply senses his inability to give her electricity like her sister enjoys. "Lettie, as soon as the war gets over in Europe, I am sure we will be able to get electricity out in the country where we live."

That remark turned the minds of the men to the war raging in Europe. Mark's dad predicted, "With Americans sending military supplies to Britain and the possibility of the US getting into the struggle, it might be some time before we can get copper wire to bring electricity to our farms in the country."

Then their conversation changed to economics. Mother remarked, "Last week, my eggs brought only twelve cents a dozen. In the 1920s, I was receiving prices from twenty cents up to a few times a high of forty cents a dozen for my eggs. Since the big drop in the Depression years, it doesn't seem the prices have come back much. Of course, when I sell eggs to the hatchery I can get a few cents more, but that's only in the late winter or early springtime."

The teenagers were beginning to have enough of adult war and financial concerns. John suggested, "Let's go on the walking trail." He and Mark led the way with Bobby and Jimmy following them. Melanie and I stepped it off to catch up with them. Janie and Marian, seeing us leave hurriedly, caught up with their older sisters.

We entered the trail where there was a wooden structure with benches to sit on to view the Upper Iowa River below. Instead of sitting down, we looked out over the rock wall, taking in the breathtaking picturesque view below us. The river waters meandered through the lower land, twisting this way and that like a large dark snake. We looked through leafy branches close to us to see a thick jade-green bank of trees cascading down to the mat of green along the river's edge.

"God's green earth sure is a beautiful place, isn't it?" I commented to no one in particular. I just felt that I had to acknowledge this beauty.

Mark turned and stared at me with a quizzical look. "Julia Ann, you are so right. We are blessed to be able to see and enjoy the beauty God created for us. Somehow when I am out in nature… in the woods, on the river…I feel closer to my Maker."

Then as if embarrassed, he took off with John, Jimmy and Bobby close at their heels. My face seemed a bit warm, and I turned to the trail. The girls and I took our time walking. Mother had told us yesterday that we might find fossils, so I kept looking at the ground to see if I could see any interesting rocks.

I told Melanie, "Mom said that this northeast corner of Iowa was not passed over by the glaciers like the rest of Iowa. Most of Iowa got its rich dark soil from soil moved here by the massive sheets of ice as they moved across the state during the ice ages. The glaciers smoothed and flattened the land. In contrast, Northeast Iowa is hilly and has many hills, limestone cliffs, and forested areas. The limestone cliffs were laid down from the seas of long ago. As the sea animals died, their bodies decayed, forming the lime that eventually turned to limestone. Now in the limestone, one can find trilobites, snails, and other sea animals embedded in the rocks."

We examined some stones where we could see snail shapes. As this is a park, we knew that we should not take any of the rocks so that others also can enjoy finding and examining them. We came to a rocky curved walkway leading down steps to a wooden bridge over a deep waterway. Below we could hear the falling water and see the runoff from the recent rain. Water was cascading over the hillside to the Upper Iowa River below.

We slowly stepped down the steep hillside to the wooden bridge. We stood on the bridge and looked down into the rocky deep waterway with its sloping steep sides covered with greenery. I could picture wildflowers there in the springtime.

I told Melanie, "I bet trilliums, jack-in-the-pulpits, mayapples, wild geraniums, and other wildflowers can be found here in early springtime. I love looking for wildflowers in the woods in the spring."

After leaving the bridge, we even more lazily climbed the rather steep hill ahead of us. We were nearly to the top when we were shocked.

The boys jumped out from the underbrush along the walkway, yelling and scaring us nearly to death. In my fright, I stumbled on a raised rock in the path and fell on my face. I skinned my knee, tore my polka-dot dress on another sharp rock, scraped my hands, and I could feel my nose hurt. My nose was bleeding.

Mark came over and handed me a nice large white men's handkerchief. Almost in tears from the shock and my ouchies, I stammered, "I don't want to get blood on your hanky."

He assured me it was okay and began to wipe my face. The blood was still dripping. I just sat there. *What must everyone think of me? Do they think I am clumsy? Why did this have to happen in front of Mark? I must look miserable with a bloodied face, torn dress, and scraped knee.*

Mark and John helped me to my feet. My knee hurt, but I could walk; there were no broken bones. My bleeding nose was now barely dripping, but the white hanky was bloody red.

Melanie took my hand, and we started walking. The rest, a subdued group, solemnly followed behind. When we were almost back to the beginning of the trail, the boys apologized for frightening me and causing my fall.

Before I returned to the picnic tables, I found a water faucet and washed my face. By now my nose was no longer bleeding. I washed the hanky in cold water. I will take it home and whiten it before giving it back to Mark.

I guess I looked a mess when I returned to the table. The boys admitted to their part in causing my fall. Both set of parents reprimanded them playing such a prank and causing me to be hurt. Mom and Martha McDonald set out food from our baskets and boxes one more time. We all took pleasure in having another opportunity to eat the delicious picnic food. Mark came up to me as I was preparing to be the first one to get in our car to go home.

I did not expect him to say anything more to me today.

"Julia Ann, I am so sorry that I frightened you. Most of all, I feel so bad that I caused you to be hurt." He took my hand and squeezed it tightly.

"Thank you, Mark. I appreciate that." With hearing my remark, he turned and in a flash was gone.

Sunday morning, I wore my old dress to church. It was almost too small for me. *I hope Mom can fix my polka-dot dress, so the tear doesn't show. Maybe she will help me fix it.*

My knee still hurts a little bit, so I kind of hobbled up the many steps to St. Benedict's Church.

The priest standing in the elevated pulpit to the side of the altar, speaking in an Irish brogue, gave a sermon about the prodigal son. He related how the wayward boy's father welcomed him home with open arms, forgave him for his wrongdoings, and made a feast to celebrate his return. Father Dolan stressed that is the kind of love that God, Jesus Christ, offers to us if we return to him and repent of our sins.

In the back of the church over the entryway, the choir is located on a second level overlooking the pews below in the main part of the church. I like to think of the choir as angels singing over our heads. There is a large pipe organ behind them. I love to hear the pipe organ music.

At Communion, I lightly limped up to the communion rail, knelt down, and the priest placed a communion wafer on my tongue. We are not to let it touch our teeth or at least not chew it, just swallow it down. On my return to my seat, I knelt and piously said the prayer for after Communion.

The priest said the mass in Latin. I took Latin during my freshman and sophomore year in high school, but I still cannot understand the priest. Latin is known as a dead language because it is no longer used in daily life, but Latin words do turn up in the romance languages, which are French and Spanish. Many English words are derived from Latin, and Latin is used in medical terminology. I am glad I studied Latin because I think that I understand the roots of many words better.

I wonder if Mark and I will have any classes together next year. He is a year older than me so maybe not.

After yesterday, I think my family is ready for a quiet day at home. Marian is busy playing with her paper dolls. Mom and Dad are relaxing in lawn chairs on the front porch. The boys are boxing in the roped ring they made on the floor above the horse barn. I guess they think they are fighting Joe Louis. Sometimes if the battery isn't low on the radio, they listen to the Joe Louis fights.

I am happy to have some time to write in my dairy, but I have to be careful what I say. I do not want anyone to know the deep feelings of my heart. Some things are just meant to be private. They are just too secretive to be shared. Why do I feel that way so strongly? Would I be embarrassed if someone knew? Would I be teased relentlessly? Or do I feel if I think it is true and find out it isn't, I would be hurt too much?

Nevertheless, I decide to write in my diary that I am only sixteen, but I like Mark. I hope that he and my brothers do not have to go to war.

At bedtime, I kneel by my bed to say my nightly prayers. I make the sign of the cross and say a Hail Mary and the Our Father. I thank God for my mother and father, my brothers, and Marian. I pray for Grandpa Sturloff.

When I am tucked under my covers, I pray for Mark.

Will he really leave to go to war when he is eighteen years old? I hope not. But if we go to war, maybe he will be drafted into the service. Why are there wars? Why do men want to kill other men? Aren't we supposed to act like Christians? We think that we are civilized, and yet we kill just like men did centuries ago.

I am young. I want to live a good life. Can I enjoy my life if I have to worry about war, my loved ones being killed in battle, and living without the ones I love so dearly?

I turn one way and then another trying to get comfortable and go to sleep. I think of my mother's laments about society changing so much after World War I. *If there were so many drastic differences after that war, what would a bigger world war bring to my personal world? How can we as mere human beings cope with such alterations of how people live and relate to one another?*

Finally, I drifted off to sleep.

3

Summertime Activities

With the crops planted and the hay in the barn, the men are now not quite so busy, but the women are getting into a very busy season. We have been busy picking raspberries and making raspberry jam. The vegetables are coming on strong. Monday, I picked two five-gallon pails of green beans. Then I sat on the porch swing to remove the ends of the stems to ready the beans for Mom to can. As I work, I remember the good time we had at the picnic. *When will we have another fun outing like that? I wonder.*

I put my hand on the middle of my back. *Oh! How my back aches.* My back is aching from first leaning over, picking the beans, and now sitting here, leaning over stemming the beans. *When will I ever get these done? I still must cut them into inch or so pieces.*

Finally, when they are all cut, Mother takes the cut beans to place in clean hot sterilized canning quart jars. She pours boiling water to an inch of the top of the jar. Rubber bands fit around the jars, and a zinc lid is placed on each jar and tightened. The jars are then carefully placed in boiling water for so many minutes depending on the size of the jars and the kind of food. The boiling water sterilizes the jar and food to make sure the food will be free of bacteria and will keep for the winter when there will be no garden to supply fresh vegetables.

Because we had to do beans before they would get too big and tough on Monday, we washed clothes on Tuesday. The motorized washing machine is in the milk house in the summertime. I pulled the sheets and pillowcases off all the beds. Mother washed them and other whites like white shirts first.

While Mom loads the colored wash and gets the machine agitating, powered by a gasoline motor under the tub, I take a basket of white clothes to hang to dry. The clothesline is as long as our house and parallel to it. I take clothespins, wooden, like pegs, with a slit in the bottom to hold the clothes to the wire line. I picked up a heavy wet sheet and was trying to attach one end to the line. With a piercing scream, I dropped the sheet and the clothespins and ran like mad. "John, help… help…help!"

John heard my continued yelling and rushed to the clothesline. I was shaking and pointing into the mulberry tree close to the clothesline. He saw what I was motioning at and took off for his gun. He shot the snake that was entwined on a branch eating the mulberries.

There was no doubt that I had to go back to hanging clothes, but my eyes kept searching the grass and the tree for any movement. *Oh! How I hate snakes.*

Mother and I canned tomatoes. They were easier to do as they are larger than beans and peas. We scald them in hot water to remove the skins and pushed them into sterile jars, adding a teaspoon of salt on top, sealed them with lids, and put them in for a hot water bath in the copper boiler.

After they have been in a rolling boil for the required minutes, Mother lifted them out with a jar holder, being careful not to get burned by hot steam and water. Canning tomatoes goes faster, and we can put up a lot more jars than most other garden produce.

After a few more weeks, Dad came in one day and announced, "The coons have found our sweet corn. We will have to pick the corn and preserve it tomorrow, or those raccoons will leave us none."

The next day, Dad and John took the bushel baskets and headed for the sweet corn patch. Coming back with heaped baskets of green husked ears of corn, they dumped the bushels of sweet corn on the lawn.

Dad and the boys husked the corn, and Mom and I pulled off the silks. Marian tried to help us.

Pulling the silks off the ears of corn seems such a tedious task. Because of all the work we had to do, we did not talk much while we worked, which added to the monotony of the job. *Oh! How good that corn will taste next winter. I especially like when Mom makes scalloped corn.*

Mom carried the husked ears of corn to the milk house where she started cutting the kernels off the cob. When the rest of us finished cleaning up in the yard, Dad, John, and I helped cut the corn. Then Mother started putting it into jars, ready for its hot water bath. As we worked, I asked, "When will there be something fun to do again?"

"How would you like to go to the Winneshiek County Fair next week?" Dad asked us.

What exciting news for the whole family. Marian and Bobby had made artwork and school projects for exhibit in the school exhibit hall. They excitedly told us how they wanted to show their crafts to us.

Mother decided she would exhibit some vegetables and canned food in the culinary arts building. Dad and John talked about exhibiting some young pigs. Bobby said he would like to exhibit a young lamb if it was okay with Dad.

"Mom, what can I take to the fair?" I asked. She thought I should exhibit the apron that I had made in home economics class.

The more I thought about it, I felt I wanted to take something else. What could I build something out of? There were now two peach crates, one from last year and one from this year after we canned the peaches. *Could I make something out of them? I always wanted a dressing table. Could I make one by putting a board on top of each crate and long enough to leave an eighteen-inch gap between the crates?*

When I told Mother and Dad that I wanted a dressing table and explained my design to them, they said they thought it was an excellent idea. Mother said she would buy some material for me to sew a skirt to put around the dressing table and tack it to the edge of the board on top of the crates.

When we did our shopping on Saturday, Dad helped me buy some cream-colored paint to paint the boxes. Mother purchased nice crisp flowered material for the skirt. On Monday, I painted my crates. Tuesday

Mother helped me measure and cut the material. I stitched the sides and top of the skirt and hemmed the bottom. Wednesday, I tacked the frilly skirt to the dressing table. Presto! I had myself a pretty table to sit up to and comb my hair, put on my necklaces, and maybe even a touch of lipstick and perfume. Mother doesn't want me using cosmetics, or at least not much makeup. She tells me it is not fitting for a young girl. I think the flamboyant flappers of the twenties sickened Mother on very red rouge and lipstick.

The dressing table would be the perfect place to sit and put my hair up on metal curlers or make pin curls with bobby pins. Mother used to curl my hair with a hot curling iron, which she heated over coals in the cook stove. I was scared it would burn my hair off. I would rather use sticky junk to strengthen the curls on curlers.

On Wednesday, Dad and Bobby borrowed Mr. McDonald's old truck to take the pigs and the lamb to put in stalls at the fairgrounds. A very excited Marian rode with them in the truck. Mother and I washed tomatoes, cucumbers, peppers, squash, potatoes, and cut a large head of cabbage to exhibit. Mother wiped off jars of strawberry jam, raspberry jam, Whitney apple pickles, tomatoes, and corn to try for a ribbon at the fair. Some items shown at the fair might win a cash award.

We took my dressing table to exhibit at the fair by carefully loading it in the backseat of the car. We were able to find places for Mother's produce and canning. John drove our car; I sat between him and Mother.

Thursday was judging day. On Friday, we were anxious to find how the judging went the day before. Mother and I packed a picnic lunch. We piled into the Ford and left for a day at the fair. The plan was that Dad and John would go home to do the chores, the milking of the cows, and feeding of the pigs and chickens. They would return for the grandstand show in the evening.

We checked the animal barns first. Dad smiled when he saw a blue ribbon hanging on the cage holding his red hog. John's pen of three pigs received a red ribbon. Mother was unable to wait any longer to view her exhibits. She won all blue ribbons except a red ribbon for her cucumbers.

The larger items were next. We walked by furniture, which was refinished, handmade furniture pieces, and finally there was my exhibit. A large blue ribbon was fastened on the front of the skirt. "Mom, thank you for letting me do this project." I gave my mother a big hug. It feels so good to make something worthwhile. Bobby and Marian pulled us toward the midway. We had to walk through the midway containing a Ferris wheel, a merry-go- round, kiddy cars, pony rides, a booth to throw darts at targets for prizes, a tent area to play bingo, a booth to ring milk bottles, and sideshow tents. On the other side of the midway was the school exhibit hall.

There were so many interesting crafts, projects, and works of art on display. We spent much time studying pieces that interested us. There was a miniature Fort Atkinson with sticks for the stockade, small rocks in plaster of Paris to represent the block house with slots for the guns to shoot through. The story attached related how the fort was actually built to protect Indians from Indians.

My father told us, "The fort was the reason my mother's family came from Indiana to the area because there was a priest at the fort. Being they were good Catholics, they wanted to be near where they could hear mass. My grandmother was four years old on the trip to Iowa. The story is that she had to walk alongside the wagon that was pulling the belongings of the family. Well, anyway, I bet she did have to walk some of the way especially if the going was tough for the animals to pull the wagon."

I said to my dad, "Sure makes me feel happy that today we have cars to ride in." Then I laughingly said, "Horseless carriages are easier than having to hitch up a horse every time I want to go somewhere."

Dad replied, "Your grandmother Maggie used to take a couple of the younger ones and me in the buggy from the farm north of Decorah to Fort Atkinson to visit her folks."

I replied, "It is hard for me to believe only twenty to thirty years ago people traveled by horse and buggy as they had no cars or trucks."

Bobby hesitantly pointed to the wall, "There's my mill picture." On white paper with a pencil, Bobby had made a drawing of the mill my grandfather Jacob used to own and operate on Canoe Creek. To draw his picture, Bobby had looked at an old picture taken in 1912 when Grandpa sold the mill.

"Bobby, what an amazingly good job you did drawing the wooden mill, the waterway for the waterwheel, and the farmers with their buggies in front of the mill. You even drew your grandpa and my brother."

Father further explained, "Dad sold the mill in 1912 to buy wheat land in Montana. Dad and my two older grown-up brothers acquired land in the eastern part of the state. Those two brothers and their families still live out there. You know your grandma died only six years later of the flu that was so bad at the time. After that, my dad went to live permanently in Montana."

Just then Marian squealed, "Look, Mom and Dad, that's mine."

Her picture was of a kitty playing with a ball of yarn. It was quite a good drawing for her age.

We walked slowly back through the midway. I was thinking about what I would like to do there. It would be so much fun to ride the Ferris wheel with Mark. Now I am dreaming. Maybe I can ride it with Melanie or Marian.

Marian begged her Dad to ride the ponies, and we all watched as she rode a Shetland pony around and around. She waved and seemed to have a great time. Now she will want a pony of her own. We ate our lunch under a large oak tree near the grandstand.

After lunch Mother and Dad visited with some people they knew who had just finished eating at the picnic tables.

John and Bobby went back to the livestock barns to find buddies to talk to. Marian and I strolled through the midway again and took another look at the school exhibits. Someday I would like to be a teacher and help students make such great projects.

Melanie found us on the midway. She exclaimed, "Let's go ride the Ferris wheel. We can put Marian between us."

It was great looking all over the fairgrounds from that high up. The biggest thrill was coming down from the top height of the big wheel.

Mother played some bingo. She won a small lamp with a pink shade. She told me, "We don't have electricity yet, but I am giving it to you for your dressing table."

I gave her a warm hug and squeezed her hard. "It will be just perfect. Thank you, dear Mother."

Around seven thirty, we started up the ramp of the grandstand to find good seats. There was visiting going on all around us.

At eight o'clock, the show started. There was a doggie show where the little dogs jumped through hoops and did tricks. A lady dressed in a sparkly short-skirted outfit walked the tightrope. We all held our breath for fear she would fall. She didn't. Then she bowed, smiled, and waved at us. A clown did funny things, making us laugh loudly. Three women and three men performed a dance routine. They were dressed in colorful costumes. They merrily sang as they gracefully danced on the stage.

After the show, Dad told us, "You have an hour to walk around the midway and maybe have some rides. Your mother and I will stay under the grandstand, look at some of the exhibits, and do some visiting."

Melanie and I took off for the midway. It was more fun now with all the lights, the carousel music loudly playing, and the eager crowds of people of all ages. We watched young boys try to ring the glass milk bottles.

Mark touched me on the elbow and whispered in my ear, "Julia Ann, would you ride the Ferris wheel with me?"

I quickly turned, looking into his warm, smiling chocolate- brown eyes. "That would be fun."

John asked Melanie to ride with him. Mark took my hand, and we headed to the pay booth. Mark paid for his ride and mine. We stood watching the lighted wheel go around and around amid the giggles and shouts of its riders.

Mark took my hand, and helped me get into the seat, then he sat beside me, and the operator made sure we were fastened in. The wheel slightly turned a few times to allow more to get on. Then the wheel started turning more forcibly.

Mark took my hand and said, "Are you afraid of heights?"

"No, Melanie and I rode this afternoon. But with the lights, it is much more fun tonight." In my heart, I know it is more fun because he is with me.

Then he slipped his arm behind me and drew me closer. Oh! What a happy ride this is. Going up was fun and coming down was a real thrill. Round and round we went. I did not want the ride to ever end, but of course it ended too quickly.

Mark and I knew that soon I would have to go meet my parents. but we decided to circle the midway one last time. The four of us walked and watched people having a good time. For a while, we watched young people trying to throw darts at a target to win stuffed animals. We decided that would be fun. I threw my four darts, and only one hit the target. Mark threw three hits and won a small teddy bear.

"Julia Ann, I want you to have this teddy bear." He thrust the small bear into my hands.

What will I tell mama? Should I keep it?

I wanted it to remember this night, so I kept it. After Mark left, I tucked my bear in my purse. I believed John wouldn't tell because I won't tell he took Melanie on the Ferris wheel.

That night I tucked the little bear in with me. I knew I would think happy dreams tonight. We were so tired sleep came easily for not only me but also Marian.

The next days were busy getting ready to go back to school. We shopped in Decorah for school clothes. Mother bought me some new shoes, socks, and a pretty sweater. It was so much fun looking at all the pretty things in the department stores. We bought the usual school supplies, paper, notebooks, pencils, and erasers. For Marian, Mother bought Big Chief tablets and scissors with a blunt end.

Earlier in the summer, we had purchased material for Mrs. Whipple to make me three new skirts and several blouses, two with long sleeves. I am delighted with the skirts. She had sewn hooks and eyes at the waist to hold the waistband together.

My folks and Mark's parents decided that John and I would ride to school with Mark and Melanie on Monday mornings. John and I would be staying with Uncle Roy and Aunt Ida during the week. On Friday after school, we would ride home with Mark and Melanie. I feel this year will be one of my best.

School starts the Monday after Labor Day. John plays a trumpet, and I play an alto saxophone in the school band. Mark plays a trombone and Melanie the piccolo. It is planned that Dad will take us to the McDonald home on Monday at seven thirty or a bit earlier if possible. After school on Friday, Mark will drive John and me to our house.

That evening, Aunt Lizzie and Martha called on the phone. "Lettie, we want you to know the Concord grapes are ripe. Can your family come to help make Concord grape jelly? The menfolk will help with the stomping of the grapes. You and Julia can help preparing the juice to make jelly."

To me, it is exciting when the ice blocks are brought from the ice house. The big block is chipped with an ice pick, and the chunks of ice are dropped into a large pan of juice crushed from the ripe purple grapes. Hmmm, that ice-cold grape juice is delicious.

Last winter the aunts and Uncle William had ice cut from the river in the coldest part of the year. The ice blocks are stored with sawdust over them and around them in the ice house to keep them cold so that in the summer there is ice for the icebox to keep food cold. An ice block is placed behind a door in the upper part of the wooden ice box, and behind a separate door below, the food is stored.

On the Saturday before Labor Day weekend, my whole family went to the celebration at the fort in Fort Atkinson. We walked around on the grounds and looked through the slots from which guns were fired from the block house.

Indians dressed in their native attire, with feathers in their hair, danced. There were displays of guns from earlier years. There were campfires, and people dressed as if they stepped out of an earlier time.

When we arrived home, I had a big surprise. Blackie was lying near the steps to the kitchen. I rushed over to him. He seemed glad to see me. He stood. Shocked, I saw that his left lower hind leg was missing, but he was alive. I petted him, and he purred contentedly, happy he was home.

I praised God that I wasn't hurt during haying time when the horses ran away with me holding the reins. *Dear God, bless and protect my family and Mark. Do not let our country get into the war.*

Summer is over, and my thoughts turn to the school year ahead of me.

It has been a wonderful, happy summer. It is nice having a kind and good friend like Mark. I feel unsure what the school year will be like. Will Mark find another girl friend during the school year? I hope not.

4

1940 – 1941 School Year

On the first day of school, Dad took John and me to McDonald's farm so that we could ride with Mark and Melanie to high school. Bobby stayed home to help Dad and will go to high school next year. Mark stacked our band instruments in the trunk of the car. He drove with John in the passenger seat and Melanie and I seated in the back.

Band is at eight o'clock, so we will always have to be started on the road by seven thirty. After band, we have classes beginning at nine until noon. We have an hour's lunch period, which allows enough time for John and I to walk to Uncle Roy's to have lunch with his family. Classes resume at one until four.

After school, John goes downtown to help Uncle Roy in the hardware store. He helps wait on customers and stocks shelves. I go to Uncle Roy's house to help my aunt with the young children. When I leave the high school, I pick up Bonnie from kindergarten and Rickie from first grade to walk them home. Usually Randy in third grade runs home by himself.

By the time I get to Aunt Ida's, she is very glad to see me. Baby Becky, only a year old, is a real handful. Her sister, Bernice, three years old, is a little rascal too.

By helping Aunt Ida after school until about seven o'clock I earn my board and room for the week. John earns his keep by helping Uncle Roy after school. Both of us usually have homework to do in the evenings.

This fall I am taking English literature, world history, typing, and home economics. Two days a week I have gym classes. During my study period after lunch, I help at the high school librarian's desk.

My world history class is third period; I was surprised to see Mark in my class. After class he walked with me to my locker where I deposited my books.

Mark told me that he always liked history classes. He thought Mrs. West's class would be interesting. Mark informed me, "I like studying about foreign countries. Someday I would like to visit some of the lands overseas."

Is that another reason you want to enlist in the army? Oh well, I want to enjoy Mark's senior year. I will try not to think of war and his wanting to enlist if the United States goes to war.

My cousin Ruby kind of stared at me, making me feel that I was doing something wrong. Is it wrong to walk and talk with a boy? All we did was talk to each other. Does she think that I am supposed only talk to girls? Oh! well, I don't really care what she thinks. I just hope that she doesn't make it sound like something bad to Aunt Kate. Ruby, at her age, still likes to tattle; being a talebearer of such blameless behavior seems dimwitted to me.

After the noise of the hallways, the library seems like a restful haven. No one is to talk in the library. The librarian is very strict about that. She says the library is a place to study.

If I am not busy checking in books, I am free to do my homework. I am not busy today, so I have time to start reading my literature assignment. I am to read the *Scarlet Letter*, an 1850 romantic work of fiction in a historical setting, written by Nathaniel Hawthorne. It is such a sad story that points out how important purity is for a young woman. Indiscretions are vividly described with the pain of guilt known by others and never forgotten by self.

The school week passed quickly, and soon it was after school on Friday. John and I had Mark pick us up at Uncle Roy's house, so we could take our dirty clothes home to be washed. On the way home, the boys were recapping the week. They were in speech class together and were discussing the kinds of speeches they would be expected to give. I gathered that neither one of them looked forward to standing in front of classmates and giving a speech.

Melanie said that she enjoyed her English class but wondered if she wouldn't have to study hard to keep up in her geometry and biology classes. I noted that she was taking both books home with her.

Homecoming week was so exciting. On Monday, each class selected candidates for attendants for homecoming. The senior class was to choose candidates for homecoming queen. On Thursday the whole school voted for their favorite candidates.

To my great surprise, I was selected as a junior attendant. I was happy and sad at the same time. It would be such fun to dress up in a pretty formal gown, but one of the football guys would walk with me, of course, not Mark.

I called Mother on the telephone, asking, "Where can I get a pretty dress to wear? Miss Riley told all the attendants that we are to wear formals, long dresses." I think that Mom was proud of me for being selected.

She replied, "I will ask Aunt Millie if you can wear the bridesmaid's dress cousin Susie wore in her sister's wedding last summer."

I remember the dress. It was blue lacy material over taffeta with a wide blue sash and tiny red flowers embroidered on the bodice. There was a matching short blue jacket. I knew it would fit as Susie and I are about the same size. Dad would pick up the dress at Aunt Millie's house and bring it to me.

The marching band was to play for homecoming on Friday night. Being an attendant, I could not march at halftime as I would be walking onto the field with one of the football players. Whom would I have to walk with? It can't be Mark because he is not a football player. Mark will be playing his trombone in the band. Sometimes life can be rosy and gloomy all at the same time. The dress fit me perfectly. Aunt Ida told me that I looked very pretty. She purchased a blue ribbon for my hair to match the dress. Mother had sent my dress shoes and long stockings for me to wear.

The assembly in the high school auditorium was loud and noisy. The band played, and all the classes stood and sang, "On Decorah, on Decorah…" There were several little skits about winning the game. Then the candidates came onstage escorted by one of the football players.

I felt nervous. *What does Mark think of all this?* I see him in the band holding his long trombone. Oh, how I wish he was my escort, but no, it is Mickey Thronson, a very tall, blond-haired Norwegian senior boy. *Well, I am relieved at least Mickey is a very handsome young man.*

Mickey greets me and places my arm in his as we march onto the stage. There are six senior girls who are hoping to be selected queen. No one will know until the crowning at halftime which girl has been voted the queen.

Following the assembly, students and onlookers lined the streets to see the homecoming parade. Each of the four high school classes had made a float. The six senior girls chosen as candidates for queen rode in open vehicles.

Waukon High School is playing against Decorah. Of course, they want to defeat us being it is our homecoming game. Halftime finally comes. The marching band does a short marching routine and then retires to the side. They play music softly as the freshman girl and her attendant, the sophomore girl and her attendant, and Mickey, gently holding my arm, walks me onto the field, and we take our places. Then five senior girls and their attendants walk to their places. At last, the queen, Alice Wilson, a petite blonde senior with her attendant, the well-known husky football player Bert Janson, take their place of honor, waving and smiling at the happy faces on the bleachers.

In the gymnasium, we have a homecoming dance. In the beginning, the queen and her attendant dance, then the other girls and their attendants are expected to dance. So, I dance with Mickey. He is kind and pleasant to me, but he is not Mark.

After putting their instruments away and removing their marching band suits, John and Mark arrive at the gym. Mark's eyes search out mine. He gives me a wink. That makes me feel better. Perhaps he understands my situation. He must realize that I was expected to walk in with Mickey and to dance the first dance with him.

Maybe I didn't have any need to worry because I could see Mark coming toward me with a big happy smile that made my heart jump.

The hired musicians were playing "Only Forever." Other couples were doing the fox-trot to the newly popular music. *Can I fox-trot? Will Mark know how?*

"Julia let's dance this one."

Mark led me onto the gymnasium's shiny floor. He took my right hand in his left hand and placed his right hand behind my middle back. I placed my left hand on his shoulder. We started to move backward for me; one, two. As we danced counterclockwise on the floor, I began to relax. This is exciting—*No, I must not think about that. I must keep my mind on what I am doing.*

Mark whispered in my ear, "Julia, I am going to twirl you."

Before I could protest, Mark lifted his right arm, and taking my left hand in his right hand, he twirled me around. Thankfully, I kept myself on my feet surprisingly well. Then just as quickly, his right hand was at my waist, moving me backward in a graceful movement.

Happiness swelled up inside of me. I felt proud that Mark is such a good dancer, but most of all, I was happy because he is enjoying dancing with me, and I am following his lead.

"Mark, how did you learn to dance so well?"

He explained that his mother had taught him how to dance.

He even knew how to waltz. He is better than me at waltzing.

Mark danced with me a-number-of times. Then while dancing together the last slow dance of the evening, bent down and whispered, "Julia Ann, you look very pretty in blue. You are one of the prettiest girls here. It makes me happy to dance with you."

I felt like my heart must have skipped a beat. I squeezed his left hand and replied, "I am a blessed girl to have a nice-looking friend like you to dance with."

The dance ended far too soon. Mark took John, Melanie, and me home. All my worries about being a junior class attendant were for naught. I had a good time, and I had good reason to think that Mark did too.

When I crawled into bed, I reached for my little teddy bear and gave him a hug and a kiss. Dreamily, I thought someday— someday—I will get a hug and a kiss.

December was a cold month, but the most chilling thing to me was the news Dad told the family after supper one colder-than- normal evening. Dad said, "The news is that President Roosevelt asked our nation to build weapons of war for the Allies. After that presidential request, Congress passed the Lend-Lease Act, which makes money available to the Allies for them to buy American war materials and food.

Dad predicted, "This increased demand will put our nation to work in the factories to keep them humming with production. Farmers like me will build up our agricultural production to keep the armies and the nation in food. I believe the pain of the Great Depression will soon only be a memory."

I felt like a confused numbskull. I expressed my thinking. "We suffered financially in the Great Depression. Even if we could have afforded to install electrical writing in our home, we could not get electricity. We live in the country, and the electrical company could not justify the great expense to bring the wires out this far. We had to go without many comforts, even ones that others considered needs. Anything we sold was almost worthless. The money we did have was used only for absolute necessities. We struggled to make ends meet. Now we are being asked to go into hard labor to produce weapons of war. By producing war materials for the British and her Allies to fight the Nazis, won't that pull us into the war? Hitler will view us as an enemy for taking sides with the Allies.

"I do not want our country to get into a war. My brothers and our neighbor, Mark, might have to go to war. Wars can be bloody and deadly. I do not want war."

John must have been thinking along the same lines that I was, for he said, "Now we are supposed to bust our guts in producing weapons for war. We had years of not having jobs for men, and now they are going to push them into working harder than ever to produce for a war.

"Yes, Dad, people will be put to work. It is highly likely prices will rise, but at what cost to humanity? Workers will be pressed to their limits to produce. If our involvement in providing for the Allies angers the Axis, it will pull us into the war. What a high price that will be in manpower, materials, and dollars to finance the fighting."

"Yes, Julia and John, the ordinary man does not have much say when it comes to conflicts between countries. I am afraid that you both are right with your insights about this clash between nations. It is sad, but only time will tell us of the outcome of all this discord."

January was cold and snowy in Northeast Iowa. I was happy to see the month end. The groundhog did not see his shadow on February 2. Whether or not we have six more weeks of winter, I have something warm to look forward to. The high school is having a Valentine's dance on Friday night.

On Friday, after school, we do not go home to the farm but stay in town to go to the dance. Mother bought me a red long- sleeved blouse to wear with my black skirt. It was not a bright- red color and looked nice with the dark skirt. John and I walked to the high school gymnasium. The wind was chilly and sharp. I am sure my cheeks were rosy without any rouge to color them. Mother did not like me using rouge or red paint on my nails. She said it made a woman look gaudy and of ill repute. Mother was always reminding me modern ways were not always good for Christians and are often sources of sin. Well, I wanted people to think well of me, so I did as she desired me to do.

Mother did not like me crossing my legs and taught me to do so is not lady like. Keep your legs together and sit up straight, she always taught me. Anyway, it helps me have good posture. The typing teacher told the class one day that I had good posture and asked the whole class to look at me while I was typing. That was embarrassing, but it still made me feel good that I was doing something well.

A small school band was playing the music and Mark and John were in the band. John does play a mean cornet and I like to watch Mark push his trombone out and in as he plays. I enjoyed the evening watching them play songs, some of which are modern jazz.

Twice Mark left the band and danced with me. That was so wonderful, floating around the floor in his arms. I felt like I was on a cloud and a strong wind was gently pushing me here and there. We had a break time when we could get refreshments. I sat, drinking some Pepsi and eating a hamburger with Mark and John. Mark had purchased the refreshments for all of us including Melanie.

"Julia Ann, when is the prom this year?" asked Mark.

"I think that the school paper said it would be April 10," I replied.

Melanie agreed that I was right about the date.

"Julia, will you go to the prom with me?" Mark questioned.

I felt rather embarrassed that he asked me in front of John and Melanie. I could feel the color rising in my face, but I answered him in the affirmative.

"Fine, then that's a date." He turned to John and inquired, "John, are you taking a date to the prom?"

My brother John had not thought that far ahead, I am sure. He did not quite know what to say, but I think it got him thinking that it would be nice to have some young lady go with him to the spring fling. Maybe Mother and I should help him learn to be a dancer. He is so good playing his cornet, he should be good at dancing also.

Mother and I helped John learn to dance. Before Mom was married, she bought a tall dark wooden cabinet holding a crank phonograph on top and doors underneath opening to shelves for holding stacks of records. I like to wind it up and play, "Tiptoe through the Tulips." It is one of Mom's old 78 rpm records she purchased in the twenties.

We picked out some waltzes and two-step recordings to practice with. Dad and Mom danced together, then Dad danced with me and Mother with John. I think Mom and Dad had a good time helping us learn to be better dancers. It was great watching my parents dancing in each other's arms. I could see that the spark of love still flows in their hearts. How comforting to know the love that binds my parents is a strong cord.

In early spring, before Easter, Dad drove the family to LaCrosse, Wisconsin, so that we can shop for the prom and Easter. Mother wants to buy me a new long dress for the prom. We look at pretty gowns in Dorflingers, but they are all so expensive. Finally, in another dress store, I find one I really like. I feel so ladylike in it, so grown up. Mother is making more from her eggs, so she is happy to be able to buy the dress for me.

John gets a new suit jacket and slacks to wear to the prom. Dad kids him if he has a date yet. John blushes brick red. Maybe, I thought, he has asked someone. *I wonder whom he has asked or maybe whom he plans to ask.*

Mother got something new for the whole family to wear to mass on Easter Sunday. Afterward, we met for lunch in a cafeteria. What a treat to eat out. We ordered the ninety-nine-cent special: turkey, dressing, mashed potatoes and gravy with green beans, and vanilla pudding for dessert.

On Easter Sunday, Mother put on her pretty dark-blue hat with some small flowers tucked in the veiling around the rim of the little hat. Both ends of the veiling hung a ways down in the back. Mother always likes to get a new hat for Easter from the millinery shop.

My new hat is also dark blue with a wide brim and trimmed with a blue polka-dot ribbon. I feel so stylish wearing it.

In church, I can hardly keep my eyes on my prayer book. I look up every so often to gaze around the church at the pretty spring hats of all colors and various trimmings. Most of them are not large, and the shapes are round with a small brim. Most have some veiling on them. Women are supposed to cover their heads in church. That tradition goes back a long way into ancient Bible times.

I am sure back then most women wore similar coverings and they would therefore not be such a distraction at church. In olden times, it seems the veiling was a way to protect women from unreasonable attraction, and now the opposite is happening.

With prom two weeks away, the juniors and seniors are busy making decorations. The theme this year is "Hollywood." The senior shop boys made a big sign which read "Hollywood" and mounted it between two tall stepladders loaned from the janitor. The senior girls used blue crepe paper to cover the ladders, and they stuffed puffy white clouds of tissue paper between the rungs. Many silver cords from Christmastime hung from the sign, forming a free-flowing door entrance.

On both sides of the entrance, big colorful placards of movies and movie stars were placed. These were obtained with permission from the Lyric and Grand theater lobbies. The walkway up to the entrance was two deep-red ten-foot runners loaned by the father of a high school junior girl. On either side of the runners were short white picket garden fences on loan from the hardware store. Every once-in-a-while, I glanced over at Mark and John working together. and I felt that they were taking some man-like pleasure in helping make the prom special.

On Friday afternoon, tables and chairs from the lunchroom were brought to the gym. Some junior and senior girls covered the tables with large white sheets of paper. On the sheets of white paper, they laid paper cutouts of blue stars, large black music notes, and black round records with a hole in the center. They sprinkled colored confetti here and there on the white paper covering the tables.

The supervising teachers had chosen a small group of boys and girls to make a memory booklet for each person in attendance at the prom. I was asked to design the cover. I drew a picture of the Hollywood entrance for the cover. Inside there was a page listing the president, vice president, and secretary of the class. The class flower is the rose. The motto "The Song Lingers On" was written across one page with notes all around. Then there were pages to fill in for dances and other mementos.

As I worked on the booklet, I wondered how many dances I would get filled in. *Who would dance with me? Would I get to dance with Mark at the prom? With so many girls to dance with, would he notice me? I do not want to be a wallflower all evening.*

5

1941 Prom and Graduation

Getting ready for the prom was so much fun. Saturday morning, I washed my hair and rinsed it with a little vinegar to make it shiny clean. I wound my hair on metal curlers, hoping for some pretty curls for tonight.

My formal is a blue taffeta with light-blue lace overlay and tiny red rosebuds stitched into the bodice. There are small rosebuds tucked here and there into the top of the ruffle where it is attached to the bottom of the long skirt. I slipped into my white two-inch heels and whirled around. I felt so special all dressed up. My hair was bouncy with many light-brown curls. I was ready for a good time. Hopefully, I would enjoy an evening to remember.

Mark came in his father's Plymouth four-door sedan. He came to the house for me. He was so handsome in his blue sports jacket and blue trousers.

"Julia, you look very nice. This is for you." Mark handed me a little box in which was a beautiful red rose corsage. Mother helped me pin it to my left shoulder, and it looked very pretty on my dress.

Mark opened the door for me, John hopped in the backseat, then Mark said, "John, where to next?"

So, John did ask a girl to the prom. Whom, I wonder?

I was surprised when John told Mark to pick up Betty Olson. *Betty is not a Catholic, she is not a country girl, and she is Norwegian. Betty lives in town, and she goes to the Lutheran church. What will Mother and Dad think about John taking her to the prom? No wonder John never said anything about a date for the prom.*

Betty was ready when we arrived. Evidently, Mark had picked up the corsage that John gave to Betty. It was a pink rose. It looked pretty on her darker pink satin dress, which complemented her fair complexion and light blonde hair.

Mark and John acted like real gentlemen, escorting Betty and me into the prom. I placed my arm over Mark's as we walked on the red runners and entered under the "Hollywood" banner. I felt almost like a movie star myself. Oh, what fun. It was more than that; I felt warm and excited. I was with Mark.

The sophomore girls waited on the tables. The school cooks and some band mothers had prepared the Swiss steak, mashed potatoes, sweet peas, lemon Jell-O salad, and the dessert of strawberries on a slice of angel food cake topped with a dollop of whipped cream.

The music was provided by the band director and some local musicians. The first piece was announced as a two-step "Only Forever" from the new Paramount picture *Rhythm on the River* starring Bing Crosby.

Mark took my hand and led me to the floor. As I danced the two-step with him, he whispered in my ear, "Julia, did you notice one of the placards by the entrance is advertising that movie. It is playing at the Grand next week. I would like to take you to that musical comedy."

"If it has music like this, I would enjoy it, I am sure."

Mark and I danced several more two-steps and a couple of waltzes. Then the band struck up a swing piece. Several girls went out on the floor and started dancing the Lindy Hop. Everyone stood around the floor watching them. I wondered how they could jive to the music like that in their long formals. Mark reported that he had been told that the Lindy Hop was named for Lindbergh's hop across the Atlantic. For whatever reason it was named, it is a wild swing-style dance to jazz-type music. When their dancing came to a breathless stop, the crowd clapped enthusiastically for their performance.

All of us, Mark, John, Betty, and I, decided it would be nice if we danced with someone who had not danced yet. When the next slow music started, we all found different partners. I thought it was a nice thing to do for ones who did not have dates or had not danced all evening.

The end of the dancing came too soon. Music from the early twenties floated through the air, "That Naughty Waltz." As Mark and I slowly danced, the words seemed so meaningful as he held me tight and we waltzed and waltzed.

Mark drove Betty to her house, and John walked her to the door. Then Mark took John and me home. Mark walked me to the door and bent to give me a light kiss on my cheek.

"Julia, I have had a wonderful time tonight. I will pick you up on Tuesday evening to go to the movie, *Rhythm on the River*."

I gave his hand a squeeze. My strong, happy emotions made it hard to answer. I struggled to keep my emotions in check. In a low voice, I answered, "I will look forward to going to the movies with you. Good night."

I enjoyed the prom so much, it was difficult to calm down and go to sleep. I kept reliving the evening.

During the spring 1941, I enjoyed the daffodils and tulips blooming in the yard. Later the purple lilacs were in bloom. I brought a large bouquet in the house. The lilac scent filled the room with a wonderful fragrance but a bit overpowering.

Before graduation day, there was a baccalaureate service for the class of 1940. The Lutheran minister gave the farewell address to the graduating class. He told the young people, "Your whole life lies ahead of you. Your parents and teachers have done their best to teach you skills and values needed in adult life. Your church instilled in your mind biblical wisdom and knowledge. Now it is up to you to make your life the best that you can make it. I wish to remind you of Proverbs 3:13–14: 'Happy is the man that findeth wisdom, and the man that getteth understanding. For the merchandise of it is better than the merchandise of silver, and the gain thereof than fine gold.'"

I thought those verses spoke volumes on the importance of learning and using that knowledge to one's advantage in life. It is not just academic learning that is important, but it is God-given wisdom that has come down through the ages in our Bibles that is of greatest value.

On Friday evening was graduation. Mark and John looked so nice in their dark-blue graduation gowns and hats. They made sure to place the tassels on their caps where their teacher had instructed them to do so. Mark came across the stage to receive his diploma. I felt so proud of him when he pushed his tassel to the other side signifying that he was now a graduate. Later John walked up to receive his diploma, and he too remembered to move his tassel to the other side before walking off the stage.

On Saturday afternoon, my whole family was invited to Mark's home for a graduation party for both Mark and John. Mrs. McDonald and my mother prepared the food. Other graduates were invited to come if they wished. The food was laid out on long tablecloth-covered boards atop of several sawhorses in the new machine shed the McDonalds had built. It was a nice warm sunny day, and I think people welcomed being outside.

Some of the younger children played games on the large lawn. Moms and dads sat on wooden benches and chairs, visiting. The young people gathered together at a picnic table, talking and laughing.

Mark's parents gave him their Plymouth car for his graduation present. They bought a new car for themselves. How nice, now Mark has his own car. Maybe he will take me with him to picnics, dances, or just driving around.

Mark drove John to pick up Betty for the graduation party. *I would like to know what Mom and Dad thought when he came with Betty. I am sure they are glad that he has a friend, but do they know who she is? What will they say when they find out who she is? By her light-blonde hair, it seems quite evident she might be Norwegian.*

"What are we going to do tonight for fun?" asked John.

"I heard that there is a wedding dance at the Innwood in Spillville tonight," replied Mark. "How about we take the girls dancing?"

Right away, I let it be known that I would love to go dancing. Betty hesitated to answer. I think I know why. Her folks do not want her going to dances.

"Betty, would your mom let you stay with me tonight if I see that you get home to go to church in the morning? We can tell her we want to make a big day of being together. In the morning, we will go to town for mass at nine o'clock. That should give you plenty of time to get home and dress for your church service at ten."

We were happy to help our moms clean up after the last guests left. Mark and John put the boards and sawhorses in their usual places in the machine shed. Betty and I helped put the food away. We told our folks where we were going. My mom said, "Drive carefully, and do not be out too late as we will go to mass in the morning."

We promised we would follow those instructions. Betty telephoned her folks and they allowed her to stay with me all night. We piled into Mark's car. I know Mark is a good driver, so I felt secure in going off on this exciting evening. After we left Decorah, we drove on a paved road until we turned off to go to Spillville. The rest of the way was a gravel road and dusty when a car passed us.

When we arrived at the Innwood along the river, it still was daylight. We walked around the park area, looking at the river and enjoying the nice warm evening for strolling.

Before nine, we went into the dance hall.

The bridal party was ready to march into the hall. First, a cute little flower girl dropped rose petals as she walked along with a chubby little ring bearer. Next in the procession, a bridesmaid on the arm of a groom's man was followed by another bridesmaid with a groom's man. In front of the couple, the maid of honor and the best man in an army uniform marched in. Smiling broadly, the couple from St. Lucas, a German community nearby, walked across the dance floor and joined the wedding party near the bandstand. The German band started to play, and the bridal couple danced the first dance. It was fun watching them; they were such good dancers. After that dance, the whole bridal party danced, even the little flower girl and the ring bearer.

The parents danced next with their newly wed children. Then

wedding guests danced. That included brothers, sisters, aunts, uncles, cousins, nieces, and nephews.

Then we could dance. The shiny circular floor has some posts with mirrors on them. From the ceiling, a few white wedding bells hung.

John taught Betty some dance steps at the prom, so tonight she seemed to be doing a good job dancing. She was smiling a lot. I loved dancing with Mark to the waltzes and two-step music.

Then the oompah band played a polka. Step hop, step hop—oh, how those Germans and Czechs can dance the polka. We watched a little bit, and then we tried it. When it comes to music, Mark is a natural; he caught on quite quickly how to polka.

The band with the bass horn loudly playing oompahs played a schottische. One, two, three, hop; one, two, three, hop—around and around they danced. Mark and I tried it open dancing and did just fine. We danced toward the stage; the musicians were all smiles as they knew we were having a good time dancing to their music. The older woman on the piano was pounding out the music to the beat of the trumpet, saxophone, clarinet, and bass horn.

At intermission, the wedding party lined up to follow the bride and groom off floor. Mark and John led us to a booth. Mark asked what we wanted to drink. I said, "I would like a Nehi orange soda."

Betty let it be known she would also like a Nehi orange soda. When the boys returned with the sodas, they each had a Schlitz beer in their hands. *What would Mother say about John drinking beer in public? When the men are busy haying, sometimes Dad gives the men beer chilled in the milk house tank by the cold water pumped by the windmill. I know John tasted some of that, but this is different. But I guess if they just drink one, it is okay.*

There seemed to be a stir, and it was obvious that the bride and groom were leaving. The bride threw her floral bouquet, and the maid of honor caught it. A few threw rice as the couple dashed out the door.

The best man wearing the US Army uniform kissed the maid of honor. Cheers went up. It brought sobering thoughts to my mind. *Would Mark enlist soon, and would I be like that young lady kissing good-bye my best friend? Well, I am going to enjoy being with him now, and that is that.*

We danced one more dance after intermission, but then Mark said, "We better go home so we can get up to go to church in the morning."

At my home, he walked me to the door, kissed me, and said, "I had so much fun tonight."

"Thanks to you, so did I."

Mark and I said good night to each other. Evidently, John and Betty had finished saying good night, and I followed them into the house. Betty and I quietly crept upstairs so as not to awaken my folks. Once in bed, we could not keep from discussing the evening. Betty told me that she didn't think that she had ever had so much fun.

"What if your folks find out?"

"Oh, I don't think that they will. No one there knew me, I am sure of that."

"I hope that they never find out. Your parents will never let you stay with me or let you go out with John."

"I don't really think I did anything wrong. It was good fun. Good night, Julia."

"Good night, Betty."

6

Summer 1941

Early in the spring of 1941, Dad bought a B John Deere tractor. He told the family that he felt he better buy one now just in case we get into the war. If the US got into the war, he believed that all the agricultural machine companies in our country would become heavily involved in war production. He was afraid that if the US entered the war, metal would go for the war purposes, and he could not get a tractor for a long time.

Today, Dad told us how he had read an article stating the production of civilian farm equipment would be held at 80 percent of 1940's production level. He went on to tell us that the companies were encouraged to increase production of repair and maintenance parts.

He turned to Mother. "Lettie, I think I should replace the steel lugs on the tractor with rubber tires just in case of war." Later that week, he did just that. I was glad because lugs can sure tear up a road surface.

Dad's talking about war made me feel real concern for my brothers and for Mark. *Would the boys be drafted to go to war? How could we farm without their help? How could we stand having them go into battle? How could I stand not seeing Mark for weeks, maybe even months…or worse yet years…or never?*

A few weeks later, Dad and Mom came home with Dad proudly driving a new-to-us 1938 Oldsmobile. They decided John could drive their old car. John was well pleased over that news. With the new tractor, we would no longer have to solely use horses to farm our 280-acre farm. John taught me how to drive the tractor so that I would be able to drive it for haying. This year, Dad planned to hire the McDonalds to bale our hay with their new hay baler. He told me that I would drive the tractor around the field so that the boys could load and stack the hay onto a wagon.

The hay baler took two men to thread the wire through the baler to tie the rectangular bale up with the wire. Mr. McDonald and my dad shared that job. My fifteen-year-old brother, Bobby, drove the McDonalds' Oliver tractor on the baler.

Mark, John, and Jimmy would load the bales on the wagon. John will drive the tractor and the load of bales to the barn. At the barn, the boys would load the rectangular bales into an elevator powered with a gasoline engine. One by one the bales are lifted up the elevator into the hay loft. Then the boys go up into the loft and stack the bales.

One bright sunny day late in June, the boys and I sat, waiting for the baler to put out a load. Earlier the baler had broken down. It seems the wires were not threading through like they should. While the fathers repaired the machine, we young ones had time to talk.

Mark talked about the McDonalds' new Oliver tractor. He informed us, "The Oliver Company was formed in 1929 with the merger of four companies, two from Indiana, one from Michigan, and the Hart-Parr Tractor Company of Charles City, Iowa." He looked around and then added, "Bet you didn't know Charles City had something to do with the Oliver tractor."

I looked at him and replied, "No, I did not know that. So, John Deere is not the only tractor company in Iowa. I find that interesting."

"Julia, if you are going to be a teacher, you need to know about Iowa industries. Charles City, Iowa, is known as the birthplace of the tractor industry. Around 1900, Hart and Paar created the world's first successful production of the farm gas traction engine, predecessor of today's tractors. By 1907, one-third of tractors worldwide were made in Charles City, Iowa."

"Wow! That is interesting. Yes, you are right. I need to know about industry in our state. I do want to be a teacher."

Several weeks went by of haying at our farm or at the McDonald farm. One warm afternoon, while sitting in the hayfield under the shade of the bale stack we were making there, my father shocked us.

Mother had brought to the field bologna sandwiches and oatmeal raisin cookies. We were sitting there happily munching our lunch. Dad looked at Mother, winked, and then announced, "I plan to drive to Montana to see my two brothers and my father before war breaks out, and I cannot go there for maybe years. He looked at John. "Do you think you could manage to milk the cows, feed the hogs and chickens while we are gone?"

That took John by surprise, but he managed to say, "Sure, Dad, I can do that. If I get in a bind and need more help, I am sure I could count on Mark to help out."

Mark nodded his agreement.

Then Dad looked at Bobby, Marian, and myself and said, "You three will be going along, so start packing as we will leave as soon as this haying is finished. I expect we should be ready to leave on next Thursday. On the way, I plan to see the Black Hills and the faces carved on Mount Rushmore.

Dad turned to Mr. McDonald. "I think I need to go see my brothers and my father before war breaks out. Then it might be years before I could visit them. Dad sold the Springwater Mill on Canoe Creek in 1912 to buy wheat land in Montana. He is getting up in age, and I feel I need to spend some time with him." Mr. McDonald assured Dad that he would see that John would have any help he might need while we were on the trip. That declaration made me feel a little bit better about leaving John behind. I had seen Mark almost every day during the haying season on both the farms. *I wish he was going to be with us on the trip.*

Mom and I washed and packed our clothes. We made up a picnic basket and a box of food to take with us to help cut down expense.

At five o'clock Thursday morning, I felt wide awake and eager to get going on our trip. After a quick breakfast, Dad and the boys loaded the car with our suitcases, bags, picnic basket, and the box of food.

I made sure that I had my notebook in which I intend to write what I learn about on the trip. I want to make sure that I keep information for teaching school. I intend to keep in mind what Mark told me: if I plan to be a teacher, I should learn everything I can. It should be fun to collect information of interest to young children, which will help them grow in learning.

We all gave John a hug and said good-bye.

Mom hugged him last and reminded him, "John, I left plenty of food for you. Remember there is canning in the cellar. You will have milk and eggs. There is cured bacon and ham as well as summer sausage and cheese for you to eat. I left soda crackers in the cupboard and bread in the bread box. Oh! Be careful and stay safe while we are gone."

John hugged Mom back and told her, "Mom, you know I will eat well with all that food. Yes, Mom, I will be careful and stay safe. Mark will help if I have any troubles. Good-bye and have a safe journey, Mom and Dad." Then John waved as we drove away, waving back at him.

Finally, we were off in our new Oldsmobile. Mom and Dad looked happy in the front seat. Marian sat between Bobby and me. I got out my journal and made some notes about the date and the time we left.

"Julia, I will drive for a while. Then when we are on the straight highway heading west, I will let you drive for a couple of hours while I study the map of South Dakota. I want to stop at the Corn Palace in Mitchell, South Dakota."

Sure enough, after we ate our lunch at a picnic table along the way, Dad told me to drive. I guess he figured after I drove tractor all summer, I would be a careful driver. I was glad to be in the driver's seat with Dad in the passenger seat. Mom sat in the back with Marian and Bobby.

Bobby, being fifteen, I am sure was wishing he could be driving rather than sitting in the backseat with Mom and Marian's chattering.

Driving west across northern Iowa to South Dakota was easy driving. When we got almost to Sioux City, Dad took over driving. In late afternoon, we arrived in Mitchell, South Dakota. We had no difficulty finding the tall Corn Palace. We looked at the interesting corn displays. I found the souvenir shop interesting but did not want to spend my money, not yet.

We located a gas station. While the man pumped the gas, Dad studied the map. The man washed our dirty windshield and asked Dad if he should check the tires for air pressure.

We drove for a couple more hours. We stopped in a small town where we found a cabin to stay in for the night.

Dad let us know that today we would drive through the Badlands located in southwestern South Dakota. He told us that we would be seeing something that we never have seen before. Dad was careful to make sure we always had plenty of gas because the farther west we traveled there was a greater distance between towns.

When we started driving into the Badlands, I was surprised to see the eroded areas of land. As we drove along, we saw sticking up here and there buttes, pinnacles, and spires. They were fascinating shapes and sizes. No one lived on such desolate places. In places there were stretches of undisturbed grassy prairies. It seemed like we would never drive out of the Badlands.

From a brochure that I picked up, I found plenty to write in my journal. I learned how scientists found much important information in the Badlands about ancient animals and their surroundings from different geological periods. Fossils that remain from ancient times include animals and birds that lived in that era.

While Dad drove, he told us, "Next will be the Black Hills and Mount Rushmore. On Mount Rushmore is the world's greatest mountain carving. The four faces are carved five hundred feet up, and the faces are sixty feet high, looking out over the forest of evergreens, birch, and aspen."

The lodge near the faces of Mount Rushmore had a deck from which one could view the faces. An older lady offered for me to view them through binoculars that were secured to the deck in which one puts money to use the machine.

I was shocked with what I saw. I could see the men working on the carvings. I could even see the buckles on their overalls. I wondered how anyone could work that high up carving on stone. Who could crawl around five hundred feet above ground and do work while being that high? I could see the ropes they were using. But who but the very brave could risk such a task?

The heads of the four American presidents were huge. It was easy to see that they were the well-known faces of George Washington, Thomas Jefferson, Theodore Roosevelt, and Abraham Lincoln.

I thanked the kind lady for giving me an unforgettable memory. I believe my gratitude was reward enough for the gentle woman. She smiled very sweetly at me.

Dad put a coin in the binocular so that Bobby and Marian could have a look. Then he put another coin in so Mother and he could have a good view close-up.

We spent some time in the gift shop in the lodge. I bought several postcards of the faces of the four presidents on Mount Rushmore. I quickly wrote one to Mark and another one to John. I briefly wrote that I was having a good time. I told Mark I was collecting information for teaching.

Mother, with her box camera, took several shots of the faces. The five of us sat on a bench near the lodge, and a tourist was kind enough to take a picture of us on Mom's box camera.

We drove away from Mount Rushmore and found a cabin for the night. We enjoyed the food Mother had packed. We had Van Camp's pork and beans, summer sausage, bread, and raisin oatmeal cookies with applesauce.

We located a gas station, and Dad bought some orange pop for the kids. We found we could not drink the water. It tasted awful. Mom said it was because it had a lot of sulfur in it. Guess it tasted rotten like eggs. Marian complained the most.

Mother had picked up a brochure at the cabin last night, and from it she started reading. "In 1874, gold was discovered in the Black Hills, which set off one of the last large gold rushes. By 1876, many miners came into the northern Black Hills looking for gold. Some came across a gulch with lots of dead trees and luckily a creek full of gold. The site became the town of Deadwood."

When we approached Deadwood, there were many cars, trucks, and even some horse-drawn carriages on the road. We stopped at a filling station and learned that the town was getting ready to have their "Wild Bill Days." We were just in time to view the parade. We found a place to park the car and joined the line of people along the parade route.

We learned "Wild Bill Days" was a weekend celebration of the life and times of Wild Bill Hickok. When the parade started, there were musicians marching, playing lively music. There were lots of horses with colorful riders—authentic-looking cowboys and colorful-shirted cowgirls riding their silver-decked bridled horses. They wore huge smiles and waved enthusiastically at the crowd.

What I found so interesting was the hearse—yes, the hearse. It was a long dark black enclosure with glass windows on the sides loaded on a wagon pulled by a pair of sleek black workhorses plodding down the cobblestones.

There were full-skirted ladies with colorful large-plumed hats riding in stagecoaches. Some fancy ladies in bright-colored billowing long skirts and tight bodices, holding pretty cloth parasols in their hands to shield the sun from their faces, promenaded along.

There were a-number-of stagecoaches, wagons with gold panning equipment on them, and many young and old appropriately dressed for that time period. Toward the end of the parade, a tall man representing Wild Bill Hickok rode, smiling and waving at us.

My whole family could not believe our good fortune to come just in time to see the parade on Deadwood's historic main street. It is a memory I am sure I will not forget.

As soon as we could get out of town, we left for Spearfish. We wanted to get there to attend the evening performance of the Passion Play.

Mother informed us that the *Black Hills Passion Play* is in its ninth year of summer performance in Spearfish, South Dakota. The production is an American version of the Passion Play that was brought here by immigrants. They claimed it had been produced in Europe since 1242.

The Passion Play held our attention. There were so many people and animals to watch. Even Marian was enthralled with the dramatic presentation of the Passion of Jesus Christ. However, it wasn't easy watching the sufferings and death Jesus went through, but the colorful robes worn by different characters, the large cast of people, and the many animals riveted our interest. The music made it all seem so special.

It was so different being in an outdoor amphitheater, a half circular seating area rising gradually from the lower level to a higher level in the back. It was a beautiful warm evening and very pleasant looking down and watching the lights and action on the low-level stage.

After we were in our cabin for the night, Mother commented that the Passion is a long established part of Lent in the Catholic church. The tradition is also found in some other Christian denominations.

"Mother, I heard the story of the death of Jesus many times, but seeing it acted out was such a privilege. I am so glad that you and Dad took us to see it."

From the look on their faces, I knew my parents were thankful I recognized the Passion Play was a moving experience to treasure forever in my memory.

On Sunday, we went to mass before we drove out to Uncle Bill's ranch. They welcomed our travel-weary group with open arms. Aunt Bertha had a chicken meal ready for us. Grandpa Sturloff was there. He hugged my dad and then us kids.

The adults ate in the dining room. Bobby, Marian, and I ate in the kitchen with Bettie, my eighteen-year-old cousin. Uncle Bill and Aunt Bertha's older children, Ben, twenty-four, and Margaret, twenty, ate with the grown-ups.

Bettie just graduated from high school. She told me during the school year, her mother and her had stayed in their house in town during the week so that she could go to high school. From the ranch during the winter, she could not have gone to high school.

On Monday, we went to see the wheat fields. The wheat was tall, almost as tall as Marian. Uncle Bill, Ben, and hired help were combining the wheat. Ben drove the combine. The wheat was unloaded from the combine hopper onto a truck. A hired ranch hand hauled the wheat to the elevator in Glendive.

We visited Grandpa Sturloff at his small house on his ranch land. Dad seemed happy to have time to talk to Grandpa. They discussed other wheat harvests and fishing.

Tuesday we were asked to stay to watch the cowboys bring in a herd of Herefords to give each head of cattle a brand. The cowboys roped and brought down a head of cattle. Another cowboy came quickly with the hot branding iron and put the ranch brand on the back-hind quarter of the animal. The animal let out loud protesting bellowing and was then released. It walked off, the worst over.

"Bettie, write to me." She promised that she would.

It was sad when Dad said good-bye to his father. I had the feeling that he felt he would never see him alive again.

Dad headed the car toward Billings, so we could visit Uncle Jim. We ate a picnic lunch at a park before we drove to Uncle Jim's home. Billings is an interesting place as it sits low with a high rim around the city. Uncle Jim used to have a farm up on the rim, but because of his age, he has retired to live a city life.

Uncle Jim and Aunt Annie's children are grown and live in California. Aunt Annie made a nice supper and put us up for the night. I know Dad and Uncle Jim talked late into the night.

The next day, when we were ready to leave for the Yellowstone National Park, Dad told me, "Julia, I think you should drive. I will study the map." I knew Dad was tired, and I had a good night's rest.

Bobby could not help complaining, "Ah, Dad, I wish I could drive." Being a year too young was hard on him.

"Marian are you going to be scared of the bears in the Yellowstone?" Dad asked.

"Am I really going to see bears? I have never seen a bear. What else will I see?"

Mother answered, "You will see brown, cinnamon, and black bears, and even the huge grizzlies can be found there. Other animals that we might see are deer, elk, antelope, mountain sheep, coyotes, moose, and buffalo, known also as bison."

She added, "There are over two hundred species of birds that find sanctuary in the park. Finding sanctuary means the animals and birds are protected in the park. It is possible to see eagles, wild geese, and ducks. Graceful white swans and pelicans can be seen on the Yellowstone Lake.

"The majority of the trees are evergreen such as pine, Douglas fir, spruce, and juniper. One can also find aspen, cottonwood, birch, and alder. The forests add to the beauty of the park and give shelter to the animals and birds."

Dad teased, "There are some things in the park that you have never seen before, but I am not going to tell you what they are."

"Dad, there's a bear. See him on the edge of the road. Please stop," yelled Marian. "Oh! He is standing up to the window of that stopped car."

Mom tells her, "That is why it is not a good idea to feed the bears. After all they are wild animals and could hurt a person."

Further on, we see some deer grazing. Then Dad tells us to look on the right. "What is that steaming place?" asked a puzzled Marian.

"That is the surprise you have never seen before. It is steaming water from hot springs flowing over rocks. There are nearly three thousand geysers and hot springs in the park. Soon we will see the largest geyser, Old Faithful."

Old Faithful was just shooting into the air as we left our car and walked toward the geyser. Marian, in awe and astonishment, shouted, "Look how high it is going. Wow! Isn't that something?"

"Marian, it is hurling columns of hot water high into the air from deep within the earth," Dad explained.

We drove by Mammoth Hot Springs with its tiered, descending layers of mineral deposits. Hot water flows over the edges of the terraces. That looked scary as the water must be real hot.

We drove up to a wall of rocks from where we got a good view of the falls of the Yellowstone River. The falls have carved out a deep wide canyon with colored rocks on its sides.

Dad asked what our favorite thing in the park was. Marian's favorite thing was the furry bears. Bobby liked Old Faithful best. I think my favorite was the falls of the Yellowstone and the canyon. Before we left the park, we got to see a buffalo herd. What big shaggy animals they are. I think Bobby was ready to change his favorite thing to the buffaloes.

We drove miles away from the park before we found a vacant cabin for the night. That evening I had a lot to write in my journal. I wrote that the Yellowstone Park was created by Congress in 1872. It is the largest and oldest of our national parks. Practically the entire region is volcanic. From a brochure I picked up in the lodge near Old Faithful, I have much more to write in my journal. If I get a chance, I have so much to show Mark about what I have learned on this trip. I hope he will see that I am following his suggestion that I keep records of interesting facts to teach to my students someday.

We got up around 5:00 a.m., and Mom fixed bacon and eggs for breakfast. I found a toaster in the kitchenette small cupboard and made toast. Mom advised us to make sure that we packed all our belongings. Dad told me to start driving as he was studying the map. He told me how to take the right road heading toward Salt Lake City, Utah, our next major stop.

Dad was driving when we arrived in the late afternoon at the Salt Lake. Marian, in disbelief, pointed to a man half sitting in the water. "Dad, look. How can that man be sitting in the water reading his newspaper?"

Dad explained that the salt in the water was holding the man up. "Evidently, Marian, you are not the only one delighted with this feat. It looks like the man's wife is snapping his picture to prove to friends that her husband could read a newspaper sitting in the lake."

Dad drove around Salt Lake City. We saw the Mormon temple, but, of course, we could not go in it. We are not Mormons. Mom told how the Mormons came west because of being oppressed for their religious beliefs. She revealed that their journey west was part of Iowa history. I perked up when she said that. I got out my journal and starting writing notes from what Mom was saying.

Mother went on to tell us, "The Mormon Church was started by Joseph Smith in 1830 in New York. Later, members of this church gathered in Nauvoo, Illinois. Because of persecution, in the cold of February 1846, the Mormons began to leave Nauvoo. In the beginning of the trip, they had spring-like weather, and then the snows came. They were ill-prepared for freezing temperatures and snow, but one good thing came out of the sub-zero temperatures. The mighty Mississippi was frozen over, allowing many to cross over to Iowa soil on the frozen river.

"Once on Iowa soil, it took the main camp 131 days to trek the 300 miles across Iowa. A year later, it took a company only 111 days to travel 1,050 miles from their winter quarters in Nebraska to the Great Salt Lake Valley. However, in 1846, in their hasty departure, there was not time to develop sound organization for such a long journey. The consequences of that was especially felt in their lack of well-planned supplies especially food. Those ill preparations and the inclement weather, which brought snow and later rain, made the trip across Iowa difficult. When the spring rains poured down, the ground became muddy and difficult for the oxen and wagons to pull the loads. Some people even pulled their belongings in carts."

We located a cabin for the evening. After our supper of Van Camp's pork and beans, summer sausage, bread, fresh peaches and cream, I wrote some more in my journal about what I am learning.

The next morning, we headed east toward Denver, Colorado. We traveled through some more badlands. Out west there sure is a lot of land that cannot be farmed.

In Grand Junction, Colorado, we took the United States Route 24 east toward Denver. As we came closer to the mountains we could see them on the horizon rising skyward. The curving highway winds along beside water rushing westward. As we are starting to climb, one can sense the car pulling harder. I found it entertaining to watch the many-shaped rock formations jutting out of the mountainsides. It seemed I could not get enough of viewing the high mountain peaks, odd-shaped spires, colored rocks, the high places, and the deep areas between them. We saw a lot of evergreens looking like emerald splotches of color up the sides of sloping mountainsides. The road continues to get higher and higher. The trees are getting shorter and farther apart.

"Dad be careful. That looks a long way down." Marian is getting scared. I must admit I wish there were more barriers between us and the sheer decline to the canyon bottom.

At the higher levels, the trees are smaller and farther apart. I try to look out the window to see the tops of the mountain peaks as we motor along. Where the mountains dip, known as passes, we view picturesque little villages nestled in the lower hills. Sometimes we see abandoned mining sites and ghost towns left behind after mines go useless. I keep busy writing the details of what I am seeing in my journal. I note in my journal the kaleidoscope of colors I saw in the rocks exposed on the sides of the mountains.

We ate the lunch Mom packed this morning at a lookout along the highway. One could look for miles. What a panoramic view. How can I adequately describe it? The large sweeping landscape makes one feel very small in relationship to the immense size of the backdrop.

"Mom, why don't you take our pictures here?" I wanted Mark to get some idea of the beauty that I am seeing.

We stopped on the east side of the mountain in a quaint little village. I think Dad was getting tired of driving in the mountains. I spent the evening trying to find words to describe how I felt being in the mountains.

I enjoyed so much watching the white-water glisten as it bubbled over the rocks in the mountain streams rushing downhill to larger waterways. The majesty of the mountains is overwhelming. *No wonder God is known as the Rock of Ages.*

I wish Mark and John were here to enjoy with me the majestic beauty of the mountains. My journal will prove to Mark I am not just learning about Iowa but other states for when I teach school. I hope he will enjoy my journal. For only ten days on this vacation, I have been gone from Mark. I will be so unhappy if Mark leaves to serve in the army and is gone for not just days but months and maybe several years.

7

Fall 1941 – Julia's Senior Year

On Saturday, we planned to drive all day. I think everyone was glad the Oldsmobile was steered toward home. Dad and I took turns driving. Because he was pushing to get home before dark, he did not want either of us to get overtired driving. While we drove steadily along, Mom was deep in thought and busy figuring in her notebook. When we were within a few miles of home, she turned to Dad and said, "Sam, how much do you think the gas on this trip added up to be?"

Dad just shrugged his shoulders and kept his eyes on the road.

Mom answered the question.

"The total gas bill added up to $56.80, oil $6.76, cabins and other expenses came to $37.04. I think the trip was well worth the cost."

"Lettie, I appreciate your keeping such good track of our expenses. Your record keeping has always helped a lot. Your financial records were especially helpful when we went through the tough years in the early thirties during the Great Depression."

He paused awhile and then added, "It looks like this year will be the most income that we have ever had. I am thankful that we could afford a new car and this trip."

At that moment, I felt very proud of my parents for their perseverance during the Depression years. I have often heard them tell of the low prices for hogs, cattle, cream, eggs, and anything they sold off the farm. They must feel deep satisfaction in knowing they brought the family through such trying times. I felt the warmth of my love for my parents.

When the car pulled into our yard, Mom noticed right away the old car was gone. "Oh, where is John?" Her voice betrayed her anxiety.

"Lettie, I am sure John is all right. After all he is a young man and wants to have a little fun. He probably is out with Mark."

Are John and Mark out with girls? I did not want to think that. I guess I did leave, so maybe Mark started dating someone else while I was gone. My mind seemed a whirl of confusion. I cannot blame him for wanting a good time; I sure did have a nice time on the trip. But how could I stand to see him dating some other girl?

Dad quickly unloaded the car. Mom put some things away and the dirty clothes in the milk house for the Monday wash. Dad checked the barn, hog house, and chicken house. When he returned to the house, he reported, "Looks like John did a good job taking care of the place while we were gone."

The next morning, a sleepy-eyed John was happy to see us safely home again. He told us that there were no major problems while we were on the trip.

After mass, Mark came up to me. His eyes seemed to twinkle when he warmly smiled. *He must be happy that I am safely home again. He is glad to see me. I am so happy.*

Mark asked if he could come over in the afternoon. He said that he would like to have a sing-along fun time and asked if I could play the piano for it. I was delighted. *Maybe he did not date while I was gone.*

When Mother heard about the young people getting together, she invited Mr. and Mrs. McDonald to come also. Both mothers planned a lunch for after the singing.

Mark, his sister Melanie, John, Bobby, and Jimmy sang while I played the piano. We all sang out lustily the new hit, "Deep in the Heart of Texas." The lyrics were so much fun to sing. We clapped to the music—*clap, clap, clap, clap.* It was such fun.

After a break of a few minutes from singing and clapping, I played the piano and they sang, "Five Foot Two, Eyes of Blue."

Then John got out his trumpet, Mark his trombone, Bobby the saxophone, and Jimmy the clarinet as they prepared to enjoy playing their instruments. I accompanied them on the piano, and Melanie sang as we made music together.

Both sets of parents came into the living room to enjoy our music. They joyously joined in the singing when we played the Christian hymn, "Onward, Christian Soldiers."

> Onward, Christian soldiers, marching as to war,
> With the cross of Jesus going on before.
> Christ, the royal Master, leads against the foe;
> Forward into battle see His banners go!
> *Refrain*
> Onward, Christian soldiers, marching as to war,
> With the cross of Jesus going on before.

Then the boys played their rendition of "In the Mood." They definitely are not Glenn Miller's band, but they are good for amateurs.

Mrs. McDonald had brought a salad and cake. Mom had made sandwiches. The adults and the two younger ones ate at the picnic table. The rest of us sat on the grass to eat our food.

Mark leaned over and asked, "Would you like to go to the movie at the Grand tonight?"

"Yes, what is playing?"

"*The Grapes of Wrath*, a story of the early 1930's Dust Bowl in Oklahoma forcing a family to leave their drought-stricken state and migrate to California to seek work. Henry Fonda plays the son in the movie."

So, Mark, John, Melanie, and I leave for the movies. I go into the seats first, and Mark sits next to me. So maybe he didn't have a date last night.

Before the movie started, there were video clips of war news from Europe. The legs on the marching soldiers looked jerky as they paraded. I guess the cameraman didn't have the best camera or film. The news emphasized Hitler's invasion of Russia in June. There were pictures of Hitler and men saluting him "Heil Hitler" with their arm stretched straight up toward the fuehrer. It looked like the salute is performed by extending the right arm to at least eye level and straightening the hand so that it is in line with the arm. Usually, an utterance of "Heil Hitler!" will accompany the gesture.

Mark leaned over to whisper that the arm salute represents a sword. That reminds me of the knights of old who used swords in their fighting.

After the movie, we stopped for treats at the A&W Root Beer stand. Over our root beer floats, we discussed the movie. I let it be known that I thought it was a dark, sad, and gloomy movie.

I went on to explain, "First, the farm family had to leave Oklahoma because of the drought and resulting Dust Bowl. Without crops, they financially could not continue farming. It was an extremely tough time with little money to reach California and possibly find work. Once there, the Depression made it a struggle just to live. As migrant farm workers, they faced violence and prejudice. That forced them to move from one camp to another. But the best part was that despite it all, the poor but decent people sought dignity. I did like how the son unwaveringly reached for self-respect."

I added, "It reminds me of what St. Paul said in Philippians that whatsoever state he is in, he will be content. I guess that is a good lesson for all of us to live by."

That night I looked up in my Catholic Bible to record in my journal the words that Paul said about being content in whatsoever conditions he found himself.

> Not that I speak because I was in want. For I have learned to be self-sufficing in whatever circumstances I am (Philippians 4:11, Douay/Confraternity Version).

I pray and hope that I can be like that no matter what I face in my lifetime.

My parents fear that there will be tough years ahead if we get into another world war. If I face adversity in my life, can I be strong like the people from Oklahoma during the Dust Bowl days? I guess no one wants to have to live through real trying days. Dear God, protect my loved ones in the years ahead.

The following days I found myself very busy getting ready for my senior year of high school. Dad took Mom and the three of us, who are going to school this year, to La Crosse shopping for school clothes. Mom purchased a good pair of dark-brown leather oxfords for me. I found a black-and-white checked woven wool skirt with a matching short jacket with a peplum. I just love that peplum with its short-flared ruffle attached to the waist of the jacket. Mom picked out a lovely red wool sweater that I can sometimes wear with the skirt instead of the jacket. We found some nice light-beige knee stockings for me to wear.

One evening in August, Mark took me to the fair. We sat in the grandstand and watched the program on the stage. Then we rode several rides. When we arrived at my house, he pulled me close, gave me a hug, and a quick kiss on the cheek. He walked me to the door and kissed me again. I felt very happy.

School started the third Monday in August before Labor Day. Melanie drove Bobby and me to school the first morning. Bobby and I are staying with Uncle Roy and Aunt Ida again this year during the week. We will ride home on Friday night with Melanie or with Dad if he happens to be in town.

This year I am taking speech, home economics, and a class on reading and literature for teaching. Another one of my classes is on how to teach mathematics to grade students. I am finding my classes for teaching very interesting. In the evening, I am copying in a notebook a collection of poems for young people. In the math class, I am making flash cards for teaching addition and subtraction. Later I will make them for multiplication and division.

I think Aunt Ida is very happy to have me help with her three little girls. I am reading some of my poetry collection to them in the evenings. I have some nursery rhymes in my notebook, and I think they like them best.

After mass on the second Sunday in September, Mark suggested, "Julia, let's have another musical session this afternoon." Then he added, "In the evening, I would like to take you to the movies."

That evening, before the movie started, war clips were shown. The war news told how the United States, even though they formally are acting nonbelligerent, they really are aiding the British in their battle against Nazi Germany.

"Mark, it seems our country is dangerously tempting fate, and it looks like we might get into the war in Europe."

He quietly spoke back, "Yes, it does look serious."

The movie came on. It was a new movie, *Sergeant York*.

Mark, in a barely audible voice, enlightened me. "The story is supposed to be a true story. That should make it interesting."

As the story in the movie unfolded, we learned that the main character was a pacifist, yet he was drafted into WWI from Tennessee. In the hillbilly country, he learned to be an excellent shot. His sharpshooter ability made him a war hero. Sergeant York was one of the most decorated American soldiers in World War I.

We discussed the movie on the way home. Mark seemed quite impressed with the war hero. He went on to say that with the war heating up in Europe, it might not be long before the United States is drawn into the war.

Mark stopped the car by my front gate. He leaned over, took my chin, and turned my face toward him. "Julia, what would you think if I enlist as soon as my dad's corn crop is harvested?"

I felt numb. I dreaded the thought of war. Now my best friend is telling me that he wants to enlist.

"Why do you want to enlist?" I finally got out.

"I think we are going to be in war soon. I might as well enlist rather than wait to be drafted. I want to do my duty to protect our country and to protect the people that I love."

"Oh, Mark, I would miss you so."

"Julia, you will be teaching next year. You want to teach. After a couple years, I will be coming home again. I hope then I will be able to start farming for myself. Julia, we are too young now to be too serious. Don't you see you will get your chance to teach and I will fulfill my duty to my God, family, and country?"

"Why do you say your duty is 'for God, family, and country'?"

"We live in a great nation that protects our religious freedom, our families, and our land."

I leaned toward Mark. "I am proud of you for wanting to protect all that we love so much. Maybe we won't get into war, and you will not have to go into battle."

"Julia, we have to be realistic. War looks inevitable. You and I have a strong faith. We must believe that we can save our nation. We must believe that faith will see us through."

He kissed me, and we said good night to each other.

That night sleep did not come easily. The movie, the war clips, and most of all Mark's words came again and again to my mind. The reality of the war clips was hard to accept as affecting me so far away in America. The movie made war look very dangerous. The killing of men in battle is terribly tragic. We are civilized people, yet we are acting in battle as if we are heartless brutes.

How can I let my best friend go away for weeks and maybe months? I will miss him so much. I love to sing and play music with Mark. He takes me out to movies, dances, and for other fun activities. He teaches me many interesting things. We share good companionship. *Dear God, I pray don't let this happen to me. I don't know if I can stand it. Dear God, give me strength to face the days ahead.*

Marian complained to me that Dad wouldn't let her listen to her radio programs because he wants to keep the battery for listening to President Roosevelt give his fireside chats. Marian is upset because she cannot listen to the Lone Ranger and Jack Armstrong. Mom went to the library to get her books to read instead.

Dad's listening more to news on the radio makes me realize he is concerned that we might be close to war. He reads the *Telegraph Herald* every day.

While I am at Uncle Roy's during the week, he listens every evening to the news. I am glad that Aunt Ida and the girls keep me busy. Sometimes I help Rickie with his second-grade work. He needs some help in reading. I think that is good practice for me to be a full-time teacher someday. I also drill him on the memorization of his addition and subtraction facts.

Sometimes Aunt Ida lets me take her kitchen electric radio to my room to listen to music. I like to hear the latest songs. Then I can better choose the sheet music I want to buy for the piano at home. Some day we will have electricity at home, so I can have a phonograph or a radio to play music.

Dad and Mom went to the electric co-op in Cresco to see about getting electricity out to the farm. They were told with the threatening war news that no one would get wiring at this time. If we get into war, that will mean we have no electricity until after the war.

At least I am happy that in the evening at Aunt Ida's, I can hear music like "In the Mood" and "Blueberry Hill" by Glenn Miller and Bing Crosby's voice as he sings "Only Forever".

The second weekend in September was very warm for that time of year. Mark asked me if I would pack a picnic lunch as he would like to take me to a park on Saturday about eleven o'clock.

Mark drove us to Dunning's Spring. I had never even known it existed. The parking area and picnic grounds were not large. But oh, how beautiful it was there. Mark suggested we hike the path up to the falls. Recently, it had rained heavily, so there was much water racing down the hillside. The incline was a bit steep. In places, Mark would lean back to me and grab my hand to help me over a slippery rocky area. The trees were still green leafed.

I gasped, "Mark, this is such a lovely place. Where is this water coming from?"

Mark found a large rock to sit on and motioned for me to find a seat also. "Julia, remember learning in Iowa history that the northeastern corner of Iowa was not passed over by the glaciers that covered the rest of our state? In this area, the limestone bluffs are not worn flat by ancient ice sheets. Like other springs here about, Dunning's Spring wells up out of the limestone cliff and tumbles down to lower ground."

I looked down at the ways we had climbed and up to the sparkling cold spring water issuing forth from an opening in the bluff. The glistening water is cascading over large boulders and rushing in fanned out streams of water over rocks to the picnic area below. "How far do you think the water falls?" I asked.

Mark looks up and replied, "Probably the water drops over several hundred feet. I am glad we came here today. You are enjoying it so much."

"It is so refreshing sitting still near this natural spring and listening to the water gurgling over the rocks."

We slowly continue along the path to the spectacular falls. We are now close enough to feel some spray of cold water. I look down to the parking lot. "At least it will be easier going down. All this scenic beauty, I wish I had brought Mom's box camera."

Mark reached into his light jacket and pulled out his camera. "Stand there, Julia, so I can take your picture with the falls in the background."

Another couple was climbing up, so we waited for them intending to ask if they would take a picture of Mark and me. They took several pictures of us, and we did the same for them.

Going down was easy, but we had to be careful that we did not go too fast and lose our balance. We found the spring water was very cold. We agreed it would be a good place to come on a very hot day in July.

The lunch I packed included sandwiches made of ham salad with cut-up sweet pickles, potato salad, carrot sticks, and angel food cake. After lunch Mark said we are now going to Ice Cave.

We did not have very far to go. Near the Ice Cave and close to the road, there is a stairway made of limestone rocks. From the steps, a path leads up to the cave entrance. As I approach the cave entrance, I could feel colder air.

We enter the cave. Not very far in, I could feel ice on the walls. "How can there be ice in here?"

"Julia, in July, the hottest month in Iowa, one can come in here and touch walls of ice even though the temperature is over a hundred degrees outside."

He went on to tell that part of the cave has collapsed and no one can explore beyond that point. Mark's flashlight shone on the shiny walls glistening with a film of water atop the ice.

"Julia, you are claustrophobic. You do not want to go farther anyway," teased Mark.

I poked Mark. "You know I think this is captivating, but I want to be careful as caves can be dangerous. Take care, the floor looks slippery."

"According to information I read in the library, this is one of the largest ice caverns in the Midwest. Most caves consistently maintain a temperature equal to the average yearly temperature of the area. During the winter, cold air circulates in the ice cave, cooling the rock walls to below freezing. Warm air escapes through cracks in the cave ceiling. After thawing weather on the surface, water is turned into thick layers of ice. The entrance of the cave is higher than where the ice is located so the ice is trapped. Thick ice formed can last until August or September as there is little circulation to bring in summer heat."

Mark and I follow the road from the Ice Cave along the banks of the Upper Iowa River. Before long we are ascending a road winding through the trees up a very high bluff. At the top, I was astonished at the view of Decorah far below.

In awe, I declared, "It is good that the glaciers missed this part of Iowa. We have so much beauty in Decorah because of the high limestone bluffs flanking the river. I am thankful that forward looking people preserved this beauty by establishing parks along these bluffs."

Mark and I found a rock lookout from which we could view the city below. I pointed out the courthouse, some of the churches, the library, and some of the streets.

From our lunch basket, we took a couple of apples and sat on a picnic table, munching them. "Mark, I have had one of the most fun days ever."

"Before I leave for service, I want to take some more day trips to other close-by places of interest."

My heart seemed to stop or skip a beat or something. *How much I enjoyed today, but it is frightening to think of what will follow these enjoyable times.*

The following Saturday was another beautiful day, and Mark picked me up at ten, and we headed for Spillville. In the small Czech town, we easily found the brick-front building housing the Bily Clocks. The bachelor Bily brothers carved working clocks from wood during the winter months for fifty years. In the summertime, they were farmers. The two Bohemian Czech farmers created their large clocks with animated wooden figures and built-in music boxes.

The Czech composer Antonin Dvorak and his family lived on the second floor of the building in 1893. There are on exhibit items and memorabilia related to the artist. We found the intricately designed clocks fascinating, and Mark, being the musician that he is, enjoyed the Dvorak part of the museum.

Mark learned while Dvorak was in Spillville, he composed the String Quartet in F Major and String Quintet in E Flat. It is claimed that Dvorak asserted those pieces of music would never have been created if he had not visited America.

We saw the old stone mill on the Turkey River. In the Riverside Park, we ate the lunch I had packed. Then we drove to Fort Atkinson to see the fort. The corner stone houses with slots for guns to shoot out of were of interest.

It was another fun day to write about in my journal but another day closer to when Mark would be leaving. It is almost October, so the corn will be all husked soon. Until then, all the men and boys are needed in the fields to husk corn by hand and store it in corncribs with slats, openings between the boards to allow air to circulate and dry the corn.

This year, Mom agreed to let me drop band and return to taking piano lessons. I think that I will put to good use my piano skills as a teacher. I hope that there will be a piano or organ wherever I teach.

Dad, John, and Bobby finished picking corn the third week in October. I leaned from John that the McDonalds hope to be done in a day or two.

Three days later, on a Saturday, Mark came to my house. "Julia, I would like to take you to the movies tonight."

I had mixed feelings. Sure, I wanted to go with him to see a movie, but what would he have to tell me tonight?

The movie was an Alfred Hitchcock movie, *The Foreign Correspondent*. It was a suspense-filled espionage story that involved chasing spies and suspecting Nazi spy ring involvement. All the talk of spies and Nazis did not help my state of mind, but the worst was the conclusion of the film. The film ended with an unforgettable radio speech, an outright plea, for the US to join the war effort. Will this make Mark more determined than ever to enlist? I already know the answer to that.

We stopped for root beer floats before going home. Mark sat across from me. After we finished our ice cream treat, Mark got my attention.

"Julia, on Monday I plan to enlist in the US Army. I will miss you, but I feel I need to do this. I will be home on furlough after my basic training. It isn't that I wouldn't ever see you while I am in the service."

I felt like crying but didn't want to. I thought of protesting but knew that Mark expected me to be as brave as he was in serving his country. Then I thought of the verse I wrote in my journal about St. Paul being content in whatever circumstance he found himself in.

"Mark, I will miss you so." I barely whispered. Then I rallied, "I will try to keep busy and be content while waiting for you to come home." I paused. He did not speak either, then I spoke. "It may not be easy, but faith will see both of us through these times."

"Julia, I am relieved that you understand. It would be so hard to leave if you didn't. I will write often."

Mother helped Mrs. McDonald put on a farewell party for Mark. They made all kinds of good food. The invited neighbors, relatives, and friends came laden with more food. There were people all through the McDonald home, in the kitchen, dining room, living room, and screened in porch. Janie and Marian took some of the young girls up to Janie's bedroom to play. Bobby, Jimmy, and some of the young boys were out in the machine shed talking about school, trapping, and whatever.

On Monday, John and I went to the bus depot at the filling station to see Mark off on the bus with other young enlisted men. Last night, Mark and I had gone to the movies. At my door, he hugged me close and kissed me. "Julia, I will miss you. May the memory of this hug and kiss be with you until I am home again." When the men started getting on the bus, Mark took my arm and said, "Good-bye, Julia. Write to me." He hugged his mother and kissed her. Then he hugged his dad. Next thing I knew, he was gone.

Mark is gone. How can I face the many days ahead without him in my life? I feel numb, like this cannot be happening. *It cannot be true. My best friend has walked out of my life.*

I have to force myself to remember the happy times. I must hold in my heart the smiles, the twinkling eyes, dancing in his embrace, and the love he has shown to me.

I know life must go on. Dear God, give me the strength to face each day. Please, God, protect Mark wherever he is and from any danger that lurks around him. Bring him safely home someday. I feel that he is my best friend. It is too difficult to think of life without spending the rest of our lives together.

8

Wartime Activities

Not only me but my parents felt the sadness of Mark's leaving. They care about Mark. But are they fearing that John will be next to go?

Marian says that Dad listens every day to the news. Mother and Dad daily read the *Telegraph Herald* for news of the war in Europe. Dad made clear to the family President Roosevelt's Navy Day Speech on October 27, 1941. He explained that the president said Hitler was trying to frighten the Americans by torpedoing one of our ships carrying supplies to aid the British. Then from the newspaper, he read some of the concluding words of Roosevelt's message.

"Today in the face of this newest and greatest challenge of them all we Americans have cleared our decks and taken our battle stations. We stand ready in the defense of our Nation and the faith of our fathers to do what God has given us the power to see as our full duty."[1]

A chilly feeling rippled through my body. *That sounds close to a declaration of war.*

In the news, it is becoming more and more evident how we are actively involved in producing and providing weapons for fighting men on the battlefronts. Our nation is supplying military equipment and materials of all kinds.

The march of Hitler's troops through mainland Europe is shocking. Some nations without much struggle yield to Hitlerism. Mark is in boot camp. I received his address. He did not write much as he is kept so

---

[1] http://www.patriotfiles.com
President Franklin Roosevelt Navy Day Speech, Oct., 27, 1941

busy. I try to write something every day in a letter but plan to mail my writings only two or three times a week.

This week is Forty Hours at the church. With all the talk of war on the news, Father Dolan, the priest, told us that we need more than ever this time of continuous prayer before the Blessed Sacrament. He reminded us that Forty Hours is reminiscent of the forty hours between our Lord's burial and his resurrection.

During Forty Hours, we are encouraged to go to confession, take care of the penance that the priest gives each one of us, and go to Holy Communion.

The devotion begins with a Solemn Mass of Exposition and ends with the exposition of the Blessed Sacrament and a procession. The Blessed Sacrament remains on the altar in a large gold container. For the next forty hours, the parishioners come for private or public prayer. The devotions end with the Mass of Reposition, a procession, benediction, and reposition of the Blessed Sacrament.

Saturday afternoon my entire family goes to the church to confession. People are standing in line waiting to go to confession. The confessionals are in the front of the church, one on either side of the altar. The confessor goes in a tiny room, closes the door. In the dark, the person waits for the priest on the other side of the wall to slide open a small door when he is ready to hear the confession.

In my pew, I examine my conscience. I mentally search very intently so as not to forget to mention any sin. I think hard to remember how many times I did something I should not do. When I feel prepared to confess my sins, I stand in line to wait for my turn to go into the confessional. Because of Forty Hours, it is a long line of waiting people.

When it is my turn, I open the door of the confessional and go into a tiny room. I kneel and wait in the dark for the priest to slide open a small door that covers an opening covered with a dark cloth. As the priest is listening to a confession on the other side of him, it takes a while before he slides open the door on my side of the confessional.

In the dark, I fervently pray that I remember all my sins and how many times I sinned. I feel anxious about remembering every sin. I try to remember how many times I did a sin. Did I say a naughty word? I know that I did not eat meat on Friday because Mother makes fish on Fridays to eat.

After a few more minutes, the small door slides open. The priest can hear me but cannot see me through the dark cloth. The priest listens to my sins and gives me my penance. Then I recite the Act of Contrition.

When I leave the confessional, I go back to my seat, kneel, and repentantly bow my head and say my penance. Tonight, I am to say five Hail Marys, five Our Fathers, and the Act of Contrition. Afterward, I feel a significant feeling of peace.

On Saturday, December 6, Dad, with a long wire with a hook on the end, seized a rooster from the hen house. He squeezed the rooster's head between two large spikes driven into a chopping block. With one stroke of an ax, he chopped the neck of the bird, cutting off its head. The bloody head fell to the ground, and the beheaded rooster's body flopped around on the grass.

Mom had hot water ready to dunk the rooster in to get its feathers good and wet, so we could easily pull the feathers out and not leave too many pin feathers. Then on the bare ground, she lit crumpled old newspapers; they suddenly became a blazing fire over which she rotated the plucked chicken to singe off any remaining pin feathers. With the naked-looking chicken, Mother and I went to the old gray table in the milk house to cut up the chicken.

"Julia, I think it is time for you to learn how to cut up a chicken." I felt queasy but knew it was time I learned to do this job.

Mother patiently told me how to cut the bottom end of the bird to remove the innards—the guts, gizzard, and other organs. I warily stuck my hand in and pulled them out. I kept the heart, liver, and the gizzard. I had to try hard to cut and almost divide that tough gizzard in half. Then I cleaned out the bird's last meal and the grit (sand or small stones) used with the muscular thick-walled motion of the gizzard to grind the food for digestion.

Then I severed off both legs and the wings. I started at the back end of the chicken and divided it, cutting off the back from the lower part. That was not easy to do. Each of those parts I also cut apart.

Mother told me to wash carefully each piece of edible chicken in cold water several times. After that I put the chicken in a covered pan and placed it in the cellar to keep cool until we would cook it.

"Julia, you did a good job cutting up that rooster. We will keep the chicken cool until we fry it tomorrow."

Sunday morning, December 7, Mom made oatmeal pancakes with Karo syrup for breakfast. When Dad left the house to go milk the cows, Mom and I washed the dishes. Later I could hear Dad bringing the cream up to the milk house to put the large metal cream can into the water tank to keep the cream cool. I knew it was time to hurry and get ready to go to church.

At St. Benedict's, the long dark wooden pews were filled with families this peaceful Sunday morning. In the balcony high in the back of the church, the organist was playing a beautiful hymn. The large circular organ pipes of various sizes reached toward the ceiling. Accompanying the organ music, the voices of the choir floated over our heads, making me feel as if it was celestial music from heavenly angels.

At home, Mom and I leisurely set about preparing Sunday dinner.

"Julia, coat the chicken with flour, salt, and pepper. Then brown the chicken in two pans on the hot stove. After that put the chicken in this blue roaster to bake it in the oven while we boil the potatoes and heat green beans on top of the range. I will make an apple salad."

Mom directed Marian, "Go to the apple bin and get several large yellow apples. From the high wooden fruit shelf, bring up a jar of pickled Whitney crabapples to have with our evening meal." Earlier in the fall, the whole family picked apples to store in thin wooden boxes in the cool cellar with a dirt floor under our house. We thankfully are now reaping the fruit of our orchard that was set out seven years ago.

After I put the chicken to bake in the oven, I took a large pan to the potato bin in the cellar. I picked out potatoes to peel for making mashed potatoes for dinner.

Because it was the Sabbath and we had gone to church, the dinner was put on the table later than usual. We had just finished saying the blessing before meals. "Bless us, O Lord, and these Thy gifts, which we are about to receive from Thy bounty, through Christ our Lord. Amen." We were startled by the ringing of the big brown wooden phone on the kitchen wall. People usually didn't call at mealtime and especially not on Sunday. The shrill rings definitely were meant for us, one long ring followed by two short rings.

Mother answered the phone and turned to Dad. "It's your brother Roy." Dad took the receiver from Mother's hand and leaned to speak into the mouthpiece on the phone.

"Hello," he said. Dad listened closely to the caller. I could tell by Dad's ashen face something was terribly wrong. It seemed like forever before he spoke again in a trembling deep low voice, "Roy, are you sure?"

Dad slumped down in his chair at the table. He solemnly looked around at the family. *I felt like I could hardly breathe. What happened that is so bad?*

"A few minutes ago, Uncle Roy was listening to his radio. The program was interrupted to inform Americans that Oahu, one of the Hawaiian Islands, has been bombed by the Japanese. There is scanty news yet, but Roy thinks it is true that the Japs were able to reach Pearl Harbor by plane."

We had made a delicious Sunday meal, but no one felt like eating any of it now. *What will this mean for our lives? How will things change? An unknown, uncertain, frightening future lay ahead of us.*

On the late evening news, Dad learned the attack occurred in Hawaii just before eight o'clock Sunday morning. It was a complete surprise to the US military and civilians on the island.

I wonder what Mark thinks of this attack. Where will he be sent in the war? Will he now be sent to islands in the Pacific, or will he be sent to the battlefields in Europe?

Bobby and I rode to school with Melanie Monday morning and came home to the farm with her after school. With all the talk of war, I guess we just wanted to be at home.

Monday evening on the news, Dad heard words from President Roosevelt's address to both Houses of Congress. We learned how that day the president summoned the US to war.

On Tuesday night, Dad knew President Roosevelt was to make a broadcast to the nation on the declaration of war with Japan. My father claims he has never missed one of the president's fireside chats since the first one in 1933, during Depression times. Dad made sure that the radio battery was strong so that evening we could listen to President Roosevelt's fireside chat.

It is now two days after the bombing of Pearl Harbor. My family gathers around our battery-powered radio to hear President Roosevelt give his nineteenth fireside chat directly to the American people. I know that many families just like ours are listening tonight. From his previous fireside chats, we have learned to feel like he is a close friend talking to us in our living room. Dad says that tonight it is not just America listening but the world.

In his speech, Roosevelt is preparing the nation for war. He warns us of what is ahead—dark days, hard work, sacrifices, casualties, and setbacks for all of us. Production for war is to be speeded up by work in the plants seven days a week. War materials will be produced in existing industrial plants large and small, and new plants will be built. At this time, articles of food would not be curtailed but that there would be a definite shortage of metals for civilian use. In President Roosevelt's own words, he declared: "Every citizen, in every walk of life, shares this same responsibility. The lives of our soldiers and sailors—the whole future of this Nation—depend upon the manner in which each and every one of us fulfills his obligation to our country."

After the speech, I felt very somber about what I had heard. *What lies ahead of us? Will Mark be in grave danger? Will my brothers be drafted?*

Dad brought up the factories turning production to war equipment. He acknowledged how glad he was that he bought the tractor and the car last summer. Otherwise, he feared that it might be years before he could buy a tractor.

What lies ahead of us? How many sacrifices will my family have to make? I am so glad I was here with my parents to listen to the president tonight.

Every day Dad listens to the news and reads the paper to glean more information about the attack on Pearl Harbor. As it is now past mid-December and Christmas vacation time, I am home for several weeks.

In the evenings, Dad gathers the family around the kitchen table; he reads or tells us war news. Dad always encourages us to participate with our questions or thoughts about the war.

We understand that the Japanese planned the surprise attack on Pearl Harbor to wipe out rows of battleships in the harbor and planes lined up wing tip to wing tip on the airfields. The Japanese dive bombers had easy targets to cripple with no time for the US to take defensive action.

We discussed previous Japanese aggressive actions of waging war throughout Asia. That aggression strained relations with our country. It seemed evident the Japanese hoped to curtail our ability to stop their conquests.

This year, it was hard to get in the spirit of Christmastime. A week before Christmas, Mom put up our small artificial tree. Mom and I hung colored cords around the tree and put on bright colored Christmas balls. *Within my heart, I just could not feel joyous.*

It is a family tradition to have hot oyster soup on Christmas Eve. Afterward, on the way to midnight mass, it was lightly snowing. The church was packed. People who came later than us had to stand in the entryway.

During the last four weeks, the church has been in the period known as Advent. It is a time of spiritual preparation for believers to prepare for the coming of baby Jesus. The crib is set up but Jesus is not placed in it until Christmas. The beautiful red poinsettias are not placed on the altar until the day before Christmas.

During these weeks of Advent, the church is not very colorful; actually-- it is very drab looking.

The December weather was cold and the skies bleak looking, which just added to my depressed emotional state of mind. *I must force myself to find joy in the little things of life. We have plenty of good food to eat. Our home is warm and comfortable. I feel the warmth of love just being with my caring family.*

Tonight, in sharp contrast to the last seventeen days, Christmas Eve is a glorious, joyful experience. The church is filled with the almost overwhelming powerful pipe organ music as we find our seats in the wooden pews. I picture the organist using her feet as well as her hands to create rich strong music at times and simple pure delightful sounds at other times from her keyboard, and with the foot pedals, she controls the tone, pitch, and loudness of the large ranked pipes.

Tonight. for Christmas, Father Dolan and several visiting priests from neighboring churches are celebrating a High Mass. I know the mass will be longer. The priests will sing many prayers and psalms.

One of the visiting priests goes to the pulpit, a raised structure from which he reads from the Bible the story of the birth of Jesus from Luke 2. After the reading, Father Dolan speaks to the parish of the true meaning of Christmas, the birth of our Savior to save us from our sins.

At Communion time, the people in the front rows of pews pour into the center aisle and approach the long communion railing, kneel, and wait for one of the priests to lay the communion host on their tongues. We are to swallow the wafer without it touching our teeth or chewing it. After partaking of the Christian sacrament of Communion, each of the communicants goes to one of the side aisles and returns to his or her seat.

As I follow the line to Communion, I marvel at the beauty I am seeing. The altar is banked with rows of bright-red colorful poinsettias. Father Dolan is wearing a beautiful white robe trimmed in gold. While the people file up to Communion, the choir is singing familiar Christmas carols, "It Came Upon the Midnight Clear," "Away in a Manger," and "O Come, All Ye Faithful." I feel the angelic spiritual music is changing my anguish over the war news into joy for tonight anyway. This holy night, I believe others must feel the same way.

Just for now, everything seems peaceful. The baby Jesus is in the crib. We have biblical assurances that he will not fail us nor forsake us.

With the beauty of the Christmas mass warming my thoughts, the crisp cold night did not chill me to the bone. *I wish Mark could have been at the service. Where is he tonight?* Christmas should be a happy, joyous time of year. I felt that way tonight in the well-lit church filled with blissful music, but now out in the dark of the countryside, I am starting to feel very sad.

The Christmas best wishes I wanted most to be given, I did not receive. Why did I not get a Merry Christmas card or letter from Mark? Why did I not hear from him for Christmas?

On Christmas morning, we opened our presents. Most of the gifts were practical ones—items we needed for clothes or some activity. Bobby received some trapping equipment. John was given a hatchet for hunting and money to buy new tires for his car. Dad wanted John to have new tires because he was worried we soon would have trouble getting tires because of the war. Marian opened packages containing paper dolls, a checker game, a puzzle, and a new sweater. There was a long toboggan for all of us to use. Most likely, Bobby and Marian would get the most use out of that.

I was given a Lane cedar chest. Mom said it was time that I start my hope chest. She had made me several very pretty crocheted doilies and a set of embroidered pillowcases with crocheted edgings on the opening end of each one.

We enjoyed our turkey and dressing meal including mashed potatoes, gravy, candied sweet potatoes, cranberries, apple salad, and pecan pie with whipped cream. Mother had made pinwheel date cookies, cut out white Christmas cookies with colored frosting, homemade fruit cake, and chocolate fudge for us to enjoy during Christmas vacation.

The day after Christmas, Mark's Christmas card was in the mail. I was happy to learn when I would see him next. He wrote he would be coming home in mid-February and would give me his Christmas gift at that time. *I will count off the days until then.*

In January, from Uncle Roy and Dad, I was kept posted on war news. The first American soldiers arrived in Europe on Irish soil. The Japanese were striking hard at European colonies in Southeast Asia. Colonies are lands other countries maintain to harvest raw materials from. The Japanese had few raw materials on their small islands. The Japanese captured Manila. They declared war on the Netherlands. It seemed the whole world was getting involved in the war.

While I was at school, I was so busy I did not have time to think about the horrors of war. I was busy preparing materials for my six weeks of practice teaching. I made flash cards of often-used words such as *the, in, up, on, from, here, there*, and others to use for teaching reading. I made and added multiplication and division to my stacks of flash cards for arithmetic.

Pictures were cut from old magazines to paste on one side of a flash card, and I wrote the name of the picture on the other side. Hopefully, these cards will help my students learn word recognition. I made a collection of pictures to put up on a bulletin board in the classroom. Pictures to use were found from old greeting cards, calendars, magazines, old signs, and boxes.

I copied nursery rhymes and poems in a notebook to have students read or memorize. A poster was made of the vowels and a picture for each to help identify the sound of that specific vowel. I knew once I started teaching that I would be so busy working directly with students that I would have little time to make teaching aids.

On Friday, the day before Valentine's Day, Mark was to come home for a week. All day at school, I had trouble keeping my mind glued to my work. *Will Mark still want to take me out? If so, will we have much time to spend together?*

After school, Melanie was excited to get home to see her brother. She drove Bobby and me to our home. How I wished that I could stay in the car and go home with her.

Not long after I was in the house, the phone rang a long ring and two shorts. I eagerly ran to the kitchen phone. *I just knew it would be Mark. It was him.*

"Hello, Julia, would you like to go to the movies this evening?" Seems I could not decide what to wear. *Should I wear my black-and-white checked suit with the peplum at the waist or my new red, light wool dress?* I loved wearing the suit with the peplum and decided on that. I fussed with my hair. I combed it this way and that, finally fluffing it up on top and combing down the sides, curling the fronts to my face.

Mark looked taller and was so good looking in his olive drab green army dress uniform. His greeting smile was as enchantingly warm as ever. His eyes looked over me and seem to light up his face. He took my hand, and we walked out to his car.

I commented on his insignia on the sleeve of his uniform. He laughed and said, "I am no longer a private but a corporal. When I go back, I will be given additional training, and then I will receive a higher rank. I am being sent to school for mechanics in Fort Hood, Texas."

At the start of the movie were pictures of the ongoing war, a regular part of movies nowadays because of the war. We saw short clips telling us that after the Japanese triumph at Pearl Harbor, they went on to attack the Philippines, Aleutian Islands, and British colonies in the East. Their aim was to drive General MacArthur and the Americans out of the Philippines. The news informed us that the Japanese hoped to curtail any interference the allies might give them in their advances in Asia.

From listening to Dad and Uncle Roy, I knew the allies were Britain, the United States, and any other nation standing with them against the Axis powers of Germany, Italy, and Japan.

The new release, *Mrs. Miniver*, starts on the screen. I become engrossed in the wartime movie. The story is of the great trials, dangers, and sufferings of a small British village during the war. There is bombing; a shot down German wounded pilot parachutes into their lives.

Toward the end, when the family heartily sings "Onward Christian Soldiers," Mark squeezes my hand. I think we felt their singing as a message of belief that there would always be an England. In our hearts, we felt the belief that there would always be a United States.

After the movie, we went to the Eat Shop next door for malted milk. Facing me in the booth, Mark told me about his basic training. It was decided that he was to go to Fort Hood near Dallas, Texas, for further training in being a tank mechanic. "Julia, I guess my years of being around Dad's tractor and repairing machinery gave the military the belief I would make a good mechanic on large tanks. Anyway, with my past farm experience, I think that it will be interesting."

"Mark, I am happy for you that you are doing work in the military that you enjoy doing. I am proud that you have the mechanical ability that is so needed during this wartime." *On Mark's face, I am sure I can see his pleasure in hearing me acknowledge his capabilities.*

After a short silence, he informed me, "Dad told me that the tractor plants are now manufacturing tanks. Massey-Harris is building several kinds of tanks, aircraft wings, and truck bodies. John Deere is building transmissions for medium-sized tanks.

They are manufacturing parts for aircraft and ammunition. Our nation's industrial plants have been transformed from civilian production into producing all kind of materials for war purposes." After a few minutes of silence, Mark reached into his coat pocket and handed me a small wrapped package with a red bow. "Julia, I wasn't home at Christmastime to give you a present. So, I bought something for you for Valentine's Day."

I gently opened the pretty package to lift out a gold cross necklace. "Oh, it is beautiful. Thank you, Mark."

We made plans to go dancing the next evening. I knew that Mom would not like me going to DanceNite dance hall on Saturday night, but maybe this once would be okay. Mother calls it a bad place because people go drinking and carousing on the night before the Sabbath. Then they can't crawl out of bed for mass the next morning. I explained all that to Mark. We agreed that we would leave the dance at midnight.

On Saturday night, Mark and I enjoy the dance music. We know that we do not have a lot of time to talk alone, so we find a booth away from the dance floor. We can still hear the music, and we can talk too. Mark tells me about his training so far. He admits it was hard at first. He was kept so busy there was hardly any time for him, no less write a letter.

I shared that I might have a chance to teach in the home school next year. Mother heard that the teacher there now is getting married to her enlisted boyfriend. The way Mom heard it, it sounds that she wants to live on the base where he is stationed. Her future husband is an officer who trains inductees and so will likely stay put awhile.

I told Mark, "In April and the first two weeks in May, I will do six weeks of practice teaching in the brick school, the one closest to the home school. Dad or John can drive me to and from school every day, unless John lets me drive his car. I hope he lets me drive once-in-a-while, maybe when the men are busy in the fields."

Mark remarked, "John was blessed at Christmas to receive new tires before the rationing went into effect last month. Also, your dad was smart to buy a new car last summer as the government is starting to ration cars this month."

We wondered how much more we would have to learn to do without on the home front as more materials were needed on the battle fronts. We danced some of our favorite dance numbers and left about a quarter to twelve. Mark reminded me that John would visit with him after mass in the morning. Then both boys are to come to our house for a beef roast dinner. Afterward, the McDonalds are coming to my home to listen to Mark, John, Melanie, Bobby, Jimmie, Marian and I play and sing.

For supper, my family is invited to the McDonalds for a chili supper. Afterward, we are going to play cards.

Sunday evening, while getting ready for bed, I felt thankful that I was with Mark so much on the weekend. Tomorrow I have to go to school. I picked up the box of chocolates that Mark had given me for Valentine's Day. *How sweet of him. He is kind and thoughtful. That's why I care so much about him.*

How can I go to school every day this week knowing Mark is at home and I wouldn't see him until Friday night? Tonight, we made plans to go to a movie at the end of my work week.

Friday night, Mark and I went to see a movie at the Grand Theater. The news clips told how German subs are cruising the Atlantic in efforts to hold off American aid to England. German forces occupy much of European Russia. German armies are moving in lands bordering the Mediterranean Sea. The strategy was for the Germans to move east and the Japanese to move west planning for Axis control of the oil fields.

The movie is about a couple trying to plan their escape from the Nazis. I find it hard to concentrate on the movie plot. I keep thinking unrelenting thoughts. *This is the last movie that Mark and I will be together at for a long time. Tomorrow he will be on the bus to Fort Hood, Texas. When will be the next time that I see him? Will I ever go out with him again?*

Before we say good night to each other, Mark and I talk a bit. It is too cold out to sit in the car and talk very long, so we try to say as much as we can in a short time.

We talk about missing each other. Each of us promises to write as often as we can. Finally, we walk to the door. Mark gives me a strong hug, kisses me, and he is gone.

Sleep didn't come very fast once I was snug under the flannel sheets and a thick quilt with a wool batting inside. *I must focus on finishing my high school courses and do my practice teaching. Maybe if I keep real busy, I wouldn't have that much time to think about missing Mark.*

It being Saturday, Mother let me sleep. I did not wake up until nine o'clock. When I saw the time, I knew Mark was already on the road to Texas. *How can I get up and face the day? My best friend is headed South and going farther and farther away from me.*

9

Julia Does Practice Teaching

The first week in April, I started my practice teaching with Miss Nelson. It was her fourth year of teaching, so I felt quite confident that I would learn a lot and get much experience working with her. I was glad it was springtime, so we did not have to worry about keeping a stove going to keep the school room warm.

There were eighteen students in the school. Two students were in kindergarten, and they sat in one of the small double desks. Miss Nelson asked, "Julia, is it all right with you if you start by teaching phonics to first through third grades? The kindergarteners are also part of the beginning of each phonics class. Then they go to their seats to work on their letters and simple words.

"The older ones in the phonics class write word families, for example, start with the word 'fun' and underneath write other words that end in the 'un' sound like *bun, sun*, and *run.*"

With all the phonics students sitting on the recitation bench, each day we drilled together letter sounds. We went through all the sounds of the consonants in the twenty-six-letter alphabet.

I believe knowing well the vowel sounds are main keys to good reading skills. I would hold up picture flash cards as cues for the students to remember the short vowel sounds. In my normal training reading class, I had made picture flash cards showing the sound of each short vowel sound. I had drawn an apple for the short *a* sound in *apple.* There was a picture of an egg to remind the pupils of short *e* as in *egg.* A card with an Indian in an Indian headdress illustrated the short sound of *i* and for the short sound of *o* an octopus. For the short sound of *u*, I had drawn an open umbrella. Most of this lesson was just a review for the youngsters, so we moved along quickly.

We reviewed the short vowels sounds. The students know that if I put a small cup above a vowel, it has the short vowel sound.

We repeated together *ă*, the short vowel sound in *bat, cat, fat*; the short *e* like in *bed, Ned, wed*; short *i* as in *sit*, *hit*, *mitt*; short *o* in *not*, *cot*, *hot*; and short *u* in *nut*, *hut*, *cut*, and so forth. I found it fun working with the students. We had fun rhyming words like *small, tall, wall*, and so on.

As we progressed with our sounds, we built the sounds into words. When we had a stack of word cards, we wrote sentences on the blackboards using the words from the cards. The children were growing in their learning, and I was having a great time teaching them. We would giggle at some of our nonsensical rhyming words and the funny sentences that we created together.

After phonic class, the teacher had me listen to the lower grades read their reading books. Because of their phonics training, they were little "experts" at sounding out new words except for ones like *gnat* that have silent letters in them.

While Miss Nelson worked with the regular math lessons, she had me drill lower-level grades on their addition and subtraction facts. Fourth and fifth grades recited their multiplication and division facts. I would say, "Recite your multiples of six," and they would say, "Six, twelve, eighteen, twenty-four, thirty, thirty-six, forty-two, forty-eight, fifty-four, and sixty."

Then I might have all the fourth- and fifth-grade students form a circle. I would tell one student to begin saying the eights and they would say "eight," and the next student to the left would say "sixteen," the next would say "twenty-four," and so on. If one student did not say the correct answer in a few seconds, that student would have to sit down. The one who stayed standing would be the winner. If students were having much trouble, they were encouraged to take their flash cards to their desks and study them.

Sometimes we played the game that if you had to sit down, in the next round if you knew the answer, you could stand up again. When they became very good with the answers, we speeded up the time for giving the correct answer.

The first few weeks, while the regular teacher taught English, history, and science, I would help students with math or any other subject that needed one-on-one help.

Every Friday, we had music class. I could play the organ for the singing. Ms. Nelson was happy that I could play as she claimed she was not very good at playing the organ. While I played the Scottish song, "You take the Highroad," Miss Nelson and the students sang, "Oh! Ye'll take the high road, and I'll take the low road, and I'll be in Scotland afore ye."

Sometimes we sang, "Row, row, row your boat gently down the stream. Merrily, merrily, merrily, merrily. Life is but a dream." At noon, the students would go to the entryway that was partitioned off from the classroom to retrieve their lunch buckets. They would sit in their desks to eat their cold lunches. Their lunches would contain such things as sandwiches, fruit, cookies, pieces of cake, pickles, and maybe some sauce in a jar.

After lunch, Miss Nelson and I played games with the students. As it was springtime, we usually played softball. Miss Nelson played on one team, and I played on the other one. The two older boys took turns choosing who would play on their team.

After the noon hour, Miss Nelson asked me to read a chapter from a book every day to the students while they rested from their active playground games. I enjoyed reading a book about Daniel Boone and his pioneer experiences.

In the afternoon, we taught English classes. The first two weeks, I worked with the younger students, and the rest of my practice teaching time I spent with the older students.

One week we would teach science for the whole week, and the next week we taught health classes for the week. The health classes had workbooks in which they read and then filled answers in blanks.

We taught history and geography for four days. On Friday, we gave spelling tests and taught handwriting. After afternoon recess on Friday, we had art class.

This year, my senior year, I sat with Melanie during the prom dinner. *Last year's prom was so much fun. It is not exciting without Mark. I do not like watching happy couples having a good time eating and talking.*

I stayed awhile to listen to the music. When the memorable music "Only Forever" filled the auditorium, I became teary eyed. *Oh, how I wish Mark was here to dance with me our song, the one we danced to last prom. How could a year's time make so much change in one's life? What is Mark doing tonight?*

Shortly after that song, I said good night to Melanie and went home early. My heart wasn't in having fun without Mark.

Being springtime and a sunny warm day, Miss Nelson and I had each student grab a lead pencil and a tablet to draw outside. Some students sat on the steps going into the school. Others sat on the grass. They drew trees with leaves. Some created a picture of the schoolhouse. One drew a very good likeness of the road and the farm place in the distance.

When it came time to say good-bye to the children in the stone school, I found myself tearing up. The little ones hugged me and said they would miss me. After the students went home, I hugged Miss Nelson good-bye. She told me, "You will make an excellent schoolteacher. I will give you a high recommendation to your high school supervising teacher and to any school director or superintendent you wish me to contact. You are not only knowledgeable about teaching methods, but you are patient and compassionate with students when they have troubles understanding."

John honked the horn to hurry me. I thanked Miss Nelson and ran to the waiting vehicle. I should not keep John waiting. Gas is being rationed this month, so I am lucky he is willing to give me a ride home.

Mother bought me a new dress and dress heels for my graduation. I was surprised when she gave me a pair of full-fashioned nylons. "Mother,

I thought you couldn't buy nylons now. Isn't all the nylon from the DuPont Company going to make parachutes, tents, and tires?"

Mom replied, "Julia, at Christmastime I bought extra pairs of new nylon stockings for you and me. Now I am very glad I did." Mom had a new garter belt for me to hold up my mid-thigh stockings. When I dressed for graduation, I hooked the garters onto the tops of my stockings. I tried to look to make sure the seams in the back of my stockings were straight up and down.

The commencement speaker told us that we had our whole lives ahead of us. He urged us to use our education to make a good life for ourselves and our loved ones. I felt a thrill when my name was called and I walked across the stage to receive my diploma, but I was most relieved when the long ceremony was over.

At home, I was very careful removing my nylons. I put them away to wear when Mark comes home. It is summertime, so in the warmer weather now I can go barelegged.

The next day, Mom and Dad hosted an open house in the afternoon for my graduation. Some of my high school friends, neighbors, and relatives were there. *One person did not come— could not come—the one that I wanted most to be there.* With Mark's folks there, I missed Mark more than ever.

The Monday after graduation, I drove John's car over a mile out to the main road to see if I had any mail. Our mail is delivered to a metal box on a post alongside the graveled road. There were several envelopes addressed to me. One was from Mark. I was anxious to get home to read my mail.

At home, I went up to my room to see Mark's card. It read, "Happy Graduation to a Dear One." In his letter, he wrote how he wished he could have been home for my graduation and the celebration afterward. He felt it would be another couple of months before he would have any chance of a furlough. I tucked his card into the top drawer of my dresser where I could find it to look at and read often.

There were cards from relatives in Montana and Illinois. All those cards contained money for my graduation. I thought I will buy bonds with my graduation money. I remember seeing the posters at the post office encouraging people to be patriotic and buy US war bonds. Before movies, I had viewed government ads telling that the uniformed men were making the greatest sacrifices; we should be helpful in buying bonds to put more money into defense purposes. *Someday I can cash my bonds to buy some furniture for a home of my own.*

As sugar was now rationed, Mother had to apply to get extra sugar for canning purposes. The purpose of rationing was to try to give a fair distribution of goods to the people.

In the spring, Marian had helped our parents plant a small garden near the house. They planted a larger garden in the rows lining up with rows of corn plants, so Dad could plow between the rows to weed the garden when he cultivated his cornfield. That saved a lot of weeding. Marian called the garden the Victory Garden. The government was telling people to plant Victory Gardens to provide food for civilians so other foods would be in supply for the military.

The June strawberries were plentiful this year. The whole family helped pick them every other day. I brought the berries to a boil, added sugar and the jar of pectin, and brought the mixture back to a rolling boil. I skimmed the scum from the top of the berries and poured the hot mixture into odd-sized jars. On top of each jar, I placed hot wax thick enough to seal the jars.

I had just finished sealing the jam jars when the local school director knocked on the door. He had a contract for me to sign to teach the home school. I was so happy because I can live at home this year. I couldn't wait to write Mark to tell him the good news. Mother, Marian, and I spent many days picking and preparing foods to be canned. We canned many quarts of tomatoes both as either tomato sauce or whole tomatoes. We placed many glass quart jars of vegetables and fruits on shelves in our cellar.

Mom made lots of dill pickles. She placed sprigs of fresh dill in the bottom of the jar then small-sized cucumbers over which she poured hot vinegar. Then she put rubber bands around the top of each jar, and she tightly screwed a zinc lid over each to seal the jars.

Mark's letters came regularly every three or four days. He sent me a small picture of himself by a huge tank. Another picture was of him and an army buddy. His training was almost over, and he was to have another furlough near the end of July.

That was good news and not so good news. If his training was almost over, would he be sent overseas? I did not want to think about that. If he did go overseas, would he go to Europe to fight against the Nazis? Maybe he would be sent to battles on islands in the Pacific Ocean. He would be so far from home. He could be in grave danger in such places.

One of Mark's military buddies, Jim McClury, from Waukon, Iowa, was also coming home for a furlough. As he owned a car, he drove Mark directly to the farm. Mark spent an hour with his parents and then came over to see John and me. He asked me to go to Spillville dancing that night. Somehow, John talked Betty Olson into going to the dance with us. *So, John was still sweet on Betty.*

We had such a great time dancing and lots of fun watching some dancers doing the swing dances. We tried it too and found it exhilarating but fun. Glenn Miller music was popular with the swing crowd. Glenn Miller could be heard several times each week on the Chesterfield radio program, so people who enjoyed his music were very familiar with Miller's big band sound of music. The band played the current popular "String of Pearls" followed by "Chattanooga Choo Choo," and the happy dancers did swing to the beat of the music.

After dancing a waltz, fox-trot, polka, and schottische, the band played "In the Mood," another Miller big band favorite. I think Betty Olson enjoyed the dance as much as the rest of us.

On the way home, we planned to go caving after mass on Sunday. Betty and I volunteered to bring picnic baskets.

We went to the local cave first, the Wonder Cave, which is only a few miles from our house. When I was younger, I rode my bicycle over there a couple of times. I was anxious to go in the cave again. Betty had never been in the cave. She was apprehensive about going in. Going in is especially scary as the only way in is to go on ladder steps straight down. John went first and warned Betty to come down slowly and carefully.

As we walked farther into the cave, the walkway was wet and the walls were dripping. Some water trickled along by the pathway. We saw a white salamander. Betty was surprised at the stalactites on the ceiling of the cave and the stalagmites on the floor of the cave. In some places, they had grown together forming a column. After some time walking underground, we came to an iron railing, which stopped us from going any further. Below us was a huge water-filled area and above was a wonderfully beautiful high underground waterfall pouring water into the big hole. We stood there mesmerized by this astounding, beautiful underground falls. When John and Mark were in high school, they did some caving. They would tie long barn ropes around their waists and keep a few feet of rope between each person. One end of the rope they would tie to a tree on the outside of some noncommercial cave or hole in the ground. Sometimes they went into sinkholes on our farm. One time they had explored a long way underground, and they felt they were headed toward Wonder Cave. Feeling it was too dangerous to go any further, they did not go on.

Mother had always worried when they went exploring holes in the ground. Rightfully concerned, she warned them of the danger of falling rocks and getting trapped in the cave. I was glad when they gave up that interest.

John turned to Mark and asked, "Do you remember hearing that someone once poured dye into this hole, and dyed water turned up in the spring at Dunning's Spring Park?"

"I remember hearing that, and I don't doubt it. This water has to be going somewhere. Besides, it probably has already traveled underground for a long way."

We drove to Dunning's Spring and ate our picnic lunch that Betty and I had packed. After lunch, John drove to Highway 52, a highway built only ten years earlier. We were on our way to see Niagara Cave near Harmony, Minnesota. I had been in the cave as a little girl when Mom and Dad had taken Mom's aunt from Chicago there. I was only three, so I did not remember it.

By now Betty and I were both excited to visit this much-larger cave.

Sometimes the boys held our hands while we walked in the cave. If I came to a wet or rough spot, Mark would seize my hand and help me cross over. John did the same thing for Betty. We both appreciated that as we did not want to fall on the slippery floor of the cave and dirty our dresses.

On the way home, I think the boys thought we were such good sports going into the caves that they decided to try another adventure with us. They talked about wanting to canoe the Upper Iowa River from Kendallville to Bluffton. Betty and I agreed that we would like to go with them.

So, plans were made to go canoeing on Tuesday. Betty and I would pack a picnic lunch, and the boys would see about renting two canoes. Betty and I decided that we would wear pedal pushers and a blouse over our swimming suits.

Tuesday John loaded Betty's picnic basket and his old inner tube into his car. Mark packed my basket and his inner tube into his dad's car. We drove to Decorah where the boys rented two canoes. One canoe was tied on to the top of each car. We drove to our takeout point near Bluffton and left Mark's locked car there with our picnic baskets inside. As John's car was the older car, the boys thought it was best to tie the second canoe on the top of it. We drove to where we would put the canoes in the Upper Iowa River, near Cresco. We loaded our water and snacks into each canoe. John and Betty pushed off in one canoe; Mark and I started floating in the other one. Each one of us had a paddle.

John taught Betty how to hold the paddle and demonstrated how to use it in the water. Mark patiently taught me the same thing.

In some places, limestone cliffs lined the riverbank. Swallows would fly out of cracks in the rocks. As it was almost August, the river was not very high. The worst part was several times we came to where there was barbed wire across the river. Some farmer did not want his dairy cattle wandering away. The boys took turns holding up the wire so we could pass under. I wouldn't want to be caught on barbed wire; it would make an ugly tear on the skin. As we leisurely floated along, we just enjoyed being in such pleasant surroundings. One feels close to God in nature. In places, the trees blocked our view so all that we could see was the river ahead of us. In places, the river barely flowed over the rocks but still enough to keep us afloat. Coming around a bend in the river, we came to what the boys said was a big hole where the river would be very deep. We were careful not to tip over in that area. Mark explained that sometimes when the water is rushing around as on a bend in the river, it whirls, and a hole is formed underneath the surface. Such areas can be dangerous to people swimming or wading in the water.

We decided when we reached our takeout point that we would try swimming in the water. It was so peaceful floating along with the current; I did not want the canoe trip to end.

The boys started splashing water at each other. The canoe I was in started rocking. "Mark and John, stop. I do not want to tip over."

They did stop. I was relieved. Boys that they are, they probably would have enjoyed tipping each other and getting soaked. I had never been canoeing before, but I knew that several years ago, John and Mark had canoed on Canoe Creek in the spring when the water was high enough.

I was enjoying the float so much that I did not want to quit canoeing when we got to our takeout point near Bluffton. The boys helped Betty and I disembark from the tippy canoes and unloaded our belongings. The boys pulled the canoes up on the bank.

Then John and Mark left in Mark's car to go back to get John's car at the spot we put in the canoes. While they were gone, Betty and I had time to talk.

"Julia, do you think that John will enlist before long? I know with Mark home it is on his mind to do his duty too. I shudder when I see those posters, 'Uncle Sam Wants You.' You know, the ones where Uncle Sam is pointing a finger like it is meant for me. How does a young man feel when he looks at that poster?"

"Betty, I think as soon as John can get away from fall work on the farm that he will enlist. Bobby is older now and can help Dad almost as well as John can."

"That's what I am afraid of. How do you stand it when Mark is gone for so long? Don't you get lonesome for him?"

"Of course, I do. War is not fun for anyone."

"Well, I am glad that I have my job at the telephone office. It is a good job with good pay. I am buying bonds with my money I can save out of my wages. As I live at home, I do not have many expenses, only my clothes and some toiletry items."

I asked, "What do you think of the girls working in the war production plants? Many young girls and women are flocking to cities to work in the industrial plants."

"I don't think I could do work like Rosie the Riveter. It just seems so unladylike to get greasy and dirty welding and bolting machinery."

"Betty, I suppose some of the women have husbands, boyfriends, brothers, or sons who have gone to war. Maybe they believe that they are helping their loved ones by making ammunition, airplanes, and other supplies for them."

"But how can mothers justify being away from the home and their young children? I hope that I never will have to do that. What a sacrifice for a mother to have to make."

"I cannot fathom what that would do to young children. Having fathers in the war is bad enough. Children need both parents in their lives. A daughter not only needs her caring mother, but she also needs the protection and love of a father. A son needs the nurturing of his mother and thrives on the manliness of his father. The feminine makeup of the mother and the masculinity of the father help promote the healthy mental growth of a child to maturity."

"Yes, Julia, you are right. What will this all mean for our country in the years ahead? The Bible in the book of Proverbs says, 'Train up a child in the way he should go, and when he is old, he will not depart from it.'"

We were having such a good time visiting that before we knew it, the boys were back with both cars. Betty and I pulled off our pedal pushers and blouses in the backseat of John's car. Then all four of us headed to the river. The water was quite shallow close to the bank. The boys ventured out into deeper water, but Betty and I only went as far as waist-deep water. I didn't want to get my hair wet. I don't think Betty did either. We dog-paddled for a little while and then Betty and I just walked around in the warm water.

Betty and I walked back to John's car, dried ourselves off, and changed into dry clothes. The boys were still swimming in the river. Betty and I laid out a cloth on the grass and set out our food. We called to Mark and John, "It is time to eat." That brought them out of the water in a hurry. They dried off in the backseat of Mark's car and pulled on dry clothes.

The food tasted ever so good after being all afternoon on the river. I wondered if I got sunburned. Betty looked as if her face was getting red from being in the sun so much today.

The boys were talking about what we could do on Thursday. John thought of going to Effigy Mounds and riding along the Mississippi River to McGregor and having a picnic at Pike's Pike. He knew we would enjoy the high bluff and park area, known as Pike's Peak, overlooking the mighty Mississippi River. John told us, "You will enjoy the sights from Iowa's beautiful Pike's Peak even though it is not as high as the well-known mountainous Pikes Peak in Colorado." We all agreed that is a great idea. If the boys can provide the transportation, Betty and I will pack the food. John claimed that he had not driven much and would have plenty of ration stamps for gas. Mark said he would try to borrow his dad's car.

Thursday, we picked up Betty in Decorah. She was able to get the day off from work. She traded days with another girl. We drove Highway 18 to Waukon. From there, almost to the river, the road ran along a high ridge. Beautiful rolling hills sloping to deep ravines could be seen along both sides of the road. In places, one could see for many miles. The wooded hillsides were like scenic paintings of various shades of green.

We drove north along the mighty Mississippi to Effigy Mounds. Near the mouth of the Yellow River, we drove into Effigy Mounds. The four of us climbed the large hill to the top where we could see Indian mounds in the shapes of animals. It was a lot easier going back down.

Next, we returned to the Mississippi River and went south to Marquette and then continued on to McGregor. There the car followed a steep road to Pike's Peak. We walked to the lookout area. What a breathtaking view! The wide Mississippi stretched for miles below us. In that expanse, we could see trees covering small areas in the water and stretches of water extending in all directions for miles. One could make out the main channel as there we could see barges moving down the river. We could see a few smaller vessels on the water.

Betty and I laid out our lunch on a table close to the edge of the cliff. We wanted to enjoy the view while we ate. As it was a weekday, there were only a few people at the park.

When Mark took me home, he said, "Julia, I very much would like to have a picnic in Phelps Park tomorrow, just you and me. The afternoon I want to spend with my parents, but in the evening, I would like to take you to the movies."

When Mark picked me up Friday morning at nine o'clock, I was excited. I am going to actually hike the trail at Phelps Park with Mark alone. I remembered how two years ago I wanted so to hike the trail with him.

On the way to the park, I relayed to Mark what Mother had told me about the CCC and what they had done in the park last summer. Mom said that they have made the park so much nicer.

"My little sister, Marian, asked, 'What is the CCC?' Mother told us CCC means Civilian Conservation Corps. It is a major part of the WPA (Works Progress Administration). After the Great Depression hit this nation hard in 1929, the value of the dollar became almost worthless, and millions lost their jobs. By 1933, President Franklin Delano Roosevelt knew something had to give. The 'New Deal' came into being. It was a series of programs to stand unemployed men back on their feet and give a monetary shot to the economy. The men were to help with federal, state, and local government-building projects across the nation. They were paid from $15 to $90 a month to help to build American infrastructures such as bridges, highways, parks, and such projects."

"Julia, that is right. The CCC was a public relief program for young men from the ages of seventeen to twenty-eight. It provided unskilled labor for projects involving conservation and the development of natural resources."

"Mark, I remember last summer seeing the men around the barracks they lived in on the fairgrounds."

"They were given a place to stay, clothes, and their meals. Being they were in tough times, those benefits were a good thing to them.

Besides they were paid $30 a month, but $25 had to be sent home to their families."

As we drove up to the park, we appreciated looking up at the high limestone entrance put there by the CCC. Then we became engrossed in looking at the stacked and layered stone wall along the roadway made of limestones lining the driveway. After parking, Mark took my hand and led me to the trail along the scenic view of the Upper Iowa River.

Happiness seemed to flood me with exciting joy. We walked to the main lookout structure made of limestone rocks below on which straight-up wood supports held wood rafters overhead. We sat on a bench and took in the beauty of the trees and the meandering river below.

Mark pulled me to my feet, and we started walking on the trail. We saw rocks stacked on their sides to form walls, rocks laid flat to create steps and walkways. Then we came to a picturesque rocked stairway made of many steps descending downhill to a bridge overlooking waterways to carry runoffs to the river below. I was charmed by the attractive stone curved stairway and felt like a fairy princess on the arm of my prince descending the stone stairs to the intriguing stone end posts of the bridge. The limestone posts by the bridge were craftily built. I just wanted to stand there and etch on my brain forever the exquisite beauty of it all.

Mark led me to the center of the bridge. We gazed down at the waterway many feet below.

The last time I was here, I was thinking of wild flowers. Today, it is just a pleasure being with Mark. It's like a dream to be here in this scenic beauty with my best friend.

"Julia, do you remember when we were here two years ago?" Mark put his arm around me and pulled me close. "I think that is when I first really realized how much I care for you."

"Mark, I remember very well. I wanted so bad to walk with you that day. But the wait makes this day even more special."

Mark gave me a big hug and a quick kiss. "Julia, this morning has been real special to me. I will be gone for a long time, but I want you to know that I will never forget today neither will I ever forget you."

Mark and I sat in one of the lookout structures with wooden seats and areas from which we viewed the panoramic scene below. We ate the lunch I packed. While we ate, we remarked on the wonderful natural beauty surrounding us.

I think the love we felt for each other made us more keenly conscious of the magnificent wonders of nature and life itself. I am glad Mark admitted to me that he cared for me two years ago when we were at this park. It made the thrill of today even more special. It will give me much pleasure to remember today while he is gone.

Friday night Mark and I went to see the musical movie *Yankee Doodle Dandy*. It was a vaudeville song-and-dance film with fancy foot movements and unforgettable flag-waving tunes. The patriotic singing lifted spirits, swelled happy hearts, and made one feel proud to be an American.

We were both highly impressed with the movie, and I doubt if we ever forget the impact it had on us. I am glad that we saw a musical tonight rather than a war story. It put us in a lighthearted frame of mind

We went to the A&W Root Beer stand. We slowly drank our floats and talked. Mark told me he thought he soon would be sent to Europe or Egypt. *Those are just the words I did not want to hear.* He explained if he was sent overseas that he might not be home for a long time. The chills started below my knees and spread up into my chest.

How long would he be gone? What terrible experiences would he have?

"Julia, I think the world of you. I want you not to worry while I am gone. I will pray for God to keep you in the shadow of his wings. I will pray you enjoy teaching school and all goes well."

"Mark I will pray for you too. It is hard to think that you will be many hundreds of miles from me. I don't want to think of you in harm's way."

In the yard at my home, Mark stopped the car, leaned over, and pulled me to him. He hugged me tightly. "Julia, I love you. When I come home, I hope to marry you." He slipped a ring on my finger. He pushed the switch on his flashlight, so I could see the ring. I looked down to see a deep-blue-colored sapphire, my birthstone.

"Julia, I hope when you look at your ring, you will see it as a symbol of my faithfulness to you."

"I will wear your ring every day. I will think of you whenever I look at it."

Mark kissed me. He walked me to the door and kissed me once again. I threw my arms around his neck.

"Oh, Mark, I wish you weren't going. I will pray every day for your safe return. I care very much for you."

He held me close again and kissed me.

"Julia, I will be leaving in the morning, but I will be home again. I love you very much. Good night."

We simply clung to each other and held very tight. He patted my shoulder, turned away, and was gone all too soon.

I don't think Mark, or I wanted to draw out any longer the inevitable that he had to leave. I feel like my heart will break for him and myself. Dear God, help us both live through this.

Will I ever see Mark again? Will he still want to date me when he returns from being overseas? Will I still be his girlfriend?

Can our love for each other last even if he is gone for months and even years? God, only my reliance on your strength will carry me through what is ahead for me. Dear Lord Almighty, please bless us and strengthen us with your mercy.

The next morning, when Mom and I were cleaning up after breakfast, Mom noticed my ring. "Did Mark give you that beautiful ring?"

I stuck out my hand, so she could see it. "Yes, last night he gave it to me just before he left."

"Dear, that was nice of him. Mark is a very nice young man. I pray that he can stay safe when he goes overseas."

"Mom, I hope to pray for him every day. He told me not to worry and that he will be home again."

"Julia, I am afraid that John will be leaving soon."

10

Julia Starts Teaching

Fall 1942

The weeks flew by. I was so busy getting prepared for the start of the school year. I felt very happy that I was to teach the homeschool. I was thankful that I could live at home. I was hoping I could save much of my salary for my future home.

Several times I went to the schoolhouse. The director and his wife had cleaned and scrubbed the building. I was thankful for that. A large bag of oiled sawdust was in the entryway and a wide broom to sweep the floor with. There was a new oilcloth covering a table near the big, thick crock water fountain on metal legs. A metal can with a lid to carry water in stood nearby.

The large room had rows of seats screwed to the floor. There were two sets of double desks. All of the larger desks had inkwells in which to put the bottles of ink so they would not spill while the older students were using their ink pens, which they dipped in the ink bottles to write on their papers.

The teacher's desk was in the front of the room. On the wall behind her desk, heavy slate blackboards were mounted across the wall to write on with chalk. On the left side of the teacher's desk was a tall bookcase with two doors above and two doors below. To the right of her desk was a tall Victrola, the brand name of a phonograph, and a piano for music classes.

A few feet in front of the teacher's desk was a long recitation bench.

To the right of that, a rectangular table with chairs around it was placed. That is where the students did lessons with their teacher. In the classroom, the desks had been scrubbed and the teacher's desk as well. The old piano and wood cabinet holding the phonograph player were free of dust.

I put up some of my collection of pictures. I chose fall pictures to tack on a board mounted to the wall.

In the large bookcase, I found a couple of empty shelves on which I put my teaching materials. I picked out some books that I could read to the younger students. There was a good collection of nursery rhymes and poetry for young children.

When I went to the meeting of rural teachers at the Winneshiek County Courthouse, I brought back a box of books from the county library. I positioned the books on the shelf between the upper doors and the lower doors of the large storage cabinet. I chose one book to read to my students after recess each day. The book was *Little House in the Big Woods* by Laura Ingalls Wilder.

I sorted the workbooks that I received for my students. There were soft-cover workbooks for health, English, spelling, and phonics. There were smaller workbooks on the Palmer handwriting method. For reading, arithmetic, history, geography, and science, the students had hard-covered books. All the students used the same music books. I sorted the books for each grade level. Then it would be easy to hand the books to each student on the first day.

This year there are brand new books for arithmetic. I am excited to teach from these new *Iroquois New Standard Arithmetics.* I am glad to see after each unit there is a Testing Your Progress page so I can accurately assess student progress and reteach some areas if necessary.

On my teacher's desk, I placed the daily schedule. I put each student's name in the large grade ledger and put it in one of the desk drawers. I sharpened pencils for my desk.

I laid out sticks of chalk on the ledge of the blackboards. I wrote "Miss Sturloff" in my best cursive handwriting high on the chalkboard. Underneath I wrote "Welcome Back."

School started the third Monday in August. I was at the school early. I brought a pail of water from home so no one would have to go to the neighbor's farm today to get water. I placed my tin cup on one of the hooks above the water crock. I put my black lunch bucket on the shelf above my coat hook. There were high hooks for older students and lower hooks for the young ones.

All sixteen students were there awhile before nine. I marked all present in my school register. All of them I recognized as they are neighbors to our farm. They chattered among themselves. At nine, I rang the brass bell on my desk, and the students found seats. Most of them chose wisely. I helped the younger students to make sure their feet touched the floor and their desks were not too high for them to write comfortably on.

I welcomed them to the 1942–1943 school year. I hoped that they had a fun summer. Some were eager to tell about their summer, so I let them briefly tell us.

Then I asked Mary, Tom, Susan, and Ben to help me pass out the books to each student. The students became acquainted with their new books and wrote their names on their soft-backed workbooks. I started a phonics class with the younger students. Then I had them write their names on a piece of paper and draw what they did for fun in the summer. I told them I wanted to put their pictures up on the bulletin board.

I started with first grade and had Patrick and Tim read a paragraph from their readers to me. I wanted to know where they are in their reading ability. I continued that way with each grade level. By recess time, I was getting a good idea of the reading levels of my students.

At ten fifteen until ten thirty, they were dismissed for recess. They fairly flew out the door to play tag in the front of the school. While they were gone, I tried to organize for math classes.

At ten thirty, I rang the brass hand-bell to signal recess was over. Some rushed off to the little house out back. There was one for the girls and one for the boys. In a few minutes, all were in their seats again.

I told the older students, fourth through eighth, to work the first page in their math books while I worked with the lower grades. I started with kindergarten. I asked them if they knew any of the letters of the alphabet, any of the ABCs. Susie triumphantly rattled off the ABCs, but Jack looked like he was ready to cry, so I suggested that Susie help

Jack learn his ABCs. Jack's expression changed from hopelessness to maybe school isn't so bad. There was a small table near a window. I told them to work there. The two of them huddled together while Susie helped him learn his ABCs. I asked Mary if she minded keeping an eye on them. She seemed pleased to help.

Patrick and Tim, first graders, were next. I asked them to count to twenty-five for me. Patrick did well, but Tim got to nineteen and seemed lost. I gave them each a paper with 1 to 25 written on it and told them to write the numbers under each one and then write them several more times.

Alice and Jim, second grade, brought their second-grade workbooks to class. They had worked the first page, so we corrected it. They both had done a good job. They happily left to go back to their seats to work in their new spelling book.

Teresa, third grade, had her first page in math done, and it was all correct. I told her to work the next page for tomorrow.

Janie and Robby, fourth grade, each had only one math problem wrong. We discussed why it was wrong. They said the fives for me. I marked off on the fourth-grade skill sheet that I made that they both knew the multiples of five.

Billy, Marian, and Dan, fifth graders, also had finished the first page of their math workbooks. They appeared to be good students. I asked each of them to say the multiples of nine. They faltered on the task. I wrote the multiples on the board and had them copy the numbers to the top of a sheet of paper. They were to copy them underneath and learn them. I told them I would mark their individual skill sheet when they could say them correctly.

Susan, Tom, and Ben had their work done, and it was almost all correct. I went over the problems with them that gave them trouble. Mary handed her work in to me as it was noon and time for lunch.

The students decided to eat their lunch outside on the steps up to the schoolhouse. I ate out there with them.

Then the older boys, Tom and Ben, brought out a bat and a softball, and each boy took turns choosing players for their team. The four youngest were happy to play in the sand in an old iron ring under a tree near the schoolhouse. I played on the team that I thought might be at the most disadvantage.

At one o'clock, I rang the bell. The students lined up at the water cooler with their metal cups to get drinks. One by one they filtered into the classroom. I started reading *Little House in the Big Woods*, and soon everyone was listening intently from their desks.

Today I read longer than I will later, but I thought let's ease into the schoolwork. I read until I felt the young ones might be getting restless.

I told my students if they need to sharpen a pencil, they could raise a finger. I would nod an okay. If they needed a book from the library, they could go one at a time to get a book. If they needed to go to the little house out back, they were to raise two fingers and get my nod meaning okay. If they needed my help, raise their hand. If I am busy, go on to something else and try again later. If they need a drink, quietly go get one. Only one person at a time should be out of their seats.

I told the students that I needed some helpers and would appreciate some volunteers. Tom and Ben offered to go next door each morning to get the pail of water for the water cooler. Susan offered to wipe the blackboards at the end of each day. Mary offered to help with the kindergarteners. She will help them get ready to go home each day and sometimes help them with their work.

Billy offered to shake the erasers every Friday before dismissal time. Each Friday, or more often if necessary, Ben offered to shake oiled sawdust over the floor. The oiled sawdust helps pick up dirt and other material on the floor, making it easier for me to sweep and keep the floor clean.

Beth offered to help the little ones keep their pencils sharpened. Marian wanted to read to the kindergarteners every afternoon after last recess, except Friday when we have art class. I told the students I would make a chart with their name and their duties.

The English classes were short, just enough time for me to assign work for them to do at their seats. I told the students they were responsible to fill in the first lesson in their spelling books and to study for a test on Friday.

At two fifteen, they were dismissed for recess. I was glad for a break. The fifteen minutes went quickly. At two thirty, I rang the bell again.

After recess, I had the older students read out loud from their history books. I let each class read to me for fifteen minutes, and then they were to finish the rest of the reading at their seats. During the time they read, I made sure they could pronounce any new or unfamiliar words.

While the older students were doing history, I let the younger ones write their spelling words on the chalkboard. Marian read to the kindergarteners.

The parents came for the younger ones at four o'clock. The older students walked home.

Whew! I made it through my first day. Once I get to know the abilities of my students, it will be easier to assign work to them. It will take some time to assess the skills that they know and the skills that are lacking. But I am fortunate that all the students seem like bright young people. I do not think any of them are slow learners nor have any serious behavior problems. All students are capable of being a problem at one time or another, but not to have any major problems that is good.

The next day, classes went much easier. The pupils were more aware of the schedule and what I expected of them. I put the volunteer task chart on one of the two doors going into the entryway. The names were placed in slots next to the tasks. With the names in slots, I can move them if later I wish to do so.

That evening, I had a letter waiting for me in the mailbox. Mark wrote that he is being shipped overseas but he could not give me any other details.

Oh, Mark, I will not be able to see you once more before you go overseas. How cruel can life be to separate us because of a horrible war. The weight of this unhappy news and the stress of my first days of teaching are too great a burden on me.

Last night I was too exhausted to write. Tonight, I felt I had to write. I described for Mark my first three days of teaching. I told him that I am praying every day for him. *I do not want to make Mark more homesick than necessary, so I better not tell him how very much I miss him. But already I do miss him so very much. Maybe he would rather know that I miss him so.*

The days seemed to fly by. It is now the third week in September. I feel that I know more about the abilities of my students, and I am more aware of the areas where they need more teaching and experience. The first day, I felt I was grasping for busy work for them just to keep them busy. Now I feel I am giving them work that is consistently building their skills.

Some good news, the Germans were defeated at the Battle of Stalingrad. There are still fierce battles going on in North Africa. *Is Mark on his way to Europe or Africa? How much good would it do me to know where he is going? It would not bring him back.*

It is customary for a teacher to put on a school program for the parents and to raise money for the school. I started planning skits, songs, and poems that my students will say, sing, or perform in front of their parents, grandparents, and neighbors. I plan to have the program the first Friday night in November.

John enlisted and is scheduled to leave for basic training the first part of November. The corn picking will be done by that time. John is letting Bobby drive his car to high school, so Dad will still have a son to help him with farm chores. During the coldest months, Bobby plans to stay with Uncle Roy in town. Melanie plans to stay with her aunt.

I know John is still seeing Betty. I am glad for him that he has someone in his life, but I dearly know how it hurts to be separated. Will Betty soon face life without John?

Mother is quite upset but tries not to show it in front of John. I know she will dearly miss her son. He has never been away from home but a day or two. It is hard for her to accept that her first baby, her oldest child, is going off to war, a war that has grown to encircle the world—a world war so large it is hard to envisage its size. It is a war that has already brought untold misery to thousands of people worldwide.

The Saturday before my school program, John leaves on the bus for basic training. Mother and I tearfully hug him good-bye. Dad hugs his son and wishes him well. The big bus pulls away. John is gone.

With both Mark and John gone, I feel such emptiness in my life. How can I shut off the ache in my heart? It seems so unfair to my young years to have to shoulder such dark and gloomy sadness, but I know I must accept this burden and go on living the best way I can. It will not do John, Mark, or anyone any good unless I go on living as joyful as I can. In my spirit, I will try to be cheery and happy for my own sake and for others. It will not be easy.

My school program is keeping me busy. I don't have much time to think about Mark and John. Every day the students practice their skits, songs, and recitations. Now the reading of their parts or sayings is our reading lesson for the day. The speaking with good pronunciation and voice production is an important part of speech training. Monday morning Dad and Bobby bring some wooden blocks and large boards to make a stage in the front of the room. They help me hang the curtains around the stage and hook them on large hooks already on the walls for that purpose. The curtains form two dressing rooms, one on each side of the stage. In front of the stage are two curtains, one to pull left and one to push right.

The students are excited to practice on the stage. This week they giggle and laugh as they dress in the clothes that they have brought for their parts in the plays.

Alice, in second grade, is to open the program with her recitation.

We're glad to see you,
bet you didn't know
We entertain too
Get on with the show
(Throws up arm).

Jim follows her with his poem.

Full-grown we're not,
But talent we've got.
About many a thing,
We talk and sing,

Melanie and Betty have volunteered to help this evening. Each of them pulls a front curtain to the side. All the students are lined up. On the piano, I play "You Are My Sunshine."

The students strongly sing out "You Are My Sunshine." *I wish singing could bring my sunshine home.*

A play about the meaning of Thanksgiving followed. The four oldest students have the main speaking parts, and the younger students have very minor parts to play. All the students are on the stage for the final scene to portray the first Thanksgiving.

Next, I accompanied the students on the piano as they sang "God Bless America," and while they sang, the older students in the back row waved small American flags. The smaller pupils in the front row waved short crepe paper streamers of red, white, and blue.

A short comical play about a boy and his grandparents followed. Tom was dressed like an old man with a hat, and Mary had on her grandmother's old dress, hat with veil, and carried a pocketbook. Their grandchildren, played by the fifth graders, had come for a visit.

Grandpa was telling what it was like when he was a boy. Grandma kept interrupting, "Now, Ole, that wasn't the way it was." Then she would give her version of the story.

The final song was "America." We sang the first and third stanzas. I asked the audience to sing the two stanzas again with us. With the ongoing war, everyone put their heart and soul into the singing about freedom, liberty, and the protection of God. The strong blending of young and old voices in the patriotic and spiritual meaning of the words was awe-inspiring.

Jim spoke the final words.

We're so glad you're here
on our special night.
We aim to cheer
Hope it's been jes' right.

Later that night, I wrote to Mark that I was happy the program had gone over so well. I believe the parents, neighbors, and friends really did enjoy it.

In the November news, I learned that American and British troops are invading French North Africa to oppose the Axis powers that have taken control there. In my most inner gut feeling, I know that Mark is one of those American soldiers. *Oh, God, I pray you keep him safe.*

December 9, I received a letter from Mark. He wrote, "I cannot tell you where I am, but listen to the news." From that I felt sure that he is in North Africa. Mark wrote, "Because of my mechanical abilities, I am kept busy keeping tanks and sometimes other equipment in operation. My superior officer tells me he is very much aware of my knowledge about engines and what it takes to keep vehicles in good repair. Most of the time, he is using me to advise and supervise the work of other mechanics.

"My superior officer told me it takes technical ability to do what I am doing. He said, 'You are doing more than driving and braking vehicles. You have the knowledge and capability to repair heavy machinery like the different kinds of tanks.' My training under my dad to keep our farm equipment in good running condition has paid off for me as I have a technical job and less of what the army calls a grunt job."

Mark ended his letter telling me how much he wishes he was home and could be with me. "It would be so nice dancing with you in my arms to the music 'Only Forever.'"

Mother gave me a copy of the Ninety-first Psalm typed on a five-by-eight-inch card that another mother of a soldier had given her. She told me that it is known as the Psalm of Protection. The story is that in World War I, a Colonel Whittlesey encouraged his regiment to memorize and daily recite the Ninety-first Psalm. During more than four years' time, he never lost a man despite engaging in three of the bloodiest battles of the war.

I asked one of my high school friends, now a secretary at the high school, if I could use one of the typewriters to type the Psalm 91. When the secretary read what I was typing, she wanted a copy of it also to send to soldiers and sailors serving from her church. She said that she would give a copy to her minister.

I neatly typed copies of the Ninety-first Psalm on five-by- eight-inch cards.

That night, after I had written my letter to Mark, I wrote on the bottom of my letter, "I hope that saying this psalm daily will help you rest safely in the shadow of his wings." I tucked two copies of the psalm with an explanation about Colonel Whittlesey's regiment in the letter.

I read the first lines of Psalm 91: "He who dwells in the shelter of the Most High will rest in the shadow of the Almighty." Reading those lines brought to my mind Psalm 36:7: "The children of men put their trust under the shadow of thy wings."

The more I thought on it, words started coming to mind. I grabbed a tablet and starting writing. The next couple of days, on and off, I worked on my attempt to write a poem for myself. Finally, I felt it was finished, not perfect, but the best I could do.

In the Shadow of His Wings

In the shadow of His wings,
Your heart truly sings.
Live above your pain and strife,
Rebuff anxiety over life.
Do you often fret and stew?
Just know what to do.
Cry unto God on high,
Trust His help is nigh.
Believe He will surely answer
Heartfelt, faithful, fervent prayer.
His truth will see you through,
Your point of view is up to you.
In all sadness and catastrophe,
Lean on Him and you will see
His truth and laws prevail
In any heartache and travail.
For God's commands are true
Wisdom and blessing for you.
Your heart truly sings
In the shadow of His wings.

When worries overwhelm me, I know that I need something to calm my spirit. I will try to remember what I wrote when I start to feel down. It seems like every so often I must read such writings to keep me on the right track.

Mother and I started making goodies to put in boxes to send to Mark and John. The first weekend, we made baked fruitcakes using dried fruits and nuts. We wrapped each loaf individually and placed each one in a metal box. On Sunday afternoon, Mom and I made peanut brittle and stored it in cardboard boxes lined with wax paper.

The next weekend, we baked date pinwheel cookies and oatmeal cookies with dates. Mother made fudge while I made divinity. We carefully wrapped the cookies and candy in waxed paper and placed them in tin boxes and made sure the lids fit tightly on the tins. Sunday evening, we packed the cookies and candy in a box for Mark and one for John. We had used every wooden, tin, and cardboard box we could find in the house.

On Monday, Dad shipped the boxes off to the boys. I hope that both boxes arrive without too much damage to the goodies inside. Mother told me, "Mrs. McDonald is also sending a box to Mark. If he gets more than he can use, he can share with his buddies who may not get anything."

This year Christmas seemed a lonely time. Midnight mass was again as beautiful as ever, but it just wasn't the same. Our family exchange of Christmas gifts just seemed something we had to do as the whole family seemed very sober, not joyous. Of course, we should think of the real reason for the season. Jesus came to earth to give sinners salvation.

11

1943 – V-Mail, Slogans, Rationing

The news of the Desert War in Egypt was that the British and American allies had Italian and German armies in retreat. In the Pacific, the Americans are struggling to recapture Japanese-held islands.

Fuel oil has been rationed since October, but the school director is able to get enough for the oil burner in the schoolhouse. I am glad; I vividly remember having to bring wood from the wood shed near the school to put in the wood-burning stove when I was in grade school. I am relieved that I do not have to labor with that drudgery.

The letters from Mark are few and far apart. It is taking almost six weeks for the letters to reach me. At the post office, I was given V-mail forms to use to send letters to Mark. I cannot go to the post office every day for my two sheets of the forms, but learned I can buy them in stores. So, I went to a store and stocked up on V-mail forms.

The government wants people to use V-mail (victory mail). The V-mail form is uniform and can be microfilmed and sent on to the recipient; it is a way to expedite delivery. By eliminating the volume of heavy and bulky WWII mail, space is freed on ships and planes for materials crucial for the war.

On inquiry, I found out that there is a network of V-mail plants located in various places in Europe and the Pacific. From them the V-mail is processed coming in and going out. I think this method of sending letters does not sound private, but I will use it if my letters will get there faster.

Several times a month, Betty and I meet each other to have a good talk. Sometimes we go to the Eat Shop for malted milk. Her mother has invited me a couple of times to eat with them on Sunday. Betty has been to our house as well on Sunday for dinner. The first part of February, John came home on furlough for a week. Mom and I made some of John's favorite foods for Sunday dinner including Swiss steak, mashed potatoes, and pecan pie for dessert. We invited Betty, and that pleased John.

Betty was able to get the week off from working at the telephone office. We had no snow that week, and temperatures were unseasonably warm. One day, Betty and John went to LaCrosse, Wisconsin, to shop. Another day they visited his army buddy, Jake Halsted, who was also home on furlough, at Cresco. They went to several movies and the dance on Saturday night.

John had pictures of life in the military that he showed us. We had a good time talking with him. He had so many military stories to tell us.

Mother was happy to learn that he was to take some additional training in radio operations. Betty was relieved that at least he was not going overseas right away. John believed he would like to study radio communications.

Too soon, it was time for him to leave. He promised to write soon and let us know his new address. He hugged Mom and I. Dad hugged him and gave him a pat on his back. He hugged and kissed Betty. His buddy from Cresco helped him with his duffel bag. John crawled in the passenger side, waved, and Jake drove away.

In Mark's letters, he often told me how much my letters meant to him. He told me he had memorized parts of the Ninety-first Psalm. He wrote, "Julia, your letters help me endure being so far from you. You make me feel less lonely. You give me strength to face the uncertainties of war. Julia, when I come home and can be with you again, I will be a happy man."

In my next letter, I reminded Mark of Ephesians 6 being known as the soldier's chapter, especially verses 10 through 20. I told him how when I was confirmed that the bishop slapped me firmly on the cheek and told me to be a soldier for the Lord Jesus Christ. For the ordinary person, we are to "put on the armor of God" so that we can stand strong against the devil's work in our lives. For the soldier, it is good to be "strengthened in the Lord and in the might of his power."

I described to Mark the many posters I have seen that our government created to enliven and heighten patriotism. A good example is "Americans Will Always Fight for Liberty."

"You buy 'em, We fly 'em" promotes the sale of war bonds. We hear slogans such as "Loose Lips Sink Ships" to remind us not to tell everything we know for security reasons. "Do with Less So They Will Have Enough" buoys us up to do without so there is plenty for the fighting men. The poster, "Rationing Gives You Your Fair Share" helps Americans be willing to share resources.

Because of her Victory Garden, Marian likes the poster that reads, "Your Own Vegetables All Year Around If You Dig for Victory Now."

A rather shocking poster is Rosie the riveter showing off her muscles with the slogan "We Can Do It." We are not used to seeing a woman doing a man's job. Some slogans such as "It's a Woman's War Too" encourage women to enlist in the US Cadet Nurse Corps, the Wacs, or the Waves. Throughout history men have tried to protect women and children from the horrors of war. Now it is hard for me to believe women are being asked to serve in the army and navy.

Some other slogans are "Save Your Cans, Help Pass the Ammunition" and supports recycling of metal for the war. "Repair work is vital to the war effort" persuades people to repair machinery rather than want new.

"Sew for Victory" encourages home sewing. I have heard of mothers transforming old adult clothing into children's clothes. At a meeting Mom went to, women were told to take, for example, an old coat, turn it inside out, and use the inside for the outside of the new garment. The inside of the wool from a coat is protected by the lining and looks like new. Mother said that women also did that during the Great Depression when they could not afford a new coat for their child.

Mark,

I wish I had a typewriter. They have been rationed now for a year. It would be nice to type; it would be easier to write when I have so much to tell you. I have written so much today that my arm is tired. Be good to yourself.

Love, Julia

April 19, 1943
Dear Mark,

Every letter you send, I read and reread them. It helps me feel closer to you. Your letters fortify my heart as food does my body. I miss you.

Lately my letters are long, but I want you to know what I am doing.

Earlier in the spring, I had the students studying plants. We planted some seeds including beans, tomatoes, and marigold flowers. When the bean seeds started growing, it was fun for my students to watch how quickly they grew and the seeds themselves split apart.

We studied the parts of a flower. The students drew a flower and labeled the parts.

Yesterday was a nice warm spring day; we took a field trip to woods nearby to look for wild flowers. It was a happy time for me as I remembered the times that you and I went on such field trips with our teacher to enjoy the wild spring flowers.

The leaves were not out yet, making it the best time to look for woodland flowers. In a week or two, the leaves will be out, and the flowers cannot get light, and they will be gone.

Tom thought he knew where there was a jack-in-the-pulpit. Sure enough, he found it. I felt we were so lucky to have found a jack-in-the-pulpit. Most of the students had never seen one. The little ones got a big kick out of seeing the jack-in-the-pulpit. I told them not to pick it as we want it to stay in the wooded area, so we can enjoy it another time.

For a while Tom searched for trilliums. When he found them, he showed the others how all its sepals, petals, and leaves are in whorls of three.

I explained that tri is a prefix meaning three. I looked at the smaller children and said, "like a tricycle." Then I asked, "How many wheels does a tricycle have?"

With knowing smiles, they shouted, "Three."

Two of the young students eagerly pointed to blue violets. Marian found wild geraniums.

Dan delighted the kindergarteners when he pointed to the britches on the Dutchman's-breetches. He showed them the two white points that look like an upside-down pair of pants. How those youngsters did chuckle about that.

Susan found a flowering bloodroot. She pulled it up to show the others that when she breaks off the stem near the root, an orange-reddish juice issues forth. She explained, "When I squeeze the root, the liquid that comes out looks like blood, so that is why it is called bloodroot."

When Janie found a buttercup, I asked her why she thought it was called a buttercup. She looked up at me and said, "Is it because the color of the flower looks like butter?" I nodded that she was right. She smiled back at me.

Mary showed us the clusters of tiny blue bells on the flowering bluebells. Those pretty flowers brought back happy memories. Do you remember you picked a bouquet of bluebells for me when I was in the seventh grade? Maybe you don't remember, but I do.

Another flowering plant we saw was the hepatica. I pointed out features of this delicate flower with its three- pointed lobed leaves and six to ten petals of pink, blue, lavender, and white.

We examined the wood anemone. I drew their attention to it being a low-growing plant. The leaves have three to five leaflets. The plant has no petals, but the five white sepals look like petals.

I think we were too early to find the bellwort with its drooping yellow flowers.

Mark, I enjoyed being in the woods so much. It brought to mind many thoughts to reminisce about our own grade school years. It was so much fun seeing the same flowers that we hunted for as kids. Hope you enjoyed the field trip with us.

Be good to yourself. Know that I think of you often.

Love,
Julia

May 9, 1943
Dear Mark,

Today I took my students on a field trip to Decorah for the day. Mrs. Johnson and Mrs. Peterson volunteered to help drive the students to the places we planned to visit.

First, we visited the Winneshiek County Courthouse. We went to the different offices and the courtroom. The students got to see the library where I find books to bring to our classroom. Next, we walked to the *Decorah Posten*, a well-known Norwegian newspaper. We got to see the printing presses running. A man told us that not only did Decorah Norwegians read the newspaper printed in the Norwegian language, but many people in states around Iowa subscribed to the paper. For some time, it was the largest Norwegian newspaper in the United States.

For a break, we went to Phelps Park. While the children played on the slide, teeter-totter, and swings, the mothers and I laid out the lunch. We covered the top of a picnic table with an oilcloth.

We started a fire in the fire pit with a metal grill above it. When we got the fire going, we heated wieners, which Mrs. Johnson bought. Mrs. Peterson heated on the grill her homemade baked beans. Mother sent two jars of applesauce and oatmeal cookies.

Our next stop was the Nehi bottling company. The children like to watch the bottles circle on the metal track as they were being filled with pop. From there we walked to the Vesterheim Norwegian Museum. A sweet gray-haired lady revealed that Vesterheim was the word Norwegians, who came from Norway, named their homeland in the West.

The students learned Decorah was settled in 1849. Many Norwegians came to settle in Decorah in the 1850s. In 1940, the population of Decorah was 5,303.

In 1861, a Lutheran College was established and became known as Luther College. The Vesterheim Norwegian American Museum is the largest museum in our country dedicated to one single immigrant group.

The children were fascinated by the exhibits of what life was like in Norway. We saw what the inside of a house in Norway looked like. There was a stone fireplace, spinning wheel, wooden furniture, cooking utensils, tools, toys, and more. It was interesting to compare those displays to what life was like when they first came to Decorah to live. We saw a hand-carved wooden pioneer altar on which was carved the Last Supper, the crucifixion of Jesus Christ, the Nativity, and Jesus teaching in the temple. I enjoyed seeing the rosemaling artwork, paintings in color on wood.

Behind the museum is the stone mill, which was used to grind grain for humans and animals. I find the mill interesting because my mother lived as a child across the street from the mill. Did you like going on the field trip to Decorah with us? I hope so.

Pray for you every day.

Love, Julia

It is the middle of May. Tonight Dad announced that the generals of the Italian and German forces in North Africa have surrendered.

I looked at Dad and asked, "Does that mean the battle in North Africa is over? If that is where Mark is, will he be coming home?"

Dad replied, "Julia, it only means the war in North Africa is over. The battles with Italy and Germany are still raging on. Only the campaign in North Africa since 1941 to now is finished. The Italians and Germans are still fighting the Allies in Italy and north of there to Germany."

Dad rather sadly went on to explain, "At the start of that three- year war in North Africa, Britain attempted to keep Mussolini ruler of Italy from getting control of a strategic area of the world. Hitler sent forces to Italy's aid. The German Commander Rommel, known as the Desert Fox, put up mighty hard offensive battles against the Allies. In March, Rommel withdrew from North Africa. He left the African Corp in other hands, and they kept on fighting.

"Yes, those forces have been defeated but just in that area; there are still battles to fight in Italy and north into Europe. So, it is doubtful while there is a battle to fight that military personnel will be coming home."

Melanie graduated with honors. She was valedictorian of her high school class and gave a valedictory address. Melanie told how education meant so much to her. She said her teachers not only taught her practical and interesting subjects but they instilled many words of wisdom to develop outstanding character traits in her and her classmates. She said she was happy that her teachers taught her the importance of the great American documents to protect our liberty and freedom. She finished by saying she is proud of her brother who is now fighting to protect those liberties and freedom. Her parents were justly proud of her.

I felt pride well up at hearing Melanie's address, and I know how proud Mark would have been to hear his sister's speech.

That night, in my letter to Mark, I told him all about Melanie's honor and her great address to the audience. I am sure his mother wrote of the family's pride in her accomplishments, but I wanted Mark to hear how pleased I was with Melanie's achievements.

> May 22, 1943
> Dear Mark,
>
> Since late winter and early spring, I really worked with Mary, preparing her for her eighth-grade exams. Most of the time, I included Susan, Tom, and Ben as they will be taking the test next year. We drilled on fractions, decimals, long multiplication and division, percent, and simple geometry. We drilled on the measurement tables.
>
> Our new arithmetic books this year dealt with a broad range of practical situations of vital importance to the home and community. There were lessons on arithmetic in the home, business, and daily life. That practical understanding of arithmetic would help Mary on the examination.
>
> In language, we reviewed parts of speech, capitalization, punctuation, verb tenses, and we did diagramming of sentences.

With the four students, I had spelling contests. They really worked, wanting to be the speller remaining in each contest.

We reviewed many reading skills such as vocabulary and comprehension. We worked with prefixes, suffixes, and root words and how they are used to build words. They memorized meanings of prefixes such as mis, pre, in, pro, etc. They did the same thing with word roots and suffixes. For science, history, and geography, we talked about where to find the table of contents, index, and glossary. We discussed study helps like pictures, graphs, charts, maps, and vocabulary specific to each subject. We studied basic facts in each subject area, for example: When was the Declaration of Independence declared? What are the names of the continents and oceans?

Mark, it paid off. Mary got a very high score on her examination. Mary's parents were very proud of her at eight-grade graduation at the Decorah High School. Mary was recognized for her outstanding academic achievement. In addition to that, she received the Palmer Handwriting Certificate for her beautiful handwriting skills.

Yesterday, we had our end-of-the-school-year picnic. I am sure you remember such picnics when you were in school. How we looked forward to that day.

Mom baked her famous baked bean recipe again this year. Dad went to town to get ice cream packed in a metal container inside of a container of dry ice to keep the ice cream cold. I am sure you well recall that is the traditional treat the teacher gives at the end of the school year.

Other families brought delicious food: meatloaf, salads, pickles, homemade buns, cake, cookies, and pies. I think that everyone, even the kids, had all the ice cream they wanted.

We played softball with some of the parents joining in the fun. It was a pleasurable day for all.

Wish you could have been here today for the fun and ice cream.

Hope you are safe and well.

With my love,
Julia

Most of the following I wrote in letters to Mark:

Dad was notified that a truck was coming to load any scrap iron or old tires we might have to recycle for war materials. I went down in the hog pasture to pick up an old tire. I lifted it high above my head and looked up. Horror! A snake was dangling out of the tire. I quickly tossed that tire and yelled like it was the worst scary thing that I'd ever seen. Bobby came running and laughed at me. He killed the snake and took the tire to the truck.

Already on the truck was the last of the iron taken off no-longer-used machinery in the old mill on Canoe Creek. Behind some of his farm buildings, Dad had some scrap iron that was loaded on the truck.

John called that he was coming home on furlough before being sent overseas. We were so glad to see him again. He told us about his training in radio work.

Betty's mother invited John for several meals. Mother and I tried to cook his favorite foods while he was home.

When John told us that he thinks he is being sent to Britain, Dad informed John that the British people think Prime Minister Winston Churchill is a great decisive leader. He inspired that nation through the blitzkrieg and the bombardment of English soil. Churchill didn't crumble under such weighty stress. Churchill is committed to victory for the Allies. You will be helping further that cause.

John and Betty spent time together going to movies, a dance, and they took a boat trip on the Mississippi River. One day we had a picnic in the Phelps Park and invited Uncle Roy's family, the McDonald's, and Betty's family.

The next day, John was prepared to leave. Mother, Dad, Betty, and

I were at the bus depot to see him off. We all gave him a big hug. He gave Betty a quick kiss and swung up onto the bus. We waved as the bus turned and drove off. I cannot speak for all four of us left standing, but I know I felt a chilling loneliness that had no bounds. My dear brother was gone out of my life.

What will he endure before I see him again? Seeing John leave this time was hard on me, for now both Mark and John will be overseas, so far, removed from the rest of the family.

Summer work will keep me busy. In the fall, I will have my second year of teaching to keep my mind off thinking of the war. That is good.

12

Waiting for Mail

Summer 1943

A short letter arrives from Mark. He wrote, "I am well. The food is not so bad, but the weather is hot and dry. I wish I was there with you. Gal, we have a lot to make up for when I get home again. Keep singing and be happy." The letter was signed, "With my love, Mark."

Saturday when I went to town, I bought some new records to play on Mom's phonograph. I bought "When the Lights Go On Again (All Over the World)." I like the words in the song about boys coming home and wedding rings. I also bought two more records, "Praise the Lord and Pass the Ammunition!" and "In the Mood." As often as we can, Betty and I meet on Saturdays to do something together. Sometimes she must work, and then we plan an activity for Sunday. We have gone to several movies. We saw *The Song of Bernadette* and *My Friend Flicka*.

Marian has joined 4-H, and I help her some with her garden, baking, and sewing projects. She is planning to take vegetables to exhibit for 4-H at the county fair. I am helping her learn to sew on Mom's treadle machine. She is making a simple gathered skirt for the fair.

Sewing on the treadle machine is tricky as one's foot works the treadle to power the sewing machine while one's hands are busy pushing the material under the needle. Someday I hope we have electricity and I can have an electric sewing machine.

Dad is still saying how blessed he was to get his tractor before the war started. Tonight, he told us, "Case is producing wings for B-26 bombers, aftercoolers for Rolls-Royce airplane engines and thousands of artillery shells."

"Dad, what is an aftercooler?" I queried.

Dad answered, "It is a device that cools compressed air coming from a compressor. It also is a type of heat exchanger that removes moisture. This year Case had far-reaching impact with their Case-built aftercoolers made for use in fighter aircraft."

I continue to buy war bonds. I am trying to save as much as I can for my future home someday. This summer I feel that I can only buy stamps for my bond book as I do not get money in the summer as I am not teaching. When I start teaching in the fall, I will be able to buy bonds each month.

We did not get a lot of strawberries this year, so Mom, Marian, and I picked gooseberries and blackberries in the woods. While we were picking wild gooseberries and blackberries, we wore long cotton stockings over our arms to protect them from tearing scratches from the thorns on the wild berry bushes.

Gooseberries are small green berries, and it takes a lot of them to fill an old corn syrup gallon can. We put the handle of the tin can over our arms while we pick the berries. The clusters of the gooseberries can be grasped with one hand and forced off the plant in a hurry with the other hand. We canned gooseberries for making pies. The wild blackberries made tasty jam. We mixed some of the wild berries with our scanty crop of strawberries to have more fruit for jam.

With John in the army, Dad hired men to combine his grain. It sure is a lot less work than it used to be when I was a young child. I remember Dad cutting the oats with a binder, which tied the stalks in bundles. I used to help Dad put those bundles into shocks. We would pick up the sheaves of grain and stack them upright in a cluster to dry in the field for threshing day.

On the big day, a huge tractor, maybe a Hart-Paar, would pull the very large threshing machine into our yard. The men would set it up. Neighbors would come with horses and wagons to load the oat or barley bundles in the field to bring to the threshing machine.

A long belt, which circulated from the power of the tractor, made the threshing machine run to thresh the oats and barley. One summer, one of my cousins tried to thrust his head between the belts. Lucky for him, a quick-thinking neighbor grabbed him just in time to keep him from injury.

That same bratty city kid found rotten eggs that some hen abandoned and threw them at the threshers as they drove their teams pulling a loaded wagon up to the threshing machine. Well, that boy deserved a threshing, and all he got was a good talking to and scolding. Dad didn't want to upset the kid's parents, Mom's sister and her husband.

One day while Dad had combiners working in the fields, he and Mom went to town to get groceries. Mom hooked the screen door that opens into the living room. She locked the kitchen door. Ordinarily we did not lock the house, but with strangers on the property, Mom felt that she should lock up the house.

When Marian came home, she could not get into the house. She could see the hook on the screen door. Then she found a wire to stick through the screen to lift the hook.

When Mom got home, she questioned, "Marian, how did you get in the house?"

"Mom, I was hungry, so I used a wire to unlatch the hook."

Mom reprimanded her. "Marian, you will make a hole in the screen, and the flies will get in."

"No, Mom, I used a wire to push the screen wires back in place, so no one can see the hole."

The next day, when Marian came home from school, Mom and Dad were gone again. Dad had taken Mom to a ladies' aide meeting at the Springwater Church, and he had gone to town for some repairs, so the doors were locked again.

Marian was shocked to see that the hole in the screen door was bigger than when she had fixed it yesterday. This time when she went into the house, she did not repair the hole in the screen, so she could show it to Mother.

When Mom came home, Marian showed Mom the hole in the screen door. Mom suspected someone had come in the same way that Marian had, so she told Dad.

"Lettie, I was afraid of this very thing happening. I have treated the combiners to some of my homemade wild grape wine. Maybe their thirst for it got the better of them and one of them went in to get some more."

That evening Dad took the whole family to a wake in town for Mr. Olson, an older neighbor man who had died the day before. Before we left, Mom sprinkled flour on the cellar steps. If someone wanted wine, they would have to go down those steps to get the wine from a large wooden barrel in the cellar.

When we came home, the dining room flour looked all smeared with a whitish-gray covering. Mom knew someone had tried to wipe up the tracked flour from the cellar steps. When the flour was wiped with water, it turned milky colored and did not wipe up clean.

Early the next morning Mother made breakfast. She had hot black coffee ready and offered the hired man a cup when he came for breakfast. Then Mom accused, "You went into the cellar last night to get some of Sam's wine, didn't you?"

The young man tried to deny it. Mom determinedly retorted, "You did, and I know you did. You left tracks all over the dining room floor, and you tried to wipe them up."

The young man tried to gulp his hot coffee. He got up. Mom backed him into the corner with her insistence that he is guilty. Dad quietly told the young man, "Today, when the combining is finished, your help will no longer be needed."

We did plenty of canning this summer. Mom supervised the usual canning of tomatoes, string beans, and kernels of corn. Later, potatoes, carrots, squash, and pumpkins will be stored on the dirt floor of the cellar.

With so much work to do in the summer, the days were flying by, but I was not getting any mail from Mark. I kept sending my letters at least twice a week and sometimes more often as it is easier to write this summer as I am not teaching.

In July, a new song came out, "Comin' In on a Wing and a Prayer." It is quickly becoming a hit. I bought the sheet music for it.

No letter from Mark again today. Why am I not getting any letters? I decide to call Betty to see if we could get together for a visit. We decide to meet, after she gets off work, at the Eat Shop.

"Hi, Betty. I am really glad to see you."

We talked for a few minutes about ordinary things. Then I brought up that I have not heard from Mark for five weeks. She is surprised and I think concerned for me.

"I would feel worried too if I did not hear from your brother for such a long time. When did he last write to you?"

"The last letter came the first week in June, and I have not heard anything since. I pray that he is okay and wherever he is that he is safe. Maybe he is so busy that he does not have time to write."

Betty and I talk about her job at the telephone office. She tells about helping place calls between servicemen and their families. I tell her about helping Mom with canning and helping Marian sew a skirt.

"I just finished helping Dad and Bobby with baling the hay. I am sure Dad really missed John's help. The neighbor came with his baler and two men to sit on either side of the baler to tie wires on each bale. I drove the tractor while Dad and Bobby loaded the bales on the flat rack."

I was sad when it was time to separate. It was good to have someone to talk to about missing Mark. I knew Betty missed John too.

Dad related the war news to the family, "On July 10, the Allied forces invaded Sicily. It sounds to me that Sicily is a stepping stone to the invasion of Italy. The Allies are making progress in the war against Italy."

I felt somewhat good over that news, but where in that entire fracas is Mark? Was he in the thick of battle for the island? Did he get injured or killed? I shuddered at that thought. Oh, if I just knew if he was all right.

One rainy day, Marian came home from playing with Beth. Marian seemed quite excited. "Mom, when we couldn't play outside because of the rain, Beth, Jim, Susie, and I went up to the attic to play hide and go seek. When I was hiding, I saw two one-hundred-pound bags of sugar and four rubber tires hidden in the attic. They aren't supposed to be hiding rationed sugar and tires, are they?"

"No, dear. Sugar and tires are not supposed to be hoarded. I imagine the Johnsons bought the sugar and tires before rationing started. I doubt that they would have paid a high price for them on the black market.

"Marian, the Johnsons are our neighbors, so please do not talk about what you saw. We do not want to cause any trouble between our families. The Johnsons are good people just trying to take care of their family like we are trying to do the best for our family."

On Sunday evening, Mother suggested we start saying the Rosary and pray to bring an end to the war and bring our loved ones home again. I knelt on the living room carpet, my arms leaning on the seat of a chair and my rosary in my hands, ready to say the Rosary with my family. Mother led the Rosary.

Tonight, Mother picked the Five Sorrowful Mysteries to concentrate on during the reciting of the Rosary. One of each of the five mysteries is said before each decade of the Rosary consisting of the Our Father, ten Hail Marys, and the Glory Be to the Father. Afterward, I stayed kneeling a few more minutes to say my own prayers for Mark and John.

Tuesday morning Mom and Dad left to go to the funeral of Mrs. O'Reilly, a lady whom my mother knew when she was a young girl. I was to do the ironing from the wash we did yesterday.

Mother helped me get the gas iron ready to use before she left. I am glad I do not have to use the flatirons that I used to use. Those I had to let get hot on the range. There was a handle that would fit over the hot irons. With the handle attached over a hot iron, it was ready to use. The other flatirons could be heating to use when the one being used cooled off. It was tricky ironing; one had to keep the stove hot to heat the irons, and the iron in use cooled off too soon.

I have Mom's, Marian's, and my good dresses to iron. Also, I have Dad's and Bobby's white shirts to do. Mother put bluing in the wash water to whiten the shirts. I sure don't want to leave brown spots by scorching those pure white shirts. I must be careful that my iron is hot but not too hot.

I start by placing the left side of the yoke of Dad's white shirt over the end of the waist-high ironing board on legs. I iron the left yoke and then right yoke. Next, I iron one side of the front of the shirt and then the other side. I iron the large back. I iron each sleeve and the cuff. I must be extra careful not to iron wrinkles in some part of the shirt at the same time I am pressing wrinkles out on the side I am ironing. I don't want to press wrinkles in as I am ironing them out. Last, I iron the collar and then hang the shirt on a wooden hanger.

My legs get tired standing, ironing is not fun. I think how much nicer it would be if we had electricity. I wouldn't have to worry about the gas in the little cylinder-shaped tank on the iron.

Finally, a very short letter arrives from Mark. He hopes that I know about the fierce fighting where he is and that I realize he could not get a letter to me sooner. He wrote just enough to let me know he is okay but busy. The note ended, "Julia, you mean everything to me. I keep your picture in a leather pouch in my pocket and look at it often."

Dad, bless his heart, keeps me informed on the war in Italy. He and I both know that is where Mark is, and if not yet, he will be there soon.

Dad related that the Allies want to eliminate Italy from the war so that the Mediterranean would be in British hands. A war in Italy would draw Germans away from the Eastern Front to defend Italy.

On one hand, Dad's news reports make me feel that the American effort in the war is making a big difference in the battle for freedom. On the other hand, I realize the tears, blood, horror, deprivation, and miseries of war are unbelievably inhuman. I try not to agonize over the images of war. Life is for the living; we need to go on and do the best we can.

My biggest apprehension is over the well-being of Mark and John. Are they in the thick of battle wherever they are at? *Are they in considerable danger of being killed? Do they have enough food and water? Are they sleeping in tents or muddy foxholes?*

It is a good thing school starts soon. I have gone to the county library at the courthouse to get books for my students and a box of library books for them to read.

Around my classroom, I placed signs. One read, "A true friend is the best possession" by Benjamin Franklin. Another sign was, "God grants liberty only to those who love it and are always ready to guard it," words of Daniel Webster. I want my students to learn from the wisdom of great men and women.

Marian will be in sixth grade this year. I am glad my sister does not mind having me as her teacher. She has already asked if she can help correct papers from the kindergarteners and first graders. That would be a big help to me. I am planning to read to the students, books about famous pioneers and frontiersmen like Daniel Boone and Davy Crocket and women like Florence Nightingale and Clara Barton. I want them to know the strength of character that made those men and women well loved.

Bobby and Jimmy are seniors this year in high school. They are planning to drive to high school together so that they can be home to help their fathers. Melanie is going to nurse's training in Cedar Rapids.

I am glad school is starting this week. It will help me not think about the war and the lack of mail from Mark.

Mother is receiving mail regularly from John. That is making it harder for me. *There must be something wrong that I am not getting any letters. I write at least three letters to Mark each week or sometimes more if I have the time.*

13

Julia's Second Year of Teaching – Fall 1943

Susan, Tom, and Ben are in eighth grade this year. I have no seventh grader, three in sixth grade, two in fifth, one in fourth, two in third, two in second, two in first, and one in kindergarten. This year I have sixteen students, the same as last year. I will have only one kindergartener, Peggy O'Brien.

The lower three grades are thoroughly drilled on addition and subtraction facts. Fourth and fifth graders must not only be quick to know multiplication and division facts but be able to do long multiplication and division problems. In addition, they learn to do fractions and decimals. The sixth graders must have mastered the lower-grade arithmetic and now add to it percent, measurement, geometry, and algebra problems. Seventh- and eighth-grade arithmetic makes use of many practical problems involving measurement, banking, insurance, the workplace, and home.

I feel strongly that if the lower grades master the memorization of basic number facts, it is much easier for them to grasp higher-order mathematical problems. It is much easier for them to think in their heads the answers to everyday problems such as how to make change in money transactions, the estimation of a grocery bill, the amount off on a percentage discount, and so on.

Teaching is enjoyable to me. I like to see my students improve in knowledge and ability. It is exciting to hear my young first graders sounding out previously unknown words. Phonics gives them the tools to make sense of the words. That is why in the beginning of the year, I have phonics classes to train and drill them on phonetic skills. Those skills are not only vital to good reading abilities but also to success in spelling.

My following stories about the vowels were new to them, and I think they enjoyed learning a new way to think about the short vowel sounds. I asked the primary-grade students, "What do you say when someone knocks you in the belly. Don't you say 'uh'?" I tell them, "You just said the short *u* sound. I call it the knock-'em-in-the-belly sound." The little kids laugh, but they don't forget the sound of short *u*.

I show them that the short vowel sounds are indicated with a cup over them. To demonstrate, I write *ă, ĕ, ĭ, ŏ, ŭ* on the blackboard.

The primary students practice pretending the doctor is using a tongue depressor to hold their tongue down. I ask them, "What do you say? Yes, you say "ah," the short sound of *o* like in cot."

"The short *e* is what the old man says when he can't hear and holds his hand behind his ear." I demonstrate, "'Eh, eh, what did you say?' The short sound, *ĕ*, like in *bed*." The pupils try that one also.

"The short *i* is what the old lady says when she is terrified seeing a mouse in the corner. She can barely speak, the only sound coming out is 'i' as she is so afraid. The short *i* sounds like in *sit*."

We talk about the *ă*, the short sound of *a* like in *cat, bat, mat* and *pat*.

To help me through this time of not knowing about Mark, I wrote the following verse in my journal to look at frequently. Betty had copied the verse and given it to me. "He is the Rock, his work is perfect: for all his ways are judgment: a God of truth and without iniquity, just and right is he" (Deuteronomy 32:4, KJV).

God is my Rock to help me stay steady in troubled times. Lately, I am thankful for my blessings of having a wonderful family to love and care for me. I have a kind, sweet mother who has an understanding heart. My father is watchful to protect and provide for our family. I have a loving family to uphold me when things do not turn out the way that I want them to.

This fall, the country school teachers are asked to have students collect milkweed pods. The rural students are to collect bags of milkweed pods for the making of parachutes.

One sunny clear fall day, I gave my older students gunnysacks, and we took off for the pastures and woods on the Larsguard farm close to the school. The Larsguards had already given me permission to bring the students to search for milkweed pods. We picked the sticky pods of milkweed and stuffed them into our tall burlap bags. Some of the pods had broken open and the brown seeds were popping out among the white feathery insides. It was fun talking and working quickly to fill our sacks. As soon as one bag was full, another one in which to push the five-inch pods was handed over to replace the full one. The students were delighted to get outdoors away from our studies and the confinement of the schoolroom.

Toward the end of our search, several ran gleefully and recklessly down a long hill in a grassy pasture. Running very fast and swinging her partially full bag, Marian ran with breakneck speed into coiled barbed wire lying treacherously hidden in the tall grass. The barbs on the wire ripped through the flesh on the calf of her leg. She screamed with instant pain and from the sight of bleeding from her injuries.

I hurriedly rushed her to the Larsguard farmhouse, a large square, two-story structure. Sara, a kindly, loving older woman hurried Marian to the kitchen and sat her down on a hefty solid oak chair by the large kitchen table. From her pantry just off the kitchen, she brought a bottle of disinfectant, and she poured some over Marian's wounds. Then she carefully washed away the blood and disinfected the area again. At first, Marian winced in pain when the disinfectant stung, but at the same time, she felt relief that this capable, caring person was helping her. Finally, when the bleeding stopped, Sara carefully poured disinfectant on a large bandage and placed it over Marian's deepest wound. Around

Marian's leg and over the bandage, Sara skillfully wound strips of white gauze. Then she taped the bandages to Marian's leg.

My mother had often spoken of Sara's family with whom she had boarded when she was the teacher at Canoe No. 8 in 1917– 1921. Back then, one night at a school program, there was a box social to raise money for the school. Some of the guys knew Dad wanted to buy Mom's lunch box so he could eat with her. They bid the box up. My father bid until he bought my Mom's lunch box. Dad continued to court Mom and married her in 1921.

After Sara married, she continued to live on her parental home place, which was close to the farmstead where my parents lived. Mother and Sara remained friends over the years. Many times, as a child, I had played among the rows of carefully cared for trimmed decorative shrubs on Sara's front lawn. Some of my fondest memories are of her tasty homemade fruit sauces, which she canned every year.

So, I was comfortable with Sara's nursing of Marian's injuries. I felt confident that Marian's injury would heal without taking her to the doctor.

Today I give thanks to the Almighty for people like Sara who can calm the mental anguishes of a young frightened person while they repair serious physical damages to the body. Marian will have a long scar to prove that finding milk pods for the United States government defense purposes by rural school students was not all fun and games. May God bless saintly Sara for her prompt action to sanitize the injured tissues and bring about healing without any infection. Sara's experience and expertise helped Marian's sores to heal without needle and thread to sew together the torn flesh.

In mid-October, I finally get a letter from Mark.

> Dearest Julia,
>
> I pray that you understand that I am not writing because I don't want to write. I pray that you understand

> somewhat of the situation here. We don't have the comforts of home. I am constantly busy with the men keeping vehicles in running order. It seems there is activity day and night. I grab rest when I can. Hope your school year is going well. How I wish I could be home for Christmas and not spend another Christmas away from you. Your letters are like a lifeline to me. Keep on sending them. Julia, I think of you constantly. You help me keep going no matter what is happening around me.
>
> Love,
> Mark

This year I decided to do a Christmas performance for the annual school program. I planned it for December 5th. I hope the weather will hold out, so we have a nice night for the entertainment.

The day of the school program, Mom said, "The weather looks good for the program tonight."

Dad and the school director put up the stage again this year. The older students hung the curtains. Now I hope the young people remember their lines without prompting. Betty and Mother are helping me behind stage.

Jim in third grade started the show with his little poem.

We're so glad you're here
Catch our Christmas cheer.
Just for you we sing
And joyous tidings bring.

All the students sang "Jingle Bells" while I accompanied them on the piano.

Next there was a play about a little boy who did not think he would get anything for Christmas. An old lady teaches him the true meaning of Christmas, the celebration of the birth of Jesus. Later, unbeknown to the child, she sees that he has toys and food for a happy Christmas.

Again, I play the accompaniment as the school children sing "Silent Night, Holy Night" and "Hark! The Herald Angels Sing." Nine of the students do an acrostic exercise on what each letter in the word "Christmas" means. Robby started out with "*C* stands for *Christ*," Teresa "*H* stands for *holy*," Patrick "*R* stands for *royalty*," Alice "*I* stands for the *inn*," Jim "*S* stands for *star*," Tim "*T* stands for *treasures*," Jack "*M* stands for *manger*," Susie "*A* stands for *angel*," and Peggy "*S* stands for *song*." When each child held their letter in front of himself or herself, they said the letter name, the word it stands for, and a line or two about the meaning of the word the letter stood for. For example, the last child said, "*S* stands for *song*, so let us sing and be of good cheer. Remember to keep in mind what he taught. Try to live the way we ought."

We ended the program by singing "Away in a Manger" and "Go Tell It on the Mountain." I asked the audience to join us in singing the last song one more time. I think the rafters shook. The audience loved singing with us.

Dad received a red, blue, and white 11" × 13½" "Certificate of Farm War Service," which read, "This certifies that this family is enlisted in all-out farm war production, 1943," signed by Claude R. Wickard, Secretary of Agriculture, and Leo Herold, County USDA War Board." Such recognition helps all of us to continue doing what we can for the war. People who are appreciated for their efforts are more likely to continue putting forth their best endeavors.

Two more letters came before Christmas from Mark. He spoke of it being cold and wet where he was. He wrote, "Living in a tent is not much like home. I cannot complain about the food as we have plenty to eat.

"We do not find much time for anything but work. It is hard to even find time to write without some interruption. I hope that John is in a better place. I pray this is the last Christmas I spend away from home and you.

"Julia, your letters are so interesting. It makes me happy that you enjoy teaching so much. Janie must be in your fifth-grade class this year. Hope she is not grown up before I see her again. She is my little sister in my mind.

"Julia, merry Christmas. I will not be able to send anything but will make up for that when I get home. I love you more than I can say. You are in my dreams. Please send another picture of yourself, this one is getting tattered."

Christmas this year was sad without Mark and John. Mother and I made cookies, fruitcake, and candy for the boys again this year. We sent the boxes more than three weeks before Christmas.

We tried to have as joyous a Christmas Day as we could. I know we wanted Marian and Bobby to have a nice vacation.

Betty and I got together several times. Once we had a fun time singing songs together while I played the piano. We went to a movie, but the best times we had were when we just talked about our letters, our hopes for the boys to come home, and our plans for someday when they do come home.

Winter 1944

January 1944 was a very cold month with heaps of snow. Dad had to harness Bill and Bud our two workhorses, to take Marian and I to school in the sled, a wagon box loaded onto runners for going over the snow.

Marian and I sat in the box, tucked under the heavy horse blanket. On one side of the blanket is a wool blanket, and it is attached to a hairy horsehide on the other side. We are kept snug and warm under the heavy covering.

On this gloomy winter day, Dad, bless his heart, stands tall with the leather reins in his hands, facing into the cold wind and tiny pellets of stinging sleet. The sled easily slides over the crusted snow.

At school Dad makes sure the fire in the oil burner is still going, and he checks the oil tank outside the school to make sure we have plenty of fuel oil. *How could I do this without his help?*

Again, this year Dad took a head of cattle and two hogs to town to be butchered. With John gone to war, it is so much easier to have the locker butcher the animals and store the meat in the locker. When we go to town to get groceries, Dad goes to the locker to get some of the meat double wrapped in white paper to bring home.

Mom still gets some of the lard for making homemade soap. She heats the fat in the oven to melt the fat. After she prepares the soap with lye, she pours the hot liquid soap in cardboard boxes to cool. Before the soap is completely cooled down, she cuts the soap into bars.

Dad brings some of the freshly butchered beef home. He and Mom cut it up in two-inch chunks and can the meat in fruit jars. Nothing beats the taste of that home-canned beef. With it one can easily make a delicious quick cooked meal. Just grab a jar off the shelf, heat the meat, and stir in flour to make beef gravy to eat over bread or boiled potatoes.

I write the ordinary activities of my family to Mark. I continue writing at least three times a week and sometimes more often. I write even when I do not hear from him. A few times, I have received several short letters from him on the same day.

> Tonight, I wrote:
>
> I wish you could see the large snowman the students made at school today. The weather was warmer, and as the students rolled the balls of snow, they grew bigger quickly. We placed the snowman down at the end of the school yard so that cars turning right or left at the Y in the road can enjoy the jolly snowman.
>
> Tom found some pieces of coal in the woodshed for eyes. The coal had been left in the old woodshed since the days when coal and wood had been burned in the

potbellied stove in the classroom. Susan donated the carrot from her lunch for the nose. Ben stuck his old red stocking cap on the guy's head. Marian stuffed wads of red cloth into the face for a mouth. Billy put nuts from the woods in the back of the school on the front of the middle-sized snowball to look like buttons. Alice and Jim found forked sticks to put on for arms and hands. Dan completed the snowman's sporty look by tying his red scarf around the big fella's neck.

It got colder again last night, so I think Mr. Snowman will be around for a while. Hope so. We all have gotten to like his company even if he is speechless. Ha!

Last night I planned a different activity for today. I brought to school all the ingredients for making homemade ice cream, an empty gallon syrup can to put it in, and plenty of clean spoons to stir the ice cream while it is freezing. I brought bowls and teaspoons to eat it with afterward.

I wanted my students to enjoy the delight I felt as a kid when Mom made homemade ice cream and my brothers and I got to stir it. We willingly went out in the cold to stir the ice cream because we could lick the stirring spoon afterward. Hmm, was that good.

There was a nice clean white snowbank near the steps where we nestled the can of ice cream. Only the older students were permitted to stir the ice cream to keep it creamy and not crystallized. I did not want one of them tipping the can when the lid was off.

Mark, I am sure I don't have to tell you that treat was a big success. I don't think the kids will ever forget the joy of eating ice cream that they made themselves by freezing it outside in the snow.

Mark, for lent this year, I am praying the Rosary every day for you and John's safe return soon. I doubt if Marian appreciates having to say the Rosary every day, but she does because Mother expects her to pray with the rest of the family.

I am not getting a new hat this year for Easter. I put wax paper on the veil of my old hat and ironed the veil. The wax from the waxed paper stiffened my veil, and it looks and feels as nice as new.

I had all my students clean out their desks on Friday. What messes some of the desks were—papers, broken pencils, and stubby pieces of crayon stuffed into corners. I had Susan and Marian help the younger ones clean up their cigar boxes in which they should keep their crayons. The girls threw away tiny broken pieces of crayons and the bits of paper that once had protected the crayons. I like to keep my classroom in good order. It is good for the pupils to learn how to keep things organized.

I feel sorry for my mom washing clothes in the cold of winter. It is too cold for her to hang the wash on the lines outside. When we have a warm day, sometimes we do hang the flannel sheets and heavy clothes like overalls on the line, but if it gets toward evening and colder, we have stiff board like sheets and garments to bring into the house. Then we use every available space to try to completely dry them. The smaller articles of clothing are hung on the tall clothes rack, which can be opened wide, spreading the wooden rods so there are more hanging spaces.

But the worst is winter clothes washing. When cold weather comes, Dad must bring the washing machine from the milk house into the kitchen. Sometimes Dad helps Mom pump cold water for the wash water from the cistern beneath the kitchen floor. Rain water runs into the cistern from eave troughs on the house. Mom heats the water in the copper boiler on the kitchen range. Dad helps her put the hot wash water into the tub of the washing machine and cold water into the rinse tubs. Mom adds shavings off her bars of homemade soap to form suds for washing. Then Dad starts the gasoline motor. The exhaust hose must be put through the kitchen door to the outdoors, so the fumes will go out of the house. With the door open only inches, it still gets cold in the kitchen. Mom with cold fingers takes the warm clothes and pushes them through the wringer into the rinse tub. Then she puts the rinsed clothes through the wringer again into the second rinse tub to get out as much suds and water as she can before hanging them to dry.

How Mom will appreciate electricity to run a washing machine. If this war would just end, then copper would be available again to wire our home for electricity.

At least in the winter, Mother does not wash every Monday like she does in the summertime. In the winter, with the white clean snow, clothes do not get as dirty as in the summer. In cold weather, one does not get sweaty and dusty like in the heat of a dry summer.

A few days later, I wrote to Mark:

The three eighth graders are being drilled for their final grade school exams. I try to review with them as much as I can. They are sharp minded, so my work is easier. They are to go to the Lutheran church basement to take their exams with other eighth graders from the rural schools in the Winneshiek County. I feel confident that they will pass and go on to high school next year.

All three of them passed in the upper levels of achievement. I was proud of them when the county superintendent handed them their eighth-grade diplomas.

14

Normandy Landing – June 1944

Dad, with emotions close to the surface and with guarded disclosure, told Mom, Bobby, Marian, and me about the British and Americans' amphibious landings on the coast of France. He explained that high-level military officials believed an invasion of France would speed the end of the war. Dad didn't want to frighten us because he knew we felt John was in that landing on Normandy beaches.

For months, we had known of American industry supplying the British war machine. Much news of British planes opposing the Luftwaffe, the German Air Force, had reached our ears. From that information, one could surmise an invasion to retrieve ground lost to the Nazi would be undertaken. We knew that John was a part of that buildup of armed forces in Britain to retake lands that Hitler's Germany had insatiably seized.

Dwight Eisenhower, commander of allied troops in Europe, delivered this message to allied forces just before they embarked on the Normandy invasion on June 6, 1944:

> Soldiers, Sailors, and Airmen of the Allied Expeditionary Force! You are about to embark upon a great crusade. The eyes of the world are upon you. The hopes and prayers of liberty-loving people everywhere march with you.

We felt pride in knowing that John was one of those soldiers in this mighty crusade for freedom, but our hearts were weak with the fear of his safety.

In John's last letter, he had written, "I have reason to believe Jake might be close to where I am. Jake was a good buddy while we were in training. I miss him. At least he was someone who grew up near my hometown. I felt a kind of a connection with him because of that."

The days slipped by without any word from John. Then one day, local news became ablaze with the news that Jake Halsted from Cresco had been killed while taking part in the landing at Omaha beach. My family felt deep sorrow over that tragic news. Knowing that Jake might have been close to John made our concerns even greater for John. We wondered more than ever where John is.

Mom, Dad, Bobby, Marian, and I attended the funeral in Cresco. We followed the funeral procession to the gravesite. Old WWI soldiers gave a graveside military service in honor of Jake. One older gray-haired man blew taps on his trumpet, and in a short time could be heard the echo of taps from another trumpet in the distance.

With the American flag draped on the casket ready to be lowered into the grave, Mother broke into tears, and Dad took her off to the side. The American flag was folded by military men and given to Mrs. Halsted. Many came forward and put flowers on the metal casket. Then the minister led Mrs. Halsted and her husband away as the casket was lowered into the ground. The tears flowed unashamedly down my face. "Oh, dear God, bless the repose of Jake's soul. He gave his utmost sacrifice for me to live in a better world."

The days since Jake's funeral with no word from John are making it harder to believe that John is still alive. After supper, I wrote Mark that I placed the following writing of my thoughts and feelings in my journal tonight. I sent the original to Mark and kept the carbon copy for myself. Someday I will make a typed copy to keep for my hoped-for future children and grandchildren.

Days without End

It is early June 1944. Dad's ears are glued to the battery-operated radio in our nonelectric rural home. The news is full of the reports about the American and British military forces landing at Normandy on June 6. The entire family believes my dearly loved brother is involved in that landing. He is a highly trained radio operator. Would he have gone ashore with the infantry? Which beach landing was he involved in?

Dad described the landing at Omaha as the toughest. Germans hidden in the rocky hillsides found easy targets of the infantry pouring inland off the vessels in which they crossed the English Channel.

In the days following, Hitler's army fiercely fought to defend their hold on France. The Allied forces are attempting to liberate France from the clutches of the German Nazi armies and force them back over the Rhine River.

Days go by. There are no letters from my brother, no word of any kind. Is he wounded? Is he alive? Why don't we hear something?

The anxiety of not knowing is hard on Mother. She looks pale and tired. Even though Mom looks weary, I know that she is a strong lady who goes to her Lord in prayer. She knows he is the rock from which our strength comes. Daily she searches the Scripture to find verses to give her hope and the energy for daily tasks.

My dearest friend, my childhood sweetheart is in the mountainous terrains of Italy. Sometimes it has been days, even weeks that I do not hear from him. So, I have two very dear to my heart loved ones, whom I deeply miss in my life, in harm's way.

In the evening, sitting up in my bed, writing in the light of my kerosene lamp, I underline with my fountain pen scripture that helps me keep living above my troubles. Each evening, I find those underlined verses and repeat them to myself. They reinforce my fortitude and faith. A calming peace pervades my soul, and I feel that God is carrying my burdens for me and has not forsaken me.

But in the wake of each day, I have all I can do to keep going to the classroom to teach. But in one way it is a blessing. I am kept so busy helping my students that I have less time to be troubled over the war news and lack of hearing from loved ones.

Each day I push myself to do my daily routine, thereby keeping my mind busy to keep out the tendency to worry. Worry, like anger, can weaken the vessel it is stored in. It will not do any good to endanger my health with excessive troubled thoughts.

My father appears to be undisturbed, but I know better. Beneath his stoic exterior, I am sure he feels much concern for his son's welfare. Dad is like a strong oak in the winds of an unrelenting storm. Dad wishes to protect Mother and not increase her worries by adding any of his own to her already overburdened despair.

Every Wednesday evening, Mother asks the whole family after supper to kneel and pray the Rosary. Mother leads us in prayer. We recite after her by saying, the Our Father and ten Hail Marys for each of the five decades of the Rosary. We pray for the safe return of my brother, our neighbor boy, and the end of this dreadful war.

As each day passes with no message of big brother's wellbeing, it is a real trying of my faith. The following verses are like lifesavers to me when I feel I am drowning in a sea of misery; these words buoy me up.

> Knowing this, that the trying of your faith
> worketh patience. But let patience have her
> perfect work, that ye may be perfect and entire,
> wanting nothing (James 1:3–4, KJV).

Will we ever know what happened to my brother? Is he already buried by caring comrades in some shallow grave in France? Has he been taken prisoner by Nazi soldiers? Is he nearly starving in some concentration camp? Are his captors torturing him with inhumanly cruel Hitlerian torments?

This time of the unknown seems endless. Dear God, let us know soon where my brother is. I pray that he is still alive somewhere and there is a reason why we do not hear from him. This waiting to get answers to our questions seems endless. Please, dear God, let it end soon.

Mark, I hope that you appreciate my musings about the war. It will be so good when all this is behind us.

Another week goes by and then my parents receive word about John. "Oh! Sam, at least we know that he's alive. Let's pray his injuries are not life threatening."

My parents learn that John has been wounded. Nothing else did they learn, just that John was in a hospital with injuries.

Some more time passes, and then word is received that John is in the states in a military hospital. Finally, Dad is able to reach John by telephone. The story is pieced together. John told Dad, "I survived the Normandy landing. With my infantry unit, I was following the tanks traveling into French countryside. The Allied forces were rapidly pushing the Axis forces to the Rhine River. With the swift movement of the Allies, some pockets of Nazis were encircled."

One day as John was marching along, a young German soldier jumped from his hiding place and pointed a gun at John. One of John's buddies not far away yelled, which took the Nazi soldier's eyes off John as the gun went off. John was wounded, tearing flesh off his lower right leg. John's buddy, grabbing John's radio, called for medical help. He tried to stop the bleeding as best he could. Another comrade captured the trembling young German soldier and took him as a prisoner of war.

"Dad, I owe my life to my buddy who saved my life twice that day.

He distracted the Nazi with the gun who tried to kill me, and he got immediate medical help to keep me from bleeding to death."

"Son, I am thankful that you are still alive. Your friend Jake did not fare so well." Dad told about Jake and the funeral. John had not heard that his friend had died. Afterward, Dad thought maybe he should not have told him yet, but it was better John heard it from family than a stranger.

John told Dad, "My wounds were left uncovered so that they would heal better. We can see the bone on my lower leg. The doctors said if they tried to sew the remaining flesh together, my leg would have a large hole on the lower leg. They said that by leaving the wounded area uncovered, in time the flesh would fill in on its own. Later, I will have skin grafting from my thigh to my leg."

Mom wanted to hear John's voice. He told her, "Mom, I will be sent home in a couple of weeks, but later I have to return to a military hospital for skin grafts and physical therapy."

Mom and Dad seemed so relieved to think John was soon coming home. I called Betty to give her the news. John had already talked with her. She sounded so happy. "Julia, I never gave up my faith that John would return. He has a wounded leg, but he is alive."

That night I wrote a long letter to Mark telling him why we had not heard from John and all about his leg injury. "Mark, I continue to pray for your safe return home."

"Mark, I have added these new releases to my sheet music collection, "I'll Get By (As Long As I Have You)" and "Comin' In on a Wing and a Prayer." Yes, Mark, I will get by as long as I have you. The song is very meaningful to me. I enjoy listening to the lyrics, and I like to play and sing the song. Betty came over last Saturday, and we played and sang. It did us both a lot of good.

"Music calms and uplifts my spirits. I feel happy and joyous when I am singing or listening to music. I long for the day when you are home again so we can play and sing together like we used to."

"Betty has John coming home soon, and you are still gone. Take care, and hopefully you'll soon be home also."

Mark would often write that he was busy and found it hard to write. What did *busy* mean? What was he not telling me about the war in Italy?

One day Dad told me that when Mark was in Africa, the tanks were greatly valuable in the desert war, but in the mountains of Italy, it was much more difficult terrain for tanks to traverse. Dad further commented that keeping the vehicles necessary in a war in good working operation was sure to keep Mark very busy. He added, "Mark is so busy that I am sure it is difficult for him to write. Living in a tent or finding shelter in a foxhole is not conducive to finding time or a place to write letters." I know Dad was trying to help me understand why Mark's letters are slow in coming and explain why the letters are short.

John's coming home was wonderful. He looked healthy despite his injury. I did not like looking at his deep open red-looking wound on the side of his right leg. Every day Mother or I had to twice daily use disinfectant and clean the wound. I was glad John did not flinch when I dressed his wound. That helped me have the courage to do it.

Betty came to our house often to visit with John. I am sure that did him much good. John told her that he would like to go to college and planned to enroll at Luther College in Decorah.

A week later, John went to see Father Dolan about his going to Luther College. Father Dolan told him, "A Catholic should not go to a Lutheran school." John came home quite depressed. It would be difficult for him to go to college farther from home.

Mom and Dad sat down and had a lengthy talk with their troubled son. John explained how the priest warned him that under the Catholic Canon Law of 1917 he would be excommunicated if he went to a protestant college where he could be educated in another religion. My parents realized the seriousness of the warning to John not to attend classes at Luther College. They were worried that their son would not be able to go to communion in the church. If John went against the stance of the church it could affect the whole family. My parents knew that it would be very difficult for John to go away to school at this time and yet they had never had any serious problem like this with their church before and it weighed heavily on their minds.

Many times my mother, when asked by neighbors or friends, has attended ladies' aide meetings or special services in another Christian church. When invited to the wedding of a neighbor or friend, my family goes to the celebration even if it is in a different denomination. They have attended in other churches the funerals of family members of friends or neighbors. In Decorah are a-number-of denominations including Lutheran, Methodist, Presbyterian, Congregational, and some other smaller denominations. The Springwater Church used to be a Quaker church. The Christian people have learned to live side by side and have respect for the religious beliefs of their neighbors. After all, we believe in the same God and his Bible.

Mother and Dad decided not to stand in the way of John attending Luther College. Hopefully, the priest will never do anything further to stop John's attendance at the Lutheran school.

Father warned, "It is still possible that the priest could stop John from going to Luther College."

John was regularly seeing Betty. Betty's parents in the past have been cool toward the relationship. Betty had confided in me numerous times her concern that her parents disapproved of her dating a Catholic. Betty privately told me that many times she has read her Bible and prayed for the blessing of her parents on her relationship with John.

John shared with me his deep feelings for Betty but feared her folks would stand in the way of a marriage between the two of them. How can Christians harden their hearts in such situations? It is hard for me to understand how parents who love their child would deny her the love of her life.

John started the fall session at Luther College despite his crippled leg and the knowledge of further surgeries to restore the leg to a healthier condition. John applied himself diligently to his studies. He wanted to study business. I think he would like to have a store of his own someday, maybe one to sell radios. His training in radio operations has interested him in radios. The demand for such communications will most likely grow greatly in the years ahead.

During the month of October, John had to return to the Veteran's Hospital for skin grafting from his upper thigh to his leg and have some physical therapy. He had already made arrangements with the college that he could do his college classes by correspondence during that time.

Dad had to hire help with the corn picking, but with John's injured leg, he would not have been much help even if he would have been home at that time.

Most of the following that I wrote in my journal I also wrote to Mark. I started my third year of teaching school. This year I have fifteen students. Colleen O'Brien and Mike McGuire are kindergarteners. Marian is in the seventh grade. She is like a mother hen with Colleen and Mike. It tickles me how she works at teaching them the school routine.

I have no eighth graders, so that will take off some pressure as I will not have anyone to take eighth-grade exams in the spring. Of course, I will strive to teach all I can to the seventh-grade students, so they will be ready for their eighth-grade year.

Mark, I hate to tell you that Bobby wants to go to service now that John is home. Mother does not want him to, but he feels that it is his duty. John is in college, but he will have school vacation next summer to help Dad. I know Bobby is determined to go into the army.

Bobby has a girlfriend, Becky; she wants to go to Iowa State Teachers College at Cedar Falls for two years. In two years, she will have a teaching diploma to teach in town schools. Mark, I have enjoyed teaching rural school. Teaching all the grades has been interesting to me. Sometimes I feel I am learning right along with my students. With teaching so many grades, there is never a lack of interest in knowledge. Mark, I guess that I am a born teacher as I love it so much.

Mark, you know how I hate snakes. This fall there are garter snakes that sun on the cement steps leading into the school. Marian screamed loudly one day when she was leaving the building to use the little house outback. There were several large snakes lying on the steps. She was terrified. Dad told her they will not hurt her; they are just garter snakes, harmless snakes. I hope that I never step on any, not knowing they are on the steps.

Another snake story involved your sister, Janie. The kids were playing hide and go seek. Janie was trying to hide herself in the tall grass on the high embankment from the school grounds down to the main road. She crouched down in the tall grass and then saw the snake beneath her body. She let out blood-curdling screams. It scared me as I didn't know what had happened.

Then just a week after that, a ball game was going strong when Teresa doubled up in pain. She was trying to catch a fly. Billy, tearing wildly into second, ran into her. I ran to Teresa; she was having trouble breathing. That almost made me feel helpless, but that will never do for a teacher who is in charge. I tried to calm Teresa and quiet the children. In a few seconds, Teresa was gasping for air. Billy had knocked the wind out of her. She quietly sat on the steps the rest of the noon hour. By the time school started again, she was almost back to normal.

Dear Dad, he always informs us of what is going on in the war. Tonight, he explained to the family the importance of the struggle going on in Italy. He told us that the Allies are struggling to eliminate Italy from the war. The Italians fighting with the Germans have come back to their native land to protect it and left the battles in Russia, weakening the power of the Axis in that front.

Today I purchased the sheet music for "Dance with a Dolly (With a Hole in Her Stockin')." I wrote to Mark, "I can't wait until you come home to dance with you to this music. With the shortage of nylon stockings, I am sure I can wear a pair with a hole in 'em. Ha!"

I told Mark how thankful I am to have a mother like mine. She has taught me to have a deep faith. That, I believe, is a most precious gift.

Mom is an excellent cook, and I am trying to learn from her. I am copying her recipes in a notebook to have when I am a wife someday with my own family to feed.

Recently, when the Watkins man came, Mom purchased two copies of *Watkins Household Hints* from him. It is a book of over two hundred pages giving household hints to help a woman become a better homemaker. I am thankful she purchased a copy for me as well as for herself.

Mom always stresses eating lots of vegetables to stay healthy. She feeds us fresh vegetables in the summer and her canned goods and stored vegetables in the winter. She is a strong believer in eating good nutritious food for nourishment.

Mother raises Rhode Island Reds as she believes that a heavy chicken lays a larger, healthier egg. In good weather, the hens run free and peck away at the green grass. Eggs from those chickens have a deeper orange-yellow yolk, which does look healthier than the pale yolks of other eggs.

I pray that I can be good wife someday like my mom is to my father. I want to be a first-class mother like she is. Her homemaking skills are resourceful and proficient; I am striving to reach such goals. She is my Proverbs 31 model for me to follow throughout my life.

15

An Accident – End of 1944

Bobby has finished his basic training. He came home for a few days and returned to his base to learn he was being shipped out to the Pacific theater. Mother is praying hard for her second son to serve in this war.

John confided in me that he is still seeing Betty. He said that he often picks her up when she gets off work at the telephone company. John told me that he took Betty to several wedding dances at Breezy Hill in the early fall, but now that it is colder, there are no dances there. In the winter, the closest dance hall is DanceNite dance hall. He said they have gone to a few wedding dances there.

We both know how much Mother hates for us to go to DanceNite dances especially on Saturday nights when they have the weekly dances. We've heard Mom say too much alcohol is drank there, causing rowdy behavior. It is not a decent place for a lady, but even worse is that Betty's mother doesn't want her dancing at all. "What am I to do, Julia? I want to keep dating Betty. She and I enjoy dancing, but we do not want to upset her mother. If her mother found out, she might refuse to let Betty go out with me. Julia, I think that I want to ask Betty to marry me at Christmastime. I don't know if her mom will allow Betty to be engaged to me."

"John, I understand your concerns. I have wondered about it for a long time myself. When you were in service, I went to the Lutheran church with Betty one Sunday. The next Sunday, she went to St. Benedict's

Church with me. I knew Betty was uneasy about the difference in your religious backgrounds at that time."

"Do you think that she would join the Catholic church for me? You know Mother would want any children of mine to be brought up in the Catholic faith."

"John, you know that I cannot speak for Betty, but I will tell you this. I believe she thinks a lot of you. She waited for you to come back to her. When Betty went to church with me, she asked a lot of questions. She told me some of the service is not that much different than in her church.

"After all, Martin Luther had been a Catholic priest when he left the Catholic church and formed the Lutheran church. It is understandable that some things could remain similar. Mark, both churches believe in God and his word in the Holy Bible. We say a similar Our Father and strive to gain the same salvation for all eternity."

"Marian, you make it sound simple, but it is not. People get set in their beliefs and feel their way is the only way. I think Betty is more open in her thinking than that. Maybe there is hope for us to marry someday."

"John, why don't you just outright ask Betty if she would join your church?"

"Well, I don't know about that. I think that Betty is afraid of her mother. She's afraid that her mother might send her away if she wants to marry a Catholic."

Julia, with the look of a frightened child, questioned, "John, her mother would not do that, would she?"

"Recently Betty told me that her mother has a brother in Rockford, Illinois. He is older than Betty's mother and lost his wife in the last year. He asked if Betty could come to live with him for a while. He said that she could get a job there in the telephone company. There would be plenty of opportunity for her to meet young people. He would see to that."

"Oh, John, that would be awful. I don't think Betty would ever do that."

"Well, I don't either, but then again, if Betty's mother wanted to stop our relationship, she might just push Betty into leaving Decorah."

The only hope I could give John was to remind him of what Mother does when she encounters problems. Our mother turns to prayer.

I told him to remember the verse, "Behold, I stand at the door, and knock: if any man hear my voice, and open the door, I will come in to him…" (Revelations 3:20, KJV).

That conversation stayed in my mind for days. *What can be done to change the situation?*

Finally, I received a lengthy letter from Mark.

> Dearest Julia,
>
> In early fall, I caught pneumonia. I tried to keep going, not realizing I had pneumonia. Most likely, I came down with pneumonia because of the cold and wet weather we were having at the time. At first, I tried to get warm. I never felt so cold in my life. Stacks of blankets did not make me feel warm. A buddy insisted I go to the doctor.
>
> My fever was 104 degrees. I was put into the hospital. For a few days, I did not do anything but sleep. The doctor gave me penicillin. I am fortunate as in WWI, there was no penicillin to treat pneumonia. I believe that it has only been the last few years it has come into common use.
>
> As soon as I left the hospital, I went back to my unit. A couple of days later, I had a relapse. I had gotten up to get a drink of water, and I blacked out. The water splashed all over me, and the container it was in crashed to the floor. Another soldier heard the noise and came to help me. I was taken back to the hospital unit.
>
> I was sicker than the first time as I was now more rundown. I was in the hospital a week. When I went

back to my tent, I was too weak to do much. I needed a lot of rest. Days went by before I felt like working. I had to push myself to keep going, and it took great effort to work.

Dear Julia, I did not write of my illness at the time as I did not want to worry you.

Now my strength is almost back to normal, and I am back on full duty. My original unit has moved on. Hopefully someday I will be reunited with them. I miss my best buddies that I worked side by side with for months.

Julia, I had your picture with me the whole while. Looking at your pretty, kind face warmed my heart. It gave me reason to want to get well. Someday this will all be behind us, and I will be home again. Then I can take you in my arms and whisper how much I love you.

Your letters are all tucked in my old metal ammunition box. Sometimes I get them out and reread them. I am so glad that you kept writing even when I could not write to you. Thank you for your faithful caring about me. I will someday make it all up to you.

Of course, it was not just my pneumonia that kept me from writing. Before that, sometimes we were on the move, and there was no way one had time to write letters. Living in a tent or worse, sleeping in a foxhole is not helpful to keeping up with correspondence. I pray that you understand.

I wish I could tell you more about where I am. I would like to describe the area. But for security reasons, I cannot do that.

Keep the letters coming; they are pleasing to me like candy to a child. At the sight of a treat, a child's eyes light up with delight, and so do my mine when I see your mail. I think of the music we used to play and sing. Those were the good days. I am glad that you are buying sheet music of current hits that we can sing when I come home.

Good night dearest one,
Mark

It was unpleasant to learn that Mark had been sick, but it was wonderful to have an answer to why his letters were so long in coming. Now I could think about the problems on the home front.

The last Friday night of November, I had my yearly school program. The students gave recitations and did two plays. While I played several Christmas hymns, the pupils sang. Last I played "White Christmas," a currently very popular song. My students and I sang it, and then we asked our audience to sing it again with us. Everyone sang heartily as all of us are looking for merrier and brighter days. Music lifts spirits and gives hope.

For the third Christmas Mark has been away, I mailed date bars, Christmas decorated sugar cookies, and homemade candy. I tucked in a few trinkets that might bring him joy.

Just before Christmas, I received another long letter from Mark. He wrote how he missed Midnight Mass, the Christmas tree and gift exchange at home, and his mom's big Christmas dinner with all the extra good food.

This year, he would settle for "a large baby doll alongside the Christmas tree—a real live doll, not a paper one will do—and she looks just like you." That made me smile.

At Christmas time, John did not ask Betty to marry him. He did not give her an engagement ring. He decided that he would give it some more time.

Betty did join us for our Christmas exchange and Mother's delicious home-cooked dinner with all the trimmings. Mother had crocheted two large doilies, one for Betty and one for me. She told us both that the doilies were for our hope chests. Betty blushed hearing that. There were gifts of clothes, games, and other items that each person wanted. John gave Betty a single- strand pearl necklace.

Privately, John told me that he had decided to wait awhile before asking Betty to marry him. I told him I was praying every day for a solution to the dilemma. He replied, "Julia, I am praying daily. I do not want to come between Betty and her mother. I know Betty loves her mother and does not want to break her heart."

The third week after Christmas, the weather turned bitterly cold. Morning lows dropped below zero degrees. One such harsh winter morning, as John drove to his college class, he noticed Betty's wool scarf on the seat where she had left it the night before. He glanced at his wristwatch and decided he had time to drop by her house and leave it off. It is so cold she needs the scarf.

He knocked at the front door. No one answered. *Betty is gone to work by now, but her mother should be home.* John walked around the house to knock on the back door.

As he came around the corner of the house, he was stunned to see Betty's mother lying on the ground. He ran quickly to her side. She was knocked unconscious.

Birdseed was scattered around her. John realized she had come outside to put out food for the birds and slipped on the icy steps. When Mrs. Olson fell, her head hit the edge of the cement steps, knocking her unconscious. Her right leg was twisted under her, and she fell on her right arm.

John quickly went in the back door and telephoned an operator at the telephone office. Betty was the operator who took the call. He told her to put the call through to the hospital for medical help to go to her home. Briefly he explained that her mother had fallen, and he hung up.

Off the living room divan, he grabbed a wool blanket, and in the kitchen, he grabbed several white kitchen dish towels. He covered Mrs. Olson with the blanket and used the towels to wipe the blood on her face and to try to stop the bleeding. She would briefly gain consciousness and then be out again.

Betty arrived at home just before the medical help got there. She knelt in the snow beside her mother, tears welling up in her eyes. "Mom, can you hear me? I am here to help you. Do not move. Men from the hospital have come to help us."

Betty stood and stepped aside so that the medical personnel could attend to her mother. Both men determined that her right leg and arm were broken as she had landed heavily on them. They carefully lifted her onto a stretcher and carried her to the waiting vehicle.

John took Betty's hand and led her to his car. They followed her mother to the hospital.

"John, why did you go to my house this morning?"

John explained that she had left her scarf in the car last night. He thought she needed it, and he decided to return it before class.

"John, you are missing your morning class."

"Betty, that is okay. Your mother needs our attention right now. How did you get away from your job?"

"The supervisor told me to go. She would fill in for me."

At the hospital, we waited in the waiting room for news of Mrs. Olson's condition. "John, what would have happened to Mom if you had not found her? It is so terribly cold today. Even if she had regained consciousness, could she have gotten into the house to phone for help?"

It was not long until Mr. Olson appeared in the waiting room.

He looked very worried. "What happened?"

Betty told her dad, "Mom went outside to put out seeds for the birds. Evidently, she slipped on the icy steps and hit her head on the cement steps, knocking her unconscious. John came to our house to return my scarf that I'd left in his car. Mom did not answer the front door, so he went around the corner to knock on the back door. He found Mom and called for help."

Betty's dad came over to John. Mr. Olson shook John's hand while he told him, "Young man, you probably saved my wife's life. She could have frozen out there in the cold before I would have gotten home at five-thirty, or she could have caught pneumonia lying there in the cold. How can we ever thank you enough?"

"Mr. Olson, if Betty would not have left her scarf in my car last night, I would not have come to your house this morning."

We waited quite a while before anyone came to tell us how Mrs. Olson was doing. Finally, a nurse came to tell us, "The doctor is setting Mrs. Olson's broken leg and arm. He fears that Mrs. Olson had been in the cold for some time. We will carefully watch her for any signs of pneumonia.

"It will be some time yet before you will be able to see her. Mrs. Olson is not very coherent yet, but the doctor thinks that she had only a slight concussion. The shock of her accident is most likely causing her disorientation."

John left to go to his afternoon class. Betty and her father stayed at the hospital, so they would be there when Mrs. Olson was put in a room. They would be there to try to comfort her.

16

The Blizzard – January 1945

When I came home from teaching, I found John anxiously waiting to talk to me. He told me about finding Betty's mother unconscious, calling to Betty, and going to the hospital. He asked, "Do you think Mrs. Olson will think better of me now that I have saved her life today?"

"John, you know that I cannot answer that question. Many came to this nation for religious freedom but even here find it difficult to acknowledge other churches than their own. To Mrs. Olson, you are like a foreigner because you have been brought up with some different religious teachings."

"I was hoping today might have made a difference. I think for Betty's father it did. He thanked me for saving his wife's life."

"John, we must pray about this."

"Well, at least I don't think we have to wonder anymore that Betty might leave to go to help her uncle in Illinois. She will be kept busy helping her mother until her mother can get around again and do her housework."

The next day, Mother made an angel food cake and a large pan of scalloped potatoes with ham for John to take to Betty's house.

Mom called Betty to tell her that she was sending the evening meal to her home. Just after Betty came home from the telephone office, John brought the food to the Olson house. Betty asked John to stay and eat with her and her father.

After the meal, John helped Betty do the dishes and clean up the kitchen. Then Mr. Olson drove to the hospital. John and Betty followed in John's car to the hospital to see Mrs. Olson.

"Mother, you look so much better than you did last night."

"Yes, I feel much better. My leg is rather large with this cast, and my arm is clumsy." She looked at John and smiled. "But I am fortunate to be alive. I do not know how long I lay there in the snow and cold. John, if you had not come along, I don't know what would have happened to me."

Betty let her mom know of different acquaintances who sent their best wishes for a speedy recovery. Mr. Olson told his wife some business news. An hour went by quickly. John took Betty home, and Mr. Olson stayed a bit longer with his wife.

"Betty, do you think your mom will have a better opinion of our relationship after what happened?"

"John, I would like to think so. I think my dad really likes you, John. Now with your saving Mom from getting pneumonia or freezing to death, I am sure he thinks more highly of you."

"Betty, I enjoy being with you. You are important in my life. I don't know what I would do if I could not be with you." John pulled her close in a big hug and kissed her. He took her arm and walked her up the slippery sidewalk. He waited until she was safely behind the closed door before returning to his car.

For the first few days, John took Betty every evening to the hospital to see her mother. When Mrs. Olson came home, Mr. Olson had an older woman hired to be with Mrs. Olson during the day and make her meals.

On Sunday evening, John visited with Mr. and Mrs. Olson awhile before he left to take Betty to the movie. When they left the house, it was spitting snow.

John and Betty went to the movie at the Grand Theater. After the movie, John and Betty were astounded to see how much snow had fallen while they were in the nice warm theater. John hurried Betty to the car, opened the door for her, and helped her in the car. The streets were filling up with snow.

"John, maybe you should stay at my house tonight. You could sleep in the spare bedroom. Dad and Mom would understand because of the weather. It's too dangerous to drive."

"No, Betty. I better go home so I am there to help Dad milk our cows in the morning."

He quickly walked Betty to the door, kissed her good night, and watched to see that she got in the house.

John started up the Locust Road. He had six miles to go to get home. The snow was getting deeper on the road. Out in the country, the wind was whipping the fluffy white flakes into drifts. John could not drive too fast but kept going. He breathed a sigh of relief when he got to the Y in the road by the white schoolhouse where Julia teaches.

He drove behind the school and started on the last mile to home. Going up the small hill, the snow was deep, but he made it through okay. When he came to the woods, the road was protected by the trees, and the snow was not deep. Then he came to a long open area. A snow fence had been put in the field along the road. The windblown snow had piled up behind that snow fence, so there was not much snow in the roadway. Next was the hill leading down to the farm buildings. The road was deep between two small hills. The windswept snow had piled in between those knolls.

John tried to buck through but packed the snow in the front of the car. He tried to back up, but the vehicle was wedged too much into the snow. He knew that he could not go any further in his car.

He pulled earflaps down over his ears. Taking his long scarf from his neck, he put it over his cap to hold it on and tied the ends of the scarf around his neck. He put mittens over his driving gloves and reached into the glove compartment for his flashlight.

By now it was snowing so hard, he could hardly see. *This must be what they call a whiteout, when one cannot see in the storm.*

He forcibly pushed against the snowbank to open the car door and got out of the car. He sank into the deep, almost-waist-high snow. The cold snow came down into the tops of his boots. Even so, he was thankful he had on his tall rubber boots over his dress shoes. It was a struggle just to take steps. The wind was strongly beating on his body, making it hard to make any headway forward. Once he turned away from the wind just to get his breath and some relief from the powerful wind. When he turned back again, he wondered, *Am I going the right way?*

The flashlight did not do much good. The light just glared on the falling snowflakes. *What am I going to do to make sure I am heading in the right direction and can find my way to the house? Maybe, I can find the woven fence and follow it. I will have to be careful not to touch the barbed wire above, so I don't get hurt from the sharp barbs.*

John knew that Dad had put a woven fence in along the pasture when he had sheep to keep them in. With just a barbed wire fence, the sheep could run between the barbed wires and leave hunks of wool hanging on the fence, but the sheep would be running free.

Groping along where he figured the fence must be, he found the woven fence and started walking along it. It was tough going as the snow was almost as high as the fence in places and sometimes higher than the fence. It was strenuous just lifting one boot after the other. It seemed he had walked for too long a time without knowing where he was.

Finally, he felt a round wooden post. Then he touched a wooden gate. He knew where he was. The gate leads into the small field near the house yard. He went on past the gate, knowing that the next fence was the house yard fence. If he followed that and turned with it, he would come to the gate in front of the house.

Once safely inside the warm kitchen, John had a time getting off his boots. They were packed with snow. He carefully wiped the snow from his right leg. All that cold snow was not good for his injured leg. He found it hard enough to keep good circulation in his leg without all the coldness in it right now. He just sat there for minutes, rubbing his leg with a heavy towel. The injured area of his leg, he patted carefully to dry it. He worked to bring warmth to every inch of the leg.

He shook his coat and hung it on a hook behind the door to dry off. His gloves, scarf, and socks were wet. He laid them behind the kitchen range to dry in the heat from the stove.

After crawling into bed, he gave thanks to the Almighty that he was able to get home safely. He slept soundly.

After John drove away into the blizzard, Betty wondered how he could ever get home in the storm. The snow was coming down so thick that one could hardly see the road.

Dear God, please help John get safely home. He is my best friend. I could not stand it if anything should happen to him. He saved my mother's life. He is a good and kind person. Please, God, protect him tonight.

When Julia awoke, she could not see out her window. Snow piled on the roof over the porch and almost covered her window. She thought, *If we had a lot of snow last night, I will not have school today.*

In the kitchen, Mother was making pancakes for breakfast. The night before, she had put oat groats in a pan covered to a few inches of the top with water. She left the pan of oats to cook all night toward the back of the stove. This morning she took some of the cooked oatmeal and added some beaten eggs, salt, soft butter, and honey. Then she stirred in some flour with baking powder and buttermilk to the right pancake consistency. She poured the batter onto the griddle already hot from the heat of the fire underneath the iron lids on the cook stove.

On the table was sorghum or honey to put on the pancakes. With the shortage of sugar because of the war, we used honey or sorghum to sweeten foods. There was a pot of hot coffee to warm a person up with.

Mother said, "Dad and John should be coming in for breakfast soon as they have been gone considerably longer than usual to do the morning milking." When the men appeared, they were covered with snow and came in stomping the snow from their boots.

Both Dad and John brought in an armload of wood to put in the corner to the right of the door. In this weather, they did not want to have to go out again very soon to keep enough wood for burning in the kitchen range and living room stove. Stove pipes from the stoves extend up through the ceiling, through the upstairs bedrooms, and out the chimney on the rooftop. The stove pipes warm the upstairs bedrooms.

While eating breakfast, John told the family about his following the fence line to find his way home last night. Mom asked, "How is your leg this morning?"

John answered, "Your nice warm quilts warmed my legs and the rest of me quite nicely last night. I sure was glad to be out of that storm."

Mom told us, "I treasure my quilts and wool blankets because they are made from wool sheared from our own sheep. Your dad got tired of the sheep running through the barbed wire fences and eating the grass too short in the pasture for his cows, so he sold the sheep a couple of years ago. We will not have any more wool to make wool blankets and battings for quilts."

"I think I should call Betty and let her know I got home okay last night," announced John.

"John, the phone is not working this morning. I tried to call Sara to see if everything was all right over there this morning," explained Mom.

"With this snow and the gusts of strong winds, I suppose either the lines snapped or a telephone pole is down," Dad reasoned.

After breakfast, Dad sat near the stove, looking at the paper and his farm journal. John was studying his college books. Mom was crocheting a lacy edging around pillowcases for my hope chest. I was crocheting cotton thread into dish rags to add to my hope chest for future use in my own home someday.

"Mom, can we make homemade ice cream?" begged Marian.

Mother answers her, "That is a good idea as it is only in the cold part of winter that we can make it. If we had an electric refrigerator, we could make it anytime."

Hearing the conversation, John offers to go to the milk house to bring in some milk and cream. Eating homemade ice cream with its delicious vanilla flavoring is a wintertime pleasure for all of us. Marian went into the cellar for the eggs.

Mom asks me to help Marian make the ice cream. "Marian, I not only want you to know how to make the ice cream, but I want you to have the satisfaction of making this well-loved dessert for your family."

I know that Mom thinks that the ice cream will give all of us something to look forward to on this cold, dreary day with the wind howling around the corners. Also, she senses that John is troubled that he cannot let Betty know that he is home safe.

"Dear, are you concerned that you could not go out in the storm to get to the telephone company?" queried Mrs. Olson.

"A number of the telephone operators live across the street from the telephone company, and I am sure those girls are able to get there and fill in for the rest of us who cannot get there," answered Betty.

"Well, you act anxious, and I am wondering what is on your mind this morning."

Then Betty described the cold furious winds and heavy snow through which John had brought her home after the movie. Then with tears dropping down her cheeks, she wept, "Mom, I asked him to stay all night. He wanted to go home. I tried to call the Sturloff home, but the phone does not ring. The lines must be down. I am so worried if he got home last night. He could be out there stuck in some snowbank. Could he live through the night in this storm?"

"Betty, dear, you really like this young man, don't you?"

"Yes, Mother. he is so kind, thoughtful, and good to me. He has been my best friend for a long time. We were good friends in high school."

"But Betty, he does not belong to our church," protested Mrs. Olson.

"I know, Mom, but he is a believer. He goes to mass every Sunday. He has a fervent faith in the Lord Jesus Christ. To me, his love is like the unconditional love of parents. He is like an earthly rock I can lean on. I do deeply care for John."

There is a silence. No one speaks. Mrs. Olson leans back in her wingback chair. Her head lies against the cushioned back of the chair, and her eyes are closed. Finally, she leans forward and speaks. "Betty, forgive me. I have not been very nice to John. He saved my life. I owe him so much. But you, dear girl, are my only child. I love you beyond measure. I want only the best for you."

Betty stood still. It was like she could not breathe. *What would Mother say next? Did I want to hear it?*

"Today I can feel your love for him. True love is a precious, priceless, freely given gift. One cannot easily find faithful love and harder yet, maintain a lasting, tender, passionate love.

"You have known him for years and still think of him as your best friend. It appears the caring between you and John has lasted through the test of time.

"Betty, I love you so and want the best life for you. I could not have chosen a better helpmate for you. John has proven he possesses the qualifications of a good husband as listed in the Bible. Betty, you have my blessings to marry John someday if that is what you both want."

"Mom, last night I could not sleep with worrying about John. I prayed a lot in the night for his safety. Help me pray that he is safe at home."

Then Betty rushed to her mother, gave her a hug, and told her, "I will be so happy to tell John how you feel about him. Dear Mother, I love you, and I am thankful that you now understand John is a good Christian man."

On Tuesday evening, Mom is making homemade vegetable soup for supper, and she asks me to make graham gems. She told me to use graham flour, not white flour, in the gems.

Even though Mom keeps white flour in the left side of her kitchen cabinet, she much prefers to use whole grains. When she fills the bin, she pours a fifty-pound bag of flour into the top of the container. Underneath is the sifter she uses to sift the flour as she removes it from the storage bin above. Mother says it is healthier to use whole grain flours, but they do not keep as well as white flour. The whole grains have the germ and bran still in them. The germ contains the oil in the grain, and with its removal, the grain will keep longer.

While we work together in the kitchen, Mom teaches me, "The bran is roughage for the body to sweep the colon clean and leave it healthy. A healthy colon makes for a healthy body. When pure white flour became the desired flour to bake with, Mr. Graham promoted the use of his graham flour, a less-processed wheat flour, for health reasons."

At suppertime, everyone enjoyed the good-tasting graham gems. They are so much more flavorful than white biscuits. The hot soup was a welcome meal on the cold night with the blizzard still going on outside.

After supper, I reread some of Mark's letters. I wrote him a lengthy letter, telling him about Mrs. Olson's fall outside in freezing weather and John following the fence line home in the blizzard last night.

Wednesday the sun was trying to peek through. The wind had diminished. There were only a few snowflakes now and then. The blizzard had drained itself out.

Dad told John that they would have to try to pull his car home with the tractor. Dad does not want the snowplow to come with John's car in the roadway. Because our house is the only one on the end of our road, the snowplow plows other roads with more houses before plowing ours.

Right after finishing milking and barnyard chores, Dad and John took the John Deere tractor and a log chain to pull John's car home. I feel for John. He is so upset that he cannot let Betty know that he is okay.

One thing for sure, with being snowed in, Mom and I kept the family happy with good homemade tasty food. For dessert after supper tonight, I made a jelly roll. I like making jelly rolls. They are easy to mix and quick to bake, but it is a bit tricky tipping the large hotcake unto a towel sprinkled with powdered sugar. Then one swiftly spreads strawberry jam on the surface, rolls the cake several times before it cools very much, and wraps it in the towel to cool. When I sliced it, the rolled cake with the spirals of red jam inside looked nice, and oh, was it good to eat with the powdered sugar on each piece.

I will have three letters to mail to Mark when we are plowed out. *Maybe tomorrow the snowplow will come through on our road. Hopefully in the mailbox will be mail from Mark.*

17

Wintertime Problems—Winter into Spring 1945

The snowplow did not come on Thursday. I spent the day writing Mom's pickle recipes in my recipe book. I wrote recipes for making all kinds of pickles: dill, 14-day sweet, chunk, bread and butter, beet, green tomato, and mustard pickles using green beans, cauliflower, carrots, small cucumbers, and onions. I also copied to my pickle recipes peach, apple, watermelon, and turmeric pickles.

If our phone was working, we would not feel so isolated from other people. I wish I could call over to Sara's and talk to Anna who graduated with me from the Normal Training Class. She is now teaching in the brick school and lives with Sara, so she is close to the school.

With Melanie gone to nursing school and John seeing Betty, I need to be a friend with Anna. She and I are both teachers so we have much to talk about when we are together. Besides, I think she gets lonesome for the company of her peers while staying with elderly Sara, dear soul that she is. Anna just needs someone her own age to talk with. When the roads are passable again, I will invite her over for a meal and a good visit.

Friday still no snowplow has come to plow us out. Today I copy mom's cake recipes to my recipe book. I penned cake recipes for chocolate, yellow, white, sponge, marble, sugar, sour cream, burnt sugar, spice, gingerbread, and angel food.

Later I will add cookie, pie, pudding, and doughnut recipes. In the front of my recipe book, I already have meat, vegetable, salad, soup, casserole, and sauce recipes.

Friday afternoon the snowplow comes through. The plow barely can push the snow aside, making high snowbanks on either side in the area where John got stuck. The snowbanks are higher than a car and the path between just enough room for a car to pass through.

As soon as the road was plowed out, John left for town. He planned to take some of his written work to the college and go to see Betty.

Dad and Mom left to go to get more groceries in case we might get more bad weather. Marian asked Janie, Mark's sister, to come over to go sledding. I worked on my recipes but felt anxious for Dad and Mom to come home with the mail. *I hope there will be a letter or letters from Mark.*

When Marian and Janie came in to get warm, I made them hot cocoa with marshmallows on top. I enjoyed the hot cocoa with them and fresh homemade oatmeal raisin cookies that Mom had baked earlier today.

As soon as John could get to a phone, he called Betty.

"Betty, I could not call sooner. Our phone was not working."

"Oh! John, you don't know how good it is to hear your voice. I worried so about if you made it home."

"Betty, what time do you get off work?"

"John, I have to work an hour longer today because of having several days off because of the storm. I will be off at six." So, the two made plans to eat at Betty's and have time for catching up on the happenings of the last five days.

After they ate and did the cleaning up in the kitchen, Betty and John went down to the Eat Shop for a hot cocoa and whipped cream and to have time to talk. Betty relayed to John what her mother told her on Monday.

"Betty, that is surprising good news. I am relieved that your mother is not going to come between you and me. But what about the church we will go to some day? That is another hurdle for us to cross. But tonight, let's be glad all is going as well as it is."

When Mom and Dad arrived home, Mom gave me three letters from Mark that were in the mailbox. I stacked the letters, so I would read each one in the order that they were written. Mark wrote that his unit had come through some dangerous fighting made almost intolerable by harsh weather conditions and the rugged countryside. He wrote optimistically that he felt the Allies were finally making progress.

He ended the last letter:

> Julia,
>
> This war cannot end too soon. To celebrate, I want to lift you up in my arms and twirl you around. Then I will give you a big hug, kiss you, and kiss you some more. Hope the day the war ends comes soon. Julia, I will always love you. Good night, my sweetie.
>
> With my deepest love,
> Mark

My stack of letters from Mark is now thick. It has been so many months since I last saw him. *How much have we changed? Will I still seem like the same girl to him? Will he be the Mark that left, or will he be like a stranger to me? When Mark left, he was barely out of his teens, and he will come home a man.*

His letters sound like the same Mark. I must continue believing that he is the same kindhearted, friendly, loving, and trustworthy Mark I used to know.

On the next Friday, the roads were drivable again. I called Anna to ask her if she would like to come to my classroom after school for a visit.

I knew she was delighted to get the invitation. We discussed teaching methods, behavior problems, and other instructional matters.

Anna shared with me her thoughts about the years ahead. She didn't want to be a teacher all her life. Anna liked teaching but would like to have a boyfriend, someday marry and have a family. With living with Sara during the school week and going to her home in Bluffton on the weekends, she did not have much opportunity to meet other young people.

I could understand that her desires were strong. She was frustrated because she did not see any way to change her life. I would like to help her. If she went to a dance, she might meet a young man to go out with. But I do not have any interest in going to a dance without Mark, so dances were not an option, at least for me.

I asked her if she knew anyone that she was interested in. She shook her head no.

"Maybe Sara would let you have a sledding party on the big hill near her farm. You could make hot cocoa and serve cookies afterward."

"Julia, that's a good idea. I could invite some of my friends from our high school days. They could bring their own sleds or toboggans. Maybe I could invite some from the Bluffton area also. I will ask Sara if I could use her kitchen for a while when I invite everyone to come in for a break and to warm up."

"Anna, I think Sara would enjoy having the young people come. I am sure she will give her approval."

Later I learned from Anna that she had the sledding party on a Sunday afternoon, and eight young ladies and ten young men came to the party. Only four out of the group were still in high school. The older guys who came were ones who were not drafted into the military for health reasons, or they were needed on the farm. Most of the young ladies were working gals in town.

"Julia, thank you for suggesting I have the sledding party. I think Sara delighted in having so many young people around. I have been asked to go to several parties and out to the movies. Thank you for helping me renew old friendships and make new ones."

It made me feel good to see Anna excited about her life. Anna is a bit shy; she just needed some encouragement to step out and enjoy her life. Helping someone else certainly can make a person feel good.

My students are all going over to Sara's hill to slide during the noon hour. Sometimes I give them a longer time to slide because they are having such a good time being outside in the clean cool air.

Days when it is stormy and very cold, they must stay indoors. Then they use white chalk on the blackboards to play tic- tac-toe, draw, or play a guessing game. Sometimes we play fruit basket upset or musical chairs. Another game they like to play is the squirrel-and-nut game where the students lay their heads on their desks, shut their eyes, and stick out their hands. One player without a desk to sit in goes around the desks and drops a small thing in someone's hand. That person must give up his seat and run around the desks trying to beat the one dropping the item back to the empty seat. The one not getting the seat is the one to drop the object in the next go around.

Marian loves to play hopscotch. The numbered squares for the game are drawn on the dark wood floor with white chalk.

Today was warmer with bright sunshine. The students pulled their sleds to Sara's hill to slide. Dan Swartz liked to ditch sleds as they came down the hill. He especially got a kick out of ditching Marian's sled. I tried to watch him and make him quit doing it. Well, he ditched Marian one time too many.

The next thing I knew, Marian was screaming and crying for help. Her sled was in the snowbank. I rushed to her side. Marian's right wrist was wedged between the steering bar and the metal front of the sled. I helped her remove her hand. Her face looked white, and she was squinting her eyes. She was trying not to reveal the pain she was feeling. She did not want to get her classmate in trouble or be in trouble herself.

I told Billy to bring all the students back to the schoolhouse. I took Marian and Dan with me directly back to the classroom. I called Mom and told her, "Mom, I think Marian's wrist is broken."

She calmly said, "Julia, your dad just finished eating dinner. We will be there as soon as we can. If she is still hurting, we will take Marian to Dr. Koontz."

Next. I called Mrs. Swartz, Dan's mother, and told her what had happened. She said she was sorry that Dan's prank caused Marian to get hurt. She assured me that she would talk to Dan when he gets home after school is out.

The rest of the afternoon, all the students were very well behaved and quieter than normal. Some of them told me that they felt bad that Marian got hurt. I think it scared them that something can go wrong so quickly.

After the afternoon recess, I asked, "Would anyone like to make a get-well card for Marian?" Soon they were busy making construction paper cards for my sister. It gave them an outlet for their concern over the accident.

Marian came home with her right arm and hand in a cast up to her elbow. She was in quite a bit of pain and went to bed. Mom took supper up to her.

Mom told me later, "I think Marian is quite upset and not just about the pain. She feels bad that her good friend is in trouble for causing her to break her arm."

Later in the evening, Mrs. Swartz called Mom. She apologized for Dan's improper behavior. Mr. Swartz evidently gave Dan a whopper of a talking to about his misdeed.

"John, how is Betty's mother doing?"

He answered, "Betty's father hired an older lady to come in every weekday to help Mrs. Olson. That frees Betty to continue with her job at the telephone company."

"Well, sometime when she is feeling better and can easily walk again, I would like to invite her, Mr. Olson, and Betty to come out for a meal."

"That would be real nice, Mom. It would be good for both families to get to know each other better, but it will have to wait until I get home from the Vet's Hospital. I will be taking my class work with me again on this visit."

"I hope and pray this will be the last surgery you will have to have. I am thankful the surgeons could save your leg and that you can walk on it."

John came to the schoolhouse to take me home. He came in and asked if I had time to talk with him. Of course, I told him I had time right now.

"Julia, I don't see how Betty and I can get married very soon. Mrs. Olson will need Betty's help for some time until she can walk on her own again. I have my leg surgery coming up soon. I am going to college, so I do not have a job to support a wife. Dad needs help on the farm until Bobby comes home again. Sometimes I just don't know how to figure this all out. I am a man, the one who should provide for his wife and protect her in our home. How can I when I do not have a job?"

"Wait a minute, one thing at a time. I know you want to marry Betty. You want to get a college education so that you can make a better living for yourself and future family. Remember, dear brother, anything worthwhile takes time and effort to achieve.

"Betty has a good job now and lives at home, so she probably is saving for her future home. That's what I am doing, and I think she is too.

"The upcoming surgery will most likely be the last one on your leg. In a few months, you will have one year of college behind you. With the Allied forces pushing the Axis armies like the news is declaring, maybe this terrible war will be over soon. Maybe in another year or so, Bobby will be coming home from service. I know that he wants to farm and will work with Father.

"Now you cannot go to summer school because of helping Dad in the summertime. But if Bobby comes home in another year, you could go to summer school and finish college in three years instead of four."

"Julia, that is a good idea. In May, I will have one year behind me. Looks like the biggest obstacle will be next year. Do Betty and I want to go on as we are now, or do we want to marry and somehow get through the next academic year together?"

"John, you and Betty have to make that decision. With either decision, you will have sacrifices and struggles, but you have to decide which one you will both be most happy and comfortable with."

"Thanks, sis. You helped me see my situation more clearly. It reminds me of in the Bible where it says, 'We see through a glass, darkly' (1 Corinthians 13:12, KJV). We do not always see things clearly. Guess too often we see the problems and not the solutions."

Dear brother, I pray that you will work out your problems in planning how to make a good living for you and Betty. I know it is so dear to a man's heart to provide well for his wife and children. I feel that Mark will have the same inherently deep desire to ensure a good life for his future family.

18

Turn of Events

This year Lent started on Valentine's Day. The family went to early morning mass on Ash Wednesday. Each person at mass went up to the altar railing to have the priest mark the sign of a cross with ashes on their forehead while he said, "Remember 'Dust thou art, and into dust thou shalt return'" (Genesis 3:19, Douay).

After mass, Mom bought fresh still-warm rolls from the bakery, so Marian and I would have something to eat before we went to school. As we are not to remove the ashes from our forehead, Marian and I went to school with the ashes plainly visible on our foreheads.

One of the younger children said, "Miss Sturloff, your forehead is dirty."

An older student asked, "What is that on your forehead and on Marian's forehead too?"

I simply told then that we had been to church this morning and the priest put the ashes there. I did not want to tell them the meaning was to remind us that we are mortal beings because it might disturb them. I instructed them to get busy with their work, and no more was said about the black smudges on the brow of either one of us.

It was a pleasant surprise being today is Valentine's Day that I discovered three letters from Mark waiting for me in the mailbox.

Dearest Julia,

Happy Valentine's Day! You are my sweet valentine. I want to make you my lovable valentine forever. Next year, I will be home for Valentine's Day. We are pushing our way through to defeat the enemy on their soil. The war hopefully will be over soon. I cannot wait to get back home. We will make up for the years we have been separated.

I will be happy to sleep in a real bed, have not had that pleasure for almost three years. Living on the move is not like living in luxury at the Ritz.

At this time, the local people are welcoming us as their saviors and are helping us to purge the country of their foreign enemies.

Faithfully yours,
Mark

On the evening of Valentine's Day, John takes Betty out to a nice restaurant in Decorah. He pulls out her chair for her and helps her get seated. Betty mentions how much she enjoys the white tablecloth and being waited on. Just before their dessert comes, John takes Betty's hand.

"Betty, I love you. I cannot live without you in my life." He looks her in the eye and lightly squeezes her hand. "Betty, it would make me happy if you would be my helpmate, my wife forever. I love you."

Betty feels the tears rising as if from bubblers in her eyes. Through her glistening eyes, she looks lovingly at John and softly answers, "John, yes. Yes, I do so want to be your wife."

John gets up and lifts her up. He gives her a big hug and kiss. Then he grasps her hand and holds it while he slips a sparkling diamond on her finger.

Betty feels dazzled by the ring's brilliance and tells John how lovely it is. She excitedly asserts, "John, the diamond ring's brilliance is like sunshine bouncing off snow crystals. I never dreamed I would wear such a gorgeous ring. Thank you for the best Valentine's gift ever."

Over their dessert, they give loving smiles to each other like a couple of lovestruck teenagers. They feel completely immersed in their world of love.

"Betty, in a week I want to remind you I have to go back to the Vet's Hospital to have, hopefully, my last skin graft and repair done on my leg. When I come back, we will have time to make plans for our future."

At home for dessert at the evening meal, Mom had made an angel food cake on which she put red raspberries and whipped cream. The raspberries we picked last summer, put in waxed boxes and froze in the town locker box. Last Saturday, Dad had brought some raspberries home, and we kept them in the metal box in the snow to keep cold until we thawed them for today.

Later in my bed, when I pulled the thick quilt around me, I was thinking of Mark. *Where is he tonight? Is he warm? He wrote "faithfully yours" at the end of his letter. He must consider me his one and only. Dear God, I pray that we have not grown apart in all these months. He has experienced the horrors of war, and I have continued living in the shelter of my parental home. How different our lives have been in this time of separation. Will Mark have changed so much that we can never take up where we left off with each other?*

It seemed impossible to shut down my mind. Marian was sleeping so soundly my restlessness did not seem to bother her.

Tonight, Dad informs us that the Allies in the Pacific theater have taken Manila, and American Marines have landed on Iwo Jima. With military persistent effort, many Pacific islands are being taken from Japanese occupation.

Mother sighed, "That is good news. Hopefully, Bobby is safe

wherever he is. It is bad enough that John was shot and will have a bad leg the rest of his life."

"My heart goes out to the mothers who have lost a loved one in this war. How can one know the grief and sorrow of the Waterloo, Iowa, mother of the five sons who went down with their battleship?"

Dad gave additional details. "Since D-Day in 1944, the British and American forces have pushed hard to liberate European countries from the Nazis. The Russian military have hammered Germany from the East. The Allies are approaching from the South through Italy to pressure Germany toward defeat. The end of the war in Europe has to be in sight."

In late March, Dad prepared his simple greenhouse to raise plants from seeds to later transplant to the early small garden and the large garden in a corner of the corn field. He dug two holes in the lawn about a foot deep and almost the width and length of old storm windows that he placed over the top of the freshly dug planting area. The windows allow light to come through for the young plants. The glass protects the fragile young plants from the cold weather.

Dad and I planted cabbage, tomato, and pepper seeds in the ground. I planted petunia and marigold flower seeds. When the weather becomes warmer and the plants are developed enough to transplant, we will set them out in the garden.

Digging in the soil and watching plants grow is so refreshing to the spirit. From creation, God gave us a garden and told man to dress it and keep it. No wonder that people believe farming is the best occupation. I know that my Dad believes he has the most fulfilling job on earth.

Mark's letters are so full of hope for the end to come soon. He wrote, "The enemy had dug in for the long haul, now they do not want to give up the fight. Hitler's visualization of a strong indestructible nation was deeply embedded in the minds of his soldiers. Now it seems almost impossible for them to face the undeniable truth that they are defeated, so they fight on more fiercely than ever. But the truth is we are out maneuvering them with greater military strength and supplies.

"Victory is in the air…I can feel it. Darling, I will soon be able to come home. All these months of not being able to see you and talk to you have been like the worst nightmares a man could have. Dearest Julia, I believe our faith has carried us through this traumatic time in our lives. At night, going to sleep, hearing the weapons firing in the distance, I pray to God to keep me safe throughout the night. All my thoughts are focused on returning home to you.

"In the future, I pray that God will richly bless us for our fortitude in these trying times. Julia, we have better years coming. I want us to have a happy, fulfilling life together. Dear one, I want to make you happy. I will be *forever faithful* to you, my dearest darling."

This wonderful letter is the most endearing one I ever received. Mark will be coming home soon. He has promised his faithfulness to me forever. That promise is a priceless gift of love.

I read and reread the letter. I will keep it forever.

Today John came home from the Vet's Hospital. After the students left my classroom, he came in to talk to me. He pulled up his pant leg to show me where the skin graft was put on his lower leg. He told me that his upper leg was raw and red from where the skin graft was taken. He had been given physical therapy for the past several weeks. John was in a good mood and anxious to see Betty as soon as she would get off work at the telephone company.

"Julia, I intend to talk to Betty tonight about whether to plan to marry soon or wait until I have more education hours behind me. As the government is helping me get this education, I would be foolish not to take advantage of it. Do you agree with that?"

"John, yes, I think that you are right in wanting to get your college education. You know what our dad would say about your decision."

Julia went on to explain, "Dad always says that one can only know real happiness when a person accepts life's bumps. Everyone has ups and downs in this world. We must learn to patiently endure the bumpy parts of life. With the right frame of mind, we can be happily walking the road of life whether that road is smooth going or rough going."

"Yah, you are right, but doing it is another thing. I don't know what Betty's parents are thinking about losing their only child to marriage. I feel that she will want to live close to them. They are good people. Betty's dad is a kindhearted man and is generous in his love and wealth to her. Will I be able to support her in the style that she is used to?"

"John, don't put roadblocks in front of you. You are a good person yourself. You are working to get a college education, so you can provide a better life for yourself and a future family. Betty is an only child, but I am sure whom she wants for her husband will weigh heavy in the thinking of her parents. You will see…it will all work out okay."

"Thanks, sis. I appreciate your thoughts on this. By the way, I wrote to Mark before I went to the hospital and told him to write to me there. He wrote that the going has been really hard through the mountains. I had dangerous fighting in France, but at least I wasn't there long. Mark has been in the thick of it in Italy for several years. I pray that he comes safely home soon."

"John, I pray for him every day and for Bobby too. Dad thinks the end of the war is in sight, even in the Pacific, and I pray that he is right."

Easter Sunday 1945

This year I bought a new $6.07 hat for Easter, a new coat for $17.29, and a pair of dress shoes for $3.06. My purchases took $26.42 out of my $100-a-month teacher's salary, but I felt well- dressed to go to mass on Easter Sunday.

John brought Betty to the early mass. Betty looked so cute in her perky navy hat with a crisp veil and a white flower attached to the hat's band. She wore a petite-sized navy suit, carried a small navy leather pocketbook, and wore cross-strap wedges. Don't think that I ever saw John look so happy as he escorted her to the pew where our family sits.

When the family got up to go to Communion, Betty stayed sitting in the pew. I hope she enjoyed the beautiful organ music and singing coming from up high in the rear of the church.

After mass, I saw Melanie was home for Easter from nurses' training. I was so happy to see her and realized how much I have missed her. I gave her a big hug. "Melanie, how about getting together this afternoon for some music like old times?"

Melanie looked as glad to see me as I was to see her. She answered, "I would love to bring my clarinet."

We talked to John and Betty, and we planned a fun afternoon. Mom told Melanie to bring her family. Mother and I prepared a roast leg of lamb and all the side dishes to make a superb Easter meal for our family. We missed having Bobby at our Easter celebration, but we welcomed Betty as one of the family. Betty and John are invited to her mother's for Easter in the evening.

That afternoon, John played his cornet, Melanie her clarinet; Betty played an alto saxophone, Jimmy his clarinet, and I played the piano. In the last couple years, there have been so many great songs. Today one of our favorites was "When the Lights Go On Again." I especially liked the lyrics about the boys coming home.

While listening to the radio on April 12, Dad was shocked to learn that President Franklin D. Roosevelt, only three months into his fourth term, died that day. The president died from a stroke while on vacation in Georgia. The vice president, Harry S. Truman, would now be the president of the United States.

Dad was soon to learn that would not be the only April death of a major leader in World War II. On April 30, my father was stunned to hear that Adolph Hitler, the fuehrer of Germany's Third Reich, committed suicide in his own highly structured bomb shelter by shooting himself in the mouth.

I found it interesting from a woman's point of view that Eva Braun, Hitler's mistress, finally got her wish to marry Hitler. On April 29, the day before their deaths, Eva and Adolph were married. Later in their wedding day, Hitler found out that disgruntled one-time followers of

Mussolini had him put to death along with his companion Clara Petacci. Hitler resolved to kill himself rather than be taken alive. Cyanide, a deadly, rapidly acting chemical, ended Eva's life.

Tonight, after the students left, I straightened up my desk. Just before school was out, Billy had sprinkled oily sawdust on the floor. I took a wide broom and swept up the dirt caught in the oily sawdust. Just before I was getting ready to lock up the schoolhouse, John stopped to talk with me.

"Julia, I have some good news." His face glowed with his excitement. "Betty's father had a long talk with me early Tuesday evening. Betty and her mom had gone to a baby shower. We sat in the Olson living room. Mr. Olson started by telling me how much his daughter meant to his wife and himself."

John went on to try to relate exactly what Mr. Olson told him. "Julia, Mr. Olson told me that I must have had a very good Christian upbringing to have the moral values and work ethic that I possess. He said that he and his wife are very pleased that their daughter has chosen me for her future husband. He explained that he and Mrs. Olson feel Betty could not have done better. He declared that they have learned to think very highly of me."

"That's great news, John," I exclaimed. "I have always known you are one great guy."

John continued to speak, "Mr. Olson said being Betty is their only child, he wants to help her as much as he can. He feels that I have a good sense of business. He is pleased that I am going to college to better myself.

"Julia, he revealed that he and his wife intend to make me a partner in their insurance business. He feels that way he can ensure a good life for his daughter and her husband.

"Furthermore, he claims he needs someone in the office that is knowledgeable about farming. He was raised in town and believes I would be the ideal person to handle his insurance business relating to the needs of farmers. Julia, he intends to hand over the agriculture-related insurance to me."

"John, how can you handle going to college, working in the insurance agency, and working for Dad?" questioned Julia.

"Julia that is some more great news. Dad and I talked this over. He feels that Mr. Olson's offer cannot be turned down. Dad said it is an extraordinary opportunity for me. After Dad thought for a while, he assured me that he will get by until Bobby comes home. He said, 'I know that your younger brother wants to farm. I will hire help if I need extra help during planting and harvesting until Bobby returns home.'"

"What does Betty say about all this?"

"Betty knows that I want to get into business. She is thrilled that her father would give us this chance to better ourselves."

I looked at John. "Do you and Betty expect to marry soon?"

"We have discussed getting married. She and her parents need time to prepare for the wedding. Betty is thinking we could get married during my college Easter vacation. She suggested the Saturday after Easter.

"I plan to start working for her father right away in the insurance office. I will go to college in the morning and work in the office in the afternoon. I will carry a lighter load at college for a while as I will need to take some insurance training also. Later, to catch up on college work, I will go to summer school next year. If that isn't enough, Betty's father has offered to buy a two-story brick family home located near them. Betty dearly loves her parents and I am sure would enjoy being close to them. If Betty and I give our approval, Mr. Olson is going to go ahead with purchasing the house. He will outright give a half share to Betty. When I graduate from college and can afford to make monthly payments, I will pay back the loan for my share of the property. In the meantime, we will not have rent or a property loan to pay. Betty wants to stay working as long as she can at the telephone office to help with expenses. In the beginning, my salary at the office might be small until I learn the business and can build a clientele."

"I am happy for you. Sounds like you and Betty are getting your life together well planned. When are you and Betty going to look at the house?"

"We are scheduled to look at it Saturday afternoon. The owners are close neighbors of Mr. Olson and have privately offered the sale of the home to Mr. Olson. They are older people and plan to move to a smaller home."

"I hope things work out this smoothly for Mark and me when he comes home from service."

"When do you think he will be coming home?"

"He should have been up for discharge before this, but with the big push and need for every soldier to end the war, he could not be sent home. It sounds like the government doesn't want to just send the soldiers home even when the war is over. The officials want to make sure there are no dissensions in occupied lands by keeping the military there."

"But surely he will come home sooner than some as he has been overseas for so long," objected John.

"Let's hope you are right. He has been gone far too long." In my mind, thoughts were whirling like a tornado sucking up anxious thinking. *Will I know him? How much will he have changed? Mark went in just out of his teen years and will come home a mature man. Will we feel comfortable together like old times?*

John seemed to sense my uneasiness. He tried to reassure me that Mark will come home just the same Mark we have always known.

I will always remember what I was doing on May 7, 1945, the rest of my life. I was dusting the furniture in the dining room. Next to the large oak divan with leather back and seat is my dad's large radio. The radio was on. Suddenly the news blared over the radio that Germany had surrendered. The radio broadcaster described the people exuberantly celebrating VE Day.

Victory in Europe means the war in Europe is finished. Now Mark can come home. Mother came in to listen to the welcome news. She said, "Go to the machine shed and tell your father."

Dad was working on his corn planter. Every year, he wires it together so it will plant corn yet another year. When I gushed forth with the news, he took off his cap and wiped his brow. "Julia, maybe soon Bobby and Mark will be coming home. This dreadful war in Europe is finally over. The end for the Pacific war cannot be very far away. With both Germany and Italy defeated, how can Japan continue to fight?"

Today I made a rhubarb custard pie. The red stalks of rhubarb are sharp-tasting, but with the eggs, sugar, and homemade pie crust made with lard and flour, it is a very tasty pie. This recipe I added to my recipe book.

"Julia, the rhubarb is like a spring boost to the system. It just seems so good to have something fresh from the earth to eat. Before the weather gets hot and the rhubarb won't be so good anymore, we will make rhubarb cobbler, rhubarb crisp, and rhubarb sauce."

"Mom, we will soon have lettuce, radishes, and green onions from our early garden. Dad and I are planning to set out the plants from Dad's homemade greenhouse tomorrow.

Then this summer, we will have plenty of fresh vegetables to eat. I can't wait until the early potatoes Dad and I planted and the early peas are ready to eat. Nothing tastes so good as new potatoes topped with creamed freshly picked green peas from the garden."

Every so often, Dad and Mom went to Cresco to the REA to see about getting electricity to our property. Late in May, the REA dug in tall posts and hung wires to bring the electricity across the fields to the farm buildings. Dad purchased for $12.70 from the REA a tall pole. It was dug deeply into the ground near the house for the electrical wires to attach to it. On that post, Dad had an electrician place a yard light. Earlier in the spring, Dad had hired a man to wire the house, barns, hog house, and chicken house. He wanted to have the wiring done so when the REA wires reached our property, we could turn on the lights and power right away.

I will never forget the trouble the electrician had to wire the house.

The original house had log walls a log's width thick. Those are thick walls. To get the wires through, he had some tough drilling to do.

Mom and I were thrilled to think that soon we could cook with an electric stove and have an electric refrigerator to keep our food in. The day Dad took out the old cook stove in which we had burned wood for heat was a big event to us. No longer would we have to keep plenty of wood in the stove to have a fire hot enough to cook with or to heat the oven to bake.

The white electric stove with its four electric coil burners and large oven even with a light in it seemed just too good to be real. Dad put new linoleum in before he brought the stove and refrigerator into the house. Under the old stove, the floor was worn and needed new covering.

"Julia, isn't this simple? One just turns a knob, and the heat is there to cook with. No longer do we have to get wood to build a fire to make a meal."

"Mom, I like having the refrigerator so handy. I do not have to go to the cellar for butter, milk, or eggs. These appliances will make our life so much easier in the kitchen."

Mother sighed. "To think we had to wait so long to get electricity when people in town had their homes wired years ago. The war caused us lots of problems."

Cooking on the stove seemed so pleasant. The stove even had a deep well. One could put food in the well and cook it for a long time with low heat without having to watch it closely.

I think what I appreciated the most was having electric lights to read by. At night, I could sit up in bed and read without worrying about falling asleep, knocking the kerosene lamp over, and starting a fire.

No, on second thought, the best is having a bathroom in the house. This month Marian's small room, which used to be her playroom and in recent years her bedroom, is transformed into a bathroom. There is a shiny white bathtub, a stool, and sink with a cabinet above it. Storage cabinets for towels and bedding line one wall.

It seems like pure luxury to run hot water and just relax in a tub where I can stretch out my legs. The round metal washtub I used to bathe in did not have much room for the body to move.

But now I must share my room and standing metal clothes closet with Marian. *Maybe I will not have to share a room with her for long after Mark comes home.*

Mother is like a kid over the joy of having electricity. She exclaimed, "Sam, our first REA bill is $6.90. The service that money buys brings such happiness to me. Really, Sam, it is almost like it has immeasurable value."

"Lettie, I know how you feel. My new milking machine cost $351.90 and is well worth every penny to me. I do not have to milk all my cows by hand anymore."

Dad bought a combine for $475 to harvest his oats. Now that the war is close to being over he thought it was good to be able to buy farm machinery again. No longer would he have to hire someone to combine for him.

My recent letters to Mark are full of telling him how much better our life is now with electricity. Seems like I just cannot express well enough what difference electricity has made for my family. It seems like magic when lights fill every corner of a room full of brightness. Electric lights are so much brighter than the orange glow of light from a kerosene lamp.

19

Hiroshima – Summer 1945

Today at mass, Father Dolan in his Irish brogue announced that Confirmation was scheduled for the first Sunday in August. He told that there would be two weeks of summer classes at the Catholic school for all those expecting to be confirmed. For three months of Sundays after mass, Marian had been taking instructions for Confirmation. Now Father Dolan announced that country young people expecting to be confirmed could stay with the nuns for two weeks to finalize their preparation for confirmation.

On the way home from mass, Dad told Marian she would have to stay with the nuns as he was too busy in the fields to take her every day to the confirmation classes at St. Benedict's Catholic School.

I looked over at Marian and saw her wince as if she was in pain. "Dad, do I have to stay with the nuns? Sister Mary Ann and the other nuns wear those long black dresses with the stiff white collars and black head coverings so one cannot see if they have hair. They are so strict I don't think I can stay with them."

"Dear, it is only for two weeks, and you will be home every Saturday and Sunday. Besides gas is still being rationed, and we cannot use our stamps to take and get you every day. Janie is in the confirmation class and will most likely be staying with the nuns so you will have a friend."

Mrs. McDonald drove Marian and Janie to St. Benedict's Catholic School on Monday morning. Dad was to pick them up on Friday about four in the afternoon.

I was with Dad when he and Mom picked up the girls to take them home after their classes on Friday. They had so much to tell us. At night they had slept in the convent next door to the school. Sister Mary Agnes was a good cook, and they liked the food that she prepared for them.

"Mom, they made us say the Rosary followed by Hail Holy Queen every evening, and then they said the Litany of the Blessed Virgin or some other litany. After that each one would say some prayer such as for the sick, suffering, and for faith," reported Marian.

"We had to go to bed early and get up early in the morning to go to mass in the chapel at the school. We sure did a lot of praying," added Janie.

"What did you learn about your faith?" asked Mom.

"This winter we did lessons in the Baltimore Catechism, and now we are trying to finish it. Sister Mary Ann says we have to really know our catechism because the bishop will ask us questions, and we just better know the answer."

Dad asked, "Did you have any time for yourself?"

"After supper, we had about an hour to walk or play outside. When we walked, we tried not to step on the crack between the cement sidewalks. If someone stepped on the crack, someone would shout, "Step on the crack and break your mother's back," recounted Janie.

On Sunday, the fifth of August, Marian was confirmed. She looked like a little bride in her white dress and long lace-edged net veil hanging to her waist. The day before, Mother had taken her to the photographer's shop to have her picture taken in her white confirmation dress, white shoes and long white stockings, and holding her white prayer book.

Today all the young people making their confirmation sat in the front pews. The girls were on the left side with the statue of the Blessed Virgin in front of them on the side altar and the boys on the right side with the statue of St. Joseph in front of them on that side altar. The sponsors for each class member sat in the pew directly behind the person they were sponsor for. As Marian's sponsor, I sat directly behind her.

The bishop came down off the altar to walk in front of the pews where the boys and girls solemnly sat waiting for his questions. He asked them questions from the Baltimore Catechism.

Bishop O'Brien asked, "Who is God?"

The confirmation class, in unison, answered, "God is the creator of heaven and earth, and of all things."

"Why did God make you?"

Again, the class confidently answered, "God made me to know him, to love him, and to serve him in this world, and to be happy with him forever in the next."

Well, it started out easy enough, but then Bishop O'Brien started asking more difficult questions from the catechism, and the parishioners could feel the tension as the young people became terrified of being called on to give the answer. What a relief when the bishop at last returned to the altar for the finalizing of the Sacrament of Confirmation.

When it came time to be confirmed, the girls went first to line up along the communion rail. Then their sponsors followed to stand directly behind them, and each one placed a hand on the shoulder of the person they were sponsor for.

It felt good to be a sponsor, and I knew it carried spiritual responsibilities. As the sponsor for Marian, I was to see that she followed the faith she was confirmed into today.

The bishop in his gold-trimmed vestments, tall miter on his head, and carrying a decorated staff in his hand came along the railing. Marian told afterward, "I placed my card with my confirmation name, Anastasia, patron saint of healing, on the communion rail. The attending priest read my name, Marian Louise Anastasia Sturloff.

"Bishop O'Brien put the sign of the cross on my forehead with the holy oil and said, 'I sign with the sign of the cross and confirm thee with the chrism of salvation in the name of the Father and of the Son and of the Holy Ghost.' While I was thinking of what he just told me, he quickly slapped my cheek and told me, 'Be a soldier for the Lord Jesus Christ.'"

Standing as close as I was to Marian, I heard the smack she received from the bishop. I doubt if she will ever forget that she is a soldier on this earth for her faith. Like the saints of old, she is to uphold her loyalty in day-to-day life. In times of danger to her religious teachings, she is to stand strong for her faith.

Mother had invited the McDonald family, Uncle Roy's family, and Sara to our house to celebrate Marian's Confirmation. Dear Sara gave her a gold cross and chain, Uncle Roy's family gave her a cross for the wall, and the McDonalds' gift was a statue of the Blessed Virgin Mary.

The next day, August 6, 1945, international news rocked the world with the news of a single B-29 airplane dropping an atomic bomb on Hiroshima in Japan. News reports were sketchy about how many men, women, and children were killed or unaccounted for in a single explosion. Early reports were that thousands died in the horrific explosion and many more thousands would die later of horrendous burnings on their bodies, maybe as many as 90,000.

Only three days later, the world was stunned to learn that another atomic bomb fell on Nagasaki. The Japanese agreed to surrender, and on September 2, VJ Day (Victory in Japan Day), the surrender was formally finalized.

General MacArthur took command of the occupation of Japan. He felt the country needed ethical principles and religious knowledge. He penned, "The more missionaries we can bring out here [to Japan], and the more occupation troops we can send home, the better."[2]

Mother's opinion was, "I am relieved to think a good Christian man is helping to restore the Japanese people to some degree of normality.

"War on both sides seems so heartless. Men work diligently for days, even years, to build and then blow to pieces in seconds what they have created. But to take another's life—that is hard to understand. Why would a man snuff out another man's breath like blowing out a

[2] America Land I Love, in Christian Perspective, A Beka Book, © 1994, Pensacola Christian College, pages 438-439.

candle? But there's a great difference—a candle can be relit, but the breath of man is gone forever."

Tonight, after I knelt and said my nightly prayers, I wrote the following in my journal. My words are an attempt to recapture my feelings as I reviewed the days of the war up to the climactic surrender of the Axis forces. Maybe someday my children, grandchildren, and great grandchildren will realize our tremendous efforts to preserve the great American liberties and freedoms for them guaranteed to us in the Declaration of Independence and the Constitution.

Above all, our liberties are God-given, and the Bible is the source of our rights and obligations. Religious liberty is the foundation of our nation. Not only in World War II but throughout our American history, men have given their lives to protect our freedom to read our Bibles and worship God.

In my journal, I wrote:

This Day's End

> My room is almost dark; I am kneeling on the linoleum- covered floor at the side of my iron bed. My head is in my hands; they lie on the chenille bedspread covering my iron bed. I have just finished saying my daily prayers including the Our Father. The words, "Forgive us our trespasses as we forgive those who trespass against us" never had more meaning than they do tonight.
>
> "Oh Lord, how can you forgive us?"
>
> Memories like a flashflood swirl through my mind. I see thousands and thousands of daring young men, the best our country has to offer; the ones most blessed with body strength and intelligence innocently offering their lives to protect mine.

Youth drilled through demanding training to fight other men. Just young people---but taught to kill.

Some are flying aces with their girlfriends' pictures on the sides of their planes. Others are drab-green-garbed doughboys in heavy boots with their canteens hanging on their side, trudging through muddy rivers and over mountainous terrains. Some with perky sailor hats and white uniforms are manning battleships in foreign waters lined with mines.

Oh dear Lord, today women are willingly shouldering patriotic duty. Some are dressed in uniform and others wear nurse's caps. Some, like Rosie the Riveter, are toiling long strenuous hours in plants turning out warplanes, tanks, and ammunition. I see the flash of the soldering irons as metal is welded to metal.

Tractor and automobile factories are moving Sherman tanks, fighter planes, artillery, and ammunition off their production lines. These industries are in high production operating around the clock every day of the week.

The music and the lyrics of "Praise the Lord and Pass the Ammunition" and "The Caissons Go Rolling Along" gloriously carry one along in the spirit of war. Movies like *Yankee Doodle Dandy* sweep us up in musical exhilaration for patriotism.

My kid sister has her Victory Garden, and my young sixteen-year-old brother is undertaking to fill his big soldier brother's boots by helping Dad produce food so vital for the country and its military strength.

I see stacks of V-mail and packages for the servicemen. Mothers and girlfriends are mailing boxes of homemade cookies, candy, and cigarettes to sons and boyfriends.

Many are buying war bonds to support the cause. Moms are cautiously using stamps from their ration books to obtain sugar, coffee, shoes, cheese, and other goods for their families' welfare. Dads are working overtime to do their own work and that of their absent sons. Gasoline, fuel oil, and tires are rationed.

There are posters and slogans. One poster of Uncle Sam, with his finger pointing at you, reads, "I want you." Others read, "Loose lips sink ships" and "Rationing Means a Fair Share for all of us."

I vividly remember my own wartime hurts. I bring to mind my handsome high school sweetheart, Mark, hugging me tightly and affectionately kissing me good-bye. Then he abruptly turns and, holding his emotion in check, walks out of my life.

As he disappears out of sight, my tears overflow my eyelids and stream down my cheeks. My heart aches in the anguish of knowing it could be months before he will return to me. He is off to combat duty overseas.

I recall the many prayers for the safe and sound return of my dear Mark and brother John. In dread, I endured those sleepless nights engulfed in nervous apprehension. The fear that a loved one is suffering hardships, deprivation, and wounds or even facing death is torturous anxiety. Can you imagine pain like mine or worse, suffering felt by countless others and so multiplied with an immeasurable scale totally worldwide during this war?

Now my visualizations take on a frightening dramatic terror. I see results of the blitzkrieg, the terrifying air raids over innocent people, cities, and fighting men. I see twisted bodies, some with arms or legs missing. There is much destruction of equipment, buildings, and bridges.

In my mind, I relive the horrors of war. In a bombed city, I view a pile of lifeless bodies, men, women, and children. On the battlefields are corpses here and there putrefying in the sun while the battle rages all around them. There are blown-up tanks, mangled and twisted vehicles of all kinds, broken-down buildings, torn-up streets and roads.

Scenes of the Normandy Landing, the battle against the Desert Fox in the dry lands of North Africa, the hardships of crossing the mountains in Italy, and the battles to control the Pacific flash through before my eyes. Above all, the most shocking vision is the dropping of the atomic bomb on Hiroshima and another on Nagasaki.

How can one comprehend the consequences of a single explosion killing eighty thousand people?

Today, August 10, 1945, World War II came to an end with Japan's decision to surrender. The war with Germany ended when Hitler committed suicide on April 30, 1945. The people are wild with the news of the end of the war. There is singing and dancing in the streets with the overwhelming joy of victory.

What a dear price we paid for preserving our liberty. The tears, blood, death, and sacrifices are indelible memories for those of us living through these trying times of the 1940s.

We have been told that WWII would end all war. Dear God, tonight I pray that it does.

20

Julia's Fourth Year of Teaching

In early August, I started preparing for my fourth year of teaching school. First, I planned my wardrobe for teaching. I sewed a colorful cotton dirndl skirt and a red plaid wool skirt on Mother's new electric sewing machine. At the dry goods store, I purchased two blouses, a cardigan sweater, a pair of oxfords, long stockings, and undergarments.

In mid-August, I went to the county teachers' meetings. I would not have any new hard-backed school books this year because of the war. I did pick up the soft-covered workbooks that I would need for my classes. We were given our large registry book in which to keep attendance, absences, and to record grades for each student in each subject.

My school supervisor's wife told me, "We have freshly painted your classroom in a soft cream color with brown trim around the windows on each side of the room. The floors have been heavily oiled, and we hope you find them very shiny and clean looking.

"On the playground, we placed a new teeter-totter. In the large tree, we hung a rope swing. You will find a new bat, softball, and a large rubber ball in the cloak room."

I put some scenic fall calendar pictures and some other pictures that I cut from magazines on the large wall bulletin board. I wanted the room to look pleasant and inviting to the returning students.

Dad helped me make an insect-catching net. He took an old broom handle and attached a wire, holding some netting that I cut for him to use. For science this fall, I planned to encourage the students to make a collection of insects.

School started on Monday, August 20. Fifteen shining faces arrived early for the first day. Marian is in eighth grade this year and says she wants to help me as much as she can. She even offered to help sweep at the end of the day.

I do not have any one in kindergarten this year, but I do have Marian, Billy, and Dan in eighth grade to prepare for their eighth-grade examinations. They will be looking forward to going to high school next year, so they will work hard on preparations for the exams. Furthermore, they well remember when they were in second grade that Oscar couldn't pass eighth grade and had to stay in eighth grade until he was sixteen.

Also, there is small rumor that the Ericson family is moving.

If that is true, I will lose two students, Bobby and Tim.

At the end of the first day, Dan offered to take down the flag from the pole on top of the school, "Miss Sturloff, I will put it up in the morning when I come and take it down at night for you." Being Dan is an eighth grader, I felt that it would be a good, responsible everyday job for him. Tomorrow I will ask students to volunteer for other jobs. I believe it builds good character in students as it teaches them responsibility and gives them the rewarding feeling of being helpful.

The next morning, school opened with the reciting of the Pledge of Allegiance and a silent time for prayer. I had made a chart that listed jobs, and I asked the students to volunteer for jobs. In the pocket next to the job, I placed the name of the volunteer for that job. With the names placed in pockets, I could change names if someone was absent or if I decided to rotate jobs. "This year, I intend to give you daily words of wisdom. I want you to think about your life and what you want out of life. I want you to make the most of your life.

"Today my words of wisdom are: 'Who you are is formed day by day from choices you make for good or evil.'" Then we discussed that if you make good choices, you develop into a good person, and if you make a lot of poor choices, you could become a bad person. An example is if one chooses honesty, others learn to know you as a person they can trust.

A new book that I recently read, *Something to Live By*, collected and annotated by Dorothea S. Kopplin, inspired me to try to relay some of the wisdom in her book to my students. With a wide range of grade levels, I will have to be careful that I reword some sayings so that the younger students can understand, or else, I can carefully explain meanings of words to enlighten the young minds.

In upper-grade-level reading classes, I will ask students to read and prepare a reading from *Aesop's Fables* to present to the class. I believe the *Aesop's Fables* will teach impressive moral behavior without pointing fingers.

The last period of the day, I explained, "This fall we are going to make a collection of insects. In the science book, you can read that an insect has three body parts including a head, thorax, and abdomen. An insect has two antennae, three pairs of legs, and more often than not, two sets of wings. Insects include ants, bees, beetles, crickets, flies, grasshoppers, ladybugs, water bugs, and many more."

I told the students, "I picked up ten cigar boxes from the cigar store on the corner across the street from the Winneshiek Hotel. From an old paper box, I cut pieces of cardboard to fit in the bottom of each cigar box. We will stick a pin in an insect and pin it to the bottom of the cigar box. Each grade will have a box to put your insects in. If you want your own box, you can bring your own cigar box."

I said to the older students, "Ask your mothers for an old odd jar to use for the killing jar. I brought several jars I will use for the younger students. I will put some solution on a cotton ball in each jar that will kill the insects. When the insects are dead, we will push a straight pin through them and stick the pin with the insect on it into the bottom of the cigar box."

I showed them the insect-catching net that Dad had helped me make. I told them they could take turns using it on the playground to catch butterflies and other flying insects.

As the children brought in insects, we would read about that particular insect. For instance, from reading about the cricket, we learned that the male makes the chirping sound by rubbing together its forewings.

We learned to identify different kinds of butterflies and moths. One student even found a walking stick, an insect that can look like a stick. Marian one day was able to get a lunar moth that was on the screen door.

As the collection grew, we would discuss and admire the colors, shapes, sizes, and activities of each insect. The students who brought in a different insect, I would ask them to look up about that specific insect and report their findings to the class. Billy was shocked to learn how far a delicate-looking butterfly with its flimsy-looking wings can migrate.

One day, as we were discussing our collections, the door opened. Because of the entryway, we could not see who came in. It was only a short time, and the entryway door to the classroom opened. In walked the county superintendent. He quietly slipped into the largest desk in the room. I sensed he was captivated with the children's collection and study of insects. Before long, he was asking them to explain about their collections.

I asked the eighth graders to be the first to show their collection. All eight grades took their turns showing and telling about their collection. When it got to Mike and Colleen in first grade, I wondered if there was anything left to tell. Well, I didn't need to worry.

Colleen, in her sweet voice, told the superintendent, "This is the most fun thing, putting bugs in a box. The bugs are alive, but they don't live like me. They do not eat like I do. They have six legs, I have two, and they make different sounds. I can talk."

Everyone laughed, but I think the superintendent laughed the loudest. He told me after the students left how impressed he was with the insect study.

A letter was in the box from Mark. Up in my bedroom, I read his letter and the poetry he wrote for me.

The utmost emotion
Of spirit and mind,
Forever love,
Faithful and kind.

That night I wrote to him how much I liked the verse he sent:

It surely cannot be long, and you will be coming home. What a happy day that will be. Take care. Good night, dear Mark. I love you dearly.

Julia

When John stopped after school the next day, I showed him the poetry Mark had sent to me. "Sis, those lines express deep feeling. It sounds like true love to me. I am happy for you both."

"Thanks, brother. Mark has been gone for so long. Will it make a big difference in our relationship? It seems scary to think that we might be too changed to relate the same as we did. Such thoughts are whirling wildly through my mind like the out-of-control turning wheel atop Dad's windmill in a storm."

"Now, sis, who is putting obstacles in the pathway? Mark would not write such an endearing poem if he still didn't care for you. He has known you all of your life and knows your Christian upbringing. He knows you are true through and through. You know his training, that he is honest and sincere. I think you need to control your emotional thoughts."

"I know that you are right. This is a real trying test of my faith. I have always felt that my faith was like an anchor. It kept me still and calm, but after these many months, I am wearing down. I must block negative emotions and not allow them to flare up like throwing water on a grease fire."

"When Mark comes home, everything will return to normal, you will see. With the war over, we can go back to living normal lives."

"I hope you are right. What have you and Betty decided about the house?"

"Last weekend we went with her parents to look at the house. It is very nice inside. Downstairs there is a kitchen with breakfast nook, dining room with double windows, double doors leading into a living room with a curved railing on the stairway leading to the upper level. Off the living room is a closed-in porch with windows on three sides. There is a large pantry off the kitchen. A large downstairs bedroom is off the dining room. Upstairs is a large bedroom with double windows. There are two smaller bedrooms and a bathroom. Each of the bedrooms has a closet with a clothes rod and shelves above. There is a cemented basement under the house and a one-car garage in the yard. It would make a very comfortable and pleasant home. We have decided to go through with her father's offer. Being Betty is an only child, her parents feel that any of their property will be hers anyway someday. They would like to see her enjoy some of their worldly goods while they are living."

"John, I am happy for you and Betty. With your injured leg, farming would not be easy for you. I am glad that you will have an office job that will help take you off your leg. The Olsons's helping you buy the house now will ease your expenses while you are trained in the insurance business and finish your college education."

"Does Mark say what he wants to do when he returns home? I think that he will want to farm."

"No, he has not said much about that. But I don't doubt that you are right about he will want to farm."

John looked at Julia and asked, "What would you think about living on a farm?"

"I would be happy. I think it is a wonderful place to live and work side by side with one's husband. If I have children someday, it is the best place to raise a family. Children have plenty of space to run and play. They have animals to feed and take care of, which teaches them the responsibility of caring for living creatures.

"We have had such a good upbringing on the farm. Our mother was always there for us. She was close when we had a bruise to put a cold object on the bump. She was near to put disinfectant on our scratches and to place bandages over our cuts. Her hugs and kisses helped ease our hurts and angry feelings.

"When I was hurting, I could always go to the milk barn and sit on a milking stool and tell my dad what my heartaches were. He always had time to listen while he stripped the cow's udder dry.

"I enjoy working in the sunshine in the garden, hanging clothes on the clothesline, picking berries, and simply enjoying the great outdoors. I don't consider myself a tomboy, but I did like driving the tractor for haying. It felt so good to be out in the open spaces, breathing in the fresh air and soaking up the warm sunshine.

"What's more on the farm, it takes the whole family working

together to keep the farm in good operation. It makes young people learn responsibility and learn to be good workers."

"Whoa, Julia, I get the idea. I see you have made up your mind you want to be a farmer's wife."

"John, thanks. I think you just got me talking and pulled me out of my negative thinking. Yes, you are so right. I want to have a life like we had with our parents. We were so blessed to have such dear souls raising us. Our dad and mom are selfless, caring people who want the best for us. They brought us up in the Catholic faith. Mom and Dad are Christian parents. They taught us to live by God's laws. We learned that God's laws are for our own good to help us live a good life and bypass the pitfalls in life. Our parents obeyed the commandments of God as shown in their character and modeling of proper behavior. They both exemplified good work habits.

"Dad always made sure we got to mass on Sunday. If he knew we were going to have a big snowstorm, he left the car out by the main road, and he took us to the car in his large sled drawn by workhorses. Do you remember how he would tuck us under the horse blanket to keep us warm?"

Mark will be coming home soon. His last letter said that he was leaving for the States. Every day I check my hair in the mirror above the wash basin in the entryway at school to make sure I look presentable.

Today I had Billy read *Aesop's Fable* "The Lion and the Mouse," and afterward I discussed with the students the moral of this story. I tried to get them to voice what they thought the meaning of the story was.

Teresa said, "A little animal can sometimes help a large animal."

I asked, "Do you think the moral of this story could apply to people?"

Billy raised his hand. I nodded at him, and he said, "A poor man could help a rich man if his car broke down on the road."

Jim responded with, "A child with a small hand could reach through a hole in the fence to retrieve a baby chick when a big man's hand could not."

It is good that the pupils can apply these fables to real-life situations. It teaches them to think of possibilities.

The older children are reading the Grimm brothers' fairy tales to the younger children. I remember as a child how I loved to read them. When I was in grade school in this very same room, there was a book of fairy tales in the large bookcase. Some of them I read time and time again.

This afternoon, the seventh and eighth graders are taking turns reading *Snow White.* I asked the students if anyone saw the movie *Snow White and the Seven Dwarfs.* A couple of the older ones remembered that they had seen the movie. They let it be known that they thought it was a delightful movie. Everyone took a big interest in listening to the story as it was read to them.

There is something special about these old fables collected by the Grimm brothers. Some believe that they are stories full of symbolism about God's people as they journeyed west and the trials they faced. I did not tell my students that, but I find that thought interesting.

21

Prayers Answered

As soon as Marian finished sweeping the classroom floor, she started out walking home. I was happy to have a quiet classroom as I wanted to correct a stack of papers, mostly arithmetic papers of the older students.

After a day filled with the din of a normal classroom, I welcomed the silence. Teachers must have nerves of steel to withstand the endless commotion of fidgety young bodies going about their business of learning.

Sitting at my desk, correcting eighth-grade math papers, I heard a sharp knock on the door. I froze. *Who would be coming at this time of day?* The knock was not the way John knocks. Besides John always follows the tap with, "Julia, it's me." I can readily recognize his voice.

I try to look out the window to see a car. The windows are only on both sides of the classroom, so there is no way to see the front of the building.

The firm knock comes again. What should I do? I opened the door going into the entry. "Who's there?"

No answer. I picked up the softball bat and placed it next to the door. Then I opened the door just a crack.

I gasped. "Mark..." Was I trembling from the fright of the unknown, or was it the shock of perceiving Mark after more than three years of not seeing him?

Mark stepped inside. It was a good thing that he grabbed me quick as I was suddenly overtaken with weakness. He wrapped his strong arms around my slight shoulders and hugged me tightly. I felt like I never wanted him to let me go. He must have felt the same way as it was the longest hug ever. I felt my body relaxing from the shock. Then Mark gave me a lingering sweet kiss.

"Julia, I have waited months for this moment. You feel so good in my arms."

"Mark, I am so glad you're home. I can hardly believe…I am not dreaming, am I?"

"No, Julia, you are not dreaming. I hope that I did not scare you. I wanted to see the expression on your face when you first saw me. I got home this afternoon. I talked with Mother and Dad for a while. I saw Marian walking home and decided I wanted to come here where we would have a private time to be together."

I asked Mark to come into the classroom. I gave him the teacher's chair to sit in. I brought a chair up alongside the teacher's desk so we could talk.

"Julia, with my months overseas and not in need of spending much of my soldier's pay, that money accumulated. With some of that and along with my mustering-out pay, I purchased a car before I started home."

"Mark, you look very nice in your civilian clothes."

"You just don't know how good it feels to wear nonmilitary clothes again. Julia, you are my pretty sweetheart. I constantly carried your picture with me." He pulled out a well-worn picture to prove it.

"If you are finished here, let's go to town. I want to take you out to eat so we can talk some more. Do you have to go home first? Your dress looks fine to me."

I nodded in agreement, and we left hand in hand. Mark was proud to open the door on his new car for me.

We went to the Green Parrot to eat. Mark took me by the arm to lead me to a small table covered with a white tablecloth and a white napkin at each of the two place settings. The water glasses glistened in the candlelight. Yellow pansies in a crystal vase decorated the table.

With growing up in Depression times, eating out was a special treat. The atmosphere of a nice restaurant made it even more special. Tonight, with Mark as my escort, it is a night inscribed in my memory forever.

I had written so much to him about my life while he was gone. Much about his overseas life, he could not write for security reasons. Now he was anxious to fill in so much of what he wanted me to know of his life in North Africa and in Italy.

"Julia, I even saw Mussolini."

"How could you have seen Mussolini?"

"Well, I did not see him alive. I saw him hanging. Some of his men who had originally followed him turned against him. In their anger, they wanted to make sure he was dead, so they let him hang for days. Many Italians as well as military soldiers from other countries passed by the hanging body of the Fascist dictator."

I queried, "So the Italians welcomed the freeing of their country from an iron-fisted ruler who had led them into such destruction for their native land?"

"Yes, it helped in the final thrust to end the war in Europe when Axis-conquered nations helped defeat Nazism and Fascism."

Mark told Julia how the Apennines, like a backbone up the boot of Italy, made progress with men and machines difficult over the mountains and through rough terrain. The entrenched enemy fought fiercely to obstruct any northward movement.

"Julia, someday I want to take you to see the Alps. Toward the end of the war, I found the Alps so beautiful. With the big push to put an end to every battle, there was not much time to enjoy the breathtaking beauty of those mountains capped with white snow."

It was so pleasant eating off a white tablecloth. The food was delicious, but the conversation was the best part of the evening.

We lingered over our coffee, talking and talking. Mark had so much to share with me, things he had not enough time to write or truths he could not write.

He reached across the table and took my hand in his. "Julia, someday I hope to marry you. I know that we need some time to get reacquainted being we have been separated for over three years, so I will try to be patient."

"Thank you, Mark. I understand. Yes, we have a lot of catching up to do." *It seemed a relief that Mark was not going to pressure me to marry him right away. I need time to adjust to being together after so long apart. Yet in my heart, I know that I love him and want to be his wife someday.*

"I have a lot to adjust to, being home again after having been gone for years. I need to have a talk with Dad. I think that I would like to farm. What do you think of that, Julia?"

"Mark, living on a farm is the only life I know, yet I have no desire to live in town. I think life on a farm is the best life. Farm life keeps one close to nature. Living close to nature is like living close to God. My parents have always worked together. They strove for the same goals. Mom was always there for Dad to discuss with her problems on the farm. Dad was there for Mom when she needed help or something fixed. It seems to me that they were true helpmates like described in the Bible Genesis 2:18 "…I will make him [Adam] a helpmeet for him" (KJV).

Mark expanded on Julia's words, "Both our parents were good to each other. As for Adam, after his creation, God spoke to Adam in a language he could understand. God's interaction with Adam awakened in him social needs. It was the beginning of man knowing he needs to feel a kindred spirit with another person, so God made Adam a helpmate to converse with him and take part in his life."

Mark placed his hand over Julia's and said, "Dear one that is why I love you so much. You know biblical truths and apply them to your life. In your mind, you not only understand ethical principles but in your heart you live them."

"Thank you. I simply believe that the Holy Bible is the best guidebook for a good life."

"You are right, but since the disturbances of the First World War and the following years of the wild roaring twenties, it seems a great many have turned to distracting thrills and materialistic things. More and more, they find it easy to ignore the word of God."

I didn't want the evening to end. It was so good to talk about our future. I told Mark, "I don't want this night to end."

"Dearest, this night is only the beginning of the rest of our lives together."

I hope so, Mark. Oh, I hope so.

Dad and Mark helped set up the platform for my fourth school play. The students put on their performance the Friday night after Thanksgiving.

Marian opened the program by saying a poem that she had written for the occasion.

On the side of the British forces,
Our ships followed the courses
To bring supplies for the Allies,
Winston Churchill's good guys.
Brother went off to war for glory,
Mother sighed and felt so sorry.
Wounded in France, home to stay
Victory in Europe, VE day.

This year, we did a play about a little boy and girl wanting their daddy to come home from service for Christmas. The first graders Mike and Colleen were the sweet children yearning for their father to be home. They told their mommy, "We do not want anything from Santa. We just want our daddy to be home."

When the children hung up their stockings, they asked their mommy, "Will our daddy be home for Christmas?"

They questioned their mommy, "Where is our daddy? Why can he not come home? Doesn't he love us anymore? Why is our daddy being mean to us?"

On Christmas day, Janie and Robby played the grandpa and grandma who came for Christmas. The family was gathered around the manger scene. Grandma was telling the Christmas story. When she got to the birth of Jesus, Mike and Colleen together placed the Baby Jesus in the manger.

Just then, hearing the living room door open, the children looked up to see their daddy in the doorway with a large sack on his back. "Ho, ho, ho! Merry Christmas!"

The children ran to their father's arms, gleefully crying, "Daddy, you are home."

Daddy had a bag of gifts, but the best gift was their daddy home for Christmas.

Dan recited the following bit of poetry that I penned for the occasion:

The War Is Over

Songs like the White Cliffs of Dover,
Inspired us to get the war over.
Mommie's glad the war is no more
Grandpa says war can be horror.
The neighbor boy is coming home,
Sis is slickin' up with brush 'n' comb.
Big brother's home to stay.
I like it this way.
Dad declares this is no boner,
For certain sure this war is over.

Dan said the poem loud and clear. He paused in the right places and used good expression. The audience enjoyed his timely presentation.

The students sang Christmas songs. We ended the program by singing "White Christmas." My students sang the entire song, then we asked the audience to join us in singing again that popular Christmas music. With the war over, we are looking forward to Christmases like we used to know. It made me feel happy and proud to hear Mark and John's voices coming through strong and clear. I felt so happy to have them here tonight. This is the first of my programs Mark has been home to attend.

On Sunday, John and I invited Betty, Mark, and Jimmy to come to our house for a music session just like old times. We played and sang many of the popular pieces including "Over There," "Keep the Home Fires Burning," and "Bell Bottom Trousers" with the words about whom a sailor loves and who loves him too. We played and sang Christmas hymns and "White Christmas."

It was so much fun being together, playing and singing like when we were high schoolers. Betty's parents, the McDonalds, and my parents enjoyed the merriment as much as we did.

Mom had made several large pans of meatloaf and an apple salad, Betty's mom brought scalloped potatoes, and Mark's mom provided a chocolate cake with whipped cream topping. Enjoying the good food and conversation was a great time for all of us.

John and Mark related some of their wartime stories. Mark told us, "It was hard for some of the guys in my unit who received Dear John letters. Girlfriends would get tired of waiting for their guy to come home. Wanting a good time, they would go to parties and dances where they would meet someone else. Then they would write and tell their friend that they had a new boyfriend."

Mark relayed, "Some of the guys would almost go berserk with anger. Those men were fighting a war under the worst of conditions, and then their most valued relationship goes sour. They were deeply wounded and not by any weapon, but nevertheless they were stabbed in the heart."

Both men felt that the guys who had forever faithful sweet- hearts at home were more stable and better soldiers in the face of battle.

John described the day he was shot. He told us, "Around the time that I was wounded, the Allies were pushing forcefully and rapidly the retreating Germans toward the Rhine. In the fast movement of the Allies some of the bewildered Nazis were encircled. The day I was shot; a young German soldiers came out of his hiding place and tried to shoot me. Without the quick thinking of my comrade, Mike Morrison, I would have been killed.

"Mike yelled and diverted the Nazi soldier's attention. The German glanced quickly at Mike while he shot, his aim went low and the bullet hit my lower leg. Mike saved my life I know.

"Another soldier took care of the German, while Mike took my radio and contacted help. He wrapped a tourniquet high on my leg to lessen the bleeding. I was taken to a medical tent for immediate help and then transferred to a hospital in England. In a few weeks, I was sent back to a Veteran's Hospital in the United States."

Mark shared, "I was never shot at, but I had a number of buddies who were wounded. Much of my time was spent keeping vehicles fueled and in good working operation. I often worked with the noise of battle in the background.

"Nights were the worst. In the darkness, one could hear movement and wonder what it was. In the distance, one listened to spine-chilling noises. Some were gunshots. Other times, in the distance, bombs could be heard. The worst were the human voices of terror, men yelling "help" or "God help me." The saddest cries heard were from young frightened dying men calling for their mother, wife, or sweetheart.

"I prayed that I would come safely home again. I believe in the power of prayer. My faith kept me going during the toughest of times. I felt that I had to live as I had so much to come home for." He looked at me and gave me a big smile and a wink.

My heart quickened, and I felt warmth spread through my body. I was glad that I faithfully wrote to Mark even when I did not get letters from him. I did my part to give him something to live for.

With humble thoughts, I realized how brave both these young men were to go to war with so much likelihood of something going wrong. *John will suffer with his injured leg the rest of his life. Mark's memories of war will be hard to shake off and put into the recesses of his mind.*

22

Before Christmas 1945

At school, my students pasted strips of red construction paper to form a circle and interlocked the circles to make long chains to hang from one end of the room to the other. On our small artificial tree, they hung more chains. Five- or six-inch circles were cut from old Christmas cards. Four ends of the circles were folded out, then six circles were pasted together, pasting one edge to another on the circles, forming a Christmas ball to hang with red yarn on the tree.

The older girls made copies of red-colored Santa Clauses to put in each of the classroom windows. With colored chalk, they drew on the blackboard pictures of stockings hanging on a fireplace, gaily wrapped presents under a Christmas tree, and a Nativity scene. The Nativity scene was a real work of art. There was Mary near Baby Jesus in the crib, with Joseph standing beside her. There was a donkey in the background and a cow. On one side were three wise men, and on the other side were shepherds with their crooks in their hands with which they rescued their lost sheep.

In art class, the students drew pictures of what they wanted for Christmas. The pictures were placed on our bulletin board.

Innocent little Colleen with her big blue eyes looked at me and asked, "Miss Sturloff, what do you want for Christmas?"

I could feel the color rising in my cheeks. I smiled and replied, "Whatever Santa thinks that I deserve this Christmas."

She squeezed my hand and declared, "You are the very best teacher, and I think you should have a great big present."

To myself I thought, *I pray that you are right. Maybe Mark will declare his love this Christmas with a special present.*

I read the Christmas poem that starts:

'Twas the night before Christmas,
when all through the house
Not a creature was stirring, not even a mouse.

Even the older children seemed to enjoy that long poem.

In music class, we had a lot of fun singing "Up on the Housetop."

Ho, ho, ho! Who wouldn't go?
Ho, ho, ho! Who wouldn't go?
Up on the housetop, click, click, click
Down through the chimney with old St. Nick.

"Julia, we better go to a dance Saturday night before Advent starts," advised Mark.

Saturday night, I dressed in my new gold-colored crepe dress with a wide band at the waist and slightly gathered skirt. I wore my new red wool coat with mink collar. Mother had purchased me a black pair of soft leather gloves. I was so happy to be going with Mark to a dance. It has been more than three years since the last time. I felt as excited as a schoolgirl receiving her first lover's kiss.

When the band struck up "Let Me Call You Sweetheart," Mark led me to the crowded dance floor. When he took me in his arms, he led me gracefully around the floor. It felt so good to be dancing with him after so many months of waiting for just such a time as this. Mark quietly sang the words into my ear as we kept perfect step with each other dancing around the floor. He was singing that I was his sweetheart and he was in love with me. It was so good to have Mark take me in his arms, and then to hear such loving words was like a soft, warm breeze engulfing me in happiness.

I tightened my right hand in his left. I hoped my nonverbal message and my smiling face assured him of my love.

The next weekend, being it was Advent, Mark and I did not want to go to the movies or dances. Instead, we spent time together preparing for Christmas. On Sunday afternoon, we helped my Mom make candy. Mom made a cooked fudge candy while Mark and I made divinity. With Mom's new electric mixer, it was so much easier to make divinity this year. Our divinity turned out in spoonful drops of very white stiff peaks. I had added some black walnuts to the mixture, so it was very tasty. Mark really liked it.

Several weeks ago, Mom had made her usual baked Christmas fruitcake with dried fruits, citron, Brazil nuts, and pecans. She made it early so the flavors would work through and make it delicious to eat.

While Mom and I packed a box of cookies, fruitcake, and candy to mail to Bobby, Mom lightheartedly told me that Bobby is playing checkers in the Philippines. "Julia, Bobby has made friends with an older man who was a Pilipino freedom fighter during the Japanese occupation of the Philippines. When Bobby is off duty, the man invites Bobby to play checkers with him. The Pilipino likes to brag about the enemies he killed during the time that MacArthur had to leave the islands.

"Julia, Bobby wrote that he thinks the man wants him to be interested in his daughter. Bobby declares he is not interested in the Negrito girl. He says the Negritos look like kids. They are small people.

"Bobby and his friends like getting off the base and enjoy the man's stories of how the Negritos lived with the enemy on the island."

"Mom, Bobby wrote to me that he will beat us all at checkers when he gets home. Now I know why. He is getting plenty of practice."

The next Sunday, Mark and I were invited to Betty's house to learn how to make Norwegian treats for the Christmas season. Betty's mom had stocked the kitchen well for our fun day of making traditional Norwegian foods. Betty had already made a batch of potato lefse.

For dinner, Betty's mother had made Norwegian meatballs and a lettuce salad. We ate some of Betty's lefse. She told us to butter the round thin piece of lefse and sprinkle sugar over the top, then roll it and enjoy. I liked the lefse, and I could tell that Mark and John liked it also as they ate several pieces.

After eating we cleaned up the kitchen, then Betty got out the rosette irons. She told us that next we would make Norwegian rosettes. She instructed us, "The secret of making nice crispy rosettes is the temperature of the fat. If it is too cold, the rosette will stick to the iron, and if it is too hot, the rosette would fall off the iron too soon."

Betty put lard on to heat in a medium-sized deep pan and said when it is hot she will heat the irons in it. Next Betty and I mixed the eggs, milk, sugar, flour, and salt in a bowl with a flat bottom. The irons had floral-looking shapes. When the fat was hot, she dipped a hot iron in the batter and into the hot fat. She breathed a sigh of relief when the batter stuck to the iron and started baking. When the batter was a golden color, she removed the iron and dropped the rosette on a plate.

She let each of us try making a rosette. Guess we're lucky as everyone turned out good until the very end when the batter almost was gone and a couple of the rosettes did not turn out complete. Mark and John were happy to sprinkle powdered sugar on those and eat them.

With our first try a success, we were ready to try some more Norwegian recipes. Betty suggested we try making fattigmand next.

Betty and I beat the egg yolks and added the sugar. Then we added the melted butter, salt, flour, sweet cream, and ground cardamom. Betty had me take the rolling pin and roll the batter thin. Then she showed me how to cut diamond shapes.

"You boys are doing a great job of keeping the fat the right temperature for frying the batter. That is really the secret to having the end results turn out perfect," Betty praised John and Mark.

Betty and I dropped the shapes into the hot fat for two or three minutes until they were golden brown. After the shapes cooled, we dusted them with powdered sugar.

We all thought we had an enjoyable afternoon. Betty suggested, "Why don't you come again next Sunday, and we will make lefse and krumkake."

In unison, we said that would be great. I said to Betty, "I will bring the ingredients if you let me know what to bring."

Betty's mom and dad came in the kitchen just in time to hear my offer. "No, I will furnish the needed supplies. My husband and I like to have you come. It is so good to hear the voices of young people in our home. Today I want you to take the goodies home with you.

"Here are two metal boxes to put your baking in. I have already made my goodies, and they are waiting for Christmas in metal boxes. So, what you make here, I want you to take home and enjoy our Norwegian food."

Mr. Olson looked at Mark and John and jokingly told them, "We did not offer you lutefisk. Maybe you Germans"—he looked at Mark and added—"Irish folks would not like that as much as lefse and some of the baked goods."

John asked, "What is lutefisk? It must be some-kind-of fish?" Mr. Olson explained that it is usually dried cod soaked in a lye solution for several days to rehydrate it. Then it is washed several times in cold water to remove the lye before it is eaten. Mark and John agreed that they might not be ready yet to try the lutefisk, but they would like to try it some time.

Mr. Olson added, "Handled and cooked properly, lutefisk is very good and is a traditional Christmas Norwegian food."

The next Sunday, the four of us were back in Mrs. Olson's kitchen. We were looking forward to learning how to make lefse.

Betty thought we should start with making krumkake. She showed us the krumkake iron.

Betty had me beat the eggs and add the sugar, butter, cream, nutmeg, and lemon flavoring. I added the flour last.

"It will be thick," Betty warned me. Then she demonstrated how to get a rounded teaspoon of batter and place on the low- heated krumkake iron. When each krumkake is baked, roll it right away in a long roll about an inch or a bit more thick. It reminded me of an ice cream cone, but instead of shaped like a cone, it is a roll about five inches long.

Betty told us we can eat the krumkake as it is or put whipped cream or some pudding like filling in the inside.

We had to be so careful not to break the krumkake when we placed them in the metal boxes to take them home. Next, we readied the kitchen for the making of lefse.

Betty told us that she had chosen a no-fail lefse recipe. She had already prepared a bowl of mashed potatoes to which she had blended in a tablespoon of fat while the potatoes were still hot. I mixed the mashed potatoes, milk, salt, and last, I added two cups of flour.

Betty instructed me to take some of the batter and roll it out on an area of the table that was dusted with flour. Roll the batter thin, place the rolled-out circle on a griddle, and bake until the lefse is speckled with brown.

We all tried our hand at baking the lefse on the griddle. When the round circles of lefse were cool, we stacked them between waxed paper and placed each one in a metal tin.

Again we were happy to take our baked goods home with us to show the rest of our families. Mr. and Mrs. Olson invited us to come again sometime soon.

Mother invited Mark to come over to enjoy with us our traditional oyster stew for Christmas Eve. Mom instructed me to slowly heat the oysters until they curled then add the hot milk with some thickening in it and a large pat of butter. I placed the oyster crackers on the table alongside a plate of several kinds of cheese and some of the lefse that we had made at Betty's house. Mom put on a plate of Christmas cookies. The sugar cookies were cut in the shapes of stars, bells, trees, and Santas topped with red- and green-colored powdered sugar frosting. There were date pinwheel cookies and a kind of cookie with a top and bottom with a date mixture sandwiched in between.

After cleaning up the kitchen, we retired to the living room. I played the piano while Mark and my family sang Christmas carols. Mark suggested to John and me, "Let's go to town to sing Christmas carols house to house until it is time to go to Midnight Mass."

John called Betty about the caroling so she would be ready to go with us and to tell her to dress very warm.

When we got to Betty's house, we sang at the front door two Christmas songs before Mr. and Mrs. Olson opened the door and welcomed us in.

We explained that we could not stay as we wanted to sing at some more doors and bring cheer to other people.

They told us about several homes near them where there are elderly people who find it difficult to get out this time of year. Then they pointed out homes with young children who would be charmed with real Christmas carolers.

At each home, we sang Christmas songs like "Silent Night" and ended with "Jingle Bells" or "Upon the Housetop" if children lived in the house. Where elderly lived, we sang, "White Christmas." We kept warm by quickly moving from one home to the next.

At ten thirty, we headed back to Betty's house to get warm before we left for Midnight Mass. Mark and I were the first to leave for church.

Mark parked his car along the sidewalk about a block from the church. He told me that he had something important to say to me.

He reached into his pocket while he took my left hand in his left hand. In seconds, he placed a ring on my left hand.

With his deeper than normal voice, he told me,

"Dear, with this diamond ring,
I ask the costliest thing,
For your life and heart,
To join mine 'n' never part."

"Oh, Mark, you have my heart, to you my life will be forever faithful, and I love you more than words can say."

In the light from the street lamp, I could see the glitter of the diamond ring. "It is beautiful, Mark. I am so happy to wear your ring."

When we entered the church, we both dipped our right hand in the holy water font and blessed ourselves. I was happy to lead the way to a pew near where my family usually sits. I genuflected, bent my right knee to the floor, rose, and entered the pew.

The organist in the balcony was playing Christmas music on the organ. When we were settled in the pew, I looked down at the sparkling ring on my finger. I could see that the large diamond had smaller diamonds on each side of it.

Mark saw me looking at my ring and smiled warmly at me.

He reached for my hand and gave it a squeeze.

The altar covered with red poinsettias looked so beautiful. Soon, with people rapidly filling the pews in front of us, it will be hard for me to see the colorful altar.

During mass, the singing of "Adeste Fideles," the Latin wording of "O Come, All Ye Faithful," seems so overwhelmingly glorious. When the priests on the altar join the choir in the singing, it just seems to fill the church with the most awe-inspiring music.

Adeste Fideles laeti triumphantes,
Veníte, veníte in Bethlehem.
Natum vidéte, Regem Angelorum:
Veníte adoremus,
Veníte adoremus
Veníte adoremus Dóminum

From the altar, the priests slowly dragged out singing the words "Venite adoremus." I just love to hear the Latin words to music.

At Communion time, it felt so right to walk to Communion in front of Mark and to kneel at the communion rail with him to receive Communion together. Back in the pew, I said prayers for after Communion.

Tonight I became conscious that my prayer book was getting very worn. I thought when I marry Mark, I need a new prayer book.

My parents had given me this one for Confirmation. Dad's cousin, Reverend Lasance, had edited *The Catholic Girl's Guide.* As it was written for Catholic girls, my parents wanted me to have it.

In Father Lasance's book, flowers were used to describe how to grow into a beautiful person on the inside. In the maiden's wreath flowers, the lily, rose, carnation, and others were used symbolically. The peony represented the love of God, the carnation obedience, forget-me-not piety, and rose love of our neighbor. The book is filled with advice and counsel for a young woman. I read and reread parts of the book many times. That is why today the prayer book looks so tattered and is without a cover. I have inserted it in a covering to protect it.

My mind was forced back to concentrate on the music and the end of the mass. Mom glanced briefly toward me and gave me a knowing smile. I think she saw my glistening diamond ring. It made me acknowledge my blessing of having grown up in a good Christian home with loving parents. *Oh God, richly bless my parents in a long and happy life. I pray that they will live to see my children's children.*

23

Christmas Day 1945

It was not daylight yet when I could hear Mother getting up. I just snuggled deeper into the warmth and comfort of my cozy nest in the bed, but the thought that Mom needed me penetrated my consciousness, and I compelled my body to leave the snugness surrounding me. I stepped onto the cotton rag rug. Feeling the chill of the morning, I dressed quickly.

In the kitchen, Mom, with her matronly apron around her neck and tied at the waist, was busy getting ready to stuff the turkey and get it in the oven. I never cared to wear long aprons like Mom's; I tied a simple short cotton apron around my slender waist.

Last night, I had broken two loaves of bread into small pieces and covered the pieces with water. Then I sautéed white onions until they were glossy and tender. I added the onions, a couple cups of diced celery, sage, coarse black pepper and salt to the bread mixture. I stirred it well in a large pan and let it be so the flavors would work through the dressing during the night. This morning the dressing is ready to stuff in the turkey.

Together Mom and I stuffed the neck of the bird and sewed the flap of skin to cover the dressing with needle and thread. Then we salted the bird's cavity and filled it with dressing. Again, we used needle and white thread to sew the opening shut to hold the dressing in place.

We placed the heavy bird in a roasting pan and set it in the oven. The leftover dressing we put in pans to bake later in the oven. With the turkey in the oven, Mom took a good look at my ring. "Julia, it is a bright clear diamond, it's a beauty. I wish you the very best, dear daughter, always." She gave me a very loving hug. "I am so happy for you. I will miss you so much, but maybe you will not be far away if Mark finds a farm near his dad's place." Yesterday, Mom and I had made pecan and pumpkin pies. I brought up from the cellar two kinds of pickles, beet, and sweet pickle for the relish tray.

In the dining room, we placed a leaf in the dining table to extend its length. I laid a pad over the table and placed a white linen tablecloth on the table.

From the oak buffet, I took out Mom's good floral china dishes and set the table with them. From the small drawer of the buffet, I took place settings of silverware for each place at the table.

Marian brought up some apples that Dad had picked from our orchard and stored in the cellar. I cut up the apples for a salad. To the apples I added raisins and nuts. I stirred all the ingredients with some of Mom's homemade salad dressing.

John left to go to town to get Betty. Not long after he left, Mark came. He had a few colorful packages to put under our artificial tree on the top of Mom's long shiny black table in the living room. Mark asked, "Can I help?" I told him we just needed to wait for the turkey to get done, so Dad and Mark visited in the living room.

When John returned with Betty, he carried in a sweet potato casserole that Betty's mom sent out. Betty placed a few small packages under the tree.

"Julia, is it true…Mark gave you a diamond last night? May I see your ring?"

Betty showed her delight in seeing the beautiful ring. "Julia, it is lovely…really it is so pretty."

Just before we were ready to serve the meal, Dad came into the kitchen with some of his homemade grape wine. He went to the pantry and came back with his grape-etched wine glasses that he stored in the glassed top of a large dark cupboard in the pantry. He poured each of us a glass of his wine to place beside our plates on the table.

Dad lifted the turkey from the oven for Mom and carried it on a large platter to the table. Mom and I dished up the mashed potatoes, gravy, dressing, and relishes to pass at the table. Betty put her casserole on.

Dad asked, "John, will you say the blessing, please."

We blessed ourselves with the sign of the cross and repeated with John, "Bless us, O Lord, and these thy gifts, which we are about to receive from thy bounty through Christ our Lord, amen."

Mother remarked, "There is so much besides good food to be thankful for this Christmas. Mark and John are safely home, and Bobby sounds like he is having a good time and is not in any danger. This year we can really enjoy Christmas." We smiled at Mom and nodded in agreement.

Dad stood and proceeded to carve the bird. Mom started the food moving to her right, counterclockwise around the table.

The Christmas feast tasted so good. For dessert, I asked each person, "Do you want pecan or pumpkin pie?" Before I served the plate of pie, I placed on it a dollop of whipped cream with a pecan on top.

After leaving the table, Betty and I put food away. Mom started washing dishes. With all of us working to wash, wipe, and put the dishes away, it did not take long to get the kitchen and dining room back in good order.

When we were all comfortably seated in the living room, Mom said, "This is a wonderfully good Christmas. I feel so blessed to have John and Mark home. I know that Bobby is in a safe place." While smiling and winking at John and me, Mother declared, "My prayers have been answered that two of my children have found good Christians to marry."

She excused herself and went into the downstairs bedroom. Soon she appeared with a huge bundle. She placed it beside John and Betty, explaining, "This present is so big I decided not to try to wrap it."

Mom had stuffed pillow ticking with goose down and had made a set of pillows for John and Betty as well as a set for Mark and me. I always liked my down pillow so was happy to know that I would have new down pillows to sleep on in my new home. Knowing how much Mom likes to write to Bobby, I gave her a fountain pen. When I gave Dad his gift, he tore open the package. He thrust his arms through the openings on the wool vest. Waving his arms, he jokingly announced, "See it is just the right length for my arms." That made us all have a hearty laugh.

John announced to us, "I had the furniture store deliver my present to Betty's house."

I asked Betty, "What did John give you for Christmas?" She answered that he had given her a beautiful Lane cedar chest.

Mother placed wrapped identical-looking packages in Betty's lap and mine too. Each of us unwrapped our packages and lifted the lid of a white box. Inside, between the layers of white tissue paper, we found delicately crocheted pink roses attached on a set of pillowcases.

We both exclaimed, "They are beautiful. Thank you."

In other boxes, Mom gave us each two sets of embroidered pillowcases made from white feed sacks. We received crocheted dish rags and some home-sewn potholders fashioned from colorful floral-designed feed sacks.

Mom and Dad gave John and Mark each a large metal tool- box containing a hammer, screwdrivers, pliers, measuring tape, wrenches, and a level.

After the last gift was unwrapped and thanks were given to the gift givers, we gathered up the discarded wrapping paper and ribbons to burn later in the metal burn barrel outside. Now it was time to relax and enjoy some good conversation.

Dad brought up how satisfied he was this year with his income off the farm. He felt thankful that there is no more rationing of gasoline, fuel oil, and kerosene. This month tires will no longer be rationed.

Mother backed up what Dad was saying. "This has been a blessed year for our family. The war is over. Bobby is not in harm's way in the Philippines. He claims he can beat all of you at playing checkers when he comes home.

"Last summer, we finally were connected to electricity. I have an electric stove instead of a kitchen range in which I used to have to fire up wood to heat food. We now have an electric refrigerator and do not have to run to the cellar for chilled victuals anymore." I added to the list of what we're thankful for this Christmas season. "Yes, we have enjoyed the gifts that God has blessed us with this year. I appreciate the electric lights to read by. I like using an electric sewing machine, it is so much easier to use than the old Singer treadle machine."

Marian, not to be left out, squeezed in. "I am glad that I don't have to run to the cellar every time we want butter, milk, or leftovers for the table, but the best is not having to go out to the little house in the cold weather."

At that last remark, everyone had a good laugh. Everyone could well remember the annoying call of nature in the coldest weather, nevertheless a necessary requirement a number of times a day.

Marian didn't think it so funny when she soberly added, "But I still have the little house out back at school."

While the family reminisced, Mom passed some of her homemade fudge, peanut brittle, and the divinity Mark and I helped make. On the dining room table, she placed a three-tiered silver tray containing Christmas cookies, rosettes, krumkake, and some of the candy.

Dad left the room for a few minutes and came back carrying some of his farm record books. Before Mom married Dad, she had wanted to be an accountant, so she always kept good records of their income and expenses.

Dad looked at John and Mark, "I want you young guys to know how much farm prices and expenses have changed since the Great Depression. Pointing to the books, he said, "These records that Lettie has faithfully kept through our farming days prove what I am going to say."

He took out a sheet of paper. He explained that he had summarized his findings. "When Lettie and I were first married in 1921, we farmed on shares with my father. I had to turn the half share of your grandpa's over to him. Of course, it was not easy turning half of the income over to my dad, but the worst was yet to come.

"With the beginning of the Great Depression in 1929, prices began to fall. In 1930, my fattened hogs brought $11 per hundred weight (cwt), 1931 at $6.95 cwt, 1932 at $2.95 cwt, 1933 at $3.70 cwt, 1934 at $3.95 cwt, and 1935 at $8.40 cwt. In 1933, I sold my market cattle for $4.25 cwt, ten steers brought at $422.87, and in 1934 at $3.25 cwt, eight steers (6,360 pounds) sold for $206.70. "This year my hogs brought $14 to $18 a hundred weight. The year Marian was born, I received only $2.95 cwt, so you can see now I am receiving around five to six times more for my hogs over what I received during the Great Depression.

"Times were tough, but we bought only absolute necessities. Your mom and I raised our own potatoes, vegetables, berries, grapes, and apples. She canned many jars of food and stored in the root cellar cabbage, carrots, squash, potatoes, rutabagas, and apples. We had our own eggs, meat, milk, and cream. We never went hungry, as by the sweat of our brow, we could put wholesome food on the table."

Lettie spoke up. "During the Depression, I sold eggs as low as 8¢ a dozen. This year my eggs averaged about four times that amount. For the eggs I sold to the hatchery, I received 39¢ to 40¢ a dozen. Because they were fertilized eggs and would hatch into fluffy yellow chicks when placed under heat-controlled brooders, I received more money for them."

Dad was eager to explain more. "You kids were all small, so your mom had her hands full taking care of you and feeding all of us. I hired men to help me with field work. During the Depression years, a young man worked for $1 to $2 a day. He was happy to earn that much and get his room and board besides. Lettie always fed them good meals.

"We still needed to make purchases. Some of 1929 expenses included oil, one gallon 65¢, Dr. Koontz, MD $1.50, eight gallons of gas $1.60, a winter coat for John $2.25, Dr. Koontz, MD for removal of John's tonsils and adenoids $43. My hair cuts cost 35¢, note at the bank $125 with $4.95 interest, March 1 farm rent $1,200.

"There were expenses like seed for planting, machinery repair, bay team $150, harness and collar $61.05, horse blanket $7.75, and Hereford bull $65.

"I must tell you the story about that bull. I purchased the bull from a farmer near Fort Atkinson. That same day, the man brought the bull to the farm and I gave him a check on my Decorah Bank. The next day, the Depression hit home. The bank was closed, and my check was no good at the bank.

"As soon as I learned what had happened, I went to see the man, and we worked out a way for me to eventually pay the man in cash."

Looking at his notes, Dad went on to tell, "Some other expenses—butchering and cutting of meat $3, auto repair $11, smoking of a side of meat $1.44, seven throw rugs $2.80, smoking of hams $4.29, x-ray when Lettie broke her arm stanchioning a cow for milking $2.

"After Lettie broke her arm, she did not offer to help milk anymore." Looking over at Mom, Dad added, "I don't blame her as when old bossy knocked her down, her fingers on her right hand have never been straight. The fingers remain bent, and she has had a crippled hand ever since. Your mom is one determined lady. Her stiff hand hasn't stopped her from doing her housework and crocheting."

Dad looked around at his listeners. "Why am I telling you all this? I want you to know how much better the farm income is since prices rose with the demand for agricultural products during the war. Without last year's and this year's good income, I could not have afforded all the improvements we have made this year. We do have much to be thankful for."

Around five o'clock, Mark and I left to go to his house, and Betty and John left to go to her home. I felt sad for my mom and dad as we left. It must be tough to see your beloved children leaving the nest.

Mom starts early in the fall, crocheting and embroidering Christmas gifts for the family and for her sister and brother. Mom works for weeks before Christmas, making fruit cake, baking cookies, creating candies, planning her gifts, and wrapping them beautifully in Christmas paper and topped with red bows. Her dedicated work intensifies her joy of the holy season.

Listening to my parents' talk of the Depression years made me feel so blessed to have been raised by such hardworking and loving Christians. I hope that I can benefit from their training in raising a family of my own in the future.

Mrs. McDonald warmly welcomed us. She served a plump goose for her Christmas meal. Two big meals in one day. Oh well, Christmas comes but once a year. After some fasting during Advent, it is good to enjoy plentiful and great-tasting food.

Mrs. McDonald had made me a set of embroidered dish towels. She had embroidered Mrs. Hen on white flour sacks, one towel for each day of the week. On Monday, Mrs. Hen washed; Tuesday, ironed; Wednesday, mended; Thursday, shopped; Friday, cleaned; Saturday, baked; and on Sunday, Mrs. Hen and Mr. Rooster went to church.

I gave Mark a set of wrenches. He gave me a walnut jewelry chest with a lid over the top compartment and a drawer below.

Mr. McDonald presented Mark and me with a glossy oak four-shelf bookcase that he had made in his shop. He said to me, "A teacher should need a bookcase."

Mark took me home before very late as we had been late last night with going to midnight mass. When we said good night I told him, "This has been the best Christmas ever."

The week between Christmas and the New Year was a fun time. One sunny afternoon, we took the long toboggan, and Mark, John, Betty, and I rode the big toboggan down the big hill sloping toward Canoe Creek. We got all snowy and wet, but what good fun we had. Trudging back to the house, pulling the big sled, we found Mother had hot cocoa and cookies ready for us.

One evening, we played board games at Betty's house. To the party, John brought a jar of our dad's homegrown popcorn. Dad had dried his small ears of popcorn stuck on the sharp hooks of racks hung from the ceiling of the front porch. When the ears were dry, he shelled the corn.

Betty suggested we make popcorn balls. While the boys popped the kernels into puffed up balls of white, Betty and I stirred up the syrup and heated it until it was boiling hot. Once the corn was ready, I poured the hot syrup over the corn and Mark stirred the syrupy mixture thoroughly. Then we all helped form the popcorn balls and let them cool while we played our board games.

Later, while munching our popcorn balls, the boys started talking about the coming New Year. Mark told us, "I have signed up to go to farmer's night classes for returning military men. That will give me help to start farming." He elbowed his buddy. "John, if you weren't becoming a city slicker, you and I would have a good time going to farm auctions. I hope to accumulate needed items for the farm from the auctions."

Betty surprised me by announcing, "I will be starting instructions for joining the Catholic church." She gave John a sweet smile and revealed, "Mom and Dad have decided I should follow my husband's religion. They think very highly of John's character and realize that he has a deep Christian faith. They feel happy for me that I will be marrying a believer. They know that my life will be much happier with a good God-fearing man."

Mark and I both gave her a happy look, and I said, "Great! We will all be going to the same church so that we can enjoy special occasions at church together."

As an afterthought, I added, "Betty, we can belong to the same organizations at church and maybe be on the same circle to help with fundraising dinners such as the church bazaar and preparing dinners for after funerals at the church."

I felt that I wanted to say something more, but Mark has not yet talked about a date for our wedding, so I decided not to say anything more tonight. After Christmas, I will be back teaching as usual.

John remarked that he has studied hard to pass the insurance tests to be able to write policies for different kinds of insurance. Now he will get serious about selling insurance.

Then John gave us shocking news. John told us, "I have withdrawn from college because the priest found out I have been attending Luther College. He warned me that if I continue my parents and I could be excommunicated."

I was stunned. *John had to give up going to college. I could understand that with his wedding and mine coming up, he could not jeopardize our weddings. I felt thankful that at least he did get a year of college under his belt.*

Mother invited Mark and Betty to join us for dinner on the last Sunday of the year. She said, "I have to use up all the good food prepared for Christmas." She had frozen a casserole dish of leftover turkey from Christmas Day. On top of the turkey, she had placed leftover sage dressing, brown gravy and a layer of mashed potatoes. One of the pumpkin pies had also been frozen, so we had another feast of well-seasoned leftovers tastier than the day they were made.

While we were smacking our lips eating the pumpkin pie with whipped cream on top, Betty and John told of their wedding plans. John spoke up and announced that he and Betty hoped to be married the Saturday after Easter. He explained that Betty would be finished with Catholic instructions by that time.

Betty was happy to report, "My dad plans to have a dinner, after the ten o'clock wedding at St. Benedict's Church, in the large dining room at the Hotel Winneshiek. We will invite aunts and uncles along with close friends to the hotel. Later there will be a reception at St. Benedict's Church basement for all the wedding guests, including relatives and friends."

John looked at Mark and asked, "Will you be my best man?

Mark poked him and asserted, "Man, I wouldn't miss being close enough to hear you say I do."

Betty turned to look at Marian and me and asked, "Julia, will you be my maid of honor, and Marian, will you be a bridesmaid?"

I looked at Betty and answered, "It will be a pleasure to stand up with John and you, especially with Mark as best man."

Betty said to Marian, "We are going to ask my cousin's high school son from Big Canoe to be a groomsman. We plan to ask Uncle Roy's youngest little girl to be a flower girl and my cousin's little boy to be a ring bearer."

Dear Mom said, "Sounds like we are going to have a busy and exciting 1946."

24

1946 – Decisions

The first week back in school, Robby and Tim Ericson told me that on March 1st they would be moving away. They said that the man they have been renting from has died and the family is going to sell the farm, so they must move to another farm in some other school district.

I couldn't wait to tell Mark that news, but when I did, he astounded me. "Julia, I already know that because my dad is trying to buy that 220-acre farm. He has made an offer to the family estate. The two sons and three daughters of the deceased man are anxious to get their inheritance, so they want to sell the farm as quickly as they can. If Dad gets it bought, we will have a place to live and farm. When we get a good start farming, Dad will turn the mortgage over to us. If we can make a go of it, we will have our own place."

"Mark, that is good news. How soon will your dad find out?" "It sounds like there are two other farmers who have shown interest, but I think the heirs of the estate are favorable to selling it to Dad. The man's children remember that when they were young, my grandparents and my dad were good neighbors to their family."

"Have you been in the house, barn, and other buildings?"

"Yes, I have been on the place before Mrs. Schmitz died. Lonely, Mr. Schmitz rented the farm to go to live with his son who worked in a factory in Waterloo. The house is a large square two-story with a porch on the upper and lower levels. There is a newer cow barn and other older buildings including a hen house, hog house, and machine shed. Almost all of the 220 acres is tillable."

"I have never been on the place, but it does look nice from the road. Being the children were of marriageable age when John and I were little, we never really knew them. The place is on the other side of your dad's and so is farther from our farm."

That night I could hardly go to sleep. *If Mark's dad buys the farm, does that mean Mark will soon be asking me to set a date for our wedding? It would be so good to live close to Mom and Dad. I have so much to plan for a wedding, a new home, buying furniture and furnishings for a home. I need to sleep in order to be fresh and alert to teach. It seems I cannot shut down my brain.*

The next day after school, Mark was there as soon as the last student left the school grounds. The first thing out of his mouth was, "Julia, my dad signed the sale contract this afternoon." He grabbed me up in his arms and swung me around and hugged me hard. "Julia, we have a place. Now we can get married."

"I am so excited. Last night I could hardly sleep, wondering if this could come true."

We sat down and talked and talked. "Julia, when do you want to be married?"

"I have always thought of being a June bride. It is such a pretty time of year with the red and pink peonies, snowball trees with their large white blossoms, lilacs, and other annual flowers in bloom."

"Julia, that sounds like a good plan. This winter I will collect machinery and tools from the farm auctions. By June Dad and I should have the planting done on both places. It will be summertime and a good time for a wedding...our wedding."

"Outside of buying some saving bonds and a few necessities, I have saved most of my teacher's salary in my savings account at the bank. I should have enough to buy a bedroom set, upholstered sofa and matching chair, and furnishings for my kitchen. I might even have enough to buy a dining room table, chairs, and buffet."

"Dad is giving me ten bred sows to have pigs. From that start, I will build up my hog business. Mother is planning to buy extra hens and roosters so that she can give us hens to lay eggs and roosters to butcher in late summer.

"I have money that accumulated while I was overseas and had

nowhere to spend it. That savings will now help me buy a used tractor and some machinery. Dad will let me use his baler, combine, and some other machinery. As I will be working with my dad planting and harvesting, my labor will repay him for my use of his machinery.

"Julia, it will work out, you will see. The best part of all of this is you. You will help me make the farm a home for you and me as well as, hopefully, a family of our own."

"Mark when do you get possession of the farm?"

"Dad thinks that they plan to close within a month. After that, we will have possession and can plan what needs to be done to get ready to live there."

Thinking about seeing the house made me wonder if there will be painting, papering, and fixing that will need to be done. When I let Mark in on my thoughts, he reported, "Mother thinks that the house is in quite good shape despite having been rented for the last eight years. She thought that some paint and paper could freshen it up and make it very livable."

Mark came home with me to have supper at my house. At the table, Mark told my dad and mom the news about the Schmitz place. Dad was glad to hear that Mark would be close to farm with his dad and share machinery. He told Mark that maybe at times they could share some work and machines.

Mom, with a twinkle in her eye, asked, "Have you set a date for the wedding?"

Mark let me answer that question. Dad and Mom agreed that June would be a good time for the wedding. Mother thought that would give us time to do some painting, papering, and any other improvements that needed to be done.

Snuggling under my quilts, trying to get warm that wintery night, I thought, *Will the day ever come that Mark and I will be man and wife? Then we won't have to sleep separate anymore. Why, even the Bible says, "If two lie together, they shall warm one another: how shall one alone be warmed?"* (Ecclesiastes 4:11, Douay Version).

At that thought, I smiled to myself. *The Bible sure makes a lot of good sense. Yah, it is the best guidebook for living a good life.*

Being Valentine's Day fell on a weekday, we celebrated the day the Sunday before the fourteenth day of February.

After eating one of Mom's scrumptious roast beef dinners with carrots and potatoes, we had a good music session. We played and sang the new popular composition, "Cruising down the River," and other currently popular music.

Outside big fluffy snowflakes were falling, and the air was frosty cold. Inside the warm house, while we sang about cruising the river, it reminded us of canoeing the Upper Iowa.

Betty asked me if I had the sheet music for "Here Comes the Bride."

"Yes, I do." Give me a few minutes to find it in the piano bench. Mark said, "Good idea to play "Here Comes the Bride" because this year, we have two brides to walk down the aisle.

I played, and we all sang, "Here comes the bride, friends at her side."

Then the boys sang a different rendition. "Here comes the bride, big, fat, and wide."

We got a big laugh out of that version. Betty and I are slender gals, so were not offended by their silliness. I think our parents got as much joy out of our musical performances as we did in playing and singing.

That night Mark and I asked Betty and John to stand up with us. Betty was asked to be matron of honor and John best man. I will write a letter to Melanie in nurses' training and ask her to be bridesmaid with Marian. Jimmy and Mark's cousin will be groomsmen.

The farm auctions were starting, so every week, Mark and his father studied the auction advertisements in the Decorah paper. They looked for machinery, tools, and equipment Mark would need to start farming. Of course, he could always borrow from his father, but it is better to have one's own equipment handy for an activity or purpose.

Often after school, Mark would come to tell me of his latest purchase at a farm auction. I looked forward to those times when we were alone to discuss our future life together.

Every find—ax, spade, pitchfork, scoop shovel, and much more, he would tell me about. As he wants to raise hogs for market, he is still looking to find hog feeders, barrels, and water troughs. The biggest machinery need is for a reliable tractor. He is still looking for the field machinery.

"Will it be soon that I can see the house?"

"Julia, it will not be much longer. I heard the Ericsons will be moving out on the 1st of March. They are buying a farm near Calmar and cannot get possession until March 1st. I know you want to see the house as soon as possible so you can do your planning."

"Mark, I know most farmers move on March 1st as by that time most of the feed is fed out to the animals and there is less to move. In addition, many animals are fattened and off to market. Moving that time of year, they still have time to get settled before field work begins. As soon as I see the house, I will start looking for furniture. I will need to see the space for a kitchen stove, so I know what size to buy. It will be fun shopping for our own home."

Betty cut her own bridal veil from lacy veiling material and gathered it onto a sparkling like-crystal tiara. Her mother is sewing the wedding gown of lace over taffeta. The fitted bodice has a full gathered skirt and long lacy sleeves tapered over the wrists. The back of the dress has covered buttons from the neckline to below the waist.

Mrs. Olson has cut out the bridesmaid dresses for Marian and me. As soon as she has stitched them together, we will come for a fitting. I will wear a blue satin dress, and Marian will wear a pink one. The flower girl's mother is sewing the long white lace dress for the little flower girl.

Mothers of my students are taking turns bringing a hot dish to the classroom just before we are excused for lunch. Around noontime, when I hear the door open and then shortly hear it close again, I know that someone has placed the hot meal just inside the door.

The children really enjoy having a hot meal, and so do I appreciate hot ready-to-eat food. During the time of gas and tire rationing, and people did not drive any more than they had to, we had to eat a cold lunch or bring heated food in a thermos jug. Later, when the school got electricity, I heated food for the students to eat on a hot plate in the classroom. I used to heat cans of food that mothers would send in the morning with the students, such as chicken noodle soup or beans for the children to eat. I had a hot plate and saucepan in the room for that purpose. Mothers of the students took turns in sending food to school for the students and myself. Back then, I got rather tired of tomato soup.

It is so much easier to have the mothers bring the hot casseroles ready to eat. When I had to prepare the food on a hot plate, it was a bit messy to do in the classroom without running water and a sink.

It seemed that every time one Mother had to provide the lunch, she brought a large bowl of white pudding-like food with butter floating on top. I am not sure, but I think it was romme grot a Norwegian Pudding.

Mother and I decided that we would go to La Crosse to a bridal shop to look for a wedding dress for me. One Saturday Dad drove us to Wisconsin. Mom and I had so much of a good time looking at all the pretty bridal gowns. We had a tough decision to make as to which ones I should try on.

I finally picked out three and went into the dressing room. The first one was too long in the waist for me. The second one fit well, but it did not seem my style; it was too much sophisticated with its long sleek look like something a Hollywood movie star would wear. The third one and my first choice fit me perfectly.

The dress had imported French lace over satin on both the bodice and the skirt. The panels in the back of the skirt gradually widened, flowing into a long train.

We left the dress in the shop as we will come back for a fitting just before the wedding to make sure it is just right. The clerk said that sometimes a bride with the excitement of the wedding will lose weight, and the dress will not look as nice as it should on her big day without altering it by taking in some seams.

Mother and I always liked to visit the religious store. While there, I found a nice book, *Memories of Our Wedding*, with a rosary entwined around a prayer book pictured on the white cover. I can start right away to write in my family history and will get the information for Mark's family tree from his mother.

There are pages to paste pictures. I will put in photos of Mark and I, also I have pictures taken with the box camera of when we were at Dunning's Spring, canoeing the Upper Iowa with John and Betty, and snapshots of playing music together. I will add photos of other activities we have been involved in together. In the book, I will place pictures of my family, friends, relatives, and students. Mother bought me a crystal rosary. She saw me admiring the picture of Jesus at the door, so she purchased it for my new home.

"Mom, that picture will mean so much to me. One of my favorite verses is, "Behold, I stand at the door, and knock. If any man listens to my voice and opens the door to me, I will come in to him and sup with him, and he with me (Apocalypse 3:20, Confraternity version). That scripture makes me feel that I am not alone. If I ask God, he is there to listen. When Mark and John were overseas, that verse was such a comfort to me. I felt I could go to him, and he was there to hear me out and comfort me. I will place the picture in my bedroom as a constant reminder God is always there, we just must listen to his voice in our live and feel his calming presence."

"Dad wants me to buy you a family Catholic Bible for your home. Do you like this leather-bound copy of the Douay– Confraternity version?"

"Mom, you know that I will treasure it. Like you did in your Bible, I will record our family history in it. Look, here is the page to write about my marriage to Mark. Following that page are pages for recording other family history: birth, baptism, First Communion, Confirmation, children's marriages, religious life if any children enter as priests or nuns, last anointing before death, deaths, and military record."

Friday, March 1, was to be the last day for Robby and Tim to attend Canoe No. 8. At the end of that school day, their father would be taking them to their new farm home near Calmar. Having taught them for almost four years, I felt sad knowing they would not be my students anymore.

I knew all the students were feeling unhappy to see their classmates leave. So, Thursday night, I baked Mom's favorite recipe for devil's food chocolate cake and topped it with chocolate fudge frosting. Mom and Dad would be grocery shopping on Friday, and I asked them to get vanilla ice cream for the going-away party. Dad offered to bring the ice cream to the school after the last recess time. I told him to come about three o'clock.

After recess, we partied. I had the students play fruit basket upset. I whispered in their ear the name of some fruit or vegetable, giving each one a different word. The pupils sat in a circle with one student not having a seat. Then I played a musical record, and every so often, I lifted the needle from the phonograph and shouted the name of two fruits. Those students had to exchange seats, and the one without a seat was free to grab one of the empty seats. The person left without a seat was it for the next game.

Every so often, to shake things up a bit, I shouted, "Fruit basket upset!" Then everyone had to take a different seat.

After that we played a relay game. I placed pieces of chalk on the blackboard and divided the students into two teams lined up about twelve feet from the chalkboard. At my signal, the first person in the row was to rush to the ledge on the blackboard, grab a piece of chalk, rush back, and give it the person first in his line. That person is to rush the chalk to the ledge, pick up a different piece, and take it back to the first person in line, and the process is repeated until all pupils in each line have taken part. The team that finishes first is the winner.

All was going well until Colleen fell returning to her line. Marian and Janie picked her up and helped her return the chalk to Dan. Like his pants were a fire, Dan took some leaping fast steps to and from the chalkboard. His fast actions saved the day for his team. They were the winners. Colleen was soon laughing along with the rest over Dan's antics.

I thanked Marian and Janie for consoling Colleen. It is good for young people to learn to be there for each other. I want to encourage such behavior in my students. With proper training, a child should learn to be a helper, not a bully.

Knowing Dad will be here soon with the ice cream, I cut the cake. Marian offered to put it on the small plates I brought from home.

Just then Dad came with the ice cream. I opened the side of the ice cream boxes so that I could cut the brick ice cream into slices. As each child brought his plate of cake to me, I placed a slice of ice cream on it for them.

Marian and Janie helped Peggy, Colleen, and Mike get their plates to their desks without the ice cream sliding off the plate. Peggy giggled, "This really looks good."

"Miss Sturloff, this is the best cake I've ever eaten. Hmmm, it is good. You are going to make a good wife for some man," declared Billy.

Everyone laughed and looked at me to see my reaction. I smiled and offered another piece of cake to Billy. Several others took seconds of the cake.

Just before four o'clock, Mr. Ericson came for Robby and Tim. They quickly said good-bye; so eager were they to see their new home. All their schoolmates shouted good-bye to them.

You cannot teach a person for almost four years and not feel a twinge of sadness when they leave. *If I feel this sad over two leaving, how will I feel next fall knowing that I will not be the teacher for the others either?*

I know Mark does not want me to teach after we are married. I will be a wife and homemaker next year. I am looking forward to that, but I will miss teaching. I know that I will. Again, I think about Saint Paul who said that no matter his circumstances, he was content. I need to remember that and learn to enjoy life as it is at the time.

Then I remember *today is a good day too. Being it is March 1st, the Ericsons have moved, and tomorrow Mark can take me to look at our future home.*

While I was cleaning up after the party, Mark came to catch me up on what he has been doing. "Julia, you know that I offered to help the Ericsons move. I have been helping for several days and they appreciated my help."

"Yes, I know that you have been helping your neighbor move. Mr. Ericson came at the end of the school day today to pick up the children to take them to their new home." I did not tell Mark how I felt seeing the Ericson children leave; I felt now wasn't the time. *Mark needed to tell me about his business.*

"Mr. Ericson did not want to move some of the hog equipment and sold it to me very reasonable. Mr. Ericson felt moving the older hog feeders, troughs, and waterers would be too hard on them. If they stay put, they will last much longer. As I will be the new owner, he was happy to get something out of them and not have to move them.

"He also sold to me some fencing, posts, baled hay and straw in the barn, oats in the granary, and ear corn in the corncrib. Tuesday, I helped him load several truckloads of baled hay and straw that he had stacked in a shed. I drove the truck to his new place and helped him unload the truck. So, for my labor, he further reduced what he wanted for what I am getting from him."

"That is good news, Mark, Now, you can start getting some livestock as you have feed. But what is Mr. Ericson going to use for feed for his animals?"

"Julia, the farm he is buying was owned by a man who is deceased, and Mr. Ericson bought baled hay and straw, corn, and other grains that were in the buildings when he purchased the farm."

Then Mark drew me into his arms for a big hug and happily told me, "Girl, tomorrow you can go in the house to look at where you will live come June. I helped the Ericsons move their household goods today. The house is completely empty—no appliances, no curtains, and no furniture. We started loading appliances, beds, and all the other furniture early this morning. Women came to help Mrs. Ericson pack and move her kitchen equipment, bedding, and clothes."

The next morning, I was ready as soon as Mark arrived. "Mark, I can't wait any longer to see the house." Mark smiled as he turned the key in the back door, and we walked into an entryway leading into a large kitchen with oak cupboards. The house appears so empty and stark looking without cheery, pretty curtains at the windows, appliances, and furniture. Off the kitchen was a large pantry with empty shelves.

The spacious dining room has a south bay window. On the north wall, a door opens into a bedroom. In the bedroom, a door on the west wall opens into a bathroom, and a door from the entryway also opens into the same bathroom.

From the dining room, double French doors open into living room on the east side of the house. The roomy living room has two windows side by side facing the south. Near the open stairway, a door opens to a screened-in porch nearly the width of the house.

In the living room, the curved wood stair railing and three steps lead up to a landing, and then the railing and stairs ascend to the second floor. There were small rubber treads on the steps. Upstairs there are three bedrooms and a small room that has been turned into a bathroom. The big bedroom was over the dining room and has a bay window similar to the one in the dining room and directly above that one.

"Mark, this is a very nice house. I will enjoy making it a home. I was surprised to see an open stairway in the living room and a closed, steeper stairway off the kitchen to the second floor."

"Julia, I think at one time the bedroom at the top of the kitchen stairway was not connected to the other bedrooms upstairs. I believe it was used for men hired to help on the farm and so the other upstairs bedrooms were kept private from that bedroom."

"I have a pencil and paper with me to take notes of how long curtains have to be for each window. I would like to measure the opening for a stove and where to put a refrigerator. Will you help me?"

That afternoon we brought my dad and mom to look at the house. Mom suggested, "I think you should have the bedrooms freshly papered and that we should paint the kitchen, dining room, and living room walls to freshen up the house."

Dad said, "Julia and Mark, I can try to hire the man who did our wallpapering. You should pick out the wallpaper and paint that you want us to use."

"Julia, you and your mom pick out what you want for paper and paint. I know that I will be happy with your choices. Besides I am too busy with my outside planning and organizing of the farm." The next weekend, Mom and I picked dainty floral wallpaper patterns for the bedrooms. For paint we chose a cream color for the walls of the dining room and living room. We decided on roller shades for the living room, dining room, downstairs bedroom, and the large upstairs bedroom. I bought lacy white panel curtains to plan for in the bedrooms and front rooms. The ones for the living room were wider and fancier with an extra lacy piece of fabric at the top trimmed with wide lace.

For the kitchen, I chose tie-back curtains with red embroidered flowers on white and decided to hang them over shorter panels of the same material.

As soon as the painting and papering were done, my dad and Mark helped me hang new curtain rods where needed. Mom helped me press the curtains. How much more welcome the house will look with curtains at the windows.

One Saturday, Mark and I went looking for furniture. Mark let me have the final decision, but I wanted his opinion too as he has to live with whatever is chosen.

We decided on a waterfall-style walnut veneer dresser, chest of drawers, and dressing table. Solid wood would be nice, but right now I felt I could better afford the veneer finish. We asked if they could deliver the furniture after Easter as I would have that week off for Easter vacation. We were told their delivery day was Wednesday, and I thought that's great, it will give me time to clean before the furniture is put into place.

For my kitchen, I picked a white Frigidaire Cold-Wall refrigerator and white forty-inch Hotpoint GE electric stove with dual ovens. The stove has a high back with an electric clock. I think I will be able to put salt and pepper shakers on that top. Mother and Dad decided they would pay for the stove and refrigerator. That would be our wedding present from them. I was happy my parents were buying the appliances; it would help my savings from teaching to buy things for my new home. Mark and I picked out a cute metal chrome dinette set with a red tabletop and red chair backs and seats.

At a household auction, I was blessed to get the bid on a beautiful oak dining room set, a table with three leaves, six dining chairs including one armed chair, and a buffet. For the living room, Mark and I had trouble making up our minds but finally settled on a wine-colored velvety-type cushioned set consisting of a sofa and chair with an ottoman. From a farm auction, Mark came home with a large comfortable oak rocking chair with like new ribbed dark-green cushions on the seat and back.

Mark winked at me. "Julia, if you are a mother someday, you will want a rocking chair. In the meantime, we can just enjoy it."

I kidded him right back. "You probably want that chair to read the newspaper in, and I will never get a chance to sit in it."

"Well then, we need two rocking chairs. Someday we will have two, one for you and one for me. After all, when we have time to sit, we want to be comfortable."

25

A Wedding

How I looked forward to Easter vacation. It would give me some time to do some cleaning and get ready to put furniture in my new home. Also, it is so nice to have Easter vacation so close to John and Betty's wedding.

Friday afternoon I went to services to commemorate the death of Jesus on the cross. We followed in our prayer books the Stations of the Cross as the priest and altar boy went from station to station.

Mark and I went to Easter Sunday mass together. He looked so handsome in his navy blue pinstriped double-breasted suit. I felt happy to walk into church with him. I led the way to a pew, genuflected, and moved over for him to sit beside me.

The high center ornate white-and-gold altar was even more beautified with Easter lilies. The lower side altars also were adorned with Easter flowers. Bright light was trying to filter through the colorful stained-glass windows. The organ pipes burst forth, blending with the clear-cut musical voices of the choir like the very hosts of heaven were singing to us. The beauty of the church, the saintly music, and above all, the solemnity of the high Easter mass deeply moved one in a personal desire for holiness and righteousness. Jesus gave his all to wipe the slate of our scarlet sins white.

Before the priest left the pulpit after his sermon, he gave the last publishing of the marriage of John and Betty. It is hard to believe that by next Sunday, John and Betty will be Mr. and Mrs. John Sturloff.

Mark and Betty came for Easter Sunday dinner at our house. After dinner, while visiting in the parlor, Dad told us that the church in which we would be married was the same one where he and my mom were married in 1921. At that time, the large brick church was only four years old, having been built in 1917 at a cost of $60,000."

I asked, "Where did you go to church before that?"

Dad answered, "My family and your mom's family went to the old stone church on East Broadway. It was built in 1864. My grandfather came to Canoe Township in 1859, so he was here before the stone church was built. Some men offered labor to build the church. Back then, the church cost $7,000 to build. It had a stone bell tower above the entrance to the church and an iron fence surrounding both the church and the rectory.

"It was an impressive church on the inside with elaborate paintings on the walls and high curved ceiling. Gothic framed pictures of the Stations of the Cross hung from the sidewalls. The stained-glass windows of many colors looked Gothic with dark painted outlines on the inside and looked Romanesque on the outside. Gas lights in the church with ornate gas candelabras hung from the ceiling, and there was a sanctuary lamp above the altar railing.

"The main altar rose high behind the table like low part of the altar. The impressive tall part of the altar was an intricately built elaborate tall structure with gold trim. It was flanked by paintings of saints on either side. There was a statue of Mary on the left side altar and one of Joseph on the right-side altar."

Mark remarked, "St. Benedict's is a large beautiful church.

Why are you giving so much information about the old one?"

"It was a beautiful church for the time. Remember that church life was very important to early Christian settlers. Their lives revolved around the church. There was mass every Sunday, weddings and funerals to attend, religious classes for the children, and preparations for Baptism, First Communion, and Confirmation."

"But Dad, we go to church every Sunday and do all those things that you just mentioned," I protested.

"Yes, Julia, but I just want to emphasize that our forefathers left us a Christian heritage. They sacrificed a lot to build and preserve that priceless gift for their descendants. If one lives a good Christian life and strives to do righteousness, the Bible says that a person will have a blessed life. If they don't, they will be cursed."

Mother added, "Sam, that is so true. It is very clearly stated in Deuteronomy 28, where it tells of the blessings if we follow God's laws and the curses if we don't."

Later in the day, Mark and I looked up Deuteronomy 28 in my new Douay Bible. We read how if we keep his commandments, the Lord will "make thee higher than all the nations that are on the earth, and all these blessings shall come upon thee." We read together that the Lord would bless our fields, our children, cattle, barns, storehouses, labors, and our country. He would open his treasures to us such as rain in due season and that we would lend to others and not borrow of anyone.

Mark and I agreed that is what we would strive for in our marriage. We would pray to be blessed by the Almighty.

Together we read the curses that the Lord God Almighty will bring on those who do not hear his voice and do not do his commandments, statutes, and ordinances. We read how the Bible states the curses will come upon them and overtake them. The cursed ones will be cursed in the city, in the field, the barn, the fruit of their wombs, the herds, the storehouses, and in their coming and going. The Lord will bring pestilence, afflictions, miserable want, hunger and famine. He will afflict them "with cold, with burning and with heat, and with corrupted air and with blasting, and pursue thee till thou perish." The curses are numerous, including, "The stranger that liveth with thee in the land shall rise up over thee and shall be higher, and thou shalt go down and be lower."

In Deuteronomy 28, there are more verses for the curses than for the blessings. Verse 61 warns, "The Lord will bring upon thee all the diseases and plagues…till He consume thee" (Deuteronomy 28:61, Douay Version).

Mark and I felt very humbled by what we had just read. We discussed the reasons for our deep understanding of the meaning of those verses.

Mark postulated, "Maybe the war years taught us the reality of these verses. I saw the terror of frightened dying soldiers crying out to God to help them. I felt almost overwhelming oppression from the merciless and severe violence of enemy forces."

I added, "At home we suffered through the rationing, hard work of producing for the war, and the pain of separation from our loved ones."

Then we discussed the verse that says God chastises those that he loves. Does he bring the sword against us to awaken us to His truths?

We looked up Scripture in Leviticus 26, a chapter on God's promises to those who follow him and the punishments that he threatens transgressors. We agreed God gives us ample warning of what he will do if we do not walk in his ways and follow his precepts.

> But if you will not for all this hearken to me, but will walk against me: I will also go against you with opposite fury, and I will chastise you with seven plagues for your sins (Leviticus 26:27–28, Douay Version).

On Monday and Tuesday, Mom, Mrs. McDonald, and I cleaned in the house where Mark and I will live. We wanted to get the cleaning done before the appliances and furniture would come on Wednesday.

Mr. Grindeland had finished wallpapering and painting. The house smelled so fresh and clean, but we still had the floors to sweep and scrub. Mom started on the floors upstairs and Mrs. McDonald on the floors downstairs. I washed the inside of the cupboards.

In the afternoon, we washed inside windows upstairs and downstairs, and we washed the downstairs outside windows.

Tuesday morning, we hung the new curtains on the rods and hung them on the brackets my dad had tightened. I hung my frilly kitchen curtains and put a tack in each of the tiebacks to hold them in place. We finished up by noon, so Mom and I could go home to prepare for the bridal shower in the evening.

On Tuesday evening, several of the girls that Betty works with had a bridal shower for Betty at the apartment house across the street from the telephone company. A lace tablecloth covered a table with an open umbrella under which were wrapped gifts.

We played several games, and the winner of each game gave their prize to Betty. She received numerous handy kitchen gadgets.

Betty unwrapped the gifts. She received many items for her kitchen, some towels for the bathroom, and some personal dainty lingerie.

The hostesses served a white cake made with coconut, vanilla ice cream, and coffee. While eating the delicious cake and ice cream, the girls made much talk about the wedding on Saturday.

Wednesday afternoon, the furniture store called that they were bringing my furniture. Mom, Mark, and I went to the house to be there when the truck came.

Mark helped bring the furniture in, and I showed the men where to place each piece of furniture. After the truck left, Mark and I went back through the house, looking at our furniture.

"Mark, I like everything even better than I thought I would. It is starting to look like home."

"Julia, come in the kitchen and inspect your stove and refrigerator, which was delivered last week while you were teaching." With John's upcoming wedding, I had not been over to see them yet.

"Mark, I am going to enjoy the double ovens when I have men to cook for or we have company."

Mark told me that he had brought his bed from home and set it up in the small upstairs bedroom. I might stay here some as next week I will be getting baby chicks and will want to keep an eye on them for a few days."

Then he grinned at me and said, "Don't worry, I won't be cooking on your new stove before you do. I will go home to eat at my mom's table."

Wednesday evening, Marian and I went to Betty's house for our dresses finished and ready for the wedding. Betty gave each of us a single strand of pearls to wear with our dress.

Mrs. Olson and Betty took Mom, Marian, and I over to look at the red brick house John and Betty would soon be living in. Right after Mr. Olson received possession of the house, he had it papered and painted.

It looked already for its new occupants. Betty had used her earnings at the telephone company to purchase new furniture. She had encouraged John to help her decide on the furnishings.

Mr. and Mrs. Olson paid for the walnut bedroom set the young couple had chosen. It was their wedding present to their beloved daughter and her husband. The cedar chest John had given her for Christmas was in that bedroom.

Betty had already moved most of her clothes and John's into the upstairs closet off the larger bedroom. On the closet shelves were some boxes.

The shower presents were in place in the kitchen. Mother and Dad had paid for the new GE refrigerator and GE stove similar to mine. Within a month, my mom and dad had purchased two stoves and two refrigerators for wedding presents.

Betty explained, "I am not buying any more for the house until I know what I am getting for wedding presents."

Friday afternoon, Mom, Betty's mom, Betty, and I went to the church basement to decorate for the reception tomorrow afternoon. We put two tables together in front of the serving window from the kitchen. Over them, we placed white linen tablecloths. Atop of the tables, we put wedding bells and draped blue crepe paper strips to swag in front of the tables. On the tables, we set bunches of yellow daffodils in clear glass vases.

We hung streamers of blue crepe paper and white tissue wedding bells. On the other tables in the dining hall, we put white paper and placed blue strips of crepe paper running down the middle of each table. Betty laid small wedding bells here and there on the crepe paper. In the center of each table, we placed more daffodils in narrow glass vases. We arranged several tables near the door for gifts. We covered those tables with the white paper and blue crepe paper runners.

Friday evening, we had rehearsal at the church with Father Dolan. It was great practicing being I was the maid of honor and Mark was the best man.

Uncle Roy's daughter Becky, six years old, and Betty's nephew looked so cute as flower girl and ring bearer.

After rehearsal, we were invited to a buffet supper at Betty's house. Some neighbors had prepared the casseroles and sent in deserts. John told Mark where he was taking Betty on their honeymoon. I am glad that he did. Someone should know where they are going.

Mom asked John and Mark to bring in some gifts from the car that John had received from relatives in Montana, Illinois, and California. Betty showed us some gifts that she had received in the mail.

Mark and Jimmy planned how they were going to decorate the wedding car. They asked me if I had any wedding bells and crepe paper left. I did and gave them what I had.

It is too bad that Bobby is not going to be home for the wedding. He could have been the car driver for the bride and groom. Instead, John asked a cousin to be the driver.

Saturday we were all up early. We left before nine o'clock for the church. Mom wanted to get there to make sure the altar flowers arrived and were in place on the altars.

Mom pinned my corsage on for me, and I pinned on her mother's corsage. I put Mark's boutonniere on for him and placed the small flower for father of the groom on for Dad. Mark left to go to the room off the sanctuary to wait with John. He took John's boutonniere with him.

Jimmy and a cousin of Betty's, as ushers, started taking people to their pews. Betty had placed white bows on the pews for the wedding party and the parents, brothers, and sisters of the couple. Then aunts and uncles were seated followed by cousins and friends.

The church was filling up. Many of the coworkers of Betty were there. Her father's business clientele were arriving for the wedding of Mr. Olson's only child. Dad's childhood family was large, so we have a lot of relatives attending the wedding.

Just minutes before ten o'clock, Betty and her parents arrived. Jimmy escorted Mom to the front pew. Dad followed. Then Betty's cousin escorted Betty's mom to the front pew.

The wedding music started. Becky took her little flower basket full of rose petals, and as she walked, she dropped the petals. The little ring bearer followed close behind, carrying the white pillow with the rings attached with blue ribbons. The little guy was so busy looking all around him, it's a wonder he ever made it to the altar with the rings.

After a short wait, Marian, in her pretty pink dress, started down the aisle. When she was about a third of the way to the altar, I started walking down the aisle.

When I reached the waiting groom and his best man, I smiled at Mark. He took my arm and guided me to the altar where we split for him to kneel to the right of John and me to kneel to the left of Betty. Marian and her partner were in their places in the front pews as were the flower girl and ring bearer

In the back of the church, Betty, glowing with happiness, slipped her arm under her father's arm. Mr. Olson walked his daughter down the aisle. When they reached John standing alone and waiting, Mr. Olson placed Betty's hand in John's hand. John and Betty walked solemnly up to the altar and knelt together on a kneeler.

From the altar, Father Dolan opened the nuptial mass with a greeting to the bride and groom and their guests. From the pulpit, he read from the Old Testament Genesis 2:24 (Douay version), "Wherefore a man shall leave father and mother, and shall cleave to his wife: and they shall be two in one flesh." And from the New Testament he read from Hebrews 13:4, (Confraternity version). "Let marriage be held in honor with all, and let the marriage bed be undefiled. For God will judge the immoral and adulterers."

Father Dolan began his sermon by saying, "Marriage is a sacrament. Marrying and raising children is a very sacred thing.

God ordained marriage. In the beginning, God made man in his image. The man named the animals of the earth, but he did not find a helper like himself. God created woman and gave her like a help unto to Adam and united her with man in the closest companionship.

"God's word in Holy Scripture is both a safeguard and a shield to protect our lives. The church teaches the truths from the Bible to give understanding of God's laws. The church is here to encourage and support the daily walk of those desiring to lead a Christian life. Pray for the happy marriage of this couple. May their Christian upbringing be a blessing all their lives."

Father Dolan walked down the steps of the pulpit and went to stand in front of the altar. John and Betty moved to stand in front of him with Mark on John's right, and I was on Betty's left. I took her bouquet to hold for her during the wedding ceremony. The priest guided Betty and John through the nuptials. I could distinctly hear John say "I do" and Betty's firm "I do." They kissed each other.

After the nuptials are said, the priest returns to the altar to continue with the mass. At Communion time, Father Dolan brought Communion first to the newly wedded couple, the wedding party, and the parents. The rest of the people went to the communion rail for Communion.

When the mass was over, the bride and groom, with full smiles, walked down the aisle followed by Mark and me. The rest of the wedding party came next. Then came the parents of the bride and the parents of the groom.

I could hardly breathe. I was so happy to march out with my arm in Mark's arm. I kept thinking the next time we do this, we will be married.

The wedding party lined up in the entryway to greet the guests as they came out of the church. Many told the bride, "We wish you much happiness" and to the groom, "Congratulations."

The dinner guests left for the Winneshiek Hotel where Mr. and Mrs. Olson were having the wedding dinner. The photographer had the bride, groom, and attendants return to the altar for pictures. After the pictures were taken of the wedding party, Mark and I drove together to the hotel. Marian and Mike, Betty's cousin acting as groomsman, rode with us. The flower girl and ring bearer rode with their parents.

I love the entrance to the stately looking hotel named Winneshiek after an Indian chief. Just inside of the tall glassed entryway is the lobby with a circular railing overhead encircling the opening into the second floor. To me, the best part is the inlaid colored design on the marble floor of an Indian in full headdress. There is a marbled stairway to the second floor.

The meal was served in a large dining room. Mark sat to John's right, and I sat next to Betty. Father Dolan said the blessing before meals.

The food was served by two waitresses. When one is not used to being served in a fancy hotel, it was a nice experience. The Swiss steak and all the side dishes were tasteful. Dessert was coconut cream pie.

As Mark and I drove to the St. Benedict's church basement for the reception, I told him, "That dinner must have cost Mr. Olson a pretty penny. It was very nice. It was fun eating there."

"Well, I think it cost more than pennies." We both laughed at that comment.

At the church, it was comparatively quiet as the reception is scheduled to start at three o'clock. Mark and I sat along one wall and talked.

"Julia, what did you think of the wedding?"

"It was beautiful, and Father Dolan gave a very nice sermon.

What did you think of it?"

"I was impressed, and it made me think of what I would like him to say at our wedding. Maybe some time we could study the Scriptures about marriage."

"I agree with that. He did get me thinking seriously about marriage as a sacrament and its importance to a Christian."

As the people started coming into the reception, John and Betty were kept busy talking to their guests. The gift table was piling high with gifts. John and Betty started opening gifts. Marian wrote down in a wedding book the name of the givers and what they gave. Betty knew that the guests like to see what the bride gets for the wedding. They like to know if she got doubles of something and didn't get something that is a needed item.

Mark and Jimmy left around 4:40, I suspect to decorate the groom's car. While they were gone, I talked with some of my relatives.

"You will be next, Julia. What is the date of your wedding? I want to mark it on my calendar," said Aunt Ida.

"Aunt Ida, Mark and I plan to marry on June 20. I would like to ask you and Uncle Roy to be host and hostess at my wedding."

"Dear, I would like that, and I am sure your uncle will be happy to do that for you.

"Where will you have the dinner and reception? Will it be here in the church basement?"

"Yes, it will be here. Mother is asking her Rosary Society Circle to put on the dinner. We are hiring a cook from Spillville to cook the meal, and the circle will bring salads and pies for dessert. The ladies in the circle will help the day of the wedding in the kitchen and help serve the meal."

After the buffet meal and the serving of the wedding cake and ice cream, John and Betty thanked their guests for coming to their wedding. Some of the guests followed the young couple as they left the dining hall. Just when the newly wed pair appeared outside of the church doors, they were showered with rice. Waving and laughing, they ran to their car.

"Mark, did you do that to John's car? You know you are asking for trouble the day we get married." Mark only grinned at me.

There were old tin cans tied to the back bumper. Crepe streamers were floating around the car. "Just Married" was written in large letters with white soap on the wide rear window. White hearts were drawn on the backseat windows, and colorful balloons were tied to the car door handles. Car horns blew as they drove away.

26

Preparations

Tuesday after school, I went over to the farm to see the tiny fluffy yellow chickens. Mark told me, "Go in quietly so not to scare them so they do not pile up and smother some chicks."

The tiny, cute little creatures were huddled together under the hood of the warm brooder in the center of the brooder house.

Quietly I said to Mark, "When I was in the primary grades, I used to sit for a long time holding tiny chicks. Dad worried I would too tightly squeeze them. I knew I would not hurt the little birds. I would get very upset when a sickly-looking little chick would not eat or drink. In a short time, it would stretch out flat, too weak to stand. I cried when life left its tiny body."

"Julia, if we raise these chicks, we will have about three hundred laying hens this fall. You will have income for the house from the eggs we will sell. There should be about fifty roosters for butchering for meat for the table."

Cleaning eggs is not the most pleasant task, but I was glad to hear that I would have some source of an income next year. As I will not have money from teaching anymore, the egg money will be most welcome.

Mark stopped after school to tell me he had stood in the rain that day at a farm auction. He excitedly told me he bought an A John Deere tractor, plow, field disc, drag, and cultivator that day. Because of the weather and being late into the spring, his lower bids were good.

"I was beginning to think that I would have to use my dad's machinery this year. With my own machinery, Dad and I will be able to get the crops in faster on both places. The machinery all looks like it is ready to use. For weeks now, my dad and I have been getting his machines in good repair. As soon as the weather clears up, we will be in the fields."

Once the men were in the fields, I knew that I would not see Mark very often. *Hopefully, they will get the crops planted and the first cutting of hay in the barn before our wedding.*

In the meantime, I was busy finishing up the school year. For weeks, I had been working with Billy, Dan, and Marian, preparing them for their eighth-grade exams. Marian helped me organize the bookshelves in the big tall wooden storage unit in the corner of the classroom. I wanted to leave the room in good order at the end of the school year.

I was proud of my eighth graders as they walked across the stage to receive their eighth-grade diplomas. All three had scored high on the eighth-grade tests. I felt sure that they were ready for high school next year. It was hard to believe my kid sister would be a freshman this fall at the Decorah High School.

Mark, with his new tractor and plow, made a garden patch for me not far from my future home. When my mom and I went over to plant seeds, we found a nice, well-worked garden plot. I put sticks in the ground at each end of the garden rows. To the sticks, I attached twine string between a stick at one end and the stick at the opposite end. Following the straight string, I used a hoe to make a shallow furrow in which to drop the seeds. Mom and I planted flowers along the outer edges of the garden. In the rows, we seeded zinnias, petunias, marigolds, pansies, and gladiola bulbs. For vegetables, we planted seeds of radishes, carrots, beets, peas, cucumbers, green and yellow beans. I set out onion sets. Mark would plant the sweet corn, popcorn, and squash in the field at the end of some field cornrows.

Dad gave me some tomato, cabbage, and pepper plants from his in-the-ground greenhouse. It was warm enough now that they would grow in the garden without protection. Dad and I like to plant Dad's greenhouse plants in the garden for early harvesting. We like to put in the ground seeds to grow plants from which to enjoy fresh produce later in the summer.

On Saturday it rained, so Mark could not work in the field. He and I went to town and purchased apple trees to plant near our house yard. I chose some roses bushes to plant near the house. I love roses.

Mother gave me some bulbs to plant from her patch of irises and peonies. She had Dad dig up some rhubarb plants from her mature plants. We planted them along the house yard fence. There were two lilac bushes and a snowball tree in the house yard and spirea bushes along the wall of the porch. I discovered asparagus popping up on the edge of the yard.

The last teaching day of the school year, Susie looked at me and said, "Miss Sturloff, won't you come back next year? Who will teach me if you don't? I don't want anyone else. I want you."

Colleen piped up, "Why aren't you teaching us next year?

Don't you like us anymore?"

Mike jumped in with, "Who will play the piano when we sing?"

"You're the nicest teacher ever. I love you, Miss Sturloff. Please come back," cried Peggy.

I felt that I shouldn't cry in front of my students, but I could feel the sea wall holding back the salty tears about to burst. I assured them that I still cared for them. I reminded them I would be living not far away.

"You are all invited to my wedding in June. I will be happy to see you there."

The next day was the annual school picnic. Mark was able to get away to come for the dinner. I took him with me as I talked with each one of my students.

"Why are you taking Miss Sturloff away from us," questioned Colleen. "She is so nice. I want her to be my teacher next year."

Mark gave her his winning grin and told her, "She will not be far away. Come visit us some time."

Everyone enjoyed the teacher's treat, the vanilla ice cream packed in dry ice. On one or more of the desserts from the assortment on the table, the sweet treat was appreciated by young and not so young.

After everyone left and the picnic mess was cleaned up, I locked the Canoe No. 8 door for the last time. The key was handed over to the school director to give to the new teacher next school year.

A sudden sadness swept over me like when I shut my kitty in the car door and she died. It's the knowing something has changed and never will be the same again. I told myself, *You don't have time to be sad.* This is the happiest time of my life. In a month, I will marry my high school sweetheart. Yet I knew, like feeling the opposite sides of a coin, sadness and happiness can be felt at the same time.

The next Sunday was a rainy day. Mark suggested we take my new Douay–Confraternity Bible and look up Scripture on marriage. We sat on my mom's living room sofa with the Bible between us. We started with the Table of References in the back of the Bible to find Scripture on matrimony.

We searched for 1 Thessalonians 4:4 (Confraternity Version) "That every one of you learn how to possess his vessel in holiness and honor".

Then we read Ephesians 5:21–33 on the Christian home. The man is head of the home as Christ is head of the Church. Verse 24 says, "But just as the Church is subject to Christ, so also let wives be to their husbands in all things."

I like the explanation in the footnote where it explains that it relates to a right relationship between a woman and her husband: "Note well that the subjection inculcated in these verses is not a brutal or slavish subjection as to a tyrant, but that of the loved one to her lover, who is according in right order head of the family as Christ is head of the Church."

Further on we read that the man is to love his wife just as he nourishes and cherishes his own body. The wife is to see that she shows respect to her husband.

I demurely added to the discussion, "That makes good sense as a woman desires to feel loved by her man. I know how much I like your sweet kisses and warm hugs. Remembrances such as flowers, gifts, surprises, and your kindnesses mean so much to me. Your loving touches and thoughtful remembrances are to me proofs of your love."

With that admission, Mark gave me a quick hug and kiss on the cheek. "I want so much to make you happy." After a short pause, he thoughtfully said, "I also like to feel loved and enjoy giving and receiving loving kisses and hugs."

Then there was another longer pause. It was followed with Mark's admission, "From my experience, I like to feel appreciated and admired for what I do for our relationship, even the tedious jobs I do for you."

"Mark, for centuries the Bible has held the secret for a happy marriage. It is really very simple. The husband loves his wife like himself, and she respects and reveres him. They both treat each other righteously. If each husband and wife would be forever faithful in remembering their responsibility in the marriage, the Lord would bless that union."

"The bumps that come into every life interfere with the couple's resolve to have a happy marriage."

Wondering about that remark, I questioned, "The trouble in life does not have to be the ruin of a relationship, does it? I know our parents had the Great Depression and WWII to struggle through. Besides that, being farmers they had droughts, times of too much rain, hailed out crops, the dust storms from the Dust Bowl of 1934, low prices, animals dying of disease or injury, bugs eating crops, and more to contend with. Somehow, they lived through their trials. Through all their hardships, they maintained a happy life together and for their children."

"Sweetie, our forefathers had faith to pull them through, and so do we. God does not forsake those who follow him and strive to live a righteous life."

He took me by the hand. "Julia, let's go over to the farm, and I will show how much our baby chicks have grown. Then I will take you to the hog farrowing house to see the baby pigs that were born lately. These young animals will be our income next year."

Oh, Mark, I wish we could have kept talking. I know planning for our financial future is important. But also, I know being able to emotionally know each other is necessary for wedded happiness. I wanted so much to try to tell you my deepest fears. I realize our parents had trials during their lives on the farm. Those hardships I can understand.

Dear God, how can I reveal to Mark or anyone my deepest anxieties? Can I freely give Mark my love without his understanding my fearful heart?

With the corn planting finished, the men turned to haying. John came from his insurance office in the afternoons to help Dad with the haying. I drove the tractor some on the hay baler, but Marian wanted so much to be a tractor driver that I let her do most of it this year. I was glad as it gave me time to work in my garden and to plan for the wedding only three weeks away.

Mother and I went to see Mrs. Halusik, the Czech cook from Spillville, who is the main cook for the wedding. Mrs. Halusik said she would make dozens of Czech traditional kolaches, sweet yeast buns filled with fruit. I like both the apricot- and prune-filled buns, so she is going to fill half of the buns with apricots and half with prunes. She sold us some to take to the McDonalds and some for our family.

It was raining Friday evening when Mark called me. "Honey, it is raining, and we will not be haying tomorrow. How would you like to go to a wedding dance at Spillville tomorrow night?" I let him know that I would be thrilled as we had not gone dancing for so long as we were too busy with John's wedding, planting corn, haying, and preparing for our life together.

Saturday evening it was still misting a bit, but I did not let that dampen my spirits. I dressed in a summer light-blue-print dress and wore white high heels with nylons.

"Just think, Julia, most likely the next wedding dance we'll go to will be our own. The band that is playing tonight is the same one that I hired to play at our wedding dance."

The parking lot was full of cars. Striding up to the entrance with Mark felt good. We found a booth away from the dance floor but were glad to even find one to sit in where we could hear the music.

The bride and groom were dancing the first dance. I smiled at Mark, thinking in a few days that will be us out there with the whole floor to ourselves.

"Julia, how I dreamed of dancing with you when I was in Italy. Sweetie, your memory is what I hung on to no matter how bad things got. At night you were on my mind as I slipped off to sleep. Without your letters and your love, I don't know if I would have made it."

We had a wonderful good evening, dancing waltzes, two steps, and some swing. We tried a polka and the schottische. It was blissful dancing in each other's arms with time just to enjoy being together.

Later, while trying to go to sleep, my mind was swirling like a whirlpool. *Mother often mentions that since WWI there have been many changes against Christian beliefs. What challenges are ahead of me in life? How can I face them?*

How can I be strong as my parents were during two world wars and the Great Depression? But most of all, how can I withstand dangers to my Christian faith?

27

Deeper Understanding

The school families and the neighbor women had a bridal shower for me at Sara's large farmhouse. Children played on the front lawn. They had fun running around Sara's well-trimmed, fancy-shaped evergreens.

Mrs. Johnson had a fun word game where we filled words in blanks using vegetable and fruit names. Examples are "Lettuce go to the wedding." "The bride is a peach of girl." "She is a strawberry blonde," "The bride and the groom make a perfect pear."

Dessert was served on glass plates. On each plate was a piece of angel food cake with fresh strawberries topped with a mound of whipped cream. There was either coffee or lemonade to drink. The women sat around Sara's large oak table, with three leaves in it, to eat their dessert and enjoy visiting with each other.

Then the table was cleared, and pretty packages were placed on the table. I opened each one, delighted to find many useful items for my kitchen or bathroom. I thanked everyone for their thoughtfulness and kindness. I hoped they would be able to come to the wedding.

On Sunday, Father Dolan announced our final banns, the declaration from the pulpit of our intended marriage. There are only a few days now until the wedding. Melanie has completed her nurses' training and is home. I am happy for her that she obtained a nursing position at the

Decorah Hospital. She is a good friend, and it will be so nice to have her close again.

I paid Mrs. Olson to make the three bridesmaids dresses. Betty's is pink lace over a paler pink taffeta, and Marian and Melanie's dresses are of similar materials but in the color blue. The girls are having a giggling good time going to Mrs. Olson's for their fittings.

My little niece, Becky, will wear the same flower girl dress she wore at John's wedding. John will keep the rings in his pocket, so we will not have a ring bearer.

Betty and Melanie planned a bridal shower for me at John and Betty's house. They invited our mothers, my schoolteacher friends, and high school friends.

Betty gave me some frilly lingerie. Everyone had to have a look-see and asked me to hold each one up. That brought gales of laughter. The rest of the gifts were things like loaf pans, mixing bowls and such for the kitchen.

John and Mark came after the women left. They loaded the gifts in Mark's car, and Mark and I took them to our new home. "Julia, when my unit was fighting their way up the boot of Italy, I wondered if I would ever get home to marry you." Mark gave me a big tight hug. "Honey, I am so happy that you are to be my wife in a few days. You are precious to me."

"Don't squeeze me to death first," I joked. Then, seriously I remarked, "Mark, there were days when I wondered if I would ever see you again. Over three years is a long time to love someone and not see them in all that time."

"I am one blessed guy that you waited for me in all that time."

"Yah! For both of us, it took the patience of Job to live through those days."

"Like Job, we are going to reap the benefits of that endurance."

On the wedding day, I woke up early. Mom was pouring coffee for my dad and herself as I came into the kitchen. Dad told me, "Dear daughter, looks like a beautiful summer day for a wedding. The sun is shining, and the temperature is going to be pleasant, not too hot."

I was thankful to hear that. I didn't feel hungry but knew I better eat as it would be after the wedding before I would eat again. "Julia, I wish Bobby could be here for your wedding," lamented Mother. "But thankfully the war is over, and I do not have to worry about his safety like I did."

This would be my last meal before my marriage. It made me feel sad when I thought of that. I am no longer a little girl with a dear daddy and mommy to make things right for me. I am grown up now and will soon have a husband to share my life. It made me think of the Scripture that says:

> For if they fall, the one will lift up his fellow: but woe to him that is alone when he falleth; for he hath not another to help him up (Ecclesiastes 4:10, King James Version).

In marriage, Mark and I will be there for each other. In the beginning, God created a close relationship between a man and a woman. Those thoughts made me feel better just thinking about them.

Mark and I sat while Father Dolan read from Genesis 2:18 (Douay Bible), "And the Lord God said: It is not good for man to be alone: let us make him a help like unto himself."

Then Mark and I smiled at each other as Father Dolan began to read Ephesians 5:25 (Confraternity version) and finished with verses 28–33. They were the very verses Mark and I had studied together.

In his sermon, Father Dolan pointed out that "the marriage relationship represents the union of God with his people. Like Christ is the head of the church, the husband is the head of the family. As the church is under the headship of Christ, the wife is under the husband.

"Being Christ-like is all about righteousness. The husband is to show righteous behavior toward the wife, and the wife is to respond in respect and honor to that righteousness as the church should behave toward Christ.

"In Revelation 19:7, it reads, 'The marriage of the Lamb is come, and his wife hath made herself ready.' In Scripture, the relationship of God and his followers is often compared to marriage. Just as a Christian is to lead a pure and righteous life, the bride is to be pure and chaste. In Revelation 19:8, the bride of Christ clothes herself in fine linen clean and white, signifying the righteousness of saints and the bride of man dresses in white, symbolic of purity.

"The Christian home is the basic unit of the church. Good Christian homes make strong people for the Lord Jesus Christ.

"In the Christian home, children are educated in the truths of God. They learn humility, chastity, obedience, piety, truthfulness and how to love. They learn how to walk in God's laws, his commandments, ordinances, and statutes. Parents should raise up their children to know 'The fear of the Lord is the beginning of wisdom' (Proverbs 1:7 Douay Version).

"It is the duty and responsibility of Christian parents to instruct their children to 'Receive my instruction, and not money: choose knowledge rather than gold' (Proverbs 8:10).

"Christian marriages are like immortal guards of the church. A grave duty is to educate children and thereby perpetuate the family. The family designed by God is a nursery for the preservation of Christendom.

"1 Timothy 4:1 (Confraternity Version) says, 'Now the Spirit expressly says that in after times some will depart from the faith, giving heed to deceitful spirits and doctrines of devils.' The degrading of marriage is a mark of degenerate times.

"Traditional Christian marriages maintain a higher state of civilization. Pray to bless this marriage today."

Now we stood in front of Father Dolan to pronounce our wedding vows. I handed my bouquet of red roses to Betty. Father Dolan conducted the wedding ceremony. When we promised our love to each other, I could hardly breathe, but I answered firmly enough despite the enthralling joy of the present moments.

John had the rings ready. When Mark took my hand to place the wedding band on my left hand, I never felt so happy. I placed a gold band on his ring finger.

The first kiss as man and wife enclosed us in a deep warmth of heartfelt significance. In our affectionate embrace, I feel both of us sense the depth of our love and commitment. It is an unworldly sensation.

After the marriage ceremony, I took a bouquet of long- stemmed roses from a nearby vase and placed them on the side altar of the Blessed Virgin as the choir sang "O Beautiful Mother." Soon the mass was over; Mark and I were moving down the aisle. On both sides of the aisle, people were smiling at us. I am sure we looked very happy.

The rest of the wedding party followed us out. Then we lined up outside to receive our guests as they left the church.

My mother whispered in my ear, "Dear daughter, I pray that you will be as happy as your dad and I are." She hugged and kissed me.

There were so many kisses, hugs, best wishes for me and congratulations to Mark. After the last person went through the receiving line, the photographer took our wedding pictures in the church on the altar. The guests went into the church basement to visit until the wedding meal was served. Weddings are looked forward to as a great time to visit with friends and relatives.

While we were relaxing on the second day of our honeymoon, Mark looked at me and quizzically asked, "You look like you are troubled about something. What's on your mind, dear one?"

"Mark, in marriage your parents and mine lived through some tough trying years. First, they faced the cultural and moral changes in the roaring twenties after the First World War. Second, they provided for their families during the financial woes of the Great Depression. Third, we experienced with them the sacrifices and the stresses of the Second World War. I cannot help but wonder what lies ahead of us.

"Mother says that after the First World War, people openly exhibited depraved behaviors—excessive drinking, frenzied dancing, risky gambling, and the use of coarse words. The flappers redefined women—rouged cheeks, powdered faces, reddened lips and darkened eyebrows, and brightly painted nails. Dresses were becoming more immodest and less feminine. They were flat busted, waist less, with low necklines and higher skirts. Men and women wildly and uninhibitedly danced the Charleston and other jive dances to jazz music."

Mark added, "Yes, you are right. Changes were more rapid than ever in the history of man. Our parents went from horses to gasoline-powered engines and from open buggies to automobiles. They went from kerosene lamps to electricity, from wood-burning stoves to electric stoves and oil furnaces, and from radios run by batteries to electric radios. After WWI, the economy boomed allowing ordinary people the ability to purchase cars, modern conveniences, and to afford a faster lifestyle. The industrial growth provided not only cars but appliances, radios, modern-styled clothing, and much more to fuel the economy. Technology developed unheard-of inventions up to that time."

I thought for a minute what Mark just said and then questioned, "Were all those changes for the better? Formality gave way to practicality. It seems that people lost some of their politeness with each other. Architecture became less decorative and simpler looking in design. Some of the beauty of former buildings was not maintained in the newer structures.

"In the early 1900s, few had the opportunity to go to college. Now women as well as men are going on to higher education. Girls used to work only until they married, but now, after working during the war, more women want to work outside of the home. When women stayed home, they made a house a home. They raised a family, cooked, baked, cleaned, washed, and took care of the house. That made a house a real home—comfortable, pleasant, and a lovely place to enjoy. They were there to teach their children godly principles and how to live a good life.

"What will our married life be like? What cultural changes are ahead? What happiness, sorrows, challenges, and unforeseen troubles?"

"Julia, my dear, God's followers throughout history have suffered tribulation for his sake. Yes, through the centuries, God's people have had trials to face. The wicked, because of their vile nature, persecute the followers of God."

"Mark, you do agree in the years since World War I and now from World War II that there have been rapid changes in the way people behave and live their lives. Dear, I can understand natural calamities like droughts, hailstorms and such, but my biggest fear is the cultural changes in how people think and live."

Tearfully I blurted out, "Mark, I am afraid of the changes in people. I don't know if I can stand the moral deprivation, anti- Christ behaviors, and degrading of family life. How can we bring up children in such times?"

Mark put his arm around me and pulled me close in his warm, assuring embrace. He did not say anything for a while. He just held me in a tight embrace.

"Dear, I promised you that I will always be here for you. We don't know what lies ahead, but I assure you that I will be forever faithful. Above all, don't forget God's promises are there for us.

"Dearest Julia, remember that God Almighty has assured us that he is forever faithful to his followers. The love of God Almighty is more important than my earthly human love."

Mark opened a drawer of the nightstand beside the bed in the hotel room. He found a Gideon Bible placed there. He said to me, "Let me read to you from the book of Deuteronomy."

> Know therefore that the Lord thy God, he is God, the faithful God, which keepeth covenant and mercy with them that love him and keep his commandments to a thousand generations (Deuteronomy 7:9, KJV).

Mark repeated to me in his own words, "We have a faithful God who keeps his covenant with us. He shows his mercy to them who love him and keep his commandments. In other words, Julia, we have God's covenant that he is forever faithful to those who love him and keep his laws. His promise of faithfulness and mercy is for a thousand generations. In Scripture, a thousand is the divine number. In this case, it perhaps means more than a thousand and could even mean indefinite time."

"Mark, how did you know where to turn to in this Bible to find that verse?"

"When I was in the army, the Gideon's passed out Bibles to servicemen. I kept my Bible near me, and when I had a few minutes' time, I read the Bible. During the years I was in the army, I must have read it completely through at least once, and parts I read many times like Proverbs, Psalms, and chapters like Deuteronomy 28.

"During those dark days in my life, the Scriptures were something I could hold on to for strength and reassurance. I guess if we turn to God in our troublesome times, we can be lead to really knowing and understanding the word of God."

"Mark, it makes me very happy to think that I am married to a man who knows the Bible like you do." I pondered that thought for a while. Then in deeper understanding, I said, "You have learned to understand biblical truths and gained priceless knowledge about the words of God."

Suddenly I threw my arms around his neck. I spoke softly, "I love you for your strong faith. Because you are a God-fearing Christian man, I know now that I can feel safe in your earthly love that you will be forever faithful to cherish and protect me." Then I paused and thought more deeply. I acknowledged, "You have led me to a far deeper understanding of the words 'forever faithful.' Now I realize that God's covenant of his faithfulness and mercy is our heritage—if we love him and live in Christ-like righteousness."

Mark added, "We must not forget that we are obligated to keep our part of that solemn agreement that is binding on all parties. Under the covenant, God's faithfulness and mercy is there if we follow his laws and live righteously. Furthermore, Julia, do you see that the same is true in the covenant of marriage?"

"Thank you, dear husband, for leading me to the realization that I can feel security in knowing God's commandments are my blessings. If we follow God's laws, we have the best guide on how to live a good life here and in the hereafter."

Mark explained, "During times of upheaval, people who do not have faith in God turn to ungodly behaviors in search for meaning to their lives. But true love and happiness is only found in living a righteous life. Love comes from God."

Mark hugged me in a warm, close embrace and said, "The river of time just keeps flowing on, but now we have each other and God's promises to face our world. Together, trusting our love and leaning on our Lord, we can withstand the sufferings, trials, tribulations, and terrible wicked forces of this world. We have a *forever faithful God* to see us through whatever lies ahead of us."

My body relaxes in my husband's embrace. *I know deep within that he is wise and speaks God's truths. I am so thankful I am married to Mark, a true Christian man.*

Two are better than one; because they
have a good reward for their labor.
—Ecclesiastes 4:9 (KJV).

Reference

The American Presidency Project (americanpresidency.org) was established in 1999 as collaboration between John T. Woolley and Gerhard Peters at the University of California, Santa Barbara. President Franklin D. Roosevelt, Fireside Chat, December 9, 1941

McNally, Rand, edited by R. R. Palmer, *Atlas of World History*, 1957. 180.

Atlas of World Military History, Edited by Richard Brooks, 2000. Barnes & Noble Books.pp.200, 212.

Klein, Shelley. *The Most Evil Dictators in History.* 2004. Barnes and & Noble Books. p 66.

Printed in the United States
By Bookmasters